# By Lee Pini

The Boyfriend Fix
Good at People
When We Finally Kiss Goodnight

Published by DREAMSPINNER PRESS
www.dreamspinnerpress.com

# The Boyfriend Fix

# LEE PINI

DREAMSPINNER PRESS

Published by

DREAMSPINNER PRESS

8219 Woodville Hwy #1245
Woodville, FL 32362 USA
www.dreamspinnerpress.com

The Boyfriend Fix
© 2024 Lee Pini

Cover Art
© 2024 Reece Notley
reece@vitaenoir.com
Cover content is for illustrative purposes only and any person depicted on the cover is a model.

Trade Paperback ISBN: 978-1-64108-749-0
Digital ISBN: 978-1-64108-748-3
Digital eBook published April 2024
v. 1.0

# DEDICATION

*To Laura, who makes me feel like I belong.*

# CHAPTER ONE

THE BLENDER'S on the fritz again.

Jamie clicks it off and back on. His reflection is distorted by the curves and angles of the scuffed plastic—blue eyes, pale skin. A mop of shoulder-length black curls he needs to tame at some point today. New York humidity defeats most products. The rook piercing in his left ear glints as he angles his head.

Gritting his teeth, he flicks the blender off and on again. Nothing. Abso-fucking-lutely nothing. Like he should expect anything else? In his experience, third time is definitely *not* the charm—let alone the fifth or sixth or tenth time. Doing the same thing over and over again and expecting something different is the definition of insanity, right? Step one: try an action. Step two: determine action is accomplishing nothing. Step three: ??? Step four: fix blender.

"Val!" he calls, pounding the base with the heel of his hand in vain. "Val, is that extra blender still back there?"

Silence. Val is MIA.

Jamie peeks around the espresso machine. Hipster Mom and Baby are still here. Hipster Mom is almost finished with her Pynk Drink (he's waiting for Starbucks, or possibly Janelle Monae, to sue) and Baby has recently graduated from sleeping in his Mockingbird stroller to squealing and babbling. NYU Creative Writing Major is in his corner, agonizing over his laptop. There are some tourists who came in to use the bathroom, but tourists who come in to use the bathroom never get anything.

He has an hour before the lunch crowd shows up, and they'll want *blended drinks*. If he's going to look for that backup blender, he better go now. Val's probably smoking outside, and he can yell himself hoarse for all she'll care.

Even if she was in the back, he could probably still yell himself hoarse. He might find her sketching prop designs on her iPad, earbuds in. He'll feel bad and like he should give her more of a break, because she has two gigs, working here during the day and moonlighting at an

#ownvoices theater in Harlem as the property master. She designs at least half the props herself, and she's also generally an amazing artist.

But right now he really just wants to know if the spare blender's in the back.

He glances around the Daily Grind again. Still safe. He's got time. He can do this, and he's *not* going to have a line five frappe-deprived people deep when he returns, working blender in hand.

Val isn't in the back. After a few minutes' frenzied searching, Jamie determines the blender isn't either.

A box of individually wrapped knife-and-spork combos, left over from the height of the pandemic, tips off a shelf. Somehow the box flips itself upside down. The cutlery rains down on him, landing in a puddle of crinkling plastic wrappers around his feet.

He kicks the box, which isn't as satisfying as he hoped.

*Then* Val comes in, a wave of clove cigarette smoke following her. She takes one look at him, ankle-deep in sporks, and says, "Jamie, what the hell are you doing?"

"I'm looking for the spare blender," he says, sure he sounds incredibly dignified.

"Why, what's wrong with the regular blender?"

"It's broken! Again!"

"Oh." Val pushes her box braids over her shoulder. "Andy told me to throw the spare one out last week. He said it was taking up space. Anyway, the blender was working fine fifteen minutes ago. Wait, David didn't come in again, did he? You really can't hide back here from every ex you've ghosted."

"That was one time!" And what was Jamie supposed to do? Stand there and take his ex-boyfriend's coffee order like nothing happened? Like Jamie didn't blow David off the night he was supposed to meet David's parents, and like David didn't dump him via voicemail when Jamie wouldn't answer his phone?

Val shrugs. "I'll call Andy about getting a new blender."

Jamie wants to kick the box again at the mention of their boss, but instead he stalks out to the front.

There's someone waiting. "Hi!" Jamie says, slapping on his most charming    I'm-a-people-person-yes-I-*love*-people-and-yes-working-at-this-coffee-shop-in-my-late-twenties-is-exactly-what-I-always-wanted-why-do-you-ask smile. The young woman looks like an NYU student.

He probably shouldn't assume that every young person who comes in is an NYU student, but the Daily Grind is basically on NYU's campus, so he can't help it. Plus, he used to *be* that NYU student stopping into the Daily Grind for coffee.

Well, not coffee. He doesn't like coffee, and it's not even because he's sick of it. He's never liked it, and if he had a dollar for every person who thought they were being clever by pointing out that he works in a coffee shop and doesn't like coffee, he could be one of those people that CNN Money breathlessly reports on, how unlike other people his age, he doesn't spend his money on luxuries like avocados and rent. He would have put his You Hate Coffee And Work In A Coffee Shop, LOL money into the stock market, and he'd be retired by forty.

Of course, no one's giving him a dollar, and he's not retiring by the time he's forty. He's twenty-seven years old with a master's degree in Russian history, in debt up to his eyeballs, and he's working sixty hours a week as a barista *here*, at the Daily Grind, the West Village's favorite indie coffee place.

At least, that's how they bill themselves.

"What can I get you?" Jamie asks. Please not a blended drink please not a blended drink please not a blended drink.

"Can I have a chocolate mocha chip frappe with two shots of raspberry and a shot of vanilla?"

"Uh." Jamie glances at the blender. How can the West Village's favorite indie coffee place not have a working *blender*? "I'm really sorry, but our blender's broken."

"Oh, it's not a smoothie!" she chirps. "It's a frappe."

The effort it's taking to keep up this smile is probably burning a shit-ton of calories, which is good, because Jamie doesn't get to the gym much. "Yeah," he says. "I need the blender for frappes. They're, um." He resists turning around to point at the menu board. "They're under Blended Drinks."

Looking confused, she asks, "But what are you blending?"

"The ice," he says.

"Ohhhh." She makes a face. "SMH at myself. Uh, can I just get a green smoothie, then?"

"Our blender—"

"OMG *right*, you can't make a smoothie!" She squints at the board. A couple more people have come in, and he hopes they're hearing this so he doesn't need to have the same conversation with them too.

"I'll have a green tea latte?" she says.

This time, his smile's more genuine. "Coming right up. And sorry about the frappe. And the smoothie."

"It's okay!"

He starts the latte, and Val takes over so he can help the next customer. They ask for a frappe. Clearly they didn't hear the *entire fucking transaction* with the previous customer, who's currently flirting with Val.

No surprise. Jamie may be gay, but even he can see that Val can get it, with her unfairly flawless brown skin and the rich, dark brown pools of her eyes. She gets a lot of dudes comparing her eyes to the color of their coffee. The two of them started working at the Daily Grind on the same day three years ago, and they began a tally after the first two guys said her eyes were mocha-colored. Sometimes, when they go out, they turn it into a drinking game.

Since Hetero Blue Shirt in front of him wasn't listening, Jamie goes through the entire thing again. And again. And again. When he gets the odd person who asks, "Did I hear you say your blender is broken? So you can't make frappes?" he wants to kiss them.

Working in a coffee shop has a rhythm. Mornings are crazy, then things get slow. Then the lunch rush, the early afternoon lull, the midafternoon pickup as people crash after lunch, and then a slow-down again. They stay open later than some other coffee shops, but there's no dinnertime rush. Even in New York, people don't want caffeine after 4:00 p.m. Apparently if you read enough wellness articles on Buzzfeed, you start to internalize them.

Jamie's cleaning just after six, daydreaming about the paper he's been writing in his spare time, when Val says, "Hey, here comes Tall, Douchey, and Handsome. He's early tonight."

*Shit*. Jamie runs a hand over his hair. The touch is enough to tell him it looks horrible. There isn't enough time to run to the back and fix it, so frizzy it is. Normally he makes a trip to the bathroom around this time to make sure he looks good, but Val's right. Tall, Douchey, and Handsome is early.

The door opens and a man walks in. Dark brown hair with salt-and-pepper streaks at the temples, cheekbones so sharp you could cut yourself on them, a strong jaw with a meticulous goatee. He's almost Jamie's height, which at just over six feet, also makes him tall.

He's wearing jeans and a sweatshirt like always. It's nothing special, but damn, he makes it look good. He's got these nice broad shoulders and thick arms, but a trim waist. Nice hips, nicer ass. Jamie's been lusting after him for two years.

"Hi," Jamie says as TDAH arrives at the counter. He looks straight into his eyes, which are the prettiest blue. They're sharp and smart and beautiful, and Jamie's sure he could spend hours drinking from them.

"Hey," TDAH says. Jamie would kill to know his name, but he always pays cash, and they don't take names with orders. He wishes he'd asked two years ago when TDAH first started coming in, but now he feels weird doing it.

"The usual?" Jamie asks.

"Uh"—TDAH pulls his phone, holds up a hand for silence, and takes twenty seconds to respond to a text—"yeah."

Whatever he does for a living, he's really important—or thinks he is. Val and he have theorized about it. Val thinks he's a finance bro. Jamie prefers to think he's a foreigner with a shit ton of money and a Manhattan address.

Every day when he comes in, he is, at best, distant. Usually he's somewhere between mildly dismissive and asshole. He's the kind of guy who has it all going for him, and it's never occurred to him to care that everyone else doesn't have it as easy.

But he's fucking hot, and Jamie's not above letting his dick do the thinking for him. It's not like he's going to get involved with this guy, because Jamie doesn't get involved with anyone. He doesn't date. He knows better than to get invested. He doesn't even hook up anymore.

Maybe he wouldn't mind hooking up with TDAH, but TDAH is probably straight. He's good as eye candy, and sometime-whacking-off material. The things he lets TDAH do to him in his mind….

Good thing he's got the counter to lean against, because he feels things stir, and it's definitely not work appropriate. He punches in TDAH's order, black coffee with a splash of half and half, and TDAH tosses down a five. Jamie always gives him his change, and TDAH always drops it in the tip jar.

Jamie gets the coffee, adding exactly the right amount of half and half. It's all in the wrist. Once, when Jamie was out, Val did it, and TDAH apparently said to her sarcastically, "I was hoping to get some coffee with my half and half."

Jamie makes sure the lid is secure before he slides the cup across the counter. TDAH takes the coffee without saying thanks. Then he's gone, and Jamie's staring after him, watching as he strides past the windows on his way to... wherever he goes. Jamie's never asked.

The man is an asshole. It's fine, because all Jamie wants is his look-but-don't-touch, unattainable straight guy crush. Jamie's fine with that. Just like he's fine with being twenty-seven years old and working in a coffee shop. Just like he's fine with his tiny apartment, which he shares with three roommates. Just like he's fine with his MA in Russian history that he's never done a thing with it, aside from pick away at a paper about trade relations that will probably get rejected from every journal if he ever finishes it.

It's all fine. It has to be, because if it's not, he should be figuring out a way to make it better. Things don't just magically get better. The solution to his problems, to any of his problems, isn't going to fall in his lap.

Jamie may know how to make the perfect coffee, but the thing he doesn't know how to do?

The thing he doesn't know how to do is figure out how to take all the things in his life that aren't fine and do something about them.

# CHAPTER TWO

BEN'S GOING to be fucking *late* because of the fucking train. Sometimes he hates this city and all he wants is to get the hell out, except where would he go? All Ben wanted for the longest time was to live in New York, and now he can't picture himself anywhere else. His brain comes up against a mental block, and he gives up the stupid thought experiment and resigns himself to late trains and MTA drivers who don't realize they're operating a local, not an express.

Thank god he left himself plenty of extra time to get to the work thing tonight. He *cannot* be late.

Coffee sloshes in the cup clamped in his fingers, and he checks the lid for the fifteenth time since leaving the Daily Grind. The cute guy who gets his coffee hasn't ever screwed it up. He always takes a second to check to make sure the lid isn't going to come off. Ben has watched him do it. He has these long, graceful fingers, so actually it's kind of hard not to watch—is that creepy? Staring at someone's fingers? Especially when it's someone who's not a stranger, but also isn't someone Ben knows. If he encountered Coffee Shop Guy somewhere else, like… well, who the fuck knows, Crate and Barrel—if they bumped into each other, Ben's pretty sure he wouldn't even say hi.

What's the etiquette there? It's okay to not say hi to the guy you buy coffee from, right? Even if you do like his hands? Even if he's, like, kind of the main reason you go to the same coffee shop every day?

Whatever. Ben sucks in a breath. He's freaking out because he's late, and tonight is a big deal. He has to make a good impression. He has to make a good impression every day until he gets this promotion.

Neurosurgeon-in-chief. At thirty-seven, he'd be the youngest ever at NewYork-Presbyterian Hospital. No one expects him to get the job, not when he's up against Victor Dumas. Victor has twenty years of experience, and age, on Ben—but Ben doesn't give a shit. He's the better surgeon, and everyone knows it.

But if he's late to this cocktail hour, he'll make a bad impression on the search committee before interviews even start.

Okay. Hospital's up ahead. He blows through the doors, fumbles his badge out of his pocket, and swipes it to get into the staff areas. He'll stop by his office, change into a button-up and slacks, and go to the cocktail hour.

By the time he strips off his jeans and sweatshirt and pulls his business-casual wear on, he's late. Adriana raises her eyebrows when he slides into the room, clutching his coffee and breathing heavily.

Checking her watch and tucking a strand of her brown hair behind an ear, she says, "You know this started fifteen minutes ago, right?"

"I'm just being fashionable," Ben says, shooting her the crooked smile that used to make her eyes go all googley. The breakup means his most charming smile doesn't work on her anymore. But Adriana isn't the one he has to impress tonight. It's the hospital administrators and the other doctors on the search committee.

He straightens his shirt. "My train was late."

Pointedly, she eyes his coffee. "But you found time to stop at the Daily Grind?"

"Coffee makes me more palatable."

She doesn't argue, which doesn't sting anymore. It might have once, but Ben knows who he is: an asshole. An asshole who's the best fucking neurosurgeon on the entire eastern seaboard. Maybe the best in the entire country. He's going for world domination, obviously, but he's got just enough of a sliver of humility to acknowledge that he might not be the greatest on the entire planet.

Yet.

Victor Dumas is at the front of the room talking to Marie Kidjo, head of surgery and definitely on the search committee, and another woman who Ben doesn't recognize. A quick once-over of the room nets him glimpses of the others: AJ Georgas, the hospital administrator, Billy Emmett, the other neurosurgeon-in-chief, and Carl Park from the hospital's governing board.

A normal person would be nervous. Ben's not a normal person. On skill and merit, he's clearly the best choice for this job. He's devoted his entire life to this place. Now that he's standing in this room, he's completely confident. Dumas is old and washed-up. All right, so maybe he's not *washed-up*. But he's only like, three-quarters the surgeon Ben is.

Recognition pings in Ben's mind as he watches Dumas and sips his coffee, wanting to finish it before he dives into schmoozing. The woman standing next to him is his wife. Ben's met her at a function or two. Usually he stays away from stuff like that. These people are his coworkers, not his friends. He made that mistake with Adriana and he's not looking to do it again.

Now that Ben's recognized Dumas's wife, he sees other vaguely familiar faces. Did everyone bring their partners to this thing?

"So where do you put my chances of getting this promotion?" Ben asks Adriana, quirking an eyebrow. "Ninety-nine percent or a hundred?"

Adriana doesn't smile. "I have to talk to you about something."

"It can wait, can't it? I have to go do the whole"—he makes a face—"small talk thing."

Without waiting for an answer, he starts to move off. He'll hit a garbage can on the way and toss his empty cup. But she grabs his arm, hooking him around the elbow and yanking him back. "It can't wait, actually," she snaps. "Right now, I put your chances of getting this promotion at about zero percent."

All Ben can do is gawp.

Then, he laughs. She doesn't. When she keeps not laughing, when her expression, in fact, gets flatter and tinged with a glare, his own smile fades. "What are you talking about?" he asks. "I have this thing in the bag."

"You don't," Adriana says. "And if you would listen to me, then you might be able to try to... I don't know, mitigate it. Somehow."

He doesn't buy it, but she's his only friend, so he should hear her out. "Okay, what happened?"

She presses her lips into a thin line. "I was behind Emmett and Victor on the train this morning. They were talking about this job."

"Yeah, big deal."

Shaking her head, she says, "You don't get it. Emmett told Victor he's a shoo-in. That there's no way they'd give it to anyone else. He's the only candidate they expect to have the right personality mix to take over."

The way Adriana delivers this, in a clipped, matter-of-fact tone, leaves Ben fumbling. It's the kind of thing you hear and feel like someone's kicked the floor out from under you. It's the bottom dropping out of all his hopes and dreams. If he doesn't get this position now, it's going to be another twenty years before it opens up again—and then Ben will be practically sixty.

He opens his mouth to—what? Argue? Tell her she's wrong? That she misheard? That she misunderstood? But all that comes out is, "Fuck."

"Yeah." Finally, regret crosses her face. "Sorry."

Breathing too hard might knock his whole life down right now, so Ben doesn't breathe. "You said I could mitigate it."

Her eyes drift longingly to the open bar. "There's not really a nice way to say this."

"Then don't say it nicely," Ben snaps. "You just told me they're not giving me the job—they're not even going to consider me. There's nothing worse than that. Literally nothing you could say to me right now is worse than that."

A look he can't exactly read crosses her face. "The committee thinks you don't have a heart. They think you don't have what it takes to be in a leadership position in this hospital, because you lack compassion."

Ben scoffs. "I don't lack *compassion*. Are you kidding me?"

She gives him a disbelieving look. "Ben. Have you ever really looked at the way you behave when you talk to patients? Their families?"

"I talk to them like patients."

"You talk to them like puzzles. Like challenges you have to beat." When Ben scoffs again, because he doesn't know what else to do, she presses on, "Remember that kid with the gunshot wound last week?"

"The one I saved because no one in the ER had the skill to get the bullet out of his brainstem?" Ben shoots back.

Adriana doesn't back down. She never has. Ben likes that about her, usually. "Yeah, and after you saved him, do you remember talking to his family?"

Ben opens his mouth, but then he thinks about it.

Adriana nods. "You were stiff and awkward. Barely wanted to shake their hands. His mom went in for a hug and you flinched back." Ben glances toward the front of the room, where Dumas, his wife, and Kidjo are still deep in animated discussion.

"Why does it matter?" he asks. "I'm a great surgeon. Isn't that the important thing?"

"Ben," Adriana sighs, and he hears a world of screw-ups and lost opportunities in her voice. He's never regretted their breakup, but there's still something wistful about their friendship. "Maybe there are more important things than being the best."

"Tell that to someone who needs life-saving surgery."

"Lots of people can do life-saving surgery. The committee wants a human being as their neurosurgeon-in-chief." When Ben stiffens, Adriana sighs and says, "Sorry."

"No, you're not."

She tucks her hair behind her ears. "I'm not trying to be a jerk. It's just the truth. Victor comes across as a warmer person. His patients love him. Your patients...."

There's no point in her finishing the sentence. He already knows. "They're grateful for my help. But they're not sending me Christmas cards." When she shrugs and nods, he lets out a hard breath of air. "Okay," he says. And then, "Okay."

His whole life, Ben has never given up. That's just not who he is. He works harder, faster, more than anyone else. So if what he needs to get this job is a heart? Well, then he'll make the search committee see he has a heart.

Adriana follows his gaze to the Dumases. "Too bad you don't have a significant other to bring to these things. You could be all lovey-dovey with them."

He looks at her and raises his eyebrows. She snorts. "Yeah, um, no. Absolutely not. I like you a lot, Ben, but there's no way I'm getting involved with you, especially when I know you're just using me to get a promotion."

"It wouldn't have to just be for the promotion," Ben says, mildly hurt.

"Do you actually want to date me again?"

"Well...."

"Exactly."

He gives her a frustrated look. "So you're saying I have to find someone to date me and have it go so well that they make me look like a sentimental sap, and I have to do it within the next few weeks?"

Adriana rolls her eyes, and Ben has to admit that he might have an inkling of what the problem is.

"Okay," he says. "Do you have any single friends?"

"Even if I did," Adriana says, "I wouldn't hook you up with them. God, Ben. Do you hear yourself? You're talking about using someone just for a job."

Ben opens his mouth to retort, like, hey, maybe it wouldn't *just* be using them, maybe they'd really hit it off. But then he lets it fall closed. Something occurs to him. *Using someone just for a job.*

What if it was just *for the job*? What if he had a partner who knew exactly why they were being seen with Ben, who agreed to pretend to be in a serious relationship? That wouldn't be an asshole move, right? They'd have an agreement, and no one would have the wrong expectations. They'd know none of it meant anything.

Yeah. This could work. This could totally work. He doesn't know how he could meet his soul mate in the next few days, but he can definitely find someone to pretend to be his girlfriend or boyfriend. He'll have to offer them payment. Money should work. Everyone loves money, and he has plenty.

Adriana's voice startles him. "You look like you just got a really bad idea."

Turning to her with a crooked grin, he says, "Wrong. I just got a really *great* idea."

There's trepidation on her face. "That's exactly what I was afraid you would say. Don't do something stupid. There will be other jobs. There are other hospitals. You don't have to stay in New York. You could go anywhere."

Which is where she's wrong. He's Ben McNatt, and he's never been able to imagine living anywhere besides New York City.

He's going to get this job. This promotion is his. There's no other possible outcome.

So he has to do two things tonight. One, he's going to go schmooze it up with everyone on the search committee, and he's going to be his most charming, interesting, irresistible self, even though he hates events like this and has never quite gotten the hang of being charming, interesting, and irresistible.

And two, he's going to figure out where to find a fake lover.

"Thanks for the heads-up, Addy," he says. She mutters something under her breath and doesn't stop him as he heads toward Kidjo and the Dumases.

As he prepares to throw away his empty coffee cup, its logo catches his eye.

The Daily Grind.

Ben knows exactly what he's going to do.

# CHAPTER THREE

IT WAS easier to fantasize about standing up to Andy about the blender when Andy wasn't actually in the coffee shop. Jamie's boss has spent all morning draping himself on every flat surface, watching Jamie work, standing too close behind him, doing that thing where he's basically ogling Jamie, but Val always says that's just how he is, and what are you going to do? It's a job.

And she's right. It *is* a job. It's the only job he could get, so he grits his teeth and tells himself Andy will get bored and leave.

Unfortunately, it's the post-lunch lull right now, which means Andy's spending a lot of time watching Jamie. There's nothing else to do. Well, there's plenty else to do, but Andy won't do it. "Oh, but that's why I hired *you*!" he always says, like it's a hilarious joke that he might help out in the coffee shop he owns.

Andy has more money than he knows what to do with. He's a classic trust-funder, never had to work a day in his life. He's the kind of person who will wipe his ass with hundred-dollar bills because he can.

Jamie will clean every single surface, jug, pitcher, nozzle, and drip tray in this place if it means he doesn't have to engage with Andy. He's really regretting his clothing choice today—black leather pants and a clingy long-sleeved shirt he saves for days when he needs to feel good about himself.

He felt sorry for himself last night. When he got home, one of his roommates was with his he's-not-my-boyfriend-we're-just-having-fun in the living room. The walls are thin and Jamie shares one with said roommate, and that meant he had to listen to them fucking once they were done with their movie. It made him feel like an idiot for his unrequited crush on a straight man.

Feeling sorry for himself called for his favorite outfit. He just didn't count on Andy being around.

Jamie runs a mop over the floor behind the counter. It's clean, but he doesn't care. He's committed to looking busy and doing things that don't involve him bending over so Andy can see his ass, though admittedly, these pants *do* make his ass look great.

God, the guy's such a creep. If Jamie had any prospects, he'd find somewhere else to work so he wouldn't have to put up with Andy's skeeziness.

"Jamie, you work too hard. Anyone ever told you that?"

Jamie glances at Andy, who's leaning on the counter. Sprawling on the counter, more like. Oozing over it. "Thanks," he says, because it's better than the smartass retorts that crowd his tongue. He's working hard at biting those back, that's for sure.

"It wasn't really a compliment, sweetheart," Andy says, gray eyebrows waggling.

The thing about Andy is he could be forty or he could be sixty. He's all gray, and he has wrinkles, but not a ton of them. He dresses in this indescribable way, like he's trying to out-haute-couture haute couture. Val's theory is that all the latte art they make sucks out their souls and powers Andy's insatiable lust for youth.

Jamie wishes Val was here. But it's her day off, and normally Jamie works with Paz on Val's day off, but she called in sick, and Andy apparently decided that meant he should come in.

Andy manages to get a hand on Jamie's forearm, which is a feat, considering Jamie's got his butt pressed against the opposite counter, trying to keep as much distance between himself and Andy as possible. "Seriously. You've been at it for hours. Busy, busy, busy. Take a break, Jamie. Put your feet up. They must be aching. Want me to give your little tootsies a rub?"

"Er, no. Thanks." Jamie sidles out of Andy's grasp. "I'm fine. Good arch support in these shoes."

They're Chucks, so no, actually, they have terrible arch support, and anyway, Jamie's not totally sure what arch support is, or if it would keep his feet from hurting, but he would literally say anything to avoid Andy touching his feet.

Andy pouts. "You need to learn how to have fun again."

What he needs is a job that pays a livable wage and a boss who isn't trying to grope him, but hey. Like the Stones said, you can't always get what you want, right? Or need.

"I just take my job seriously," Jamie says. He's praying for a customer. Where are Hipster Mom and Baby when you need them? "Honestly, it was really great of you to come in, but I can handle things on my own. I know the drill. You know. I've got a handle on things."

Andy waves his hand. "Of course you do! But I like checking in." His eyes rake up and down Jamie, head to toe, lingering at about hip level. "Checking things out. Keeping my eyes on my assets, you know."

Jamie's chest tightens with anger and anxiety and shame, that mix of emotions that's very particular to any amount of time spent with Andy. What's he supposed to say? Andy's practically leering at him.

It's the Andy Show, though, so Andy doesn't actually need an answer. "Hey, did I tell you I got a new boat?"

"Um," Jamie says, because Andy's always talking about his newest toys. Did I tell you I got a boat? Did I tell you I got my pilot's license? Did I tell you I bought a place in Malibu? Did I tell you about my new Ferrari? How about a ride?

"You should come out on it with me," Andy says.

"I get seasick," Jamie says. Which is true. But he'd have said it no matter what.

"I have drugs for that," Andy says, looking sly. Jamie's stomach twists. Leaning over the counter again, Andy adds, "Come onnnn. It'll be fun. You know how much I like you, Jamie. We could like, make sweet music together, or whatever."

"I don't sing," Jamie says flatly. He hopes Andy doesn't corner him behind the counter. It wouldn't be the first time. Jamie won't go into the back room while Andy's here, not anymore. It's not like he can't fight Andy off, and it's not like Andy has actually tried anything, except being generally handsy and inappropriate. But if he did, and if Jamie had to fight him off, then what? No job. So he has to walk this tightrope of keeping Andy at arm's length, but not too far.

Pouting, Andy says, "But we never get to spend any alone time together. And I really *like* you. You know how much I like you. That's why I hired you, you know, because I… like you so much."

Wonderful. Like he needs the reminder that Andy's primary consideration when he hired Jamie was to try to fuck him. What does he expect, though? It's not like he doesn't know Andy's been thirsting after him since day one.

It's Jamie's own fault. He knew exactly what Andy wanted when they met and exactly what getting the job would entail. He knew Andy wanted to fuck him, and he called anyway.

"Tomorrow," Andy says, like it's a foregone conclusion.

Jamie has to get out of it, so he says the first stupid thing that pops into his head: "I can't tomorrow. My boyfriend and I are going out."

Andy straightens. His mouth forms an *O* that Jamie wishes he could put his fist through. "Boyfriend? I didn't know you were seeing someone."

Yeah, because he's not, but that's a problem for Future Jamie. "Yep," he says breezily. "We're exclusive. So, sorry." It's tempting to say something like, *We'll probably be having amazing sex pretty much every night for the foreseeable future, so I definitely won't be able to go for a* ride *with you on your boat or whatever.*

Not that he thinks exclusivity means much to Andy, but the idea of a boyfriend has clearly thrown him. Jamie gives him a serene smile and pointedly doesn't suggest he might be free another time.

Now Andy's scrolling through his phone. "I don't see this boyfriend on your insta."

"We don't feel like we have to broadcast how we feel about each other on social media," Jamie says, wrinkling his nose. "It's so *performative.*"

"What's his handle?"

"I don't really want to share that," Jamie says. "Why, don't you believe me?"

Andy stares hard. "I believe you," he says slowly. "Why wouldn't I believe you? Cute guy like you, you're probably beating 'em off with sticks, right?"

Not really. Grindr profile's set to *single* and Looking For *right now,* but he doesn't even use it much anymore. He's sick of hooking up, but he doesn't know how to do anything more. He's fucked up every serious relationship he's been in. One night when he and Val got super drunk together, he told her about how his mom walked out on his family when he was a kid, and she said, "Ohhhh, so that's why you sabotage all your relationships!" Even drunk, he didn't appreciate the psychoanalysis.

"Well, we're very happy," Jamie says with an air of finality. He's pretty sure Andy doesn't believe him, so the faster they move on to a different subject, the less likely Jamie is to slip up and make it obvious he's as single and prospect-less as always.

Cocking his head, Andy says, "You know, I'm having a thing at my place in the Poconos in a couple weeks. Maybe you and the boyfriend want to come?"

"Er." Shit. "Um, I'd hate to impose."

"No imposition," Andy says, smiling like a cat cornering a sparrow. "It's gonna be a casual thing, just some friends." He shrugs. "Didn't I hear you telling Val you were job-hunting? I think my friend has an open position at his finance firm. Not that I want you to *quit*, but you know. Just looking out for my employees. I'm all about growth opportunities, Jamie."

Of course he looks at Jamie's crotch when he says "growth," so that kind of sours the whole thing. Not that Jamie's buying this sudden interest in career development. Somehow Andy knows Jamie's lying about the boyfriend, which is really offensive, actually, that he just assumes Jamie's lying.

Obviously, Jamie *is* lying, but still.

Maybe there's a look on Jamie's face, because Andy smiles like he just won something. He pockets his phone, stepping back from the counter. "I'll text you the info, okay? I'll expect you and the boytoy there. Bring a change of clothes, it's an overnight."

"I don't think," Jamie begins, but Andy's already leaving, and Jamie's waffling refusal is addressed to his back.

Well.

Shit.

*That* backfired.

Jamie runs his fingers through his hair.

Fuck.

So now he has to produce a boyfriend, and he has to show up at Andy's stupid overnight thing in the Poconos, *and* Andy dangled the prospect of better employment in front of him, so it's not just a stupid lie now, it's also kind of his future. If he doesn't show up to the party, Andy's going to know he's lying.

A customer walks in, which gives Jamie something to do besides think about how he's screwed. And then in comes another, and another, and soon it's the afternoon rush, and of course Jamie's there by himself so he's swamped, apologizing for the wait, explaining they're short-staffed, working as fast as he can. He works feverishly all afternoon, burning himself on the steaming wand and spilling pretty much everything they serve on himself at some point.

He's blotting raspberry flavor shot off his sleeve during a lull, hoping he can get it out because he's going to be pissed if he ruined this shirt. It was stupid to wear it. He's definitely not feeling good about himself right now. He's covered in everything from dark roast to milk (soy, almond, whole, and skim) to tea to juice to about five different flavor shots. His hair is a frizzy disaster. His face is flushed and sweaty.

The door opens. In walks Tall, Douchey, and Handsome.

And he's looking straight at Jamie.

"Hi!" Jamie says, flustered. There's still a dark, sticky stain on his sleeve. "You're early," he blurts, like a fucking idiot.

Then he clamps his mouth shut. TDAH looks taken aback. "I am?"

"Er." *Salvage something about this day, Jamie.* "I mean, you usually come in at the same time the M21 goes by." TDAH looks over his shoulder at the street, like the bus is going to roll past. "Anyway." Clearing his throat, Jamie asks, "The usual?"

"Um, actually." TDAH has a funny look on his face. It's... nervous? Which is so incongruous from the way Jamie has always seen him that it's totally throwing him.

TDAH is really, extremely cute when he's nervous.

"Actually," TDAH repeats, "I wanted to talk to you about something."

Jamie looks around, like this was meant for someone else. Obviously, there's no one else there. It's just him. Him and TDAH. Still, he pokes his finger into his own chest—way harder than he means to—and says, "Me?"

"Yeah."

"Um." Jamie can't imagine what TDAH wants to talk about. Did he fuck something up? Did he make him a coffee and the lid popped off and TDAH burned his hands and he's serving Jamie with papers?

Jamie clears his throat. "Okay. About what?"

"It's kind of... a whole thing," TDAH says. Jamie's stomach twists. Whatever it is, it definitely doesn't sound good. And really, what could it be that's good? It's not like TDAH is here to tell him that actually he's not straight, and he's been lusting after Jamie for two years, ever since they first laid eyes on each other, and maybe Jamie would like to head back to TDAH's place and they could fuck each other senseless?

Meeting Jamie's eyes again, TDAH says, "Do you get off soon?"

If he keeps thinking about the two of them fucking each other senseless, yeah, he's going to get off very soon.

"We close at seven," Jamie replies. "And then I have to balance my register and clean up."

"So… eight?" TDAH asks.

"I can do most of the cleaning now," Jamie says. "I can probably be out of here by seven thirty."

TDAH flashes him a smile, one corner of his mouth tugging up crookedly, and Jamie's entire chest cavity explodes into glitter and wings. He's done. He's a goner. He knows better than to fall for straight guys, and yet here he is, reeled in and willing to do anything for a chance to have that smile turned on him again.

"Great," TDAH says. "I'll wait. Where do you want to go for dinner?"

# CHAPTER FOUR

BEN CAN'T tell what Coffee Shop Guy thinks of the dinner invitation. His eyes go wide, and he ducks his head, and—maybe he thinks Ben's hitting on him? Hitting on Coffee Shop Guy would be understandable. He's tall and cute, has great hair, pretty eyes, legs for days, and he has this super cool piercing in his left ear. Ben doesn't know the name for it, but he's definitely never dated anyone with a cool piercing.

"Dinner?" Coffee Shop Guy repeats. "With me?"

"Yeah," Ben says. "Wherever you want."

Coffee Shop Guy regains his composure. "There's a Chinese place around the corner."

"Sounds perfect."

So that's settled. Ben plants himself at a table. He's not going to order anything, because it might make the cleaning-up process longer for Coffee Shop Guy.

They should know each other's names. Ben opens his mouth to introduce himself, but Coffee Shop Guy is doing something behind the counter. He looks busy and intent, a little furrow of concentration between his eyebrows and the tiniest wrinkle in his nose.

One more customer comes in, and when the clock ticks over to seven, Coffee Shop Guy locks the doors and glances at Ben. "I'll close up as fast as I can."

Ben shrugs. "Take your time." He has to be patient and magnanimous. He's about to ask for a really weird favor from a stranger—even if they're strangers who see each other every day. Ben doesn't even know the guy's name, for Christ's sake.

He watches Coffee Shop Guy and tries to look like he's not. The closed coffee shop, lights still on but empty, reminds him of a hospital at night. It's this weird liminal space where nothing's permanent and nothing matters. Everything unique can be stripped away in a few minutes. You take the people out, you put the chairs up, you lock the doors, and it's just another space full of brushed metal and laminate flooring.

Coffee Shop Guy is crazy fast at balancing his register, all of his intensity focused on the drawer in front of him. When he's done, he disappears through a door with the money. Once he's back, he takes a wet rag and swipes it across the blackboard that lists the day's roasts and the trivia question that'll get you ten cents off if you answer right.

"Mariah Carey, by the way," Ben says as the writing on the blackboard smears. When Coffee Shop Guy looks at him, he adds, "The answer to the trivia question. What singer has had a Billboard number one hit in each of the last four decades? It's Mariah Carey."

A tiny smile twitches at Coffee Shop Guy's mouth. "You've had an hour to google that."

"Swear to god, I didn't," Ben says, holding up a hand like he's taking an oath on a Bible. He's not religious. But come on, cheating at trivia? That *is* blasphemy. "So am I right?"

"Yeah," Coffee Shop Guy says. "You'll have to come back tomorrow for your ten cents off."

"I just play for pride."

Coffee Shop Guy flashes a smile at him and slips his apron over his head. Turning back to Ben, he takes a breath. "Okay. That's it. So, uh. You still want to get dinner?"

Standing, Ben says, "Yeah, of course." He should have made a cheat sheet for how he's going to approach this crazy request, but he's been over it in his head so many times now that he could probably do a movie adaptation.

As they leave, Coffee Shop Guy punches in a code on the security system. He's been sneaking glances at Ben. Mostly, there's disbelief on his face, like he can't quite believe this is happening. Maybe he thinks Ben's going to murder him. Ben thinks about assuring him that his intentions are a bit unorthodox, but it's nothing bad. On second thought, that would sound suspicious.

Outside, they just look at each other for a minute. Coffee Shop Guy's hair is messy. Frizzy. Ben's always noticed his curls, and how he has this way of running his fingers through his hair. He does it now as his eyes tick over Ben's face, which is why Ben notices the giant stain on his sleeve.

When he looks at it, Coffee Shop Guy's eyes follow his gaze. With a grimace, he says, "No dress code at the restaurant, luckily."

"That's the benefit of scrubs," Ben says. When Coffee Shop Guy's eyebrows go up, Ben adds, "I'm a surgeon. That's… well, yeah. Kind of what I want to talk to you about. I'm Ben, by the way. Ben McNatt."

He holds out a hand, and Coffee Shop Guy takes it. His grip is warm and firm, and a jolt goes through Ben when they touch. "Jamie Anderson." His mouth twitches. "I'm not a surgeon."

Thankfully, Ben can keep his mouth shut when he needs to, so he doesn't say what he's thinking, which is *You have the fingers for it.* He clears his throat and lets go of Coffee Sh—*Jamie's* hand. Jamie.

What he says is, "You guys should have your names at the bottom of receipts. I would've known your name, then."

Jamie's eyebrows shoot up. "I'll take that to management." Jerking his head, he adds, "C'mon. The restaurant's this way."

Ben walks fast, but Jamie has a long stride to go with his long legs. It doesn't take them long to get to the Chinese restaurant. A buzzing neon sign identifies it as Jade Palace. It's exactly the kind of cheapo, nondescript place he hasn't frequented since his med school days.

Hard plastic booths line both walls. Ben squints at the menu. "What's good?" he asks, because Jamie's presence at his side is a buzz of some kind of awkwardness, which Ben's pretty sure he's partially responsible for.

"I usually get sesame tofu," Jamie says. When Ben makes a face, Jamie says, "Not a vegetarian, I guess." He considers. "Val swears by the moo shu pork."

"Val?" Ben asks. Oh god. Has he totally misjudged Jamie? Is Val his girlfriend? Shit, he assumed Jamie's gay.

"My coworker."

"Oh." Ben tries not to look relieved, but judging by the way Jamie's brow furrows, he doesn't totally succeed.

They order and grab a table, and then they're sitting and facing each other. The buzz of awkwardness gets way worse. The Formica tables aren't big, and they're both tall men, so their knees knock together. When Ben tries to move, Jamie does too, but they move in the same direction and all that happens is that one of Jamie's legs pins one of Ben's against the center pillar.

"Sorry," Jamie says, folding into himself, clearly trying to rearrange his legs.

Meanwhile, Ben's contending with the fact that having Jamie's leg pressed up against his felt pretty damn good.

"So—" Ben begins, but their number gets called. Jamie jumps up, returning with a tray of food. Even though Ben's used to spending more than fifteen dollars on dinner for two, he has to admit it looks and smells amazing.

Jamie rests his elbows on the table and doesn't touch his food. "You said you wanted to talk to me about something?"

"Uh, yeah." Ben can't decide if he should be eating for this or not. He fiddles with his plastic-wrapped utensil set, then rests it on the table. There's something about Jamie's eyes that's getting to Ben. He's always noticed how pretty they are—clear blue, like the sky on a summer morning, but now that the server-customer relationship has been removed, their intensity is making him nervous.

"Yeah," he repeats. "Uh. This is kind of weird. Maybe really weird. Like… okay." He takes a deep breath. "I know we don't know each other, but look. The story is, I'm up for this big promotion at work. Or I'm supposed to be. But the search committee thinks I don't have a heart or whatever, and I was thinking it would look better if I had, you know. A significant other to bring with me to stuff. While the search process is going on. So I can show them I'm a human being and that I like other people."

Jamie's eyebrows are so high that they're practically in his hair. "Okay…," he says. "I don't understand why you're talking to *me* about this."

Was Ben not clear? Well, obviously he wasn't, because Jamie's not getting it. "I'm looking for someone to pretend to be in a relationship with me," he says. "I don't have time for a real one. And I'm not actually looking. But a relationship would look good, so… I know it's kind of crazy, but what do you think? I'd make it up to you, obviously. I can pay you."

Jamie's gone from confused to full-on flabbergasted. "I," he says. His mouth works, like he's chewing on a tough piece of meat—or make that tofu, since he's apparently a vegetarian?—and he tries again, "I. Um. I still don't understand what this has to do with me. You want me to find you a woman to fake date? And you're going to pay me… what, a finder's fee?"

Ben blinks. "What? No! No. I want to pay you so *you'll* fake date me."

Jamie goes still. His eyes get very wide. Has Ben miscalculated this badly? Jamie gives off such strong queer vibes that Ben can pick them up from half a block away, but he's acting like the idea of the two of them pretending to date is the most horrifying thing he's ever heard.

"I… am so confused right now," Jamie finally says. "You're straight, aren't you?"

"Huh?" Ben asks. Then he laughs. "No! Oh man. I thought you were offended by the concept. No, no, I'm bi. Wait, you *are* queer, aren't you?"

"Obviously."

Ben's smile fades. "*Are* you offended by the concept?"

Taking a bite of his sesame tofu, Jamie says, "No. Where do you work? What do you do?" He hesitates. "You should know that—"

Ben grimaces. "You're not single, are you. Shit, is that going to be a problem?"

Jamie laughs, but there's a bitter, harsh quality to it. "I'm very single. I was going to say, you should know that I make a garbage boyfriend. Which is why I'm single."

"Oh." With a relieved smile, Ben says, "Well, that doesn't matter. I do too. That's why *I'm* single. That's the beauty of it, though. We only have to pretend to be good at it."

Jamie chews. He seems like he's giving it serious thought, which is—well, honestly, a huge relief. In theory, Ben could ask anyone. He could put something online. Grindr would come through for him. But the only person he could think of for the role of his fake boyfriend was Coffee Shop Guy. Jamie. And if he says no, Ben's going to be… he doesn't know. He'll feel like he's starting over. Or something.

He really hopes Jamie says yes.

"Where do you work?" Jamie asks.

"New York-Presbyterian," Ben replies. "Like I said, I'm a surgeon. Neurosurgeon."

"Are you good?"

"I'm really good," Ben says. He feels practically modest for leaving it at that.

One of Jamie's eyebrows arches. "I've always wanted to date a doctor," he drawls.

It makes something flutter in Ben's stomach. Okay, so he's not totally stupid. He knows the reason Jamie popped into his head for this charade is because he's cute and Ben's had a crush on him for a long time. But he's not going to be weird about it. It's just a little crush. Barely even a crush. He's a grown-up, and this is his career on the line. He may need a relationship to get the promotion, but actually having a relationship would do nothing but hold him back.

"Hm." Jamie takes another bite of his food, and Ben takes the opportunity to dig into his. Another couple minutes pass before Jamie asks, "What would I need to do?"

Ben's been giving that question a lot of thought. "There's a cocktail hour for candidates on Friday. I'd need you to come to that with me. And maybe drop by to see me one day at work. Just because we're like, really in love, or whatever."

"Hm," Jamie says again. It's not a super encouraging sound.

"I'll pay you for your time," Ben says. "How much do you want? I don't know what the going rate is for fake boyfriends—"

"I don't want you to *pay* me. I'm not an escort," Jamie snaps.

"No, obviously," Ben says. "I just figured, you work at a coffee shop, so you can probably use the money."

Jamie's eyes flash. "Oh," he says. "I get it."

"Get… it?" Ben asks. Did he say something offensive? Of course a barista would welcome the extra income. And he's serious—he's willing to pay. It's an inconvenience to Jamie, and it's kind of like an acting gig. He's not asking for nothing, and he knows it.

The look in Jamie's eyes gets stony. "That's why you're asking me, right? Because I'm a broke barista and you figured I'd leap at the opportunity to be your fake boyfriend?" His nostrils flare and he stabs a piece of tofu.

The turn in Jamie's mood gives Ben whiplash. "Wait. Are you mad at me because I'm offering to pay you?"

The tightness to Jamie's shoulders tells Ben he's on the right track. But he doesn't know why it's such a bad thing to suggest.

"Just because I work at a coffee shop," Jamie says, his voice low, each consonant precise, "doesn't mean I'm looking for charity."

Oh. *Oh.* "It's not charity," Ben says.

"But that's why you picked me, isn't it?"

Ben hesitates. He doesn't want to say that he picked Jamie because Jamie's cute, and Ben likes his voice and his hands and his eyes. He doesn't want to say that he could go to a dozen different coffee shops but he comes to the Daily Grind specifically because he likes seeing Jamie. Even though he doesn't date and isn't interested in the mess of letting someone into his life, he's still a red-blooded man. He likes to look.

"No," he says.

Jamie's eyes tick up to his. "Then why did you?"

Ben decides on a version of the truth. "I was drinking Daily Grind coffee when I came up with the idea."

Though he still looks disgruntled, the answer seems to satisfy Jamie. They eat in silence for another minute. Then, Jamie says, "I'll do it. But I don't want any money."

Ben smiles in relief. This crazy plan is actually coming together, and he won't have to pay for it? Perfect. It's too good to be true. But he should be a gentleman, right? So he says, "Well, let me do something for you. You name it."

A smile creeps over Jamie's face. "Well," he says, and Ben hears a note in his voice that, for the first time, sets off alarm bells. "There is one thing you could do for me, actually...."

# CHAPTER FIVE

WHEN JAMIE lets himself into his apartment, he's riding high. Things haven't gone right for him in so long, and tonight, incredibly and improbably, a solution to one of his problems fell right in his lap. Well, not in his *lap*. He wouldn't mind TDAH—Ben, his name is Ben, *Ben*—being in his lap.

The fake-dating thing is ridiculous, but it presents a neat solution to Jamie's issue with Andy and his sure-to-be-awful overnight in the Poconos. When Andy wants to see Jamie's elusive boyfriend, Jamie can trot Ben out. They'll go to the party, sleep on separate sides of the room, and Jamie can talk to Andy's friends about better job opportunities. He can get away from Andy and his dead-end coffee shop job.

It was like kismet, Ben coming to him with this proposition today.

They agreed, over the rest of dinner, to one cocktail hour and one hospital pop-in, plus the thing at Andy's Poconos house in two weeks. Ben must be pretty close to getting the job if that's all he needs, which is fine. Jamie's not exactly relishing going to this stuff.

The idea of dating a doctor, even fake dating a doctor, is… ugh. He hates being looked down on for his shit job and his Russian history MA, and he knows that's how it will go. That's how medical and science-y people are. They think if there isn't one solid answer to a question, then it's not real. They definitely don't care whether the Holodomor should be called a genocide or not (it should be, but it's not even an argument he can have with people because hardly anyone outside the world of Russian history even knows what it is). And they really, really don't care about Pskov's trading ties with the Hanseatic League during Ivan the Great's reign. Clearly Jamie barely cares about it, since at most he writes two words a week in his paper, and that's only after a lot of staring at the blinking cursor, scrolling up and down and picking at sentences to make them read better.

Which is why Jamie's making seventeen dollars an hour at a coffee shop.

His father would probably tell him to real marry Ben even if he only has fake feelings, because at least he'd be doing something with his life. Not that Dad would use those words, but the subtext would be clear. But Jamie would never in a million years tell Dad about this. He's strictly a holidays-and-birthday-phone-call kind of son. The last time they talked, Dad raved about Tyler and how he was thriving at the shop, and blah blah blah.

Jamie's happy that everything's golden for his brother. But everything always has been. That's why Tyler stayed in Hartford and Jamie left. It's why Jamie stays away, even though by most measures, he's not hacking it in the life he was so sure, at eighteen, that he was going to crush.

The job. The cramped apartment and three roommates. His stalled education. His even more stalled love life.

A pang rattles through his chest at that last one, but he pushes it down.

If he's horny, it's easy to find casual sex. Grindr will deliver them right to his door. Lately, he barely bothers. The sex usually isn't very good. Since he's not looking for an emotional connection, his hand and/ or a dildo are decent enough stand-ins.

His phone buzzes, and for a second, he thinks it's a Grindr alert. It's not—luckily—because it's a text from his brother, and Jamie really doesn't want to see his brother on Grindr.

Suppressing a shudder, Jamie opens the text. *You going to be around in a couple weeks?* it reads.

Jamie furrows his brow and types back, **Where else would I be?**

*Are you going to be busy?*

**No.**

*Ok good, Dad wants to visit for the weekend. He wanted to surprise you but I said you'll probably already have plans and won't be able to spend any time with us.*

Doubtful, since Jamie rarely has plans. He works. If he's not working, he's dicking around doing nothing. It's more likely that Tyler realizes if they try to surprise Jamie, he'll flip out and use it as an excuse to run off and not spend any time with them at all.

So it was actually very clever of Tyler to find out ahead of time that Jamie was going to be free. If Jamie wasn't so caught up in thinking about his agreement with Ben, he wouldn't have fallen for it.

Ben. A couple weeks from now. That's the weekend of Andy's Poconos thing. Talk about being stuck between a rock and a hard place. Andy's party isn't better than seeing his father and brother, but Jamie's not sure it's worse, either.

**I have a thing that weekend. Friday and Saturday.**

*So we can have dinner on Sunday*

Well, that was sensible, wasn't it. And kind of crafty. Has Tyler always been crafty?

**I guess**

It's the last thing he wants to do, actually—hang out with Tyler and Dad in New York? Play tour guide?

**Choose somewhere to eat. Idc where as long as it's not in Williamsburg.**

*Lol ok. See you in a couple weeks, buttface!*

The best thing to do is respond in kind, with excitement, or at least moderate enthusiasm. But Tyler has a knack for knowing when he's lying, even over text. So Jamie just sends back:

**Haha see you farthead**, with a heart emoji tacked onto the end.

Good enough. He plugs his phone in to charge and flops onto his bed. It's not that late, and usually he'd hang out in the communal space. But he hasn't decided what he's telling the roommates yet about Ben—if he tells them about Ben at all. He probably shouldn't, because they're only going to see each other a few times, and he's not ever bringing Ben back here. His roommates are just people he lives with. It's definitely not one of those situations where they turn into ride or dies.

That decides it. He doesn't need to tell anyone anything, including Tyler, because even if he and Ben are still fake dating by then, there's no point in introducing a fake boyfriend to his family.

Hopefully Ben will keep coming to the Daily Grind for coffee. Jamie didn't think about that. Does their deal mean the end of the meager relationship they had?

He's not riding high anymore. Between his family's impending visit and the idea of Ben finding a new coffee shop, he feels sapped.

And it's stupid. Well, not dreading his family's visit. He always dreads spending time with his family, because he never has anything to show for himself. Same disappointing life, same terrible job. At least he might have a job offer from one of Andy's friends. That's something.

But being unhappy about Ben not coming into the Daily Grind? *That's* stupid. They don't know each other. They're going to pretend to be a couple. It doesn't make them friends.

Telling himself how he feels about something and trusting his brain to believe it is how he gets through life. Maybe he just needs a good night's sleep for it to take this time.

"WHAT'S UP with you today?"

"Hm?"

Val boosts herself onto the counter next to him, where he's been propped on an elbow, staring out the window for... a while. Waving a hand in a gesture that seems to encompass all of him, she says, "You've been like... *this*. All day. What's up?"

"Didn't sleep well." Which is true. He didn't. He had strange dreams about not finishing his thesis but showing up to commencement to receive his diploma anyway. Tyler was there getting it instead, and he turned to Jamie and said, "It's not like you need it anyway, right?" And then Jamie tried to find his way to his advisor's office to explain the situation, that he couldn't finish his thesis because of his long hours at the coffee shop, but his boyfriend was a doctor and could vouch for him.

Jamie drags a hand across his face. He hasn't told Val about the deal with Ben, and he's not going to. He loves Val, but she can't be trusted to keep secrets. Oh, she won't tell the person she's supposed to be keeping the secret from. Not intentionally. Like when Jamie told her he didn't like doing shifts with their coworker, Anna, because she always said, "Heeeeey bitch!" when he came in, and then she'd insist on putting on her "Bad Bitches" playlist, which he was 100 percent certain she'd composed by googling "gay anthems."

Val didn't tell Anna. But Val did tell their other coworker, Malik, and Anna happened to come into the coffee shop while Val was relating the whole thing, complete with imitations of Jamie's imitations of Anna (which were hilarious, if cruel). So the whole thing got out, and it was a big fucking deal.

Or like when it got back to Andy that Jamie had called him old. Or when Jamie and Val were at Hardware and Jamie had obviously had a few, and he made some idiotic double entendre about wanting this hot guy he'd been eyeing all night to hammer his back door, and Val, by some horrific coincidence, knew the man he was there with and repeated it to him, who then *repeated it to said hot guy.*

So it's not that Val will blab secrets to the person who isn't supposed to hear it. It's that she has this uncanny ability to put herself in situations that will allow the person who isn't supposed to hear the secret to do just that.

There's no reason to tell her, anyway. Except to brag. But "I'm pretending to date a man so he can get a promotion" maybe isn't something to brag about.

The door creaks open and a rush of street noise floods in. Val hops off the counter and Jamie straightens up, and—

There's Ben.

Jamie feels his eyes go wide. "Um," he says. "Hi. I didn't know if...."

Okay, for fuck's sake, he's supposed to be pretending to date the man. Acting like he's shocked to see him isn't going to fly. What if Andy decides to drop by?

"You can't come here anymore!" Jamie blurts, as much as it pains him.

Val's head snaps around so fast that Jamie's pretty sure he hears it, but his attention is on the puzzled lines in Ben's forehead. Ben, who very articulately says, "Huh?"

"I mean...." Jamie drags his hand over his face again.

"Dang," Val says gleefully. "I missed some drama yesterday, didn't I?"

"No," Jamie says. "No drama."

"So I can't get my coffee here anymore?" Ben asks, sounding vaguely wounded. "But you always put the lid on really well."

Jamie stares at him. Next to him, Val's doing the same thing. Slowly, Val asks, "He what now?"

A flush creeps up Ben's neck. Jamie sucks in a breath and says, "Val, I'm taking my break."

"You already took all your breaks."

"I'm taking a smoke break."

"You don't smoke!"

"I'm taking it up so I have an excuse to take as many breaks as you do." He removes his apron and stuffs it under the counter, then says to Ben, "I have to talk to you."

"Sure." Ben hesitates. "But can I have my coffee?"

Jamie stares. Ben stares back. There's a little hint of a smile on Ben's face, just a tiny twitch to one corner of his mouth. If they were dating for real, it would be the smile Jamie couldn't resist. It would be the smile that made him fall for Ben.

But Ben doesn't want to date Jamie, and Jamie doesn't want to date Ben. What they both want is to better themselves, and they can help each other do that.

Jamie gets the coffee, feeling self-conscious as he fits the lid over the top of it. The action hasn't ever struck him as anything special. Jamie has no idea what to make of Ben thinking it is.

Once Ben pays, the two of them walk outside. When they turn down the nearest cross street, Jamie explains, "My boss. Andy. If he sees you come in, he'll know you're not really my boyfriend when we go to his thing."

Ben gives him a confused look. "Why?"

"Well." Flummoxed—isn't it obvious?—Jamie motions between them. "Because we aren't acting like we're dating."

One of Ben's eyebrows goes up. "We're going to have to change that, aren't we? If we're going to convince people?"

Jamie purses his lips. "Fine, but you didn't."

"Neither did you."

"You surprised me!"

"I come in every day at the same time."

"I know you do, but—" Wait, no, definitely not the right thing to say. Jamie snaps his mouth shut, then tries again. "I didn't... think. That you'd come in. You know. Still. Not while we're doing this." Or maybe ever again, but the thought makes him feel like he's got a nasty case of heartburn.

Ben regards him. "I wasn't planning on stopping. I like the Daily Grind."

"Well, we have the best staff in the entire New York metro."

"Not the best coffee?"

"You can get coffee anywhere." Gesturing to himself, Jamie adds, "You can only get *this* at the Daily Grind."

Ben laughs. It's the nicest sound Jamie's ever heard. Two years this man has been coming into the coffee shop, and not once has Jamie heard him laugh—not like this. Not startled and open and bright, blue eyes glittering and laugh lines and—

And Jamie needs to get a grip.

Once his laughter fades, a smile lingers on Ben's face. "This fake boyfriend stuff apparently requires a little more planning than we realized."

Snorting, Jamie says, "Apparently." They cross the street to a park, which is more like a square patch of grass with a verdigrised statue in the center and some shade trees. The trees are nice, at least. The statue's covered in bird shit.

Wordlessly, they sit on a bench. Ben sips his coffee. A squirrel bounds across the brick path in front of them, stops, and looks at them, nose twitching. "Oh!" Jamie exclaims, digging in his pocket. He pulls out a bag of Planter's unsalted peanuts and holds one out. The squirrel shuffles forward, looks up at him, and then takes the peanut right from his fingers before it scampers away.

Jamie smiles, but it drops off his face when Ben says, "What the hell was that?"

"What?" Jamie asks defensively.

"Um." Ben gestures. "You getting all Disney princess with the nuisance wildlife?"

"Peanuts are better for them than pizza," Jamie snaps. "Which for your information, I've seen them eating."

Ben is still staring at him incredulously. "So throw peanuts on the ground for them."

Over the last twenty-four hours, Jamie somehow managed to forget an important part of the nickname he and Val had bequeathed to Ben: Tall, *Douchey*, And Handsome. Stuffing the bag of peanuts back in his pocket, Jamie says, "If you still want to come in and get coffee, that has to be part of the fake dating. Because I can't give my boss any reason to think we aren't really together. He already didn't believe me when I said I have a boyfriend."

"Why wouldn't he believe you?"

Because Jamie's a mess? Because he's never once shown any evidence of a significant other in all the time he's worked for Andy? Because of the way they met?

He shrugs. "Who knows."

Ben shrugs too, like he doesn't really care. Maybe he doesn't. Maybe he's going to fuck this up for Jamie, because what does he care if Jamie benefits from this? By the time they go to Andy's thing in the Poconos, Ben will already have his promotion in the bag. He won't have any reason to play along anymore.

The thought makes Jamie's stomach roil. Has he made a bad decision trusting this man?

Hey, wouldn't that be a shock—him, Jamie Anderson, making a bad decision! Like his life isn't one bad decision after another. The actual shock would be if he'd made a good decision this time. God, now he's reverse psychologying himself. Should he call this off? Is this actually his worst scheme ever?

Not that he has *schemes*, more like… plans that require too many things to go his way for them to actually work. Like his plan to become a teen pop star, even though he A) couldn't sing, B) hated performing, and C) didn't write music. He'd read on the internet that Whitney Houston got discovered singing at a gas station, so he'd spent a month hanging out at gas stations, lip syncing to tinny music from his iPhone. Step one: get discovered. Step two: hide that he'd been lip syncing. Step three: write songs??? Step four: ??? Step five: FAME.

Or in college when he was going to become a huge podcaster. Step one: buy podcasting mic. Step two: idea for podcast. Step three: land sponsorship. Step four: FAME.

The thing is, he never fantasized about all the trappings of fame. He never wanted a fancy car or a huge house or anything. He just wanted… respect. And for people to like him.

Which is why he's working at a coffee shop, hand-feeding squirrels in a shit-tastic park, and pretending to date a man for nothing more than the promise that he's going to do Jamie a favor.

Yeah, his life really went off the rails somewhere along the line, didn't it?

Ben rotates the cardboard sleeve around his coffee cup. He's watching something. Oh—the squirrel. It's back, watching Jamie, waiting for another peanut. Jamie sighs, pulls the peanut bag out again, and offers one. The squirrel takes it and runs off to bury it.

And Jamie can't help smiling, even if this is a stupid thing and people think he's weird.

Clearing his throat, Ben says, "Yeah, of course we can act like we're dating when I come in. Least I can do."

Jamie eyes him. "Really?"

"Sure. We have a deal."

"And you'll be convincing?"

Ben looks wounded. For a guy who can be an asshole, his hurt look is awfully kicked-puppy. "I told you I want to help you impress your boss's friends. Why do you think I'm going to flake?"

"I…." Jamie stares at him. The truth is because Jamie's used to people flaking. Exes. His family. Friends. It's something about him. Something about him makes people think his feelings aren't worth protecting. Or maybe he's just too sensitive. Dad and Tyler have definitely told him that before. "Because," he starts again, "you don't know me? And maybe it was a stupid idea."

"It was my idea," Ben points out.

"Only the me helping you part."

"I was always going to give you something for your time!" Ben says. He looks even more wounded, but also indignant and a bit self-righteous.

It is, unfortunately, sort of adorable.

Jamie angles himself toward Ben. "Can I call you by a pet name when you come in?"

"Only if I approve the pet name," Ben says. There's a little glimmer in his eye. Mischief? Oh, Jamie *likes* that. "We can have a list of pre-approved pet names so neither of us blindside the other."

"Fair," Jamie says. "What about 'sweetheart?'"

Ben ponders that. "Sweetheart's fine. I submit for your consideration: 'babe.'"

"Ew."

"You don't like babe?" Ben asks. "What about 'baby?'"

"Oh my god." Jamie gags. "That's *worse*."

"But see," Ben says, "if I was dating you for real, I wouldn't be able to stop myself from calling you babe."

"Thus the pre-approved list of pet names," Jamie says. "That way, you have an easy repository of substitutes to choose from."

Ben laughs. "When you put it like that." Jamie gives him a tiny smile, and Ben leans back on the bench. "If babe and baby are out, what about… honey?"

Jamie makes a face.

"Dear? Schmoopy? Love? Darling?"

"I'm starting to realize I'm not a pet names sort of person," Jamie says.

"It was your suggestion."

"Maybe I'll just say them to you and you don't have to bother calling me anything." He pauses. "Except Jamie. You should call me Jamie. Because that's my name." What the fuck is wrong with him? He's babbling like an idiot. No, he knows what's wrong with him. Ben has this crooked little smirk on his face, and it's the kind of thing that takes a gay's teensy tiny crush to full-blown pining.

*Fake* dating. He doesn't want real feelings for Ben. Well, he has real feelings for Ben. But he doesn't want *serious* feelings for Ben.

Taking a sip of his coffee way too casually, Ben says, "So, we have 'sweetheart' for our list so far. And that's only for me." One of his eyebrows quirks up. "Maybe I'll just surprise you with one of the other ones."

"Please don't."

"Hey—how about this?" Ben brandishes his phone. "There's gotta be a listicle for this, right?"

"No." Jamie has regrets.

But Ben's already typing, that same mischievous glimmer in his eyes making its way to his smile. "Okay, here we go. 'Seventy-Five Cute Names To Call Your Boyfriend.' Darling… no, we got that one already. Ooooooh. *Stud muffin.*"

"No."

"*Yes.*" Ben's grinning now. Jamie's trying really hard to bite back his own grin, and he's about five seconds from failing miserably. "Sunshine? Pookie? McDreamy? Casanova?"

"You know what? Let's call this off," Jamie says, though it's hard to get the words out, because he's giggling. "Though I think if either of us is a 'pookie,' it's you."

Ben guffaws. "I was thinking McDreamy for myself, personally. Or"—he scrolls—"Mr. Big?"

Jamie's eyebrows shoot up at the same time his eyes flick down. "Oh?"

To his delight, red creeps up Ben's neck. "I mean… uh. It's, um… let's just move on."

Adorable.

Clearing his throat, Ben says, "Okay, I've got one for you. Hunk-a-Lunk. That's it. Done."

Jamie snorts with laughter. "Fine, *fine*, we can go with babe!"

Ben shoots him a grin. "I feel really diabolical right now. Which, gotta admit, is kind of a sexy feeling, so thanks."

"My pleasure," Jamie says, hand to his heart sardonically. He's still laughing.

Jamie realizes he has no idea how long they've been sitting there. Shit. He really *has* taken all his breaks today, and he hadn't meant for this to be longer than five minutes. But it's been—he checks his phone—oops. Twenty.

Out of the corner of his eye, he sees Ben tracking the movement. "You probably need to get back to work. Sorry for getting us distracted."

"No, it's fine." Jamie stands, sticking his hands in his pockets. An insane urge comes over him to tell Ben that this was fun, and the twenty minutes felt like five, and he'd rather keep sitting here coming up with silly pet names to call each other.

Luckily, he recognizes it as lunacy and keeps his mouth shut. He doesn't need to tell his fake boyfriend that he's having real fun hanging out. "I guess I'll head back."

"Yeah." Ben looks like he doesn't know what to do. "You know, I'm walking that way anyway. I could walk you back?"

Jamie opens his mouth to demur, mostly out of habit. Dates don't *walk him back* anywhere. If they do, it's because they're planning on coming upstairs and getting laid. Clearly, Ben isn't motivated by that. Which means he's motivated by... what? Chivalry? Isn't chivalry dead? Does Jamie need to be chivalrous? Should he politely decline Ben's offer because that would be the chivalrous thing to do?

He might be overthinking this.

"Sure," Jamie says with supreme casualness, as though he hasn't just picked over this concept like vultures cleaning a carcass. "Yeah, that's fine."

"And if your boss happens to be there, we're prepared now," Ben says.

Smiling at him, Jamie says, "I think we've got this. Can you taste that promotion?"

"Definitely," Ben replies. "We only have to do this for a couple weeks, and then we can both get out of each other's hair and move up in the world."

A couple weeks, and they can get out of each other's hair. Right. They can go back to the way things were before—just two strangers who saw each other every day and never took it any further than that.

# CHAPTER SIX

WHEN THEY get back to the Daily Grind, the glare Jamie's coworker, Val, is shooting at him could cut the glass. Jamie winces. "There must have been a rush or something," he says. "Normally she wouldn't look at me like… that…."

His wince turns to a grimace, then a plastered-on smile. Ben sees a man stroll out from the back room. Gray, styled hair, sharp, expensive-looking clothes. Designer, by the looks of them.

"Shit shit shit shit shit," Jamie's muttering.

Ben doesn't even have to ask. This must be the boss, Andy. Jamie's suddenly really sweaty. They're standing close enough that Ben actually smells the sharp tang of flop sweat on him.

The urge to ask if everything's okay bites at Ben. Except it's obviously not. Anyway, it's not his place to pry. Also, since when does he care? People's baggage isn't his thing. He's not anyone's therapist.

None of that changes that he wants to touch Jamie's shoulder and ask what Andy did for him to react to the sight of his boss this way.

Before Ben can figure out the right thing to do, Jamie sucks in a breath and squares his shoulders. His color returns to normal. Then he says, "Hug me."

"Huh?"

"Hug. Me." Ben's apparently taking too long, because Jamie wraps his arms around him before he can move. Automatically, his arms circle Jamie. Heat flares as their chests press together, as Ben feels the hard, lean muscle of Jamie's body.

It's totally unexpected. Stupid. Ben knows he's attracted to Jamie. He just didn't think—well, this is so *much*. Jamie feels really good. He smells like coffee. "Do you want me to come inside?" Ben asks, mesmerized by the way his breath makes the hair by Jamie's ear flutter.

"No," Jamie says, his tone clipped, totally at odds with their embrace. He releases Ben. "Text me the details about the cocktail hour."

"I can just tell you in person. Tomorrow?" Ben hears a plaintive note in his own voice and wants to kick himself. He's not supposed to be looking for excuses to see Jamie.

Jamie looks at him. A tiny smile flickers on his face before he appears to make an effort to snuff it out. "Same time, same place, I guess," Jamie says.

"You got it."

Jamie gives him a little wave and heads inside. The way his shoulders stiffen when Andy says, "*Ja*-mie, *there* you are!" makes Ben's throat ache. However the rest of the conversation goes, Ben can't hear it, because the door thunks shut and a bus goes by at the same time.

It's time to go, but Ben's feet are rooted to the sidewalk. Maybe it's not so bad. That's what a real boyfriend would do, right? He'd hate seeing his boyfriend walk away, so he'd stand there and gaze longingly after him. Not that Ben's gazing longingly. He's just… gazing. No, not gazing. Watching. Trying to figure out what the deal is with Andy, and if Jamie's desire to get away from his job at the Daily Grind is more than not wanting to be this close to thirty and serving people blended coffee drinks.

Through the window, Andy meets his eyes. Ben quickly averts his gaze. That's his cue. Jamie wouldn't want him standing out there, anyway. They're pretending to date, but he doesn't think Jamie's looking for a knight in shining armor. Actually, he thinks if anyone tried to be Jamie's knight in shining armor, he'd choose to remain in peril just to prove a point.

So he makes himself walk away. Andy is probably a garden variety creep, which is gross, but for sure not something Jamie needs Ben's help with.

He returns to the hospital to scrub in for a scheduled surgery. This afternoon it's a kid with a spinal cord injury to the C5 cervical nerve sustained in a swimming accident. In other words, the kid broke his neck. Multiple surgeons told the parents that repairing the damage is impossible, but Ben knows he can do it. A couple weeks ago, he was looking forward to this surgery being the feather in his cap that would guarantee his promotion. Now, it's just another operation.

After the surgery, he takes a quick shower before changing back into jeans and a sweatshirt. As he pockets his phone, a young man says behind him, "Dr. McNatt?"

Ben turns. "That's me."

There's a starstruck expression on the man's face. Ben's seen him around—he's a student, isn't he? That sounds right—Adriana definitely said something about him doing his surgery rotation. "I just wanted to tell you how much I look up to you. I've gotten to observe a few of your operations, and the way you help people, it's—well, it's really inspiring."

"Oh." He's inspiring for the way he helps people? What about the way he does surgeries that everyone else says are impossible? "I mean, thanks."

There's a silence, like maybe the guy wants to have a conversation. Is he expecting Ben to impart some words of wisdom?

"You're one of the reasons I stayed in med school," the man says. "I want to help people like you do."

A funny feeling worms at the base of Ben's skull. That's right—he helps people, doesn't he? He can't remember the last time he took on a patient primarily because he wanted to help them, though. Today's surgery was about proving he could do it, not about giving a kid the chance to walk again.

"You must love what you do," the student says when Ben doesn't answer. He looks a little awkward now. "Yeah," Ben says. Even though—no. Even doing the most difficult operations doesn't give him any satisfaction anymore. It used to. Now he just wants to be the best.

"Well, I just wanted to say that," the man says, sounding uncomfortable.

As Ben shuts his locker and leaves, nodding to the student, he wonders what it would feel like to care about helping people again. His patients. Jamie. He doesn't want the emotional investment—which is exactly the problem.


BEN OFFERS to pick Jamie up for the cocktail hour, but he'll get the train. When Ben repeats his offer, Jamie demurs again. Ben says it's no trouble, Jamie informs him that's nice, but seriously, *he'll get the train.*

At which point Ben gets irritated, because he's trying to do something nice, so he asks caustically, "Do you live in a bad neighborhood or something?"

Jamie glares. "I just prefer to take the train."

So Ben backs off. That's how he finds himself waiting for Jamie at the Wall Street station. The vibrations of trains beneath the streets rumble through his body. It's one of those things you don't think about until you're thinking about it. It's just part of the fabric of living in New York. If he ever left the city, he'd miss it. Shaking streets, pigeons, rats, tourists, and squirrels brave enough to eat out of people's hands.

Ben smiles. What a weird thing—Jamie feeding squirrels. It's something you side-eye when you walk past, right before you wonder if you should come back with a hot meal or just give the oddball on the corner a twenty.

And yet with Jamie, it's more endearing than bizarre.

He checks his watch. The cocktail hour starts in twenty minutes. The department hired out the rooftop bar at a nearby hotel for the night. He checks the estimated arrival of Jamie's train. It should be arriving now.

A flood of people emerges from the station. Ben scans the crowd but doesn't see Jamie. Maybe he didn't make this train, which means they'll be late—not fashionably so. He pulls up his abbreviated text conversation with Jamie to ask where he is.

"Hi," a voice says at his shoulder.

Ben jumps and whirls. Jamie's standing there, grinning crookedly. He looks way too pleased with himself. Fucker. But Ben can't help but laugh. "Okay, great job, you snuck up on me."

Jamie blows on his fingernails and then buffs them on his lapel, which is when Ben gets a good look at him. He looks… damn. He looks really good in a forest green suit that's so dark it's almost black. The cut is doing him every favor in the world, giving him a nice *V* shape, broadening his shoulders and tapering down to the waist. The pants hug the slender lines of his hips. It's no mystery to Ben that he's into Jamie's long legs. This suit isn't doing a damn thing to cure him of that.

His shirt is charcoal gray. No tie, but he doesn't need one. His hair is up in a bun, which isn't a look Ben's ever been into. Until now. Now he's very, *very* into it.

Ben's palms tingle. He has to clear his throat and squint up at the nearest building. At least he hasn't said something stupid, like *wow*. Or *you clean up nice*, which is true, but implies he didn't think Jamie would, when he didn't give it any thought at all. The last thing on his mind was how Jamie would look dressed up. Obviously they talked about proper attire (Ben actually said "proper attire" and it earned him a withering look), but beyond that, he didn't think about it.

"You look nice," Ben finally says, because that's what anyone would want to hear.

"Thanks," Jamie says. "So my attire is proper enough for you?"

"I'm never going to live that one down, huh?"

"Probably not." A smile flickers over Jamie's face, then fades. "Not that you have to live with the shame for long. Only another week and a half of this, right?"

Something icy pokes at Ben's heart. "I'll still come to the Daily Grind."

Jamie's mouth opens, but whatever he's going to say, he apparently decides against it. Instead, he says, "You look nice too."

Ben looks down at himself, like this is news to him and he has to confirm that he did, indeed, make some kind of effort. He's wearing a suit, but it's just black with a white shirt. He's not wearing a tie either. He chickened out with the one he put on, and he undid it and stuck it in his pocket while in the back seat of his Uber.

"I dunno," Ben says. "I think everyone's going to be looking at you."

Red splotches Jamie's cheeks. "I doubt it. You're the big deal doctor."

"Surgeon."

Jamie rolls his eyes. Ben feels like an asshole, which is... new. Normally he's just annoyed when people can't get this right. With Jamie, it's different. He doesn't know what that means or how he feels about it.

The two of them walk to the hotel. They're both silent at first, until Jamie asks, "Hey, how long have we been dating?" When Ben raises his eyebrows, he adds, "Someone might ask, right? How did we meet? How serious are we?"

"Serious," Ben says, because that's the whole point. This is a serious relationship, because he has a heart that's bursting to give love away. Or something. "Can't we say we met at the coffee shop? It took me forever, but I finally worked up the guts to ask you out."

"I like it."

"I'm glad it gets the Jamie seal of approval."

"You should be. There's a rigorous vetting process."

Ben chuckles. The story is perilously close to the truth. What would have happened if he'd found the guts to ask Jamie out? Wait— that's disingenuous. It's never had anything to do with courage. It's always been about not needing or wanting anyone else. Not wanting that messiness in his life.

The surgery from earlier in the week floats through his memory. That student looking up to him. The truth is, Ben's an amazing neurosurgeon, but if he's not that, who cares? Nothing else about him is worth it.

The fantasy of seeing Jamie every day and imagining someone that gorgeous wanting to be with him was nice, but it never could have been reality. After the past week, Ben knows Jamie is the kind of guy who would never go for him. He's way too good for Ben, for all Ben's the best neurosurgeon in the country and Jamie's a barista.

Ben glances at Jamie. "How long do you think we've been together? We have to sell it if we're serious, considering I've never mentioned you."

"Well." Jamie's eyebrows draw together feelingly, "I just *knew*. I knew the first time you walked me to my train station. The way you looked at me, it was like"—he bites his lip—"like magic."

Something stupid is happening to Ben's heart. It's *fluttering*. So is something lower in his rib cage. "Oh," he says.

A laugh bursts from Jamie. "God, you look like I just told you someone died."

Ben laughs too. Is that how he looks? Was that the expression on his face? Terror? Panic? Was that what he was feeling? Is that why that fluttering keeps beating against his ribs?

Flicking a wrist, Jamie says, "If you don't like the train station thing—"

"No, I do," Ben interrupts. "Let's go with that. It's sweet."

"Two months, I think," Jamie muses. "That's theoretically possible, right? People could fall in love in two months?"

Ben makes a face. "I guess we trapped ourselves into it."

Jamie cocks his head. "You don't think that's realistic?"

"I mean… no?" Ben shrugs. "How can you possibly know if you're in love with another person so fast? It would be easy to hide stuff. Or just not be yourself. Two months is nothing."

"I guess it depends on the person."

"Does it?"

"I mean, sure." Jamie shrugs. "If you aren't trying to hide anything? If you want to let someone in? If you're not terrified of that?"

Wow. Maybe they fake fell in love in two months, but they don't actually know each other that well. Jamie doesn't have the right to make that kind of sweeping pronouncement about Ben, even if it's spot on. Letting someone in *is* terrifying.

Before Ben calls him out, Jamie laughs mirthlessly. "I mean, I wouldn't know how to do any of that, but I guess I can pretend that I figured it out."

Oh. He was talking about himself.

"Let's go with two months," Ben says. "We can be convincing about it, right?"

"Definitely."

The two of them exchange a smile as they reach the hotel and go inside. They head for the elevators, since the bar is on the top floor. The lobby is standard modern hotel chic. Sort of minimalist, sort of post-modern, lots of curving lines and soft lighting. It's the kind of place Ben's stayed at in cities all over the world when he's attended conferences. They're all the same, upscale and sleek and exactly how Ben wants to present himself.

Jamie looks bored by it.

Which makes Ben realize he can't remember the last time he enjoyed a place like this. He's just supposed to, because that's the kind of person he is. Or at least it's the kind of person he wants to be.

They have the elevator to themselves. Ben's jacket falls open as he presses the button for the top floor, and Jamie's eyes zero in on the flash of color in the inside pocket.

Jamie's hand shoots out and snatches at the inside of Ben's jacket, whipping out the abandoned tie. Ben's face gets hot as Jamie looks at the stupid thing. He's not really into ties—doesn't like wearing them, doesn't like buying them. But he loves this one. It's pink and covered in tiny roller skates, and he bought it one day when he was really feeling like… like….

God, it sounds stupid. He bought it one day when he was feeling like *himself.* The thing is, being himself isn't worth it. He's never liked himself. He figured once he was the best neurosurgeon in the country, it wouldn't matter, because everyone else would like him.

Yeah, that's working out great. He's at this cocktail hour with a fake boyfriend.

Jamie looks at the tie. Ben's face gets hotter. Then Jamie looks up. "Did you take this off?"

"Yeah. Didn't really work with the suit," Ben says.

A crinkle appears between Jamie's eyebrows. "You need to wear this."

"No, it's dumb," Ben protests. "It's totally inappropriate."

With a scoff, Jamie steps closer. His fingers close around the collar of Ben's shirt and he flips it up, sliding the tie around Ben's neck. The tie slithers against the fabric. This close, Ben can smell Jamie. His aftershave is something spicy; his cologne is....

Before he knows what he's doing, Ben breathes deeply, inhaling Jamie's scent. Woody, spicy—peppery? Rose? He wants to close his eyes and lose himself, but that would be weird.

But god. Ben's forgotten how good men can smell.

He wets his lips as Jamie ties an effortless full Windsor, trying to make his body stop reacting to Jamie's proximity. Having an unrequited crush on Jamie, which he never intended to act on, is fine. Noticing how good Jamie smells, feeling blood rushing right below the surface of his skin and his heart beating in his fingertips—not fine. Those are Bad Things that Ben needs to put a stop to.

"There," Jamie says as the elevator stops. The doors open, but neither of them moves. Jamie straightens Ben's jacket and smooths the tie over his chest. "It looks fabulous with the suit," he adds. "I don't know what you were talking about."

Their eyes meet. Jamie's breath hitches, his eyes widen, and he steps back. Something jumps in Ben's throat.

The elevator doors slide shut.

Both of them move, Ben for the doors and Jamie for the call buttons. Ben gets an arm between the doors at the same moment Jamie punches the button for their floor. The elevator dings again and the doors slide back open.

Their eyes meet, and the grin on Jamie's face makes Ben's heart jump. Straightening up, Jamie extends a debonair arm. "After you, my good sir."

"Don't you mean 'after you, *pookie?*'"

With a loud snort of laughter, Jamie says, "Of course, stud muffin."

The elevator dings impatiently, and they hustle off. There's nothing on this floor except the bar, which Ben can see beyond a set of automatic glass doors. On the other side of the glass, Ben already sees hospital bigwigs. People Ben needs to impress are in there.

He spots Victor Dumas picking up two drinks at the bar.

Victor Dumas is here with his wife? Well, Ben McNatt is here with his boyfriend. His boyfriend whom he loves very much, who he's totally head over heels in love with, actually—and everyone's going to see a side of him they didn't know existed. The human side. The caring side. The *sensitive* side. They're going to see that Ben isn't just a great surgeon, he's a great person.

Jamie's smile has fallen off his face. Ben steps closer to him. "Hey. You okay?"

Which is the kind of thing you ask your boyfriend, not the guy who's just pretending to be your boyfriend because he's hoping to parley a party invite into a better job.

Sucking in a breath, Jamie plasters the smile back on his face. "Yeah. Obviously. Why wouldn't I be?"

An urge to reassure Jamie seizes Ben. What he should be doing is coaching Jamie on the right way to act with this crowd. Maximizing the boost he's going to get from Jamie's presence. They should have gone over it already. It shouldn't be something Ben's only thinking of right now. Why didn't he think about it before?

Maybe it has something to do with the fact that when he and Jamie spend time together, it flies by before he has a chance to talk strategy.

Now they're here, standing outside the bar, and Jamie's nervous, and Ben wants to make him not nervous.

Ben knocks his hand gently against Jamie's. "Ready?"

Jamie looks at him, blue eyes bright. A smile curves his lips. Ben's eyes linger on his mouth.

Innocently, Ben adds, "We got this, babe."

The smile on Jamie's face widens, and his shoulder bumps Ben's. The contact is a corona flare of warmth, body heat, and fizzing trouble all through Ben's body. "It was exactly that confidence that made me accept your offer to walk me to my train," Jamie says.

Ben laughs, and that's how they walk into the bar—smiling, laughing, elbows touching, looking like a couple.

They better fucking nail this.

# CHAPTER SEVEN

JAMIE WANTS a drink. It's his primary objective right now, which he has to set aside to schmooze with Ben's colleagues, rivals, and superiors. He hates this stuff, but he's good at it. "Who's the most important person to impress?" he asks, eyeing the crowd.

Ben leans in. His scent curls around Jamie, making his stomach do something twisty. When he was thirteen, waiting to have a crush on a girl and trying to convince himself that noticing when girls were pretty was the same as being attracted to them, it was the smell of boys that made him realize, *Oh*. Which is sort of sad in retrospect, because teenage boys do *not* smell good, but something in that soup of hormones and pheromones, sweat and drugstore body spray, aspirational aftershave and extra strength deodorant, Jamie breathed in and knew what attraction was.

Obviously, Ben doesn't smell like a teenage boy. Gross. No, Ben smells *amazing*. He smells like cedar and sandalwood, patchouli and spices. It makes Jamie feel swoony. He has to remind himself that they're business partners. They're not friends. They're definitely not people who should be noticing the way each other smells.

At this point, it becomes clear that Ben answered Jamie's question, and Jamie was so caught up in how Ben smells that he didn't hear him. "Um—sorry, which one is... are... they?"

It doesn't seem like Ben noticed anything. Maybe Jamie's Thirsting Face isn't as obvious as he thinks it is. "He's over there," Ben says, nodding in the direction of the windows. All Jamie sees are a bunch of people milling around. He nods slowly, trying to figure out how he's going to get Ben to repeat the name without making it obvious that he completely zoned out while he engaged in some mild lusting. But Ben saves him by repeating, "AJ Georgas. Hospital administrator. The guy by the window with the dark hair."

Jamie squints. "The dark wig, you mean?"

Ben's eyes snap back around. "What? No. That's not a wig."

"There's no way that's his real hair."

"Based on what?"

"Based on"—Jamie motions over his own head—"all of *that*. Hair doesn't do that in nature."

Ben looks like he's struggling not to laugh. He also looks mildly horrified by this fact. "You haven't heard of hairspray?" he asks.

Jamie looks at AJ Georgas, who has olive skin and what can only be described as a bouffant, though that hardly does it justice. "Hairspray can't achieve that," Jamie says.

"Counterpoint—why would anyone buy a wig that looks that bad?"

"Ben!" Jamie says, scandalized. "Did you just say the *hospital administrator* has bad hair?"

Ben snort-giggles, which is kind of the most adorable thing Jamie has ever seen. He could get used to making that happen. When Ben smiles—his genuine smile, not the fake, sardonic, vaguely sneery one—it bursts across Jamie's vision like the sun over the horizon.

"Ben, so good to see you here!" a woman's voice says from behind them.

They turn. Jamie hopes he doesn't look too guilty. Or smitten. Because tearing his eyes away from Ben's smile, from the laugh lines around his mouth and eyes, is way harder than it should be, and he's pretty sure it's written all over his face.

"Doctor Kidjo," Ben says, smiling and shaking her hand. "Great to see you. Have you ever met my boyfriend?"

Doctor Kidjo is a Black woman in her midfifties with short, tightly coiled hair. Her clothes are clearly expensive, but plain. Rich person chic. She doesn't hide her surprise at Ben's announcement that he Has A Boyfriend—and Ben may as well have capitalized it, because the way he says it, it's like he's expecting a gold star.

Well fuck, that means it's up to Jamie to salvage this. He sticks out his hand. "Jamie Anderson," he says. "It's wonderful to finally meet you, Doctor Kidjo. Ben's always telling me how much he admires you."

"Please, call me Marie," she says. Her eyes move between the two of them as Jamie releases her hand. "Ben, I had no idea you were seeing someone."

Ben sort of leans in toward Jamie, then drifts away again, like he's not quite sure if he should be that close. That's not going to work. They're supposed to be together and in love. They're going to have to touch each other.

"That sounds about right," Jamie jumps in, because Ben's floundering. They'll have to talk about the PDA stuff later. Elbowing Ben, Jamie gives him a fond look. "He's so private."

"Apparently," Marie says.

"We've been together two months," Ben blurts. Jamie wants to bury his face in his hands. Their wrists brush, and then the backs of their hands, and—is Ben *trembling*?

Okay, now Jamie feels bad. This is really important to Ben. And Jamie gets things being really important. He gets how scary it is to go for them, because you might fail.

It's easier to not go for the things you really want. That way, you'll never know if you were just going to fall on your face.

Up until now, Jamie's cared about this going right, because he wants it to go right for himself. Helping Ben has been the trade-off. He hasn't needed, in a visceral, heartfelt way, to help.

Ben's trembling changes that.

His fingertips touch the back of Ben's hand, brushing over his knuckles. He expects Ben to flinch or freeze or do something that will make Marie Kidjo wonder what's wrong with him. It's probably unlikely she's going to think, *Aha! Ben's pretending to date this lovely and handsome young man just to get a promotion!* But she might think, *What the hell is wrong with Ben; was he always this twitchy? Definitely not a good fit for this job.*

"Yeah, two months," Jamie echoes, nudging the back of Ben's hand and hoping he's communicating something.

And—he does? Because Ben looks at him, and his chest expands as he draws a deep breath. A smile flickers up on his face, which starts hesitant and gets deeper and happier until Jamie has to break the eye contact because his heart flutters in a way that he doesn't think is at all helpful.

"Two months," Ben says. Again. But this time he's gazing at Jamie and—and shit. No one's ever looked at Jamie like that.

This isn't real. Ben's acting. And that's what Jamie needs to do too. It's what he was doing before Ben turned that smile and those eyes on him and looked at him like the sun rises and sets on his command.

"I've never seen you like this!" Marie laughs. "You're always such a machine—in a good way, of course. Perfect record in surgery. I suppose you know all about that, though?"

The last question is directed toward Jamie. "I may have heard about it once or twice."

Ben chuckles. "Yeah, yeah. Can you blame me? You're hard to impress."

"And every boy wants to hear about a potential suitor's perfect surgery record." Jamie laughs, even though he actually *is* impressed. Damn. Ben's never fucked up a surgery? So they definitely have to give him this job. And the two of them have shown Marie Kidjo that he's not a machine, that he has a big heart that just needs a chance to shine.

Or something.

Once they do this with the other people on the search committee, they'll be golden.

Marie is looking between them, a smile hovering on her lips. Jamie's worked for tips long enough to know they've got her. She's buying it. She loves their love.

Gross, but effective.

God, can he get a drink?

Like Ben's reading his mind, he touches Jamie's shoulder and says, "Excuse me for a second. I have to get my boyfriend a drink."

"Thanks, pookie," Jamie says innocently.

Ben shoots him a look, which is half I-hate-you and half bitten-back laughter.

While he's retrieving drinks, Jamie tells the How We Met story. He was hoping Ben would be there, because—well, it just seems better. Ben could add his own touches and embellishments, make it *their* story. Right now, it's just a story Jamie's making up.

Plus, if they both heard it and participated, Jamie wouldn't have to remember the whole thing later when he relates it back to Ben.

He stays light on detail, and when Ben returns with their drinks, he wraps up, "And we sort of both asked each other to dinner at the same time. Right?"

"Yeah, real meet cute," Ben says, handing Jamie his drink.

It's purple. Jamie didn't expect that. He expected… what? He's spent so long thinking Ben's a straight bro that he's still making assumptions; that's what he expected. Straight bros drink martinis. Gin and tonics if they consider themselves more upmarket.

"How did you know?" Jamie says in that way you say it when it's like, *Ha-ha, obviously, because this is the only thing I ever drink.* Ben winks. Good. He gets it.

"Hey, I ran into Billy and Victor. I'm going to go chat with them. You stay here, babe."

Jamie shoots him a look, Ben grins, and then Jamie's alone with Marie. Did Ben want him to come with to talk to Billy (Billy Emmett? Jamie's pretty sure it's Billy Emmett) and Victor Dumas?

"It was sweet of you to come with Ben tonight," Marie says.

Jamie's attention is torn. On the other side of the room, Ben seems to be doing okay, though. Dumas and Emmett seem intent on whatever he's saying. Something relaxes in Jamie's chest, which is stupid. This is Ben's job. These are his colleagues. He's up for this position, so clearly he knows how to handle himself in social situations. Jamie's being oddly overprotective of a man he barely knows, and there's no good reason for it.

Or is there? Is it because he wants to make sure Ben isn't an awkward, weirdo nerd at parties? After all, Jamie's going to need him to be at his best at Andy's house.

It would be better if it was just that.

Jamie decides that's all it is.

"I just want to support him. He's...." Pause for effect and smitten, goopy smile... now. "He's amazing."

Marie smiles. "The two of you seem so happy together. I can't believe he never said anything about you."

"Well"—Jamie waves a hand—"we're both sort of private. Can I tell you something?" When she nods, he leans toward her conspiratorially. "I was *so* nervous about coming here tonight."

"Really?" she asks, laughing a little.

"Oh my god, I felt like I was a debutante or something." He's laying it on thick, but whatever. The point is to make these people like him, and by extension, Ben. "We've kept the relationship quiet. You know, no social media or anything. It's so much pressure sometimes." Especially when you're a queer guy in New York City, but he doesn't say that part out loud. He wonders if Ben feels that pressure. Has Ben ever dated a man?

Marie makes a sympathetic face, and Jamie goes on, "But it's wonderful to meet Ben's colleagues finally. You've all taken on sort of mythological status in my head."

Her skin is too dark to show a blush, but the way her eyes get a bit bright makes Jamie think this landed perfectly. Tens across the board. "Ben must really have another side to him that only comes out in private," she says.

"I know exactly what you're talking about. For ages I thought he was—well, you know how he is." Obviously, Jamie has no idea how Ben acts at work, but Marie nods. "But underneath that, he's…." Jamie lets the goopy smile cross his face again, lets his gaze unfocus, and sighs a little. This performance is Oscar-worthy. "I'd given up on meeting a good, sensitive man in this city."

Marie glances at Ben like she can't believe Jamie's talking about him. Following her gaze, Jamie sees Dumas and Emmett walking in their direction, leaving Ben standing awkwardly by himself. Dumas peels off for another knot of people, while Emmett keeps heading toward Jamie and Marie.

"*McNatt*," Emmett says, rolling his eyes, "still thinks he has a shot."

Marie clears her throat. "Billy, have you met Ben's boyfriend, Jamie?"

Emmett looks mortified. "Oh! Um, no. No, I haven't. He said something about… I just assumed he was being sarcastic…."

"I keep telling him that's going to get him in trouble someday," Jamie says, whipping out the Charming Party Smile. It's the smile that says *No, you absolutely didn't just put your foot so far down your throat that it's sticking out your ass! Don't worry! I didn't notice anything! This isn't awkward!*

Through the smile plastered on his face, Jamie realizes he's angry.

Not just angry. He's pissed off. He's pissed off that Ben's qualified and smart and good at his job and that he *wants* this, and these assholes have already dismissed him.

"Billy Emmett, right?" Jamie asks, offering him a hand. "Ben waxes rhapsodic about you."

Emmett's eyebrows go up. "Ben? I've never heard him wax rhapsodic about anything besides himself. Oh, and that Chuck Mangione song." Shaking his head, he adds, "Does Ben play the flugelhorn or something?"

Uh. Does he? Jamie's going to go out on a limb with this one. "No, he just likes the song." Remembering the way he knew the answer to the trivia question about Mariah Carey, Jamie takes another educated guess. "He loves music."

"Hm." Emmett studies Jamie. "And here I thought Ben McNatt only had room in his heart for one person."

Jamie holds his gaze. "Oh?"

"Yeah." Chuckling like he thinks he's making a hilarious joke, Emmett sticks the punchline: "Ben McNatt."

Anger bubbles in Jamie's chest again. This motherfucking surgeon, he thinks he's so much better than Ben, and by extension, Jamie. He thinks because he's who he is—straight, white, middle-aged, a *doctor*—that he's better than other people.

"Ben has a big heart," Jamie says, using every ounce of willpower he possesses not to grit his teeth.

"Sure he does," Emmett chuckles. When Jamie doesn't laugh, he says, "Oh, you're serious. *How* long have you been with him?"

"Two months."

"You in it for the money, or what?"

Marie looks horrified. "*Billy*," she hisses.

Waving, Emmett says, "Oh, I'm joking. That's what everyone assumes, right? People date doctors for the money. My ex-wife was definitely in it for the money. Gotta hand it to her, though"—he gulps at his drink—"she found herself a good lawyer."

"Ben has a big heart," Jamie repeats, hoping he sounds really dignified and like the much bigger person here. "He just sometimes doesn't know exactly how to show it. Excuse me."

The crown of his head feels hot. His fingertips feel hot. He throws the rest of his drink back, which—it's good, and he didn't even tell Ben that, because Ben trotted off to talk to Emmett, who's a jerk. Like. *Wow.* That guy is a *jerk.* Probably drunk, and maybe he's not as big of a dick when he's sober, but god, Jamie hates people who get mean like that when they're drunk. They're not putting-their-fist-through-the-wall mean drunks. They're the kind that get really snide and cutting, and really *nasty*, and then they play it off like it's a joke. Not drunk enough to have lost all good sense, but drunk enough to let down their inhibitions, which apparently are the only things keeping them from being complete assholes.

He doesn't even realize he's going to Ben until he's at Ben's side. Ben's face lights up. It's good acting. "Jamie! Do you want another drink?"

Jamie looks at his empty glass. "Yeah. And then introduce me to the rest of the search committee."

He's still burning with anger. But there's something else mixed up in that fire now: determination. White-hot, iron-hard determination. No matter what it takes, Ben's going to get this job. The way Emmett talked to Jamie, the way he talked about Ben—Jamie isn't interested in that guy getting his way.

Emmett may have already decided the committee's going to hire someone else, but Jamie's going to do everything in his power to convince the rest of them to choose Ben.

# CHAPTER EIGHT

BEN'S BUZZING when they leave the cocktail hour. If Ben was the kind of person who called things "magical," he'd say this night was magical. It couldn't have gone better. He was on in a way he usually wasn't. Having Jamie next to him made everything easier.

As they leave the hotel, Jamie says, "I was counting how many people complimented your tie."

"Yeah?"

"Yeah." Jamie arches an eyebrow. "Five, for the record."

"Guess I have good taste in ties."

"Um, I guess you owe *me* a thank you for telling you to put it back on."

Shooting a grin at Jamie and smoothing his tie over his chest, Ben says, "Okay, sure. I'll bite. Thanks. You were right."

Jamie preens. "Of course I was right. I'm always right about clothes."

And something about this exchange…. Ben can't put his finger on it. It makes something burbly and light bubble in his chest.

They reach Jamie's train station. Accomplishment or happiness or whatever's humming through Ben seizes him. He's not ready for the night to end yet. "Do you want to come back to my place?"

Shock flashes across Jamie's face, and Ben realizes how that sounds. Hastily, he adds, "Just to hang out! Not to hook up. Or anything. Just, you know." Jamie does *not* look like he knows, so Ben presses on, "I'm like, buzzed. Because this was a good night."

"Some company's nice while you wind down?" Jamie asks.

Exactly. "What do you say?" Ben asks. "I don't live far. We can walk."

Jamie looks like he's biting the inside of his cheek, but he says, "Yeah, okay. Why not?"

Which is how they end up at Ben's apartment. After the obligatory, *wow, it's really nice, this is such a great view, what a great place*, Jamie settles on the leather sofa. His mouth twitches at the way it creaks, like he's barely restraining a laugh.

"What?" Ben asks.

"Of course you have leather furniture." Jamie laughs again. "This is why I was so convinced you were straight."

"I guess I'm flattered you thought about my sexual orientation that much," Ben says. Jamie turns bright red. It's cute. Like, objectively. It's okay for Ben to think that because anyone would. And it's hardly worth noticing how the buzz in Ben's veins picks up at the idea that Jamie's been dissecting the chances of him being attracted to men.

"Can I ask you something?" Jamie says.

"Uh—sure?"

"Why that cocktail?"

It takes Ben a second to rewind his brain and figure out what Jamie's talking about. Duh, the cocktail hour, and the drink he brought to Jamie. Ben gives him a chagrined look. "Did you hate it? I realized when I got up there that I have no idea what you drink, besides coffee."

"I hate coffee."

"You—what?"

"I hate coffee," Jamie repeats.

"But you work at a coffee shop."

"*Do* I?" Jamie gasps.

"Okay, ha-ha, very funny."

Jamie grins. "So actually, you don't know what I drink at all. Why'd you choose that one?"

"It just popped into my head," Ben says. "I tried to imagine what kind of cocktail you'd like, and I thought… well, it wouldn't be something everyone else orders. It would be a little quirky, but classy. Something timeless. And striking. Attractive." He feels his face get hot. Great. Now *he's* the one blushing. He should've quit like, three sentences ago. "So, yeah. Aviation. That's what popped into my head."

"I liked it," Jamie says reassuringly. And then, "You think I'm attractive?"

Ben knows he's stupidly red right now. "I mean. C'mon. I'm not blind. You *are* attractive."

Jamie bites his lower lip, trying not to smile, and Ben forgets how to breathe.

Clearing his throat and turning away so Jamie won't see his expression, Ben says, "Can I get you something to drink? Sparkling water? I think it's blackberry."

"Yeah, that's fine, thanks."

Maybe he takes longer in the kitchen than he has to, just to give his face a chance to stop doing its best imitation of a tomato. And to let his heart slow down, because it's hammering. Because he's making a fool of himself. Putting his foot in his mouth. The only reason this whole thing isn't awkward as hell is sheer force of will on both of their parts. If they refuse to feel awkward, it doesn't have to be awkward.

He cracks open two cans of sparkling water and returns to the living room, sitting next to Jamie on the sofa and handing him the can. With a smirk of thanks, Jamie takes a sip. It's obvious the minute the bubbles hit his nose, because it wrinkles, and Ben feels a shot of pure carbonation in his blood. His stomach fizzes and flutters.

"Thanks for tonight," Ben says. "You were great."

Jamie does a little mock bow, twirling his hand several times. "I've been preparing for this role my whole life." When Ben's eyebrows go up, Jamie colors faintly and quickly takes another sip of water. "I hope I was convincing. Anyway, you don't have to thank me. Andy's thing is still coming up. It's not like I'm doing this for nothing."

"You were definitely convincing. I think everyone loved you."

"Good. That's what you wanted, right?"

After swallowing a sip of his own water, Ben says, "Technically, I want them to love you so they'll love me."

"Hm."

It sounds like there's more behind that *hm*, so Ben waits. Jamie doesn't go on, just taps a fingernail on the side of the can. If they were really dating, Ben might tiptoe around whatever Jamie's thinking. But they're not. "Okay, spit it out. It's not like you have to worry about me making you sleep on the sofa."

Jamie snorts. "If we were really dating, you'd never banish me to the sofa, no matter how much I pissed you off." The smile that flickers across his face contains a hint of wicked mischief.

A hot bolt of desire goes through Ben. Yikes. He's going to have to get *that* under control.

Setting his water down, Jamie says, "I don't think you're as close to getting this job as you think you are."

Ben crosses one leg over the other and leans back. "Well, yeah. That's why we're doing this whole thing."

"Emmett basically said you're not getting the job."

A chill sinks through Ben's gut, but he waves a hand. "Whatever. That's Emmett. He was drunk. And he's never been my biggest fan."

"He's the other neurosurgeon-in-chief. You sort of need him to be your biggest fan." Jamie sips at his water. "It wasn't just him, anyway. I was watching—what's his name, AJ?—talking to Victor."

When Jamie pauses meaningfully, Ben says, "Yeah? And?"

"And," Jamie says, before pausing again. God, he's super dramatic. "The way he talked to Victor was completely different from how he talked to you."

"Well, they've known each other longer," Ben says, but he's feeling less confident.

A muscle twitches in Jamie's face. "Ben. You're at a disadvantage. These people are already inclined to pass you over for this job because they have history with their favorite candidate. One of them's already decided he doesn't want you to have the job. Introducing me as your boyfriend a couple times isn't going to change anything."

"So what," Ben asks, bristling. The buzz in his veins has gone flat. "Are you backing out?"

"No!" Jamie glares. How did they get from blushing and kind of flirty to glaring at each other? "No, I'm saying we have to do more. We have to make them really *like* you. We need to sell this relationship better."

Even though he's still feeling preemptively defensive, Ben takes a deep breath and makes himself consider what Jamie's saying. When Adriana warned him the search committee didn't think he had enough of a heart, he thought she was exaggerating. Jamie telling him the same thing means... they might both be wrong. But if Ben's getting a second opinion, Jamie is a good one.

"Okay," he says slowly. "So how do we do that? Please don't tell me you put together a Powerpoint deck."

Jamie gives him a withering look. "Yeah, I'll send it to you from my Outlook. God, I'm trying to help you, you know. Don't be insulting." When Ben snorts with laughter, that same wicked smile flickers across Jamie's face. "Anyway. I don't think we planned enough appearances together. Can we like, be seen somewhere by your coworkers? The search committee would be better, but if it can get back to them...."

"Sure, there are doctor cafes and stuff," Ben says. "Are you taking me out to lunch?"

"Only if you're *very* good," Jamie says, and Ben feels his blood surge. His face is red again, and Jamie looks like he's enjoying himself immensely.

Clearing his throat, Ben says, "Fine, great. We'll go out more. You can come to the hospital more too. Maybe meet me when I'm leaving work."

"We should text each other," Jamie says decisively. "You know that stupid look people get on their face when they're texting their significant other? Make that face at your phone when I text you."

Furrowing his brow, Ben says, "Yeah, I'm not sure I know exactly what face you're talking about."

With a long-suffering sigh, Jamie says, "Okay—text me something."

"What?"

"Anything! It doesn't matter." He fishes his phone out of his pocket and jiggles it in his hand expectantly.

This is stupid, but Jamie's really confident, and honestly, doing this isn't going to cost Ben anything. It might even help, if Jamie's right. So he unlocks his phone and opens up his texts. His thumb hovers over the text field, and he very stupidly can't figure out what to say.

Christ. It doesn't matter. He opens up his emojis and just sends the first one in his most used, which is apparently a slice of pizza. He literally can't remember ever sending the pizza emoji, but okay, sure. Whatever.

"Watch and learn," Jamie says as his phone buzzes. He looks down at it, and—

His eyes absolutely light up, and a smile splits his face before he bites it back. But it lingers around his lips, private and happy, as he looks at Ben's text. He presses his lips together, clearly trying not to smile wider, as he types something in return, then locks his phone.

"That's how it's done," Jamie says, all business now.

His text comes through. It's a broccoli emoji. Ben smiles.

"Good," Jamie says, sounding pleased. "That's it. That's exactly it."

Ben's eyes snap up. "I'm not...," he starts. But does he really want to finish that sentence? "Got it. Any other ideas?"

"Pictures. Here—" Jamie unlocks his phone, flips the camera around, and leans in closer to Ben. "Smile," he orders.

Ben does it without thinking. They aren't touching, but Ben can feel Jamie's body heat. He still smells like a dream, traces of his cologne and... other stuff. Masculine stuff. Some sweat, not like, BO level, but just a normal amount of sweat. And skin. And there's a definite musky *man* smell, and it makes Ben's fingertips and toes tingle.

Jamie holds his phone out to show Ben. "This is okay, I guess."

Ben studies the photo. It's not the best picture of him. At least he's smiling? It's actually a genuine smile, because Jamie startled him with the command in his voice.

It's a nice picture of Jamie, though. His smile is mischievous and there's a glint in his eyes that makes Ben want to be in on the joke.

They look like a nice couple.

The tingle in Ben's fingertips gets tinglier.

"We should have more," Jamie says. "In different places. And different clothes. You need some with my family."

"Um, great," Ben says. "Except I've never met your family."

Jamie chews the inside of his cheek. "Yeah. Well. Lucky you. My dad and brother are coming into town in a couple weeks. You can meet them then." He draws a slow breath in through his nose. "I'll tell them you're my boyfriend. They'll definitely want photographic proof that the whole thing happened."

"You're seriously willing to let me horn in on your time with your family, and lie to them about dating me, just for some pictures? You really want to help me out that much?"

"Isn't that what you want?"

"Yeah, but…." Ben stares. "I don't get it."

Shrugging, Jamie says, "I guess I'm just a really nice person."

"Uh-huh." Ben eyes him, not buying that for a second. Jamie's fine, but Ben wouldn't call him *nice*. Funny, razor sharp, keenly intelligent. Charming. Good at playing nice.

It's not off-putting. Not in Jamie. It's the opposite.

"Anyway," Jamie says, "you'd be doing me a favor if you came out to dinner with us. When they come into town, it's always…."

His nose wrinkles and he doesn't finish the sentence. "A time?" Ben supplies.

Giving Ben a sidelong look, Jamie says, "Yeah."

Ben grunts. "I get that." Drumming his fingers on his knee, he says, "Yeah, sure. For the pictures. That's a good idea. When are they going to be here?"

Jamie's nose wrinkles again. "The same weekend as Andy's thing in the Poconos, unfortunately."

"Yeah, no problem. I'll be there." He doesn't even have to think about it. Meeting Jamie's dad and brother? Lying to them to help keep them off Jamie's back? Definitely. Ben's happy to do it. Maybe happier to do it than he should be… and happier than he should let on.

Jamie smiles. "Thanks."

"Shouldn't I be thanking you?" Ben says. There's a teasing note in his voice that he didn't plan on using. It just sneaks in. "Seriously. All this extra stuff—the pictures, spending more time together. You seem like…." *You seem way more invested than I deserve.* "This is way beyond what we agreed on. I appreciate it."

Jamie flicks a wrist. "It's fine. If I can't fix my own life, maybe I can fix yours."

It sounds like a joke, but Ben feels like he has his fingers jammed in a crack in Jamie's walls now, and he can just barely see inside.

And it's not a joke.

Ben knows he should say something, like… what? Your life doesn't need to be fixed? You're doing exactly what you want to be doing? You seem really fulfilled working at that coffee shop?

Could he get any more patronizing?

He clears his throat. "More hanging out, texting, and pictures. I think it's all coming together."

Jamie's eyes dart toward him. "There was one other thing."

"What?"

Jamie looks nervous. "PDA. I think we should…." He trails off and waves vaguely.

Heat rises up Ben's neck. Oh. He clears his throat. "Like holding hands and stuff? Or… I mean, I guess kissing, right?"

Jamie goes bright red. "We don't have to kiss if you don't want to," he says. "Sorry. That was stupid. And probably inappropriate. Sorry."

Ben remembers how Victor and his wife looked so happy together. That was a guy you looked at and assumed he'd care about you. You could see it in the way he looked at his wife.

People don't look at him at work like that. He's cold and aloof, which he always thought would be reassuring. You don't want the guy cutting into your brain to think with his heart—you want him logical and calculating.

Marie even said it. He's a machine.

Which is why Victor's going to get this job and Ben isn't. Unless he lets Jamie help him.

"Kissing," he says. "Yeah." Which, okay, *that* wasn't English. "I mean, no. Yes. I think that's a good idea. We should do that."

Jamie clears his throat and mumbles something. When Ben furrows his brow, Jamie repeats, "Doweneedtopracticetomakeitconvincing?"

Something is stuck in Ben's throat. His fingers tingle again. He's been going to the same coffee shop every day for two years just to see this man. He loves looking at him, from his black curls to his bright blue eyes to his sinewy arms to his narrow hips and legs for days. He's jerked off to fantasies of him.

In other words, considering he has no interest in dating anyone for real, practicing is a bad idea. He knows how to care about his job, and that's it. He doesn't know how to care about another person. Not like that.

Ben meets Jamie's eyes.

God, they're gorgeous.

"Yeah," he says slowly. "I guess we probably should. We don't want to look like a couple middle-schoolers trying to figure out where their noses go."

Jamie laughs. Red blotches his cheeks. He has faint freckles smattered across the bridge of his nose and his cheekbones. They're the sort of thing you don't notice unless you're... well, close enough to kiss someone.

"I guess we should start by holding hands?" Jamie asks. His tongue wets his lips. "We don't want to look like middle-schoolers doing that, either."

"Definitely not." If he doesn't just give Jamie his hand, then he's turning this into a thing, which it most definitely isn't. This is not A Thing and it's not going to be. So Ben sucks in a breath and slides his hand into Jamie's.

Their fingers thread together. Jamie's hand is warm and a little rough. His fingers feel strong. The way he's clasping Ben's hand feels almost at odds with the graceful way his fingers move when he's making coffee.

Without thinking, Ben strokes his thumb over the back of Jamie's hand. Just like they look like a nice couple in the picture Jamie took of them, their hands look nice together. They fit.

Ben wasn't expecting that.

"Well," Jamie says, "that seems to work fine." Ben's eyes flick up to meet his. Does Jamie sound a little too casual? Like he's trying too hard to sound like he doesn't care about what's happening? Or is Ben projecting and looking for something that isn't there, just so he feels less like an idiot?

"Yeah," Ben agrees. "So should we try the next part?"

"Um—hold on." Turning away, Jamie tries to discreetly check his breath. It's not discreet, but it's hella cute, and Ben has to bite back a grin before he realizes he'd better do the same thing.

Satisfied he's not going to bowl Jamie over with post-cocktail-party halitosis, he turns back—and finds his face much closer to Jamie's than he remembers it being. Jamie looks surprised too. "Um," Ben says.

There's still color in Jamie's cheeks. More, actually. And from this distance, his freckles are constellations to map. "Do you usually…," Jamie starts, then trails off with an inarticulate sound.

Ben's inexperience suddenly seems daunting. There was Adriana, and there was a boyfriend before her, and a girlfriend before that. He's never hooked up. One time he made out with a dude in a club after too many drinks. The dude asked if he wanted to take things to the restroom, and Ben chickened out and made an excuse to get away.

The point is, he doesn't go around casually kissing people that he isn't emotionally invested in, and he doesn't like getting emotionally invested in people—so he's not sure how to start this practice kiss.

Can't he give Jamie a peck on the mouth? That's the kind of thing people do in public.

Just as he assures himself he can totally do that, and it's cool and not weird or awkward or something to think too much about, Jamie raises a hand to Ben's face. He cups Ben's jaw in one of those big, just-the-tiniest-bit-rough hands. Suddenly it's impossible to breathe. Ben swallows, Jamie leans in, and their lips brush.

The world narrows to this space, just them sitting on this sofa, hands clasped, lips touching. Ben can hear his own heartbeat and Jamie's breathing. He can hear his own breath hitching. He can hear—he thinks—the tiniest noise in the back of Jamie's throat.

It feels like a perfectly acceptable kiss. It feels like the kind of kiss you'd do in public. They're fine, they can pull it off. No need to continue with this charade.

Ben doesn't pull away. He slips his free hand to Jamie's neck, curling his fingers around the back. His fingertips sink into Jamie's hair, and Jamie's skin is warm, and his hair is soft, and Ben wants to pull it out of its bun and run his fingers through it.

He doesn't. But he moves in closer. And he deepens the kiss.

His tongue swipes over Jamie's bottom lip. The rational part of his brain screams at him to stop and apologize for this base indecency.

The rational part of his brain didn't count on Jamie's mouth opening. His tongue slides against Ben's. A helpless, breathy sound comes from Jamie, a puff of hot breath into Ben's mouth, and ignites heat, low and insistent, in his belly. It makes his entire body ache. It makes him feel full and empty at the same time. It makes him want something he can't have, something that he's not supposed to want at all.

Jamie's fingers stroke down his jawline, over the bristle of his goatee, and down his neck. His thumb settles in the hollow of Ben's throat. Ben feels Jamie slide a leg onto the sofa, and how he lets his knees fall apart, widening his legs so Ben can fit between them if he wants to—

The rational part of his brain finally hits the panic button.

Also, he's getting hard.

Ben rocks back, dropping his hand from Jamie's neck and pulling the other from Jamie's grip. Jamie snatches his hand back from Ben's chest and snaps his legs shut. The erection is making Ben panic, and he's hiding it with an arm over his lap, which is basically the equivalent of putting up a flashing neon sign that says YOU JUST GAVE ME A BONER.

They stare at each other. Ben's lips are tingling, and the places where Jamie's fingers touched him are on fire. Jamie's throat bobs. Then, he lets an easy smile crack his face. "Pretty good, right? For a fake kiss?"

Ben laughs. He hopes it doesn't sound as forced to Jamie as it sounds in Ben's own head. "Yeah. That'll fool everyone."

There's the barest stutter in Jamie's smile, the tiniest flicker in his eyes. Then it's gone and he's checking his phone. Oh god, that's not a good sign. You don't want someone immediately looking at their phone after your first kiss with them.

Then again, it wasn't a real kiss. It was just practice.

Jamie clears his throat. "So, not to hit it and quit it, but…."

"It's late, and you have to be up early for work," Ben fills in for him, maybe a little too eagerly. "Right. Of course. Sorry, I shouldn't have kept you so long."

Jamie stands, his hands clasped in front of his hips. "Did things just get awkward?" he asks as they walk to the door. "Did I make them awkward?"

"No," Ben assures him. "No, of course not. It was a good idea." His lips are still tingling.

Jamie shifts from one foot to the other. His face is flushed and his eyes are bright. "I'm not leaving because...."

"I know," Ben says. He hears a gentleness in his tone that's not really intentional. It's just that Jamie seems so torn up, so intent on making sure Ben understands this point, even though Ben's pretty sure he *is* leaving because of the kiss. It's okay, because Ben doesn't know what to make of it and doesn't know what to think about the fact that his skin is still sparking.

"I'll text you," he says, smiling, waiting for Jamie to meet his eyes. When Jamie does, Ben adds, "Thanks again for tonight. Thanks for...." He searches for words. "For wanting to help."

"Like I said, at least I can fix *someone's* life." He says it like it's a joke again. It seems like even less of one this time. Smiling faintly, Jamie opens the door and says, "Good night, Ben."

Then he's gone. The door swings shut behind him, closing with a thunk.

Ben's skin still crackles.

# CHAPTER NINE

JAMIE MAKES it two blocks before he lets himself think about what just happened.

And then he thinks about Ben's lips on his, Ben's warmth under his palms, the way Ben's breath did that teeny tiny little hitch, and Jamie's not even sure he knew he did it, but Jamie heard it, and Jamie, he....

He needs to take a deep breath, that's what he needs to do.

He needs a plan. Okay. How's this? Step one: don't catch feelings. Step two: ignore them if you do. Step three: get awesome job. Step four: rock new, awesome job so much you don't even miss Ben when you don't have any reason to see him anymore. Step five: ????

*Are you in surgery right now?*
**I don't have any surgeries scheduled today**
Jamie sends back a thumbs up emoji.
**What does that mean?**
*I'm coming for lunch. See you in fifteen minutes*

Jamie's phone buzzes again—a bunch of times—but he leaves it in his pocket until he's in the elevator heading up to Neurosurgery at NewYork-Presbyterian.

**I can't do lunch right now, I'm busy**
**Can we do it tomorrow?**
**Jamie srsly**
**Omg you're just going to show up aren't you... you don't even know where my office is**
**I don't have to tell you**
**Gdi**
**Office # is 177**

The minute Jamie knocks on his door, Ben yells, "Yeah, come in!"

Jamie breezes in, announces, "Hi!" leans over the desk, and plants a kiss on Ben's forehead.

Ben's eyes are wide. Jamie jerks his head at the open doorway. "Where should we get lunch?" Jamie asks cheerfully.

Ben slouches over the desk. "I'm seriously busy. You can't just show up. Don't you work?"

"I'm going in late today. We talked about lunch. Remember?"

Ben tries to stare him down before he sighs, running a hand through his hair. When Jamie came in, it was all neat and perfectly in place, his bangs slicked back. Now, it's tousled and falling over his forehead.

And Jamie likes ruffling Ben a little too much. It's a challenge to stop himself from thinking about all the ways he could make him come undone.

So, yeah. Maybe he's thought about the kiss. Once or twice. Or like. A hundred times. Maybe he's thought about it on the train listening to music. Or when he's making drinks on autopilot at work. Or as he walks down the sidewalk.

Maybe he's thought about it in bed. And maybe, some of those times, he's thought about what might have happened if they'd kept kissing.

In all their texting since that night, Ben hasn't brought it up. And he was really nice after they did it. Even though Jamie was freaking out, Ben was calm and kind and obviously determined to treat it as exactly what it was, which was two mature adults making sure they could convincingly perform some light PDA.

Jamie stares at Ben's mouth before dragging his eyes upward. "I'm here to see and be seen, Ben," he says, perching on the desk.

His gaze roves the room. It's... austere. There are few personal touches, unless you count plaques and awards as personal touches. They have Ben's name on them, so maybe?

Jamie goes to look at them. There are... a lot. Smirking, he says, "So, it seems like you're a good doctor?"

Ben snorts. "For all the good it's doing me, apparently."

Bookshelves on the wall house medical texts, mostly on neurosurgery. Jamie chooses one at random and flips it open, and there's Ben's name. "You wrote this?"

Ben looks uncomfortable. "Contributed." He comes out from behind the desk and fishes the book from Jamie's hands.

"Hey, I was reading that."

"Why?" Ben shakes his head. "It'll just be jargon to you."

"Maybe I'm interested in bettering myself."

"You should read *War and Peace* or something, then. Not this stuff." Ben moves toward the door. "Lunch?"

Arching an eyebrow, Jamie says, "I thought you were busy."

Ben raises an eyebrow right back. "C'mon, babe. I'm buying."

Jamie grits his teeth and growls, but it's playful. "You're the worst."

"Uh-huh." They step out into the hallway, and Ben's hand brushes across the small of Jamie's back. A jolt of electricity tears straight up Jamie's spine.

"That okay?" Ben murmurs so quietly that Jamie barely catches it.

Jamie nods. Starbursts and lightning fire under his skin and he doesn't trust himself to speak. On impulse, he reaches out and touches Ben's back himself.

Ben shoots a look at him, and now Jamie's concerned he did something wrong. But before he can—what, apologize? They had a whole long conversation about this, and they *kissed*, and—

Shit, the kiss. Now Jamie's thinking about the kiss.

They're saved from further awkwardness by—well, possibly more awkwardness, in the form of a man walking down the hall. "Ben," he says as he slips past them.

"Mark!" Ben exclaims, sounding way too jovial. "Mark, have you met my boyfriend?"

Mark doesn't, quite frankly, look like he cares, or like he wants to stop. He's holding a paper bag soaked with grease spots and a sweating bottle of Pepsi.

With a wave, Jamie says, "Hi."

"We haven't met. You *date*?" Mark asks.

Looking irritated, Ben says, "Why does everyone find that so unbelievable?"

Mark looks like he could go on at length, but Jamie extends a hand. "Mark, right? Are you a neurosurgeon here too? I'm Jamie, by the way."

"Oh, yeah. Neurosurgery." Mark makes a halfhearted attempt to juggle his lunch and drink, then shrugs. Jamie doesn't really want to shake his hand anyway, since his choices are clammy condensation or grease. Mark gives Ben another disbelieving look. "I didn't know you were gay, either," he says accusingly.

"Bi," Ben says. "I'll make sure to keep my Bisexual Card more prominently displayed so I don't blindside you again."

Mark rolls his eyes and turns away. "Nice to meet you," he says without looking over his shoulder.

Keeping a straight face is a struggle, and Jamie knows if he looks at Ben, he's going to lose the battle. When they get to the elevator, Jamie risks a glance at Ben. Their eyes meet, and they both start giggling like kids.

"You know, *I* didn't actually check your Bisexual Card," Jamie says. "We probably should make sure that's all in order before we keep dating."

"Doesn't the requirement to present the card get waived if we have sex?" Ben says.

Jamie's palms get warm. "Oh," he says. His eyes rake up and down Ben, who's clearly trying not to turn red. "Oh," he repeats. "I see."

Ben punches the elevator button, looking like he wishes there were a few more steps to the process he could focus on. "I mean," he says. Coughs, more like. "I just. Two months."

"No, that's reasonable." Jamie's palms are still warm. "I agree. Two months. Plenty of time."

"I'm not like, an on-the-first-date kind of guy," Ben says, like this is important information for Jamie to know.

Mercifully, the elevator arrives before Jamie figures out how to politely say he's more of a Grindr hookup or a blow-job-in-the-club-bathroom guy.

"I think we slept together after our second date," he says instead.

Ben's head snaps around. "You'd sleep with me after the second date?"

The elevator opens on the ground floor. Jamie shoots him a sharp smile. "You wouldn't want to sleep with me after two dates?"

They leave the hospital without Ben answering, which is fine.

And Jamie takes Ben's hand. Which he hopes is fine.

Ben interlaces their fingers and squeezes. So that's good.

"I don't date a lot," Ben says as they walk. "Maybe I suck at it."

"Well, I don't either," Jamie says. "I used to do the whole"—he waves a hand vaguely—"Grindr thing."

"I never had the guts," Ben says sheepishly. "I downloaded it once. Made a profile and everything. But I chickened out when I got a message from someone who wanted to… uh. Maybe I shouldn't say it in polite company."

"One, I'm hardly polite company. Two, I will personally guarantee you that whatever that message said, I've seen much worse."

"Okay." Ben takes a breath. "He asked me if he could come over and eat my ass so clean that it would sparkle."

Jamie lets out such a loud laugh that people look at him. He claps a hand over his mouth. "Sorry."

A smile pulls at one side of Ben's mouth. "I panicked and deleted the app."

"Oh my god." Jamie brings their clasped hands to his heart. "That's really cute."

"It's really lame."

"Why? Because you don't want to have casual sex? Who cares?"

"I don't know." Ben stares into the distance. They walk in silence, because Jamie senses he might add something if he feels like there's space for him to. "Sometimes I guess I feel like… there's not a place for me in the community? Like, I don't know. I'm not the right kind of queer. I don't use Grindr, I don't go to clubs or bath houses or like… any of that stuff."

Jamie squeezes his hand. "You don't have to. You know that, right? There's not a checklist of approved activities for men who like to fuck other men."

With a wry smile, Ben says, "Intellectually? Sure. I know." He shrugs. "But I still stopped going to Pride. I feel too boring for it."

This makes Jamie blindingly, achingly sad, and god, he hopes he's never done anything to make someone feel like they weren't meeting a nonexistent queer standard. There's nothing like Pride in New York City, and Ben deserves to feel like there's a place for him there, and… is it bad that Jamie wants to be the one to show him that?

Pride's in a few weeks. Will they still be fake dating?

Maybe they don't need to be. Maybe they could still hang out? Maybe Jamie *could* bring Ben to Pride?

Once they have lunch—turkey melt on rye for Ben, veggie melt for Jamie—they walk to a nearby park and find a free bench under the shade of a maple. The smell of pot smoke hangs in the air, underpinned by summer-in-New-York smell. It's indefinable—the smell of exhaust fumes and sweat, sunscreen and grease, garbage and sewage, and if you're close enough to either the East River or the Hudson, water. You could pluck Jamie out of this city, blindfold him, fly him in circles, and when you put him back down, he'd know New York by that smell alone.

Jamie takes a big bite of his sandwich. Hot, gooey cheese starts to slide over his bottom lip, and he sticks his tongue out to catch it, licking to get it back in his mouth.

Is it his imagination, or is Ben staring at his mouth?

The next bite Jamie takes is smaller so he can avoid lasciviously licking his lips. "I had an idea," he says. "Remember how I said we need pictures of us together?"

"Sure." Ben's expression freezes. "Oh. Is it not cool if I go out with you and your family? No, yeah, I totally get that. It was nice of you to invite me in the first place—"

"No, you're still stuck doing that with me," Jamie interrupts. Ben's cute when he gets flustered. "I was thinking we should have other pictures too."

Ben gropes for his phone and pulls it out to snap a selfie of them. Jamie really hopes he got all the melted cheese off his face. "There's one."

"If you're not busy tomorrow, do you want to go out with me?" Jamie asks. Ben's eyebrows shoot up. "To get more pictures, I mean! I was thinking—okay, don't laugh. But I thought we could go around to a bunch of romantic spots in the city. And we can take pictures of ourselves there, like for all our dates."

"That's a good idea," Ben says. Jamie glows. Then Ben's face falls. "But we'll be wearing the same clothes in all of them. It will be really obvious they were all taken on the same day."

"Oh ye of little faith," Jamie says smugly. "I thought about that too. We can bring changes of clothing. That way it'll look like we took the pictures over the last two months."

He takes another big bite of his sandwich, which makes an avocado slice smoosh out the back. He squishes it back in, the tip of his finger disappearing knuckle-deep between the two halves of the bun.

Okay, he… isn't sure why he thought of it that way. Hastily, he pulls his finger out and sticks it in his mouth to lick off avocado and aioli, but that doesn't seem a lot better.

"What do you think?" he asks, his voice coming out a little too high pitched. He's acting like an idiot. He's *eating a sandwich*. Why is he turning it into OnlyFans porn in his head?

"Saturday?" Well, at least Ben doesn't seem to think Jamie is giving off OnlyFans vibes. "As in, tomorrow, Saturday?"

"Yeah. Does that work? I normally take Saturdays off."

"I'm not busy." Ben smiles. "Good thing I haven't made up anything about vacationing together. People would want to see the pictures."

"Do you go on vacations?"

The minute the words are out of his mouth, he wants to kick himself. It's a shit thing to say. The problem is, he feels like he knows Ben so much better than he actually does.

But Ben laughs. "Am I that obvious?"

Whew. "Sort of," Jamie says. "Your job seems really important to you."

Sobering, Ben says, "Well, yeah. It is. I guess that's not much of a surprise."

Jamie doesn't say that he doesn't take vacations either—but it doesn't have anything to do with being devoted to his job. He can't afford a vacation. Not the kind of vacation he knows, based on the apartment he saw the other night, that Ben can, if he could tear himself away from work.

Jamie finishes his sandwich. "Who needs vacation, right?"

"What about this thing at your boss's place? In the Poconos? That's kind of a vacation."

Jamie presses his lips into a line and looks away. "Yeah, not really. That's going to be more about making sure he doesn't put his hand on my ass."

There's a heavy silence. When Jamie looks at Ben, there's a troubled expression on his face. "I...." Ben starts, then clamps his mouth shut.

And okay, maybe Jamie shouldn't have said it like that. But he was going to have to warn Ben about Andy sooner or later.

Drawing a deep breath, Ben asks, "Is he sexually harassing you? Your boss?"

It's everything Jamie can do not to let out a harsh bark of laughter. Instead, he crumples up the sandwich wrapping. He opens his mouth to... he doesn't even know. Turn it into a joke? Brush it off? But it's not a joke, even if he does brush it off. Even if he brushes it off every single day, because what else is he supposed to do?

Jamie sucks in a breath through his teeth and smiles. Ben doesn't smile back. "What time's good tomorrow? I'll meet you outside your building."

Ben looks thrown by the change of subject. "I guess we should get an early start."

"Good idea."

"Eight? Seven thirty?" Realization flashes across his face. "How far do you have to come? Is it going to be a long drive? Wait—or do you have to take the train? Or a bus?"

"It's fine," Jamie says. "I'm used to getting up early."

"I don't even know where you live," Ben says. There's an odd quality to his voice, like he's... annoyed? Something in Jamie cringes, even though logically, he can't imagine what Ben's annoyed about.

Jamie stands. Suddenly his skin feels crawly. Like Ben's going to see through him if he sits here any longer. See through him to... what? That he's a colossal failure. That he puts up with sexual harassment because he's too chicken to look for a new job.

"I live in the Bronx," Jamie says. "Highbridge. The commute's not that bad."

Ben's hair is flopping over his forehead, and Jamie's heart, his stupid heart, is fluttering. It must be obvious. Somehow it's obvious, because Ben's giving him this look that Jamie can't figure out.

"I didn't know that," Ben says.

"I know. I never told you."

"I should've asked."

"Yeah, well. It's not like I'm ever going to have you over. Even if we were dating for real, I wouldn't bring you back there."

Something flickers across Ben's face, and he jumps to his feet. Before Jamie quite knows what's happening, Ben's hands skim his cheeks, and his lips brush across Jamie's.

He tastes like sauerkraut. It's not horrible, even though it should be.

"One of the surgical assistants was walking by," Ben says.

Jamie nods and tries to banish the image of Ben at his place. It snuck into his head without his permission, and thinking about it isn't going to do him any good. "Right. Practice."

# CHAPTER TEN

THERE'S A STEADY trickle of customers when Jamie gets to work, so there isn't much opportunity to talk to Val. Ben texts a few times, which is nice. Lunch got weird, which was definitely Jamie's fault. He's good at making things weird.

But Ben sent him a dumb meme, and Jamie responded with an equally dumb meme, and it turned into actual talking. Unimportant stuff. A rude customer, a funny case in the ED, that kind of thing.

"What's up with you lately?"

Jamie starts and looks up to find Val right in front of him He was staring at his phone and didn't notice her.

He sticks his phone in his pocket, closing the text from Ben. "What do you mean? Nothing's up."

Val purses her lips. "*Something* is. You've been weird the last few days. And you keep smiling at your phone. Are you back on Grindr?"

His immediate instinct is to brush it off with a *yeah, Grindr.* He doesn't want to lie to her, and that's what his relationship with Ben is: a lie.

He can't tell her the truth, and she's going to find out sooner or later that he supposedly has a boyfriend. Better for her to hear the lie from him.

"Okay, so." He must sound super serious, because the smirk drops off her face. "I didn't want to say anything before."

The door opens and a group of teenagers comes in, talking loudly. Jamie moves behind the counter. This isn't the kind of conversation he wants to yell over the steaming wand, so he makes the drinks and waits until the group claims the table in the corner.

Val looks to Jamie expectantly. "Are you coming out to me or something?"

"What? I *am* out to you. I mean, I'm out. Generally."

She shrugs. "I thought maybe you were going to add something else. Nonbinary? Aromantic?"

"You'll be the first to know if I am, but no."

Val snorts. "I'm your bestie. I better be the first to know about the big stuff."

His phone buzzes in his pocket. He wonders if it's Ben.

"I'm seeing someone," he says, and because he couldn't decide if he should say it super casually or all in a rush, it comes out too fast, all the words slurring together and inflected up at the end, like he's not sure. I'mseeingsomeone?

The expression on Val's face doesn't tell him if she didn't understand a word he said or if she thinks he's fucking with her.

Clearing his throat, he repeats, "I'm seeing someone. Like. Romantically. So, um. Yeah. That's probably what you've noticed."

Her jaw drops. "You're *seeing* someone? Oh my god, *what*? You fucking *asshole*, how dare you not tell me? *Shit*!" There's a huge grin on her face, and she thumps him on the shoulder, then gives him a one-armed hug. "Seriously, why didn't you tell me? Is this like a whole, you don't tell people about a pregnancy in the first trimester thing? You didn't want to say you were dating because it's only been a couple weeks?"

"Weeeell," Jamie says, and Val's smile falters. "That's the thing. It's actually been more like a couple months." He winces as her grin turns to a scowl.

"A couple *months*?" she demands. Good thing the teenagers at the corner table are like all teenagers—completely wrapped up in themselves. There are a few other occupied tables. The women at two of them have headphones in and seem oblivious to the drama playing out behind the bar. The man, who is clearly as gay as the day is long, is watching with interest.

"Um, yeah." Jamie runs his fingers through his hair. "I just—I didn't want to say anything. He did. But I was just kind of weird about it, because you know, I don't date anymore, because I'm not much good at it...."

If he didn't need this job, he'd turn to the guy watching them and snap, *Are you getting all this?* Because clearly, nothing this entertaining has happened to the kid in weeks.

Val doesn't look happy. "Did you think I'd judge you or something?"

"Um...." No? Yes? He hasn't thought about why he fake-hid his fake relationship. Maybe he should ask his fake boyfriend why he might fake-want-to-shout-their-love-from-the-rooftops while Jamie was fake-reticent about saying anything. "I didn't want the pressure, I guess. You know how it is. You have to post on insta all the time, and it's like, you have to have this perfect relationship. Especially for gay guys. You just... you have to look the part. All the time."

It's a lie, but it's not a lie. The pressure to have a perfect relationship is pressure he can't handle. Making it look good on social media would be the easiest part.

"I don't want my relationships to be performative," Jamie says. "So. Yeah. I didn't say anything because of that. Forgive me?"

Her face softens into a smile. "Of course, you idiot. I mean, I'm mad, and you're definitely going to have to buy me like, at *least* four drinks. Top shelf, not rail." She wraps an arm around him again. "But mostly I'm just happy you're with someone and it's going well. Right? It's going well?"

Jamie's smile, guarded but irrepressible, should be an act.

His phone buzzes again in his pocket.

It might not be an act.

"Yeah," he says, and he knows the sappy, goofy smile on his face says it all.

Val straightens the shrink-wrapped brownies and cookies next to the register. "So how'd you meet him?"

"Here, actually." Jamie looks toward the ceiling so he doesn't have to see her reaction. Or the guy at the table, still watching them. Jamie wants to get a bag of microwave popcorn for him.

Jamie clears his throat. "It's… uh. Tall, Douchey, and Handsome."

The silence of a post-apocalyptic wasteland couldn't compare to what falls between them. Val stares expressionlessly. No jaw drop. Just a flat, unblinking stare.

The teenagers laugh and break the spell. Everything starts moving again, the M21 roaring by, car horns blaring, pedestrians yelling, music blasting from open windows. The hum and hiss of the espresso machine and the coffee urns, and the drip of the leaky faucet.

"You're shitting me," she says.

Is she mad? Was there an unspoken rule he didn't know about, where they both totally thought Ben was an asshole and they definitely wouldn't date him even if they had the chance? Not that Val ever showed interest in him beyond acknowledging he's hot, but that's just, like, having eyes.

"I'm not," he says. "His name's Ben. He's a surgeon at NewYork-Presbyterian."

There's a suspicious look in her eyes now. "Okay, this is weird. Because every single day, he comes in here, and for the last two months, I never would've known you two were together. You acted like strangers."

"Like I said, that was because of me. I asked him to keep up the act."

If he sounds uncomfortable, well—he is. But at least he'd be legit uncomfortable if all of this was actually true.

She's clearly mulling over the past two months, trying to find a sign that there's been something between Jamie and Ben. "Last week," she says. "He came in, and you said he couldn't come in anymore."

"We had a fight," Jamie says.

"Oh." She chews her lip. "Sorry. Are you guys good now?"

Nodding maybe a little too vigorously—and frankly shocked that she accepted this lame-ass explanation so readily—Jamie says, "Yeah. Totally good. We worked it out when we went outside." Frantically, he tries to think of what they might have fought about. It really shouldn't be hard, since fights were a fixture of all Jamie's shitty relationships.

She chews her lip for another second, then folds her arms over her chest. "I don't need to tell him to treat you right, do I?"

Jamie laughs, and god, he wishes he could tell her that the whole thing is fake. It would be funny to have her fake-defend his honor.

"You guys don't fight a lot, do you?" she asks carefully.

"That was the first time. And it was fine. A learning experience, right? Everyone fights, you just have to learn how to fight effectively?"

Cool, now he's a book of relationship advice, or possibly a tumblr post with just over sixty thousand notes. *I don't know who needs to hear this, but....*

"Look at you," Val says, sounding impressed. Like she's proud of how mature he is. What a joke.

"Yeah. I guess when you meet someone special, you put in the work to make it last."

The door opens, bringing in a blast of street noise and a clump of customers. It cuts the conversation off, thank god. Now Jamie's fake dating someone fake special? Not that Ben's not special. He is. Jamie didn't want him to be this special. It would have been better if he kept being a dick, and Jamie wouldn't feel like he's feeling.

When he takes his break, he plops down on the chair in the back room and checks his phone. The buzzing he felt earlier *was* Ben texting.

Jamie doesn't realize he's smiling until he catches a glimpse of his reflection in the screen. When he opens up the texts, his heart stutters.

**Hey, I know you're at work so you might not see this right away, but I was thinking. It's a lot of back and forth for you to go all the way home tonight just to come all the way back to my place tomorrow morning. It's your day off, and you're going to spend it doing work. Why don't you come over tonight? I have a spare bedroom. We can get takeout and watch a movie we both like**
**Or maybe a movie we both hate? That might be funny**
**Anyway lmk**

So Ben writes novels over text. Somehow Jamie's not surprised. How is he supposed to feel about this offer? On one hand, Ben just asked him to spend the night. Sure, it's in the spare bedroom. But still. Images flicker in his mind of the two of them staying up too late in their pajamas (though where the hell is Jamie going to get pajamas?), eating snacks and watching something stupid. Maybe they'd find the absolute worst-rated thing on Hulu and see how much of it they could get through.

They'd be tired tomorrow morning, but it wouldn't even matter, because they would have had so much fun that it would be one of those nights you preserved behind glass. It would be one of those memories you got out when things were bad, and you'd hold it close and replay it and you'd remember you had one amazing night, at least.

On the other hand, Ben referred to their project tomorrow as "work," so....

He locks his phone.

He unlocks it. Stares at the message again.

**Anyway lmk**

The timestamp on that last message is later than the others, like maybe Ben was stressing and second-guessing that he'd sent the messages.

Oh, what the hell.

*Ok, that sounds cool. Thanks for offering*

He stares at his response. It's so anodyne. It doesn't capture the dance his heart's doing in his chest right now. Not that he really wants it to, but maybe like, a little more enthusiasm.

His fingers hover over the emoji keyboard. Before he thinks too hard about it, he sends a heart.

Then he panics. What the fuck? What the fuck is he thinking, sending a heart?

*That was a test! I hope you're doing the dumb 'i'm looking at a text from the bae' face*

He locks his phone and buries his face in his hands. God, he's… he doesn't know what. He's something.

The phone buzzes. Jamie takes a deep breath and looks.

*Cool*

The smiling, sunglasses-wearing emoji follows. Who knows if Ben's making the face—but *Jamie* definitely is.

*Did you really just use that emoji*
**Oh sorry. Is that not hip enough for the cool kids?**
**That was supposed to be kids**
**KIDZ**
**Gdi I hate autocorrect**
*Omg I can't believe I used to think you were suave and mysterious*
**Shit really? How do we go back to that?**
*Nope! Too late! You used it*
*To which I say...*

Jamie sends the monocle emoji and the poop emoji. Because he's an adult.

He receives the cowboy emoji back, which makes him laugh and type back, *You know that's grindr code for getting tied up, right?*

**OMFG NO**

**Omg what? I don't even get it. Because cowboys use lassos?**
**I was not propositioning you**

Jamie lets out a loud laugh that echoes in the back room. He looks up, startled to find himself there. He forgot. Texting with Ben made him literally forget where he was.

**I mean I'm not knocking bdsm, I'm sure it can be really sexy if it's all consensual and safe and stuff**
**But seriously that's not what I meant**
**I just made this weird**

Giggling, Jamie types back, *I'm fucking with you*
....................
*Still want me to come over*
*?*
**You're the worst**
**Also yes**
*Ok*
*Hey my break's over, gtg. I should be over by 8*
**See you then**

Jamie locks his phone, but then one more text comes through: a heart.

# CHAPTER ELEVEN

BEN HAS changed his T-shirt three times.

Black is supposed to be slimming, right? But he doesn't think he looks good in the black. The navy one has a V-neck that he's never been too sure about, and when he puts it on and looks at himself in the mirror, he looks ridiculous. He looks like… like… okay, well, he doesn't know *what* he looks like. It's not cool, whatever it is.

So now he's wearing a white tee. It's boring but looks fine. It's new, so it's not stretched out, and it's still a pristine, bright white. No yellowing in the wash yet.

He smooths it over his chest and stomach, sucking in his gut. He never thought he had a gut, but lately, it's struck him that he could be a lot more… if not ripped, then at least defined. Being more defined seems like a good goal. Just for him. Obviously not because he wants to look good for anyone in particular.

Which is totally why he's changed T-shirts three times. Uh-huh. Yeah. Right.

His phone lights up and his stomach somersaults. It's just an email. Not Jamie texting to say he's here.

It's almost eight, and Ben's jittery. Was this a bad idea? It seemed like a fantastic idea earlier—Highbridge isn't super far, but it's also not super close. It seemed gentlemanly to offer the spare bedroom.

When it took Jamie hours to answer, Ben thought maybe the whole fake dating thing was off. Like maybe he'd made it too weird.

He picks up his phone and opens his conversation with Jamie. He can't get over the heart Jamie sent. And that he summoned the guts from somewhere and sent one back. Normally he doesn't do stuff like that. He doesn't want to send the wrong message. He doesn't want to make people think there's more to things than there are. He doesn't want anyone wanting anything from him.

So what exactly does it mean that he sent it to Jamie?

Three dots appear on the screen. Ben's stomach flips. Again. It's doing its best to qualify for the US Olympics Gymnastics team in there. His heart pounds and adrenaline shoots to his extremities.

He makes himself take a deep breath. Whatever's going on with him, he wants it to stop. He *needs* it to stop. Changing your shirt three times? Getting butterflies? Gazing at old texts? These are not the actions of a man who has mere friendship on the brain.

*Hey I'm here!*
*Sorry I'm late. Closing took longer*
**You're not late! Food just got here. I'll buzz you in**

His pulse isn't slowing down. It's speeding up. What the fuck? He saw Jamie a few hours ago. Had he felt this way then?

Maybe it was better not to think about that. He might not like what he remembers.

A few minutes later, there's a knock on the door. Ben strides over to it and opens it, and….

His stomach definitely just qualified for the team. There's some Simone Biles level acrobatics going on in there.

Jamie looks disheveled and rumpled, but he's so handsome that he's pulling it off effortlessly. His mostly untucked shirt? A style choice. His frizzy, messy, flyaway hair? Cool bedhead. Beat-up Chucks under jeans that have come uncuffed on one side? Probably the new fashion. Post-post grunge revival or something.

"Hi," Jamie says with a bright, beautiful smile.

"Hey," Ben says, tightening his fingers around the edge of the door so he doesn't do something stupid. His gold-medal-winner stomach gymnast is urging him to go in for a hug, and it's taking way too much willpower not to do it.

*That* would make things weird. So weird.

Realizing he's making Jamie stand out in the hallway, he steps aside. "Come in! Like I said, the food just got here. I triple checked they had your order right. When he repeated it back to me the first time, he thought I got it with duck instead of mock duck."

The smile settles into the geometry of Jamie's face, soft where Ben's used to seeing sharpness, setting it apart from the angles of his jaw and nose. "Thanks. I'm starving."

He brings the smell of coffee with him as he steps inside. Ben closes the door and breathes in. It's not just coffee—it's the way Jamie smells, his skin and his hair and his clothes, and Ben wants to wrap himself up in it.

He has to shut this down. He has to stop noticing how Jamie smells like the softness of coffee when it's permeated a room and loses its bite. And how that smell mixes with the sweet sting of citrus and the tickle of pepper, and something musky but electric. Like petrichor or ozone—a thunderstorm on a summer night.

Okay, well, great—so far he's admired Jamie's clothes, mooned over his smile, and waxed rhapsodic about the way he smells. So yeah, shutting this down is going *great*.

They just stand there staring at each other. Ben's heart is beating too fast. His stomach is knotting. He has to do something.

So he blurts, "I dug out my lasso and handcuffs, and my cowboy hat's in the closet."

What. Why. What is wrong with him?

But Jamie's face cracks into a luminous grin, and he lets out this bright, happy peal of laughter. "God, I wish I could've seen your face when I told you the cowboy emoji was Grindr slang."

"Actually, you really don't. Not sure how much respect you have for me, but it definitely would have gone up in smoke if you'd seen how I looked."

"Aw." Jamie's grin settles to something more muted, but his eyes are still gleaming. "Of course I respect you."

"Yeah?"

"Yeah," Jamie replies seriously. "I mean, you're a *doctor.*"

Ben snorts. "Okay, okay."

"No—I mean, sorry. You're not just a doctor. You're a *surgeon.*"

"All right, I get it. You're making fun of me."

"You're a pillar of this city, Ben," Jamie says, a hand over his heart.

With a snort of laughter, Ben bumps his fist against Jamie's shoulder. It's not at all hard or violent. It's just the sort of little flirty touch you do when you have a crush on someone.

And Jamie's entire body snaps to attention when Ben does it.

Oh god. Should he pretend he didn't notice? Take a really exaggerated step back so it's obvious he noticed, but he's not going to bring it up? Apologize for getting into Jamie's personal space when Jamie's making himself vulnerable by agreeing to sleep here?

"Food's in the kitchen," he says, because *that's* smooth.

Jamie's chewing at the inside of his cheek. He takes a step closer and tugs the piece of hair that always falls over Ben's forehead. "My knight in shining armor," Jamie says in a campily overwrought voice. "I'm starving."

His fingers brush the hair back into place.

Ben's straight-up going to die. Just like. This is it. He's done for. He fucked this up. He fucked this up so badly. He asked this man to be his fake boyfriend and he's… oh god.

He's not even going to think it. If he doesn't think it, it's not true.

In the kitchen, Jamie reaches for a cupboard before he stops. "I guess I don't know where you keep your plates? Maybe I shouldn't just go through your cupboards."

"Yeah, thanks, I appreciate it. Most people freak out when they stumble on my collection of ball gags."

Jamie lets out a startled guffaw and bites his lip. "I keep my butt plugs in my kitchen cabinets too. Right next to the mugs."

"Well, all that stuff is dishwasher safe. It just makes sense to keep it in the kitchen, right?"

"Be honest, if I tell you that I wash my butt plugs at the same time I wash my dishes, would you want to come over for dinner at my place?" Jamie asks.

"What's for dinner?" Ben pauses. "Tossed salad?"

Jamie loses it. His body folds over the nearest counter and he's wheezing with laughter, sucking in deep breaths like he's about to get himself under control, and then failing and laughing more. Ben starts laughing too, and he ends up sinking to the floor and leaning against the wall while his whole body shakes with deep belly laughs.

This is twice in one day that he and Jamie have laughed like this.

Finally, they get it together. Jamie swipes at his cheeks, which are wet with tears. "Oh my god. I didn't think you had it in you."

Ben laughs again, an aftershock. "C'mon. I cut people's brains and spines apart for a living. You think I can't make a dirty joke?"

The way Jamie's grinning at him, his hair still frizzy, his shirt all twisted from the way he's been draped over the counter, his hand fisting at the hem and yanking it down in this totally un-self-conscious way…. It shoves all that stuff that Ben's not going to admit up to the front of his prefrontal cortex. To the tip of his tongue.

Because he's an adult, he says, "The plates are in the cabinet to your left."

They sit at the counter to eat. It's the best dinner Ben's had in… ever. The food isn't any different. He's just having more fun tonight than he's had in forever. Usually he eats alone. Half the time he doesn't bother with plates, he just eats straight out of the takeout containers. He's been known to down a Big Mac in a few bites as he strides down the sidewalk, his mind lost in work.

When he was with Adriana, he hardly ever bothered to have dinner with her.

The thought bothers him. Not in an oh-god-what-have-I-lost sort of way, but in a Jesus-Christ-I-was-such-an-asshole-no-wonder-she-left-me way.

A couple weeks ago, Ben and Jamie didn't know each other at all. Now they're sitting in Ben's apartment, talking about work and New York. The conversation ping-pongs to music, movies, and TV, and even fashion. They're in agreement that early 00s fashion shouldn't make a comeback, since surely the world had been through enough without the return of frosted tips and mesh tops.

Long after they're done eating, they stay at the table, talking. It's the kind of conversation where you feel your joints freezing up because you've been sitting so long, but you don't move because you don't want to break the spell that two people can cast between themselves.

When they eventually get up, Jamie starts loading the dishwasher. "Hey, you don't have to do that," Ben says.

Jamie shrugs. "The novelty is nice. My place doesn't have a dishwasher."

There's a buzzy undercurrent to the words, a kind of preemptive defensiveness, like he expects to be judged. When has Ben ever given Jamie any indication that he's looking down on him for not having money?

It makes him prickly that Jamie thinks something like that about him. And with no evidence! Just because it's something in his head, something he expects people to do? Ben grew up solidly middle class, but it's not like he didn't have to take out six figures in student loans to put himself through med school. He was lucky, and he's not complaining, but it's not like he came from money. When he was a kid, family vacations mostly weren't outside the Ohio state lines, except for the one year his parents took him to Disney World—and they made it pretty clear it was a once-in-a-lifetime trip.

Silently, Ben gathers up the takeout containers and empty duck sauce wrappers, and chucks all of it in the garbage. His chest pangs. There was magic before, when they were laughing and talking. And now it's just two guys in a kitchen.

"Thanks for dinner," Jamie says. There's an uncertain waver in his blue eyes, like he senses the way something fractured too.

"I couldn't invite you to spend the night and not give you something to eat."

As soon as the words leave his mouth, he realizes how he sounds.

"I mean," he says. "Not like. *Spend the night*. I mean, I couldn't let you crash here and not give it to you. Oh my god. *Dinner*. I'm just going to stop talking, okay?"

The look on Jamie's face isn't quite readable. Is it… fond? "So when you explain to people how you're going to do the whole cutting-their-brains-open thing," Jamie says, "do you typically use more or less sexual innuendo?"

"Oh, way more."

Jamie grins and things ease. It's not magic again, but they're back to something a little closer.

"I have a futon in the spare room," Ben says. "Um, it's probably not actually long enough for you. You're kind of tall for a futon."

Waving his hand, Jamie says, "I'll be fine. I slept on a futon for a year after grad school."

Grad school? Did Ben know Jamie went to grad school? How has this never come up?

"Wait a second," Ben says.

"Masters in Russian history," Jamie says, like he's reading Ben's mind. "So actually, I've read *War and Peace*." A smile twitches at his mouth. Ben feels stupid for assuming Jamie isn't well educated.

"You definitely wouldn't want to read anything I've written, then. It's just dry, boring stuff."

The last thing Ben wants Jamie to think is that he's just some dry, boring doctor. He wants Jamie to think he's interesting.

The problem is, he doesn't know if he is. He doesn't know if he's still the guy who buys a roller skate tie. But Jamie said he should wear it, and that it looked good on him. So maybe.

Jamie tilts his head. His eyes flick up to the ceiling and his throat bobs. Ben wishes he knew what he was thinking. He wishes stuff he shouldn't wish for.

Like, he wishes Jamie would suggest they practice kissing again.

"Actually, I really would like to read the books you wrote."

"Co-authored."

Jamie rolls his eyes, and this time it's definitely fond. "Whatever."

Ben's not going to argue, because the best thing is to make Jamie forget about those books and all their talk of laminectomy and foraminotomy and disks and vertebroplasty and compression fractures. Not that Ben's performed a vertebroplasty in recent memory. He doesn't do *outpatient* procedures anymore.

Maybe he should get things focused on the fakeness of this relationship again. He gets his phone out and pulls up Google Maps. "So, tomorrow. I'm assuming we should go back to your place to get a couple outfit changes for you?"

"Oh yeah, I guess so." Jamie looks like this hadn't occurred to him, and something like trepidation flashes over his face.

"We'll drive," Ben says quickly, before Jamie can suggest something like taking the train up there at the ass crack of dawn, which would totally defeat the purpose of him spending the night here. "I mean, I'll drive. Let's figure out where we're going. We can try to be efficient, hit as many spots as possible?"

Jamie smiles, but it's not the same bright smile from before. It's guarded now, which means Ben fucked up somehow.

"I'll just run in and get some clothes," Jamie says.

Maybe Ben's making it painfully obvious that his feelings might not be fake, when Jamie's made it pretty clear that's all he's up for.

He could've asked Jamie out. He's been crushing on this guy for *two years.* Except romance was anathema to being the best in his field. Having a boyfriend, being in love, sitting around in the evening talking and laughing—that's not how you get to the top.

And being at the top is the most important thing. Being the best, most respected, most brilliant neurosurgeon in the world—that's what's important. That's what he's been working toward for his entire adult life. It *has* to be the most important thing, because if it isn't....

If it isn't, then what has he been doing?

They look at each other. Jamie's frizzy hair hasn't gotten any less adorable. And then he yawns, a beat between when his mouth opens and when he gets his hand up to cover it, and... that's adorable too.

Yeah. Ben's done for.

And that's not an option.

# CHAPTER TWELVE

"YOU CAN wait here," Jamie says. "It'll only take me a second."

Ben puts his hazards on and checks the rearview mirror. There's not much traffic in the Bronx this morning, and Jamie's street is quiet. But there's no chance he's going to find a parking spot—the curb is choked with cars, most of them parked New-York-City close to each other (with the scrapes on their front and back bumpers providing testament to a long career of the same).

"Sure you don't want me to come in and help you carry some stuff?" Ben asks. It wouldn't be the first time he's left his car parked illegally with the hazards on.

"Positive," Jamie says, already unfolding himself from the passenger seat to the sidewalk. There's a look on his face when he says it, like he's ready to fight someone about something, but he's the only one who knows what it is. Personally, Ben just wants to get to breakfast. He made reservations at a trendy spot near his apartment in Nolita before he went to bed last night.

Jamie reappears a short amount of time later, a bulging JanSport backpack slung over one shoulder. He tumbles into Ben's Audi, chucking the bag into the seat behind him.

They're supposed to talk about their plan for the day on the way back to Manhattan, but they talk about music instead. Jamie puts the radio on and by some miracle finds a Barenaked Ladies song. Ben's about to tell him to leave it on, but then Jamie takes his hand away from the radio, leaving it on without prompting.

Ben says, "You like them?"

"Oh, I can keep scanning if you don't. Or wait, is your phone connected? We can listen to your music."

"No, this is totally my music!" *Dial it back, Ben.* "I mean, yeah, my phone's connected, but no, I'm not playing it right now. But I like this band." He glances toward Jamie. "Aren't you a little young for them?"

Which makes Jamie look positively gleeful. "Oh, wait, this is good. How young do you think I am?"

"Uh. I don't... um." Ben concentrates on making it across the Macombs Dam Bridge. "Thirty"—Jamie's expression darkens—"er, twenty... nine?"

"Please don't tell me you were going to say *thirty-nine*."

"I was going to say thirty!"

"Ugh." Jamie rests the back of his hand over his eyes. "My skincare routine is failing me."

"No! You look really great. There's nothing wrong with looking *thirty*. God, you're like...." But Ben trails off before he can say something regrettable. "I thought thirty because of your personality. And just the way you act. You act like you're thirty, not twenty...?"

"Seven," Jamie informs him. "I'm twenty-seven. Almost twenty-eight, actually. My birthday's this month."

"When?"

"Why, planning on throwing me a party?"

"I thought just a nice dinner out," Ben says seriously. "For my snugglelupagus."

"Oh my god." Jamie punches Ben lightly in the shoulder. "Just for that, you *can* take me out to dinner, and it better be somewhere really nice. But don't tell them it's my birthday. It's mortifying when they come out singing."

Cutting his eyes toward Jamie, Ben says, "Oh come on. I'd bring you somewhere that's way too nice for them to sing."

"As long as I still get a free dessert," Jamie says.

"Obviously."

Ben can still feel the spot where Jamie punched him. Not because it hurt, which it didn't, but because it's like he left an imprint of himself on Ben. An imprint of his warmth and the buzz of him only a foot away, and really for real, Ben wants to take him out for his birthday.

"Do you really think I act older than my age?" Jamie asks. His fingers drum on the door armrest, *tap-tap-tap-tap*, like asking makes him nervous.

"I guess a little. Why?"

Out of the corner of his eye, Ben sees Jamie shrug. "I don't hear that often. My dad and brother think I'm in a state of arrested development."

"They say that to you?" Ben asks, bristling at the thought. Can he confront them about that when he meets them? Is that inappropriate?

Jamie huffs. "Not in those words."

So probably don't confront them.

The tapping on the armrest gets a little more violent, *TAP-tap-tap-TAP-TAP-TAP-tap-tap*. "My brother—Tyler—I know he thought grad school was just me trying to put off growing up. Like the only reason I was there was because I couldn't face the 'real world.'"

"That's kind of shitty."

"Yeah, it is," Jamie says, irritation, maybe even anger, simmering under the words. "And my dad just lets him say this stuff. I think he agrees, but he'd rather pit Tyler and me against each other than be the bad guy. My dad's big on diplomacy. That's one of his favorite lectures, how the way to get ahead in life is by being diplomatic." Jamie slouches into the seat and moves his hands to his lap. His head turns so he can look out the window as they drive through Washington Heights. "I don't think diplomacy's really gotten me anywhere," he says quietly, so quietly that Ben's not really sure he was meant to hear.

"All things in moderation, maybe?" Ben says. "It seems like maybe if I'd been a little more diplomatic in my career, I wouldn't be in this position."

He sees Jamie's shoulders tense. "You and my dad can talk about it," he says. "Since you're in this unfortunate position."

And that wasn't what Ben *meant*. He said "position," and okay, sure, maybe it doesn't have the best connotation, but he never said "unfortunate." Jamie just filled that in himself. It's like he wants to hear bad things about himself, like he's incapable of believing that anyone thinks anything good about him.

Not knowing what else to say, Ben backtracks. "Well, even if your family thinks you're trying to put off adulthood or whatever, won't they be happy to know you're trying to get a more serious job?"

This time he doesn't need to see Jamie tense to know he said something stupid.

"Not that your job isn't serious," Ben quickly amends.

"No, you're right," Jamie says, a hard brightness to his voice that makes Ben wilt. "It's *not* a real job. I mean, my boss touches my ass at least once a week, he's clearly imagining me naked at least fifty percent of the time he's looking at me, and he only gives me enough of a raise when I demand one so I feel like I got something out of him and I don't quit."

The radio is playing the Smashing Pumpkins now. Jamie turns the volume up. Ben glances at him. "But he's helping you find a new job, right? So that's something."

"Yeah," Jamie agrees. It sounds like he's trying to convince himself.

Ben quits pressing. They're almost to his building, anyway. His backpack of wardrobe changes is already in the car, so they walk straight out of the garage to the street. "Where do we go after breakfast?" he asks, hoping the day won't be as awkward as the last ten minutes.

"The location of our first date," Jamie says. He seems like he's back to his normal self.

Ben goes with it gratefully. "Did you make up little stories to go with the pictures?"

"Yes!" Jamie says, sounding affronted. "Of course! If we're going to lie, we're going to do it well. What happens when people ask?"

With a snort, Ben says, "I think you might be overestimating how much people care about our relationship."

"I can't believe you'd say that. We have a fairy tale romance. People will want to know about it." There's a glimmer of mischief and humor in Jamie's eyes.

Shifting his North Face backpack on his shoulder, Ben asks, "Okay. Where did we go for our first date?"

Jamie holds out his hand. When Ben takes it, his heart skips. "You'll see," Jamie says.

And honestly? Ben doesn't care where it is. Not as long as he can feel Jamie's palm against his and their fingers interlaced.


HE CARES a little when they reach their first destination.

"The Empire State Building?" Ben groans. "Really? What kind of New Yorker goes to the Empire State Building for a first date?"

The expression on Jamie's face doesn't hold a single hint of regret, let alone shame. In fact, he seems gleeful. "But see, that's the thing, Ben," he says. "I'm not *from* New York. And you remembered me mentioning that to you one of the times you came into the coffee shop."

"So not only are we fake dating, we also had fake conversations before we dated?" Ben asks.

Jamie fiddles with his piercing. "I said I thought the Empire State Building has a lot of romance, even if it's a tourist trap. And you surprised me with a trip there."

Grudgingly, Ben says, "Okay, fine, that's pretty sweet."

Jamie holds up his phone. "I booked us tickets for as soon as it opens, so we have about twenty minutes to kill." He quirks an eyebrow. "We could take some pictures?"

They might as well, right? It gets surprisingly fun after the first few. They take a couple normal ones, with the two of them smiling, looking like they're having a nice enough time. Then, Jamie starts making ridiculous faces. He waits until the last possible second before Ben takes the picture, then crosses his eyes or sticks his tongue out. It's when he puffs his cheeks out *and* crosses his eyes that Ben totally loses it, and he snaps a picture of Jamie looking like some kind of human blowfish and himself cracking up.

From then on, Ben tries to get him back, and soon they're giggling and laughing like idiots. Jamie gets his own phone out, holds it in front of them, and presses his lips against Ben's temple as he takes a picture.

Without thinking, Ben wraps an arm around him, even though no one will be able to see it in the photos. You can tell, though, somehow. They're closer, and there's just like… this glow between them. Or something. The pictures they take after that kiss, even though it's chaste and could just as easily be friendly, are so much better.

His temple keeps tingling long after Jamie's lips are gone. It's still tingling when they go inside the Empire State Building and line up for the elevator with the other early-comers. It's still tingling as they ride to the observation deck on the 102nd floor, where they take more pictures. Standard stuff: *Look hi I'm at the top of the Empire State Building, wooo!* Super touristy. Embarrassing. Ben is embarrassed he's doing this.

Okay, actually… he's not? Well, he starts out being kind of embarrassed, feeling way too cool for this place. But Jamie seems genuinely delighted, despite how cliché the whole thing is.

And okay, the views of the city are great. Ben hasn't been up to this observation deck because it's newish. Even if he doesn't want to admit it, he played tourist when he first moved here too.

Until today, he had no idea Jamie wasn't from New York. It's shitty that he hasn't asked. Just like it's shitty he never asked about Jamie's background, so he didn't know how Jamie had a master's in Russian history.

God. Ben really only cares about himself, doesn't he? They're pretending to be super in love, and Ben barely knows anything about Jamie. All that matters about Jamie is how it relates to him, Ben.

Meanwhile, Jamie's asked about his job, about the work he's published. He's asked questions you ask a person when you really want to get to know them.

While Ben's been finding reasons he wants Jamie in his life, Jamie's probably been thinking he can't wait to ditch this asshole who doesn't bother to ask him a single thing about himself.

"Where did you get your master's?" Ben blurts out in the middle of an obliging stranger taking a photo of them.

When Jamie gets his phone back, he says, "NYU."

"What about your BA? Was that in Russian history too?"

Jamie looks amused, surprised, and a little perplexed. "I did my BA there too. It's in history. I minored in medieval studies. Why the sudden interest?"

"I should have already been interested."

Jamie blinks. He opens his mouth, but nothing comes out. Ben doesn't know what to make of the fact that admitting he messed up, that he should have asked these questions ages ago, like, years ago, maybe, is so shocking.

Maybe Jamie's not saying anything because he doesn't want to say exactly that. Thanks for finally asking. You know you could have done this like, last Christmas? When you and I were the only ones in the coffee shop? Instead we chatted about how snow was in the forecast.

By some miracle, they're the only people on the elevator down. "I thought of the perfect end to our first date," Jamie says as they get on.

The door closes. They're alone. It's a magical moment, in a totally New York City way. "Yeah?" Ben asks. His intestines are still writhing with the realization that he's given Jamie zero reasons to want to continue any kind of relationship with him after they've both gotten what they want out of this fake romance.

Jamie looks around, like he's checking to see if they're really alone. Sucking in a breath, he says, "We had the elevator to ourselves, and we had our first kiss."

Now Ben's intestines are writhing for an entirely different reason. "Um," he says. "We did?"

Trepidation flashes through Jamie's eyes and his throat bobs. "Er, maybe you don't want to do any kissing pictures."

"No!" Oh god, way too much. *Way* too much. The floors are ticking down fast, which means Ben only has about five seconds to make this right. He only has about five seconds to secure this chance to kiss Jamie. The opportunities are limited, and he needs to take every single one he can get. "No, kissing pictures—we should do those. Good idea. Sorry, I just—" But he decides to shut up, because every word that comes out of his mouth is another second gone, another floor the elevator has passed.

Ben moves close to Jamie and puts an arm around him. With his other, he holds his phone up. He can see their image on the screen out of the corner of his eye.

Jamie puts a hand on Ben's face, leans in, and kisses him.

It's not a first kiss. Like, it's quite literally not the first time they've kissed, but it's also not a real first kiss, because they aren't a real couple. But it feels like one. Ben's stomach drops out and champagne bubbles fizz through his veins.

It takes him a good two seconds to remember he's supposed to be capturing this for posterity.

The shutter noise from the phone seems incredibly loud, and Ben knows there's no way to pretend he didn't hear it. Jesus, does he have his volume turned all the way up or something? Hearing it means he needs to stop kissing Jamie. They got the picture. That was the point.

Ben doesn't pull back.

Jamie doesn't either.

At least for a second. Then Ben opens his eyes, a half-baked idea in his head that he'll try to tell from Jamie's facial expression if he wants this kiss to keep going. Because you can usually tell a lot from a person's face when they're kissing you. Christ. Half-baked was generous. More like quarter-baked.

But Jamie doesn't look unhappy. His eyebrows are drawn together in something that looks a lot like feeling. Ben doesn't want to stop looking at him. He's never wanted to kiss someone with his eyes open before. He's never wanted to *see* them. And now all he wants is to see Jamie.

Jamie's eyes open, and when he sees Ben looking at him, he makes a squeaking noise and breaks the kiss. "Sorry!" he says. "Sorry, I... um, I thought you might have still been taking more pictures."

"Oh, right. Uh, I was finishing up, but... if you want?"

The elevator bumps to a stop just then and the door opens. So no more opportunity for first kiss, take two.

Was Jamie lying? Did he really think Ben was going to take more pictures? Or did he… could he possibly… maybe… have wanted to keep kissing Ben?

What happened to the Ben who doesn't have time for romance? Who can't date, because it's a distraction from his career? The Ben who came up with this whole scheme literally just to advance his career? Where's *that* guy? That guy doesn't like kissing gorgeous, funny, smart men in elevators. That guy would never dream of doing something like that.

That guy also… maybe wasn't that happy.

They leave the Empire State Building. And then it's on to Central Park, where they take a spin through Central Park Zoo, take selfies in front of famous statues, and get a snack at the Boathouse. They stop at Bethesda Terrace on the way to Central Park West, and they look at some dinosaurs at the Museum of Natural History. They do wardrobe changes for each location. Jamie messes his hair up once and it's frankly horrifying how much Ben wants to sink his fingers into it.

They're making their way downtown (cue Vanessa Carlton), walking, because it's a nice afternoon, when Ben decides asking Jamie where he went to college is pretty much the bare minimum, and he can do better. He looks over at Jamie, and his eyes fall on Jamie's piercing.

"Can I ask you a really dumb question?" Ben says.

"I'm used to it," Jamie replies.

Ben smirks. He was asking for that. "I've been wondering what the name is for that piercing you have."

Jamie touches it, like he forgot he had one. "It's a rook piercing. Are you going to tell me a doctor's boyfriend can't have nontraditional piercings?"

"No," Ben says, in that tone you use when you want to let someone know they're asking a stupid question, but it's stupid because you love them and everything about them. "I just think it looks cool, and I didn't know the name for it."

"Oh." Jamie looks pleased. "Well… thanks."

What Ben really wants to ask is, *any other piercings that I can't see?* in a flirty tone, one that specifically angles to find out what's under Jamie's clothes. Ben's pretty sure Jamie doesn't want to know how much he's thinking about what's underneath that floral button-up and black skinny jeans, though.

The backs of their hands brush as they walk, and Ben wonders if he can get away with taking Jamie's in his. Before he has a chance to think through how he'd justify it, Jamie's fingers slip against Ben's palm. It's a little tug, a question, and the answer is yes yes god yes.

"Just in case we see anyone we know," Jamie says.

"Definitely," Ben agrees.

Jamie tightens his grip. Ben does the same.

Normally the thought of his coworkers seeing him holding hands with someone would nauseate him. But the idea of them seeing him holding hands with Jamie? That feels... really nice.

Would he rather be at a conference right now, talking about a surgery he only cared about because it made him look good? Would he rather be at some cocktail hour with a bunch of fawning people who don't give a shit about him?

A week ago, he thought that was what he wanted. He was the best, and everyone was going to know it. It was important that people knew he was a great surgeon, and that he defined himself that way, and that he didn't have time for the frivolity of friends or a relationship.

With Jamie's hand in his, he can't remember why all of that seemed so important. He can't remember why he thought romance was a frivolity. With Jamie's hand in his, he feels like a guy who can wear a roller skate tie. He feels like *himself*, and he barely even knows what that feels like. All he knows is that Jamie makes it happen.

# CHAPTER THIRTEEN

THEY FINISH the day at the Statue of Liberty, and Jamie's super proud of them for fitting all of it in.

Which he says.

Because of course he does.

Ben's mouth twitches into a smile, his eyebrows going up. Jamie's face gets hot.

All day, Ben seems like he's been making a point of asking Jamie more about himself. He asked about home, and if Jamie ever misses Connecticut. He asked about Jamie's childhood and about jobs he's had and what made him interested in Russian history.

Honestly, none of it is very interesting, and Jamie can't figure out why Ben's acting like he cares so much. So after Jamie extols the virtues of them *fitting it all in* (for god's sake), getting to the bottom of Ben's inquisitiveness seems like a perfect distraction.

"What's with all the questions?" he asks.

"Huh?"

Jamie leans back on the railing of the Liberty Island ferry, elbows propped on it. The metal is hot from the sun, but not enough to be uncomfortable. "You've been asking me questions all day."

Red creeps up Ben's neck. Jamie didn't expect *that*. Was it an embarrassing question? Is there an embarrassing answer?

"Um." Ben puts a hand to the back of his neck, then swipes it across his forehead. "I realized I don't know that much about you. And you know. That's… well, I felt like I should. Know more about you. Because like. You seem interested in… I mean, you're good at that stuff."

"Small talk?" Jamie asks wryly.

"I just thought showing some interest in your life was probably the polite thing to do." He snorts. "I guess that's something I need to work on."

Jamie makes a noncommittal sound. Now that he knows Ben, he's not sure it's politeness he needs to work on. Ben is definitely arrogant. But he's also awkward. And there's an insecurity to him, buried deep underneath the arrogance and the swagger, and maybe the arrogance is a shield to keep people from seeing the other stuff. Maybe Ben would rather people respect his intelligence and accomplishments but dislike him for them, too, instead of seeing through to the real him and disliking him for *that*.

"I'm not sure knowing I had a hamster named Snowball when I was in second grade is really giving you a window into my soul," Jamie says.

Ben's still red. He's actually *more* red. But he's smiling, and Jamie could curl up in that smile for weeks.

The ferry's engines start, churning water against the fiberglass sides and the pilings of the pier. The rumble travels up Jamie's legs to the base of his spine. The sun is setting, streaking the sky with red and orange, and it turns the Hudson into a Van Gogh painting, all thick swirls of color. Sunlight reflecting off the skyscrapers of Tribeca slice the air with fire, and Jamie squints before he looks away from it.

He loves New York City at sunset. He loves how the air gets still and quiet, and you can hear everything, every car horn and blaring stereo, every helicopter blade chopping through the air, every plane roaring as they come into LaGuardia and JFK. But out here on the water, even though the sound carries, it also fades to a whisper by the time it reaches them, settling on the surface before it bobs and disappears beneath the candy-colored current.

Ben stands at the railing next to him. Their eyes meet, and Jamie would give up a million New York sunsets for five minutes of looking into Ben's eyes. They're the most beautiful blue, crystal clear, and framed by dark lashes that fan against his cheek when he blinks. Jamie wants to let his thumb ghost over just the ends of Ben's eyelashes, to feel the feather brush of them against his skin.

"It was nice," Jamie says. "You asking me about myself."

Leaning over so their shoulders bump, Ben says, "Good. I started worrying I was coming off like a creep. Once I got started, I realized there's so much I don't know about you."

"I can't imagine you ever coming off like a creep," Jamie says. "Not in a million years."

There's a loud clunk as the ramp from the pier gets pulled on board and the door slams shut. The ferry moves away from Liberty Island, engines growling. It's fifteen minutes back to Manhattan.

Ben takes his phone out and puts an arm around Jamie. His first picture happens before Jamie's looking at the camera. He's still looking at Ben. At the first shutter click, though, he leans his temple against Ben's forehead and smiles. With the sky and water painted behind them, Jamie knows it'll be a great picture. They've taken hundreds today, but this one feels special.

Neither of them speaks as the ferry crosses to Manhattan. Jamie reaches for Ben's hand.

"Ben?" someone asks incredulously. "What are *you* doing here?"

The fact that Ben drops his hand as he turns to face the person who said his name doesn't surprise Jamie. The fact he takes it again? That does.

"Adriana!" Ben says. There's a funny note in his voice.

The woman is petite, with shoulder-length auburn hair. The tip of her nose and her cheeks are rosy with sunburn, despite her light brown complexion, and she's holding the hand of a girl who looks maybe seven or eight. The kid is wearing a hat and has smears of sunscreen on her face. Adriana is apparently big on sun safety for her daughter, not for herself.

Adriana's eyes move between Ben and Jamie. No one says anything, so Jamie decides he's going to have to break the silence. "Hi, I'm Jamie. Ben's told me so much about you. I'm so glad we're finally meeting!"

The way Adriana's lips purse makes Jamie wonder if he just made a mistake. Wait, she's not like, a homophobic bigot, is she? He didn't say *I'm Ben's boyfriend!* But they're holding hands, so, duh.

"Ben talks about me, huh?" she asks.

Maybe this was a huge miscalculation. Why did Jamie assume they were friends? Maybe they're *exes*. Oh god. Oh fuck. Can he salvage this? Can he take it back? Can he say, whoops, that was a different Adriana, ha-ha, never mind!

"I thought you were working today?" Ben says.

Shaking her head, she says, "I told my sister I'd take Harper to Ellis Island."

"Hi!" the girl says, her smile gap-toothed. Presumably she's Harper.

"Hey, Harper," Ben says. He smiles down at her, looking sort of at a loss. "You probably don't remember me—"

"I remember you," Harper says. "Aunt Adriana says *never* go out with people you work with, and that's because of you."

Jamie feels faintly hysterical. Adriana *is* an ex. Jamie just told Ben's ex that he *talks about her all the time.* Should he throw himself overboard?

He considers the distance to Manhattan from here. He can swim. He could probably make it?

"Jamie's never been to the Statue of Liberty. I said we had to do the whole thing. Right, babe?"

The turmoil probably isn't showing on Jamie's face, because this is what he's good at. Even Ben noticed. Jamie's good at small talk. So he smiles brightly and says, "Yeah. I've lived here for ten years and I never bothered."

"I come all the time," Harper informs them. "Did you know it gets struck by lightning six hundred times a year? And that it used to be *brown?* Like a penny?"

"Wow!" Ben says effusively. "That's really cool. I didn't!"

Harper gives him a flat look, and Adriana says, "She's eight, Ben, not two."

So Ben's bad with kids. Comically bad. Jamie wants to laugh and hug him at the same time.

"So Ben took you on...." Adriana's eyebrows go up as she studies Jamie. "A *date*? Do I have that right? This is a date?"

Jamie's smile falters. Ben squeezes Jamie's hand and glances at him. There's a look on his face that's trying to convey something, but Jamie has no idea what.

Turning to Harper, Adriana says, "Hey, can you do me a favor? Can you go sit on that bench there while I talk to Ben and his friend?"

"Aunt *Adriana*," Harper says, sounding disapproving. "Mason Fratelli has two dads. I know boys kiss each other too."

"Okay, sweetie, that's good—but just read your book on your Kindle, okay?" When Harper does as she's told, Adriana turns back to Ben, looking like she has a lot to say and not much idea where to start.

"That kid has a Kindle?" Ben asks. "Do you know how long I had to beg my parents for a Nintendo?"

"Ben, what are you doing?" Adriana asks, her tone biting.

Ben stares her down. "I'm on a date with my boyfriend."

"Your boyfriend. Are you serious right now?"

Something crackles to life in Jamie. He's an out and proud gay man in New York City, one of the queerest places in the world. But before

New York was Hartford, Connecticut, and even if it's a progressive place now, when Jamie was younger, things were different. He was out then too, and he got bullied and called terrible names and beat up. Now he doesn't take this kind of bullshit.

What makes him even angrier, though, is that Ben doesn't feel like he has a place at Pride. That he hasn't been in years because he doesn't feel welcome, or like part of the community. And sure, maybe some of that's coming from within him, but Jamie's willing to bet a whole shit ton of it is coming from external sources.

Jamie's willing to bet, in fact, that a whole shit ton of it is coming from this ex-girlfriend, standing in front of them with her arms over her chest like a Latinx Karen.

"Listen, I hate to break it to you, but you might have a problem when your eight-year-old niece has a better grasp on how things work in the world than you do," Jamie says heatedly.

Ben's hand tightens. "Jamie—"

"And you may have dated Ben, but that doesn't give you any right to judge him, or me, or anyone who doesn't fit into your narrow, heteronormative ideas of how the world works—"

"Jamie—"

"—so I suggest you pull your head out of your ass and find something to be concerned with other than who other people choose to have sex with—"

"Jamie!" Ben puts his hands on Jamie's face and that finally gets Jamie to shut up, because Ben's hands are warm and he has these interesting calluses that are making Jamie's heart canter.

Adriana is giggling. "Well, at least he's a knight in shining armor," she says.

There's a sheepish smile on Ben's face. "Guess so. I didn't know that at the time."

Jamie looks between them. "What's going on?"

Her expression sobers and she gives Ben an exasperated look. "I was there when he came up with this idea. I'm actually afraid I gave him the idea. You don't have to pretend for me."

"Oh." Jamie's face flames. "So you're not a homophobe."

"I like to think I'm not." Her gaze becomes more penetrating, flicking to their joined hands, then back up to Ben's face. "Ben McNatt doesn't do relationships." The way she delivers this makes it clear she's quoting Ben. "You have to realize what a horrible idea this is."

"It's not a horrible idea!" Ben says.

Adriana's eyes shift to Jamie. "I hope he's paying you really well."

"We have an arrangement," Ben says. He lets go of Jamie's hand. The absence cuts across Jamie's palm like a knife.

"So you're not paying him?" Adriana asks. To Jamie, she adds, "You'd have to pay me to date him again, even if it was fake."

"Geez, Addy, did I refer a nightmare patient to you or something?" Ben asks aggrievedly. "We don't have to re-litigate all the ways I ruined our relationship in front of my new—" He stops and takes a breath. "Can we just not?" He sounds plaintive. Jamie wants to take his hand again and smooth that sound out of his voice.

Adriana kneads her forehead with one hand. "Okay, you're right. Sorry. But Ben, this is a bad idea. You know that, right? You can't fake date your way into this promotion."

"You were the one that told me I needed to prove I had a heart," Ben retorts.

"Which I'm seriously regretting right now," she shoots back. "I didn't think you were really going to go through with it!"

"Well, I did," Ben says. "And it's working."

"How do you know it's working?"

"Everyone thinks we're really together," Ben says. Jamie's not going to be the one to point out that everyone thinking they're together doesn't mean their plan is working. Maybe no one on the hiring committee gives a damn. Maybe they don't think Ben making googley eyes at his significant other is any real indication that he has a heart. Maybe they just think it's an indication that he has eyes and a healthy libido.

With a sigh, Adriana says, "Okay, fine. Let's say it's working, which I think is kind of a stretch, but whatever." Ben opens his mouth to argue, but she goes on, "What happens when you get the promotion? The arrangement you two have ends, you tell everyone you broke up, and you continue on the way you were before? *You're faking a relationship* to get a job, Ben! You're not learning some huge life lesson that's going to turn you into a better person!"

Ben glares. "Once I get the job, everyone will see that 'having a heart' isn't what matters—it's the fact that I'm the best neurosurgeon in the country."

Oh. Okay. Right.

How many times a day does Jamie repeat to himself that this is just a professional arrangement? That sure, they have fun together. And yeah, Jamie's caught feelings. Hard.

This is just a means to an end. They wouldn't ever have ended up dating for real. Ben's a surgeon. The best neurosurgeon in the country. And Jamie's a broke barista with a pointless degree.

Once Ben gets the job, he'll kick Jamie aside.

Okay, well, no. He'll probably be nice about it. He'll probably even say they should still hang out. But it won't be the same. Because Jamie will still be into him, and he'll know it's never going to happen, *was* never going to happen, and it will be weird and awkward and Ben will pick up on that, and in the end they won't see each other. Maybe Ben will stop coming into the Daily Grind. He'll probably find a better coffee shop once he's neurosurgeon-in-chief.

Even though the day was warm and the evening is still pleasant, a chill goes through Jamie. It's cold out here on the water. He shivers and jams his hands into his pockets, barely listening to Ben's and Adriana's conversation.

"—just don't want this to blow up in your face," Adriana's saying.

"There's nothing to blow up in my face. Either I get the job or I don't." Ben crosses his arms over his chest. "I'm not doing anything illegal. Or unethical. Or wrong at all."

"You literally hired a man to pretend to date you," Adriana says. "I'd file that under 'unethical,' personally."

"He didn't hire me," Jamie says sharply.

Both Ben and Adriana look at him like they forgot he was there. Jamie shoves his hands deeper into his pockets. "He didn't hire me. I want a better job too. Ben's helping."

Adriana looks between them. The ferry slows, making its approach to Battery Park. "Well," she says, "then I guess you two are perfect for each other." She sweeps her hair out of her face, looking tired. "I don't want you to throw away an opportunity, Ben. Just think about how this would look if people found out. You might need a job from them someday if you don't get this one."

"I'm getting this job," Ben says, his voice flat.

She sighs. "I've never met anyone as stubborn as you. Please just think about what you're doing." She glances toward her niece, who's still sitting quietly on the bench she was banished to with her Kindle. "Nice to meet you, Jamie. I'd say you two make a great couple, but—well, you know."

Without waiting for a response, she turns on her heel and leaves, putting a hand on Harper's shoulder and drawing her away.

Ben stares after her before his shoulders sag and he rubs the back of his neck with a hand. "Sorry about that."

"I told your ex you talk about her all the time," Jamie says.

"Oh." Ben waves a hand. "That's okay. We're still friends. She's kind of my only friend. Anyway, she knew you were full of it. Don't worry, you didn't just set some kind of jilted-ex-lover-stalking-situation into motion."

The ferry bumps to a stop at the pier, and passengers shuffle toward the door to disembark. Jamie stays where he is, feeling stuck to the rail. His mind is spinning, trying to get traction in a pool of mud. It takes him a second to pin down the reason.

It's because it reminded him so much of talking to his family. The disapproval, the conviction of the other party that they were right and he was wrong, and he doesn't have a clue what's best for himself or how to get it. And then the fear, the suspicion, that they were *right*.

Ben's words to Adriana won't stop echoing in his head.

Once I get the job, everyone will see that 'having a heart' isn't what matters—it's the fact that I'm the best neurosurgeon in the country. The subtext is barely even subtext. Having a heart won't matter, so having a boyfriend isn't necessary—even a fake one.

"Jamie?" Ben asks. The way he says it makes it obvious it's not the first time, and that he's been repeating himself while Jamie zones out. "Hey, are you okay? Sorry about Adriana. She means well, really. Sorry that was how you met her. I think you two would get along. You know, in another situation."

"A situation where you and I actually meant something to each other, you mean?" Jamie snaps before he can think about what a colossally terrible idea it is.

Ben gets very still. His eyes flicker with something, but Jamie doesn't want to look at them. He doesn't want to look at Ben at all. He wants to claw the words back and pretend he never said them. He wants to stuff his heart back into the cage he's been so good at keeping it in.

Somehow, Ben McNatt got his hands on the key to that cage, and he's got it in the lock, about to swing the door open. And Jamie cannot, *cannot*, let that happen. His chest already aches at the confirmation that their fake relationship is just that: fake.

He has to lock up his heart again.

There's a touch on his arm. Jamie's eyes snap to the point of contact. Ben's fingers are there, resting on his bare skin. "I fucked up, didn't I?" Ben asks.

Jamie swallows hard and finally moves. They're going to get kicked off the ferry if they don't get off themselves. "There's nothing to fuck up," he says. "We just have an arrangement."

# CHAPTER FOURTEEN

HOW HAD such an amazing day gone so wrong?

Ben stands at the railing of the Liberty Island ferry for an agonizing moment, watching Jamie's hunched shoulders disappear around the corner. And then he gets his fucking ass in gear and moves, hurrying to catch up.

"Hey! Hey, Jamie!" The ramp to the ferry bounces and rattles as Jamie stomps onto dry land, and Ben has to hustle to keep up. Goddamn, legs for days, and he can move when he wants to. Ben manages to get half a step in front of Jamie and holds out his hands.

Jamie stops. His lips are pressed into a thin line, and his eyes are flashing. His eyebrows lower, and a deep notch appears between them.

"I'm sorry," Ben says.

"Do you even know what you're apologizing for?" Jamie demands.

"Uh."

Jamie jams his hands into his pockets. Again. Ben realizes he was doing it through most of the conversation with Adriana. Ben barely thought anything of it, because he was too wrapped up in proving to Adriana that he was right.

"I'm…." Ben's mouth hinges open, and Jamie's eyes flick toward him, then away. His eyebrows are cast low like he's trying to hide his eyes entirely, like he doesn't want Ben to see what's there. But Ben doesn't need to see Jamie's eyes to know what he's feeling. That's kind of the thing about Jamie—he wears his heart on his sleeve.

"I'm apologizing for upsetting you." Ben's not sure what he did wrong, but it was obviously something.

The fight goes out of Jamie. His shoulders slump and he looks away. "Never mind. It's not a big deal. I should… I should probably go."

They're supposed to have dinner. And after, they're going to a club—a nice one, where Jamie assured him "hardly anyone fucks in the bathroom—usually it's just guys making out." Now Jamie wants to end the day here, on this sour note, because Ben fucked up.

"Maybe we should call this whole thing off," Ben blurts.

Jamie's head snaps around and his eyes widen. Ben has no idea why he said it. He didn't mean to. He didn't plan on saying it. The words were just there, falling out of his mouth in a jumble that now he has to sort through.

Something in his brain must have thought there was a straight line between getting what he wanted, which was *dinner and a club with Jamie*, and putting an end to their fake dating. Because… maybe Jamie's mad about that? Maybe he's realizing that being Ben's fake boyfriend sucks just as much as being his real boyfriend would.

"Call it off?" Jamie repeats. "But don't you need the relationship to get the promotion?"

"I don't know. Maybe Adriana was right. Maybe this was a bad idea. Maybe I've been wasting your time when you could've been looking for a new job, or…." He remembers what Jamie shyly told him earlier today, that he writes papers sometimes, academic ones. "You could be working on your paper. The one about Pskov's trading ties with the Hanseatic League during Ivan the Great's reign."

"You remembered that?"

"Sure." Ben offers him a wry smile. "Did I pronounce everything right?"

"Close enough." The incredulity on Jamie's face is fading to something that Ben is having trouble parsing. "I didn't expect you to care. I felt like an idiot for going on about it."

Ben's forehead crinkles. "You barely told me anything! I wanted to ask you, but I thought you were annoyed by how ignorant I am about everything you're interested in."

"No, I'm not—you're not ignorant, I mean, and I definitely wasn't annoyed." He stops and rakes his fingers through his hair. "Do you really want to call this off? Stop seeing each other? Not *seeing each other*. You know what I mean. Stop trying to convince people we're dating."

"Do you?" Ben asks. "I'm obviously not even much good at a fake relationship. I ruined the day."

A small, genuine smile finally cracks Jamie's face. "Ben—I don't want to fake break up with you." When Ben laughs, Jamie's smile gets gentler and happier. "I shouldn't have stormed off. I just…." He chews at his lip. "I don't know. I don't know what I was thinking."

But the pieces click into place for Ben. What had Jamie said? *A situation where we actually meant something to each other.*

Ben hurt Jamie's feelings because…. Ben means something to Jamie, and he made Jamie feel like Jamie doesn't mean anything to him.

Can that be right?

"I like you," Ben says, again before his brain can catch up with his mouth. Jamie's eyes widen. "I'm sorry I made it sound like I don't. That's why you got upset, right? Because I said we just have an arrangement. That's not true. I mean, it *is* true, but I really do like you. For real. You're a cool guy, and I'm glad we're…"

He's going to say something like, I'm glad we're getting to know each other, or I'm glad we're finally out together, and I wish it hadn't taken this stupid scheme for us to finally go on a date, or I'm so glad I met you because you're the most amazing person I've ever known.

At the last second, he panics. Instead, what comes out is, "… friends. I'm glad we're friends."

Is that disappointment shadowing Jamie's eyes?

"Are we real friends?" Jamie asks. "Or just fake friends to prove you're capable of it?"

Ben laughs. An hour ago, he probably would've taken Jamie's hand. Now it feels weird, like playing with fire. It's like they're having their first fight as a couple, but they aren't actually a couple. It leaves Ben feeling confused and adrift.

"We're definitely real friends," Ben says. "If you want to be. I mean. I can't really force you to be my friend."

"Of course I'm your friend, Ben," Jamie says softly. "I thought it was obvious."

No. God, no. Nothing about this situation is obvious.

"And," Jamie says, "I don't want to call this off, for the record. No fake breakup. I want you to get this promotion."

Ben rubs his beard with his thumb. "You don't think there's anything to what Adriana said about it being unethical?"

Jamie puts a hand on his hip. "Are you the best person for the job?"

"Yeah," Ben answers immediately. "Of course. I'm the best surgeon out of all their internal candidates—and probably the external ones too."

"There you go. Looking for a job is all a performance. Your resume's a performance, the interviews are a performance. The whole thing is designed to see if you know how to act the right way. So act the right away. Give them family man Ben McNatt, who will take care of everyone who comes through his doors, because he knows how much the health of the people you love matters."

"You give better job-hunting advice than LinkedIn."

Jamie snorts. "Is that supposed to be a compliment?"

"Well, it was supposed to be."

"I'm not sure I'm really hashtag-winning if you're comparing me to LinkedIn."

"Favorably! I was comparing you *favorably* to LinkedIn!"

A smile flickers over Jamie's face, and it drills straight through Ben's sternum. Straight to his heart. Straight to—Jesus, Ben's not supposed to believe in souls. So why does it feel like Jamie's got a hold on the soul he isn't supposed to believe in?

Shifting from one foot to the other, Ben clears his throat. "So. Since we're not fake breaking up, do you want to get dinner like we planned? And, er, go to that club you told me about?"

Jamie's bottom lip catches on his teeth and his eyebrows draw together, but it's the lip that Ben's eyes snag on. The way Jamie's teeth leave little indentations in the skin, tiny blood-swollen notches, darker red in the surrounding pink. A vivid image of Ben's own teeth on those lips, or Jamie's on his, seizes him. It's a hook in his gut, hot as a brand. "Really?" Jamie asks. "Are you sure you don't want a break from me?"

"Why would I want a break from you?" Ben thought they were back on safe ground. Or maybe not safe ground, because nothing about this is safe—but more familiar ground.

"Well, not to put too fine a point on it, but the expiration date on the delightfulness of my company usually comes around pretty fast."

Ben can't help laughing, because even though Jamie's putting himself down, he's funny while he does it. An answering smile flits over Jamie's face. "I don't know what you're talking about," Ben says. He pauses for effect, then adds, "Expiration date-wise, you're like a canned meat—shelf-stable for decades."

A sun-bright grin settles on Jamie's face and he puts a hand to his heart. "No one's ever said something so beautiful to me."

"Yeah well, I'm a real poet." He takes a breath. "I would love to go to dinner. And I haven't been to a club in like—" He thinks. "—ever, maybe. Maybe when I turned twenty-one. I want to tear up the club?"

The look Jamie gives him makes Ben want to melt, or possibly float away. It's full of affection and humor, but there's this softness too. Ben can't remember anyone ever looking at him with softness. He's always assumed no one could love his awkwardness. The part of him that doesn't feel like it fits anywhere. Not straight enough, not gay enough, not man enough, not fun enough, not cultured enough, not country enough.

His heart feels like it's cracking free from a chrysalis—though that's giving himself too much credit. That implies his heart emerging from its ugly larval stage (sorry caterpillars) was predestined. That he just needed to reach the right point in his life and his heart would spread its wings, transformed into something beautiful.

But there's nothing predestined about this. He needs to make sure the chrysalis actually falls apart. He *wants* to make sure the chrysalis falls apart. He doesn't just want to pretend to have a heart. He thinks he actually wants one.

# CHAPTER FIFTEEN

"HOW ARE you so good at this?!" Jamie yells over the pulse of the bass. "You said you haven't been to a club since you were twenty-one!"

Lights strobe and flash, flickering on bodies and glittering off clothes and makeup. This club is amazing, and Ben totally isn't just thinking that because he's had four drinks. Five drinks? Does the wine at dinner count? No, wine at dinner totally doesn't count.

Bass shudders through his bones and settles in his hips, and he yells back, "Haven't I ever told you I love to dance?"

"Then you should go clubbing!"

Ben throws his head back and laughs. Someone bumps into him from behind, and he doesn't care, even though it's the kind of thing he would usually care about. Whoever bumped him grinds into him, hot, sweaty hands at his waist pressing his damp shirt into his skin.

The bass in his hips and the feel of a stranger's hard dick pushing into his ass makes Ben get hard. It's like—it's kind of nice? He doesn't want to turn around and see whoever's behind him, and in a second he's going to step away because he's not interested in dancing with strangers, or in having their dicks pressed against him for more than a few hot, sweaty seconds.

But he feels like he belongs here. No one cares if he looks like Standard Cishet Man. All that matters is he's here, and he's on the dance floor.

Has he ever felt like he belongs anywhere? In his entire life?

Is this why he needs to be the best? Because when you're the best, you're excused from needing to belong? Who needs community when the community wants to be you?

No one here knows he's a gifted neurosurgeon. All anyone knows is that he can swing his hips with the best of them.

The man behind him pulls at his hip, trying to turn him around, but Ben doesn't. Instead, he looks at Jamie, who's not looking at him. He's glaring at the man behind Ben. It makes giddiness leap in Ben's chest. It's one of those jumping fountains, heady joy leaping from his heart to his lungs to this spot on his throat that isn't even anything anatomical, but it's where Ben's butterflies have chosen to gather, wings brushing and tangling together.

Jamie reaches for Ben and grabs his hands, pulling him close, away from the guy behind him and his hard dick and his sweaty hands. Maybe it's the alcohol, maybe it's the strobing lights, maybe it's that he's dancing and it throws his balance off, but Jamie and Ben careen into each other.

They're pressed together before Ben's brain can process it. Jamie's final outfit of the day is a black muscle tank with a narrow rainbow striped across the chest, and it's currently soaked in sweat. Jamie's hair is sticking to his forehead and neck, and his eyes are bright, and Ben can smell him.

Their hands stay gripped together. Jamie glares over Ben's shoulder for a final few *fuck-off* seconds. When Jamie's eyes move to Ben's, Ben says, "He doesn't mean anything to me, baby."

Jamie grins fiercely and wraps his arms around Ben. "Good."

"Good? Wait a second, you weren't jealous, were you?" Alcohol is making Ben say things he normally wouldn't.

Jamie makes a face. Ben can't help laughing. He doesn't know what else to do. He can't remember the last time he felt this free. Jamie's arms are around him; his hands are splayed against Ben's back. Each one of his fingertips is a hot, bright point on Ben's body. Their hips brush and move together as they dance, and Ben moves closer so there's no daylight between them.

He wants to feel Jamie like he could feel that stranger behind him.

"There's people I know here!" Jamie shouts over the music.

"Oh!" Ben says. Okay? What? "Do you want to go talk to them?"

"No!" Jamie's fingers dig into Ben's back harder. It's the best thing Ben's ever felt. "I mean—I know them!"

"Right! You said that!"

Jamie opens his mouth. He closes it.

He leans in, narrows the space between their faces to nothing, and kisses Ben.

The light gets more glittery; the music gets louder. Ben tangles his fingers in Jamie's hair, pulls him closer, and opens his mouth to the kiss. To Jamie's tongue, which darts between his lips to tease Ben's tongue, to the brush of teeth, to the hot pant of breath.

Ben grinds against him and feels more than hears the noise Jamie makes. It rumbles low in his chest and Ben feels the vibration, and suddenly he wants off this dance floor. He wants to go—somewhere. Somewhere private. Somewhere he can push Jamie against a wall and get his hands all over him, get his hands on skin and maybe even the hard bulge he can feel—

The music changes, revving to something faster with a machine gun snare. Jamie pulls back. His eyes look hazy, but he grins. "Now they can gossip about how they saw me making out with someone at REBAR!"

Right. Ben's so stupid. Just because they had a real conversation about their feelings doesn't mean that Jamie has real feelings for him beyond friendship.

Do friends get boners when they make out with each other?

Wait. Do friends make out with each other?

Sounds like a meme. Fellas, is it gay to grind your dick into your friend's dick as you make out on the dance floor of a gay club?

This is maybe the worst thing that's ever happened to Ben. Also maybe the best. He can't decide, and anyway, he thinks he might need another drink. "Hey, I'm going back to the bar!" he yells over the music, a mashup of Lizzo and Troye Sivan. It slaps, but Ben's breathless from the kiss and overwhelmed by the fact that it was for show.

He figures Jamie will stay on the dance floor, but he follows Ben. It takes a while to get served, and when they do, it's because Jamie finally gets the bartender to pay attention to them. Clubs are all the same.

Grimacing, Jamie says, "I feel old."

"You're twenty-seven!"

Jamie jerks his chin toward a group of men nearby. "Yeah. Twenty-seven. Not twenty-three. A gay guy in New York is basically past his prime once he's twenty-five."

"That's stupid, and you're not," Ben says. The words slip out because *he's* stupid and also drunk. "You're better-looking than anyone else here. And I bet everyone was jealous that I got to kiss you."

Jamie's mouth opens, his cheeks flush red, and he looks really pleased, but also flustered about feeling pleased. Ben wishes he'd kept his mouth shut but also he's glad he didn't. Because it's true.

To hide his embarrassment, Ben checks his phone. There's an email from a few hours ago from—*shit*.

It's from Marie Kidjo.

Is this important? Did they make their decision? Why is she emailing him on a Saturday if it's not to tell him whether he got the job or not?

His brain is screaming at him to open the email, maybe to go somewhere quiet to read it. But what his body does is tilt his head up so he can meet Jamie's eyes. Jamie's hand is frozen with his drink halfway to his mouth, and he's watching Ben.

"Everything okay?" Jamie asks.

"Um." Ben swallows. "I got an email? From Marie? Marie Kidjo?"

Why the fuck is he uptalking?

He clears his throat. "I'm going to go read this."

"Do you want me to come?"

Jamie really cares, doesn't he?

"Okay," Ben says.

Jamie nods and puts his drink back on the bar. The two of them weave through the crowd. When the lights get dimmer and the bodies get thicker—and also more intertwined—Jamie slips his hand into Ben's and leads the way.

They make their way through a long, dark hallway. There are couples standing against the wall, some talking, a lot of them making out. Finally, they emerge into a quieter lounge lit with cool blues and purples. A bar takes up one wall, and the seating is all mid-century modern sofas and chairs. Jamie leads Ben to an empty sofa.

Ben stares at his phone. "What if this is bad news?"

"Then we deal with it, I guess."

Ben's chest feels tight. "I don't think I can do this. What if I'm out of the running? They haven't even done interviews yet, not official ones. What if I'm so not cut out for the job that they're axing me now? Who the hell *am* I if I don't get this job?"

There's the barest squeeze on his leg, and Jamie says, "Hey." It's quiet, and there's nothing commanding about it, but Ben can't do anything but drag his gaze to Jamie's. "You're Ben McNatt. You have great taste in coffee. You know all the words to 'One Week' and 'Good as Hell,' and you have a fucking amazing voice. And *moves*." When Ben chuckles weakly, Jamie gives him a bracing smile. "You're smart and you're funny and you have killer dress sense. You're interesting. And you're fun."

Their faces seem closer together, though Ben doesn't remember moving. Jamie's eyes are… so pretty. They're so pretty, and Ben doesn't want to blink, because he doesn't want to look away. He can't believe Jamie's saying all these nice things about him, and Ben's staring into his eyes and he doesn't see any lie there. Jamie *means* it.

"You didn't even mention that I'm a pretty brilliant neurosurgeon," Ben says.

Jamie's smile looks almost shy. "Well, yeah. Of course." The blue-purple lights in the lounge make Jamie's eyes look the color of the sky when the sun sinks deep beneath the horizon—sapphire shot through with violet and the first stars appearing. His fingers squeeze again. "But to be honest, I didn't think you needed to hear that. It kind of seems like you need to hear the other stuff."

Ben doesn't know what to say. Hearing this brilliant, funny, sharp-as-a-razor, beautiful man tell him that he's worth more than the only thing Ben knows how to be good at? That's like….

Well, it's kind of a revelation.

What do you say to someone when they make you feel like you matter?

"You think I have killer dress sense, huh? Wait till you see my flamingo underwear," Ben says.

So yeah, that's definitely not what you say.

Jamie goes on like, a serious face journey, but it probably has nothing on Ben's as he unpacks what he just said in the moments immediately following the words' unfortunate path from his brain to his mouth and then out into the air. Though maybe positing his brain's involvement is a little generous.

"I…," Ben says.

Yes, he has boxer briefs with a flamingo pattern on them. No, he did not think about how informing Jamie of this fact was going to sound.

Jamie bites his lower lip.

And he snorts with laughter. Ben does too, and before he knows it, he's laughing so hard he can't breathe, and Jamie's bent double at the waist, hiccupping as he loses it. His hair curtains his face, and even though Ben's stomach hurts and he's struggling to get a breath, it's so hard not to touch it. He wants to sink his fingers into it the way he did when they kissed on the dance floor; he wants to tuck it behind Jamie's ears; he wants to trace the line from Jamie's jaw to his chin and then up to his lips.

They get themselves under control, but Ben sets them off again by saying, "Wow, I got *no* enthusiasm about my flamingo briefs."

Jamie leans against him, wheezing and wiping at his eyes. After several deep, labored breaths and several giggles, he says in a sultry voice, "Oh, I can't wait to see your flamingo briefs, Ben. I'm ready whenever you are."

He's joking he's joking he's *joking*. So what are you gonna do, Ben? *Joke back.* "I keep them in the dresser with all my other underwear," he replies in the most sensual tone he can manage, which isn't very sensual, considering he's still trying really hard not to laugh.

And then. *And then.*

Jamie straightens up. He reaches out. And he brushes Ben's hair off his forehead. "I didn't mention how just… lovely you are," he says. "In case you need to hear that too."

Everything in Ben twists up in knots of longing and need and desire and this feeling that he's not sure he's ever felt before. It's terrifying and exhilarating and takes his breath away, and he *doesn't know what to do.*

How do you ask your fake boyfriend to be your real boyfriend?

How do you know when another person wants that?

"Are your loins sufficiently girded to check your email?" Jamie says, his smile crooked.

"First you want to see my underwear, now you're talking about my loins," Ben says before making himself look at the email.

*Dinner invitation*, the subject says, which Ben can't parse. That's not what he was expecting. Dinner? Invitation?

"What is it?" Jamie asks, sounding nervous himself.

"Um," Ben says distractedly, scrolling to read the email.

Ben,

I'm so sorry for the short notice, but Dan and I were wondering if you'd be free to join us for dinner on Sunday evening. Victor and Alaina will be there, and we would love to have you and Jamie as well. We had planned to have you over next weekend, but Dan had an unexpected work obligation come up! I hope you'll be able to join us, but understand if you already have other plans.

Best,
Marie

"What is it?" Jamie repeats, sounding full-on concerned now.

Ben looks up. A smile creeps over his face. "We got invited to dinner." Jamie laughs in delighted disbelief, and Ben doesn't think—he just grabs Jamie's hand. "That settles it—we're doing something right."

# CHAPTER SIXTEEN

BY THE time Ben puts Jamie in a Lyft to go home, it's just past two in the morning. Ben's bleary-eyed and keeps insisting he should ride with Jamie, because that's what a gentleman would do. He's drunk, and there's something charming about seeing someone drunk for the first time. Especially when they turn out to be a silly and fun drunk, when they just keep smiling goofily at you and making you feel like the greatest thing since sliced bread.

On the fourth iteration of *No but I really should ride with you*, Jamie grabs Ben's face and says, "Ben. I'm going to be fine. *You* are drunk and should go upstairs and have a Gatorade or something."

"You should come upstairs with me," Ben says, and knowing him, it's not a proposition—it's an offer to share the Gatorade, because Jamie's drunk too.

Drunk and so, so close to Ben's face. He can feel each warm puff of breath as Ben exhales. It would be so easy to kiss him. Maybe not kiss him like they kissed on the dance floor earlier. But something gentle and careful, something that says, *I like you; I like you so much and I don't want you to run away. I don't want to make you run away before you decide to yourself.*

Instead, he leaves the empty space between their mouths, and he gives himself one thing, which is to run his fingers over Ben's jaw, to feel the soft bristle of his beard against them. "I'll see you tomorrow for dinner," he says.

The music in the Lyft gets louder, and Jamie figures he has another minute or so before he loses the ride. Before he can step away, Ben wraps his hands around Jamie's upper arms. "That's why you should stay," Ben says. "You're coming back tomorrow. So just… stay. It's late."

And god, Jamie's chest aches with the desire to do just that. The temptation, the pull, to twine his fingers with Ben's, to follow him through the front door, to get in the elevator and go to his floor and be alone in his apartment, just the two of them, is so intense that it takes his breath away.

Which is exactly why he can't do it. Because he wants it so badly. Because it's too easy to imagine getting up there and drunkenly deciding they need to practice kissing. Because Jamie's pretty sure it wouldn't stop with kissing.

In the morning, Ben will realize it's a mistake, like everyone always does. The thought of losing Ben hurts. Jamie can't let that happen, so he won't let it get to the *oh-shit-this-was-a-huge-mistake* stage. They'll be friends. Jamie will want him. Ben will look at him like he's a revelation, and Jamie will take those practice kisses and hoard every single one of them.

"I want to," Jamie says, "but I can't."

"Yeah you can." Ben points, his arm going wide and missing the front door of his building by about a hundred feet. "We'll just walk in there."

"Ben," Jamie breathes. "You really are lovely." He kisses Ben's forehead and steps away before his brittle willpower wears away entirely.


"ARE WE sure I'm actually invited to this dinner?"

Ben glances at him, amusement crinkling the corners of his eyes. "Uh, yeah. Pretty sure. The email literally says they'd love to have you."

"Maybe you should let me read it again, just to make sure. That feels wrong, somehow." Jamie watches the scenery flash by on the Long Island Expressway. "You might have misread it."

"Jamie. I didn't misread it."

"But—"

"Babe."

Jamie's eyebrows rocket straight to his hairline and he splutters a few unintelligible syllables before managing, "Pet names in private now? Really?"

Ben shoots a grin at him. "Figured it would distract you from spiraling over a non-issue."

"I'm not spiraling. Trust me, you'd know if I was spiraling."

"So that's something you do?"

How to make sure a man will never want to actually date you: casually reveal your propensity for anxiety in casual conversation.

"Well," Jamie says, hoping that's sufficient. It's clearly not, because the silence that follows isn't normal comfortable-silence quiet. It's I'm-waiting-for-you-to-go-on quiet.

Clearing his throat, Jamie says, "Yeah. I mean, I'm on medication. But it's not perfect."

"It usually isn't." Ben slows as traffic thickens around them. Brake lights glow red through the windshield. Jamie stares into them, letting the electric crimson form a halo around each light.

It hasn't reached full-blown anxiety attack, but Jamie *is* anxious about dinner. He's good at parties, where he can flit from one person to another and never overstay his welcome. He can use the same charm over and over on different people. At a small dinner? Different story. He'll be cornered, sitting at a table and unable to duck an awkward question. What he says can come back and bite him in the ass. He'll be talking to these people long enough for things to reflect on him.

He'll be talking to these people long enough for things to reflect on Ben.

"What sets it off?" Ben asks.

The question takes Jamie so much by surprise that he can only gape at first. No one, literally no one—okay well, aside from therapists—has ever asked him that. "What... sets it off?" he repeats. "My anxiety?"

"Yeah." They've come to a dead stop now. Might be an accident up ahead. Might be roadwork. Might just be shitty Long Island traffic.

"Depends on the day," Jamie says vaguely. Dinner parties. His family. Thinking about his future. ATMs. He hardly ever uses them, and he's always worried he's going to forget his PIN when he actually has to. Which checks out. He still has dreams that he can't remember his locker combination.

"I was on Zoloft in my twenties," Ben volunteers. "Med school and my residency. All that stuff, you know? It can get kind of rough."

Eventually they arrive at a house shaded by tall maples and bordered by ornamental grasses. Not much grass in the yard, lots of terracing and gravel and gardens. It's all meticulously kept. There's another car parked in front of the three-car garage, a BMW.

Ben leans forward and kisses Jamie softly. On the mouth. With his lips. For no reason. There's no one watching. They're in a car in a driveway and not a soul is looking at them. And Ben is kissing him.

His lips are soft and full and warm. Jamie already knows this, but every time they kiss, it's a revelation all over again.

The kiss is over way too fast. Jamie doesn't have time to savor it—he barely has time to register it's happening. Ben rocks back. "Thought we should get in the right frame of mind. Happy boyfriends, right?"

Jamie forces a smile, though what he really wants to do is grab Ben's tie (not roller skates tonight—but it does have polka dots, which isn't as good but is better than Hetero Powder Blue) and pull him into another kiss. "Right. Sickeningly in love. Soppy gazing and all that stuff."

"We're nauseating," Ben says with a smile of his own.

Is it Jamie's imagination, or does Ben sound a little wistful?

Jamie's breath catches. He reaches for Ben's hand. Before he loses his nerve, he brings Ben's hand to his mouth and kisses his knuckles. He doesn't so much hear Ben's sharp intake of breath as feel it—the way something shivers through his body and there's a hitch in his chest.

Abruptly, Jamie throws the door open. "We should go in, right? I'll grab the wine."

Before he gets any bad ideas—at least, any more bad ideas, since most of his ideas consist of ways to kiss Ben again—he jumps out and gets the bottle of Boekenhoutskloof out of the back seat.

As they head up the path to the front door, Jamie can't help himself from hooking his pinkie around Ben's. "Nauseating," he says softly. Ben meets his eyes and there's something *there*.

# Chapter Seventeen

A TALL BLACK man, about Dr. Kidjo's age, comes to the door. His tightly coiled hair is threaded with silver and cropped short. A gold stud glints in one ear, a tragus piercing, so score one for the men with nontraditional piercings who date doctors.

"Ben!" The man offers his hand and Ben takes it, getting a hearty handshake in return. "Good to see you!"

The smile on Ben's face looks genuine, if nervous. "You too," Ben says. "Dan, this is my boyfriend, Jamie Anderson."

It rolls off his tongue like it's the truth. *My boyfriend, Jamie Anderson.* Jamie smiles and extends his hand. "Nice to meet you. Thank you so much for having us."

"Yeah, of course!" The man gives Jamie the same hearty handshake. "Dan Johnson. It's great you two could make it on such short notice. Come in! The mosquitos will eat you alive if you stand out here."

Jamie offers the bottle of wine. "From both of us."

Dan reads the label. "South African red, huh? The good stuff. Leave your shoes on, everyone's on the porch."

As Dan leads them through the house, Jamie glances at Ben. He looks uncomfortable. Jamie takes his hand and kisses his cheek.

The house is nice. There's art on the walls, a lot of which looks like it was done by the same artist. Plants hang in baskets from the ceiling, and near the patio is one of those tiered planters. Mementos and knickknacks are scattered around, a few on a shelf here, a few on the mantle there. They look like souvenirs from foreign travel. Jamie spots evidence of at least one kid—there's a backpack propped against the wall and a clarinet sitting in an open case in the living room.

It's all very lived-in and homey, which makes it distinctly different from Ben's apartment. Jamie feels like he knows something about Marie Kidjo and Dan Johnson, and he's been in this house for three minutes. Ben's apartment says almost nothing about him.

When they get to the porch (four season, wicker furniture, hammock, more plants), greetings and introductions are exchanged. Victor Dumas's wife's name is Alaina. She has a faint southern accent and warm brown eyes.

Marie says, "It's wonderful to see you again, Jamie," as she makes room for them.

"You too," he says, surprised by her warmth.

They make small talk for a while. It turns out that a lot of the art on the walls is by Dan, who's a full-time artist. His gallery is in the Bronx, near where he grew up. It's only a few blocks from Jamie's apartment, and the two of them spend a few minutes throwing favorite cheap restaurants back and forth. Dan tells Jamie to try the Dominican snack bar and Jamie vows to.

"Ben," Victor says, crossing one ankle over his knee, "you look… *different*. Are you doing your hair differently?"

"No." Ben glances at Jamie. "Unless you're noticing the way I changed up my moisturizing game? Thanks." Jamie wants to either kiss him or high-five him. Maybe both.

Victor chuckles. "That must be it. I thought maybe we could thank Jamie. Ben's been hiding you. We've had a number of gatherings we would have invited you to if we'd known you existed." He chuckles again. "Of course, seeing Ben at a social event is a little like getting a glimpse of Bigfoot."

Arching an eyebrow, Jamie says, "Oh, Ben's not that hairy."

Ben's just taking a sip of his beer and he chokes. Victor looks kind of scandalized. Alaina and Marie both look amused. Dan lets out a guffaw.

When Ben shoots him a frantic look, Jamie reads the room. "That joke played better here than it did with my lesbian friends last week," he says. He gets a bigger laugh.

Hopefully Ben isn't asked about these lesbian friends they hung out with last week, because they don't exist. Val is the only person in this city he considers a capital *F* Friend.

A twinge of guilt hits him about lying to her. She'd be on board with the plan if she knew about it. But the prospect of her spilling to Andy, even accidentally, is a risk he can't take.

When he tells her, once it's over, she'll think it's funny. She'll maybe be annoyed that she didn't get to scheme with him while it was going on—she has a talent for coming up with ludicrous date ideas, best enjoyed by the eccentric and criminally insane—but she'll understand. There's no need to feel guilty.

Soon, Dan goes to finish dinner. Not long after that, the tantalizing smell of whatever he's cooking draws the rest of the party into the dining room. They sit down to dinner once it's ready—crispy carnitas and homemade tortillas, with a mango salsa that explodes in Jamie's mouth. He eats this good *never*—he doesn't have the money to buy the kinds of groceries you need for a meal like this, and he doesn't have the time to make it.

He tries to pull his weight during dinner, but his reservoir of charming small talk is running dry. This is the longest he's spent in one spot, talking to the same strangers/acquaintances, in forever. It's draining. He's starting to second-guess everything he says, wondering if they'll all remember later how stupid he sounds.

After dinner, Marie sends them back to the porch while she stays behind to do the dishes. Jamie offers to help, and Marie doesn't argue. She purses her lips, smiles, and says, "A man who does dishes—I hope Ben snatches you up."

"Should I tell him you said that?" Jamie asks with a grin.

"God, no. That's hardly professional." She shoots a grin back. "But I did decide to marry Dan when he offered to do dishes the first time." Waving a hand, she says, "No, I'm sorry. You two just started seeing each other."

THEY WASH up without speaking before Marie says, "You haven't told us what you do for a living."

"Oh." Yeah. Deliberately. Like he's going to tell these people he's a barista? When they told the "how we met" story, they were vague on details, making it sound like Jamie was in the Daily Grind when Ben came in. Another patron, not the schlub making the coffee. Like he's going to tell two neurosurgeons, a really cool artist, and a successful insurance agent that he's scraping by making blended frappes and flat whites? Yeah, no thanks.

"It's not interesting," Jamie says.

She rinses a plate and hands it to him to dry. "It can't be too boring. It's hard to imagine you doing something that isn't interesting."

"Um." Why is she being so nice to him? Did she just call him interesting? "You'd be surprised."

There's a silence while she waits for him to share. Awkwardly, he doesn't. Realization—and embarrassment—enters her eyes. "Oh, I'm sorry, are you between things?"

Oh good lord. It's *secondhand embarrassment.* For *him.* For, as she's apparently just decided, his unemployed ass.

"No, I'm not!" Jamie yelps. Marie looks startled. "I'm not. Between things, I mean. No, I have a job."

*For really reals, I have a job, and it's a really great job, too!* Is he going to lie to her? Is he going to add another cardboard brick to the teetering edifice of his fake life? A serious relationship, a boyfriend who might want to lock him down because they're so happy, and a great job.

"I work at the Daily Grind," he says.

She smiles blankly, like she doesn't understand. Like he's speaking a different language. "The coffee shop where you and Ben met? What do you do there?" Mortification flashes across her face. "*Oh.* I'm sorry! Oh, that was insulting, wasn't it?"

"No," Jamie lies.

She turns off the water. "No, it was. You're a barista? At the Daily Grind?"

He wants to die. Lying was the better option. He could have made himself a scholar of Russian history. Of course, knowing his luck, Russian history is her second passion.

"Um, yeah. I've been there for years. Ever since I got my master's. I'm trying to get something different, but…."

She leans against the edge of the sink. "What's your master's in?"

"Russian history," he says. "I know, I should've gone into political science with a focus on Russia. It would've been a lot more marketable."

That's what his dad says every time they talk, at least. He's probably right, which makes Jamie hate it even more.

"Maybe." Marie shrugs. "I think there's something to be said for pursuing something that makes you happy, even if you can't turn it into a career."

Jamie snorts. "My father definitely wouldn't agree with you."

With a chuckle, she says, "Parents want their children to be secure. We worry." She gestures toward the door. "I catch myself doing it with our girls. Our oldest is starting to think about college, and I've already suggested three schools that I know have a good MBA program. She wants to be a poet. Or possibly an anthropologist."

"Her dad's an artist," Jamie points out. "So she has a good example of making it in the arts."

"True." Marie gives him a considering look. "Russian history. You know, I have a friend at Columbia who teaches Russian history. She's looking to hire a permanent teaching assistant. Someone who's interested in pursuing a career within the discipline."

Jamie's breath catches. He knows exactly who she's talking about— Nina Noskova, an up-and-coming star in the field. Since Jamie's nothing if not a masochist, he looks at the available positions that someone with a degree in Russian history might be qualified for. This is one of the few where he actually is.

But who is he kidding? He's been out of grad school for years. There's no way anyone would hire him for an academic position, even if it's objectively a shitty one. Teaching assistant? He'd barely make more than he does at the Daily Grind. It could be a step toward greater things, though—if he had the guts to apply for the position, and if he got it. He has a better chance of getting struck by lightning.

"I've seen the job posting."

"Have you applied?"

"Well—no." *Carpe diem, dumbass.* "Not yet, I mean."

She looks approving. "You're going to, though?"

"I've been thinking about it."

"Do it. I'll let her know. I think you two would work well together."

"Really? Oh my god, the opportunity just to talk with her for an hour would be amazing—" He sounds like a total fanboy. Clearing his throat, he attempts a more dignified tone. "I mean, working with her would be a dream. I've admired her for a long time. My master's thesis was inspired by her work."

With a smile, Marie says, "She'll be flattered. But tone down the hero worship in the interview. She doesn't like that."

The interview. Marie Kidjo is talking about him interviewing with Nina Noskova like it's a given. "Thanks for the advice," he manages, hoping his voice comes out smoother than how he feels. He wants to shriek like a tween girl at a BTS concert. "And just... thank you."

She hands him a plate. "It's no trouble. I like to help where I can. You don't have to tell me how cutthroat academia can be."

Yeah, but. She barely knows him. He's just some guy dating one of her surgeons. He hasn't done anything for her, nor can he imagine what she could want from him.

They finish up the dishes. As Marie dries her hands, she says, "There's something you can do to repay me, though."

Of fucking course. Nothing's free in life. People don't help for nothing.

"Um, sure?" he says, trying not to sound weary.

There's a conspiratorial smile on her face. "Can you *please* show me a picture of Ben having fun? I can barely imagine him loosening up, but he's different with you. He seems so much happier."

"You just want to see a picture of Ben having fun?" Is this a joke? How does that help her?

Then he realizes. Her saying he could repay her was the joke. He's so primed for people to use him that he can't recognize a joke. Andy has really done a number on him. Some people do things to be nice.

Good thing Jamie spent every quiet moment at work today going through yesterday's pictures, grinning goofily over them, choosing his favorites, and sending the best ones to Ben. Or just the ones that made him laugh. Or the ones where he thought Ben looked particularly beautiful.

"This was our third date," he says, handing his phone over.

"Oh." She puts a hand over her heart. "I love museum dates."

"I wasn't sure Ben would," Jamie says, like he's confessing something scandalous. "I knew I really liked him, but I guess it was kind of like a test. Because I can't date a man who doesn't like the Museum of Natural History. I just can't."

He gets lost in thought, remembering this day like it's real. Like Jamie really has a checklist for his ideal partner. Like he would ever pull something like that, because if he was looking, and he liked the guy enough for a third date, why would he devise a test that could be failed?

Fantasy Jamie has standards, though. He wants to establish that there's a solid foundation to build a relationship on.

In the picture, the two of them are standing in the Museum of Natural History lobby (they never got any farther, but obviously Marie doesn't need to know that part). They took a bunch of selfies in front of Sue, the T-rex skeleton on display. Then they started goofing around, making up dinosaur facts, then making up dinosaur facts in a Richard Attenborough voice, and finally acting out the dinosaur facts while the other narrated.

A young family nearby was watching, clearly entertained by them, and the mother asked if they wanted a video. This would be another of Fantasy Jamie's tests: was his date too uptight to have his silliness immortalized? Of course, Real Jamie froze, mortified by the idea of a video. Ben, though, Ben handed the woman his phone and said, "Yeah, thank you!"

So there was a video of Ben demonstrating the "majestic tiny arm flutter dance of the mighty Tyrannosaurus Rex, performed to intimidate rivals for the attention of potential mates."

"This one is particularly limp-wristed," Jamie says on the video, "so you can tell it's the well-attested gay T-rex."

Ben broke character and, laughing, hooked an arm around Jamie's waist and kissed him. The woman filming switched from video to photo and got several nauseatingly adorable photos of the kiss, and of the two of them grinning at each other and looking absolutely, horrifically, irrevocably in love.

The picture captures what it's supposed to, even if it's fantasy. Marie's face softens. "This isn't the Ben McNatt I know," she says. "Not at all."

"He takes his job really seriously," Jamie says. "But outside work, he's different."

A week ago, that would have been total bullshit—just Jamie saying what he needs to say. Now? He believes it with his whole heart. There's this person inside Ben who laughs without reserve, who isn't afraid to be silly in public, who will wrap you up and kiss you regardless of who's watching. He wishes other people knew that Ben. He wishes Ben would *let* other people see that side of him, because Jamie thinks that's the real him.

Maybe not the kissing part. He doesn't want other people to know how it feels to kiss Ben. Jamie wants to be the only one who gets to kiss him.

"This is adorable," Marie says, handing Jamie's phone back. "It's wonderful you two found each other. I can tell how happy you are."

"You can?" Jamie asks stupidly.

Her smile gets mischievous. "I know young people want Boomers to stay out of their lives, but the love that I see between you and Ben? That's something special. You need to hang on to that."

He has to say something. He can't just stand here gawping at her.

"Technically," he says—strong start!—"you can't possibly be old enough to be a Boomer."

Real bad finish.

Marie laughs and touches his shoulder. "I won't say anything to Ben, don't worry. And I'm sorry if I'm being awkward. I just—" She pauses. "Our world is difficult for partners. It hasn't always been easy for Dan. I want you to feel welcome. I want to let you know that it's obvious how much Ben loves you. I hope he shows it often."

Okay, now Jamie's mind is reeling. Sure, they're putting on an act, and sure, this is precisely the point, to make people think they're madly in love with each other. But they haven't even really been doing anything tonight. They've both just been themselves, mostly. Ben has seemed on edge, and Jamie's been in Charming Dinner Party Mode, but they haven't been holding hands or kissing or even making eyes at each other.

Have they? Because if they have been, Jamie didn't realize he was doing it.

"Thanks," he manages. "I appreciate that. I really—I mean, you've been so kind. Welcoming us into your home, and—the job with Nina Noskova." Charming Dinner Party Mode is clearly on the fritz. Jamie can't make it through a complete sentence. He takes a deep breath. "Thank you."

She pats him on the shoulder one more time. "C'mon, let's join everyone else."

# Chapter Eighteen

WHEN JAMIE appears in the porch doorway with Marie, Ben feels his face light up. Ben makes room on the wicker loveseat and their thighs press together when Jamie sits.

"So, Jamie," Victor says. "You never told us what you do for a living, and Ben keeps insisting he doesn't want to speak for you."

His voice and the way he says it makes Ben want to grind his teeth. Victor Dumas has never been his favorite person in the world, but being in competition for the same job has only sharpened his feelings. The way he's been acting for the past fifteen minutes while Jamie was out of the room, like Jamie's just a fun diversion for Ben to blow off steam, hones his dislike to a blade.

Jamie glances at Ben. Ben tries to convey with his eyes what he was trying to do: I didn't know if you were okay with telling this asshole you work at a coffee shop. Not because I don't think it's good enough or think it's beneath me to date a barista! But because at the cocktail hour you didn't specify that we met because you were at work at the Daily Grind, and I noticed that and didn't want to be presumptuous. I should have brought it up later to clarify what you wanted to tell people! Total oversight on my part. It's because I'm new to this whole fake dating thing and I wouldn't make the same mistake again, which I wouldn't because I don't want this to be fake dating anymore. I want to real date you. I want to feel like I have a leg to stand on when Victor makes insinuations that I'm a sugar daddy and you're only with me because you're a nice piece of ass—I mean not that you aren't, you totally are. Your ass is like… really amazing. And yeah, not the point! The point is that I want to be able to call shit like that out without feeling like a total hypocrite, and also I'm pretty sure I'm falling in love with you

He's pretty sure he doesn't get all of that across.

And wait. Did he just think the *L* word?

Interlacing his fingers with Ben's, Jamie says, "Ben McNatt, ever the gentleman."

It's loud enough for everyone to hear, but the way Jamie says it, and the way he's looking into Ben's eyes, makes it feel like it's only for him.

Turning his head to face the room, Jamie says, "I work at the Daily Grind. I'm a barista."

"No shit!" Dan says. "I used to hang out there all the time in college. I think it's changed hands since then. Probably a lot trendier now. They always had three different blends but I could never taste the difference."

Marie nudges him. "Are you telling me you'd be able to taste the difference now?"

"I'm a connoisseur, madam!" Dan says in mock affront.

Victor's head is cocked. "Side hustle. I get it. Everyone's trying to make ends meet, right? But what do you do for a living?"

"That." Jamie's shoulders straighten. "That's what I do for a living."

Victor raises his eyebrows. "I see."

Ben wants to murder him.

Okay. Fine. Maybe not murder. He just wants to hit him hard enough to bring those eyebrows down out of his hairline.

The smile on Jamie's face looks pleasant. But Ben knows—now—that smile hides a dagger. It would be really bad if Jamie went off on Victor. It would be very bad for Ben's chances at this promotion if his boyfriend caused a scene at a dinner party organized by the Head of Surgery.

"What's with the tone, Victor?" Ben snaps.

Jamie's head whips around. "Ben—" he begins, sounding way more conciliatory than Ben's feeling.

Victor's chest puffs up. "There's no tone, Ben," he replies. Yeah right. His sneer is audible, even if it's not quite visible.

"There was a tone. You think you're better than Jamie, right?"

Rolling his eyes, Victor says, "Oh, here we go." He looks directly at Jamie. "You know I didn't mean anything, right?"

"Of course," Jamie says.

"It's just the difference between skilled and unskilled labor," Victor says. "Nothing wrong with unskilled labor, right? I go to the Daily Grind. You make a mean macchiato."

Jamie's eyes are ice-cold. "Thanks."

Ben wants to call bullshit. If Victor frequented the Daily Grind, he would already know Jamie. Jamie is unforgettable.

"And," Victor says, "you have to admit, it takes a little getting used to."

"What does?" Ben asks. He's vaguely aware of the low murmur of conversation from Alaina, who is clearly trying to distract Marie and Dan from her husband's current awkwardness.

"A surgeon dating a barista," Victor says, like it's obvious. "People must talk. And the age difference, too. Isn't that a trend in the gay community?"

"I'm sorry, I'm not sure what you mean," Jamie says, sounding like he knows exactly what Victor means. "A trend in the gay community?"

Victor laughs. "Maybe 'trend' isn't the right word. I thought young gay men dated older men because they expect a certain lifestyle? And older men, well—there's no mystery why older men date younger people."

"Victor," Marie says suddenly, sharply, "can I get you another glass of wine?"

Yeah, another glass of wine is the last thing Victor needs, but at least Marie is trying to distract him. Victor just waves her off.

"The word you're looking for," Jamie says, hard and bright, "is 'gold-digger.' For me. You're calling me a gold-digger. And Ben is my sugar daddy. It's a trend in the straight community, too, if you didn't know."

Victor looks like he's been slapped. "There's no need to be sarcastic," he says.

"Shut up, Victor," Ben says. The room falls silent, and the silence sucks all the air out. "You can take your judgmental, homophobic bullshit and shove it. Apologize to Jamie."

With an incredulous laugh, Victor says, "I think if anyone is owed an apology right now, it's me."

Dan holds his hands out in a calming gesture. "Let's all take a step back, okay?"

"I have an early surgery tomorrow," Ben says. "And Jamie has to be at work at the ass crack of dawn making those *delicious* macchiatos for dickwads who think they're better than him because their paycheck has more zeroes on the end of it. Jamie, do you want to go?"

"Most definitely," Jamie says coolly, standing. Ben gets to his feet too. Jamie reaches for his hand and says, "Marie, Dan, thank you so much for dinner. Alaina, lovely to meet you."

There is pointedly nothing for Victor, and the lack has physical substance. Marie and Dan jump up and see them to the door, apologizing for Victor's behavior and insisting they'll have the two of them over again.

When they're back in the car, Ben lets his head fall against the headrest and closes his eyes. "I don't think I've ever been so close to breaking a vase over someone's head in my entire life."

Nothing but silence. Ben opens his eyes to look at Jamie. Shit, maybe he's mad? Maybe storming out was too much like a tantrum, and—

And then Jamie's pulling him into a kiss.

It's over before Ben can return it. When Jamie rocks back, he clears his throat. "In case anyone's watching. That moment deserved a kiss."

"It took me by surprise," Ben says dazedly.

"Oh." Jamie chews the inside of his cheek before a smile draws one corner of his mouth up. "Well, then."

He leans forward and kisses Ben again, slower this time. His tongue traces Ben's bottom lip, and the floor drops out of Ben's stomach. He lets his own tongue brush against Jamie's, and he knows he doesn't imagine the soft noise Jamie makes.

When Jamie pulls back, his eyes are still closed. He looks blissful and satisfied and just this side of euphoric. He looks beautiful, and Ben could stare at him forever.

He's staring when Jamie opens his eyes. Jamie blushes and says, "Sorry. I'm just—I know it's… I mean, our relationship isn't real, but I feel like I should tell you, you're a very good kisser."

"Likewise," Ben says. There's a goofy grin on his face, which is definitely saying the opposite of *this relationship is fake.*

Jamie's eyes drop to Ben's lips, then slowly track back up to his eyes. He loosens Ben's hair until a piece falls over his forehead. "I don't need a knight in shining armor," Jamie says. "But thank you."

"For what?"

"Sticking up for me."

"You're right, you didn't need me to," Ben says honestly. "I've never seen Victor look that stunned. You're amazing."

Jamie grins, but then he bites his lip. "I really hope I didn't just mess up your chances at the promotion."

A fierce swell of emotion wells up in Ben's chest. "Hey." He takes Jamie's hand. It feels natural. "Victor was the one being the douchebag. You didn't do anything wrong. You were way more polite than I would've been."

"I was actually way more polite than you were," Jamie points out.

"Exactly."

Jamie's thumb strokes the back of Ben's hand and Ben thinks he might die. Jamie, on the other hand, doesn't look like he realizes he's doing it. "They know you, though. I'm a stranger."

"They know me and they don't like me."

"That's not true," Jamie says, surprisingly forcefully, as far as Ben's concerned. "Marie likes you. She likes you more than you think she does. And if she does, then maybe other people do too."

Reluctantly disentangling their hands, Ben starts the car and puts it in reverse. "I really don't think anyone likes me at work. And if they do, it's not the real me."

Whoa. Shit. Where had that come from? Until two weeks ago, Ben was perfectly content with who he was at work. He'd tell you what you saw was what you got, that he was unashamedly himself.

And then… two weeks ago. Jamie. Getting to know him. Getting to know *himself*. Because the Ben he buried can't help but unearth itself around Jamie. The Ben he didn't think anyone else would care about, let alone like. And with that Ben's emergence, a parallel truth has come along for the ride—the person he is at work, the person he is everywhere, isn't the real him. At least, it's not all of him. It's only a carefully curated part, the part he thinks is primetime ready.

Two weeks ago, he would have said the world had told him only part of him was primetime ready. But what if he's been wrong all this time?

What if the thing holding Ben back… is Ben?

# CHAPTER NINETEEN

"OH, I THINK my iPad's dying? It might be my stylus, I don't know. I hope it's just the stylus. It's overpriced, but it's not as bad as an iPad." Val keeps up a steady stream of conversation as they fill online orders.

"Are you going to get a new iPad if it's dying?" Jamie asks.

Val flips the steaming wand on with the heel of her hand and raises her voice over the sound of milk frothing. "I don't know! I might get one of those super fancy tablets!"

The steamer shuts off, and Val portions the milk into the lattes she's making. Jamie pushes another batch of orders across the counter and gets started on the next one. "Aren't those like, insanely expensive?"

"Yeah," Val says wistfully. "A Wacom MobileStudio, though? Damn, bruh, that is the *dream.*"

Jamie snorts. "How many months of rent is that?"

She makes a face. "Two-ish?"

"Fuck."

"But," she goes on, "I'm gonna need one. Like, at some point, I'm gonna have to get one. Anyone who does art for a living gets one."

"I bet there are people out there who are making do with less than a two-months-of-rent tablet." He pauses. "Whose rent are we talking, here? Yours or mine?"

"They're almost four thousand dollars."

"*Four thousand dollars?*" Jamie feels faint. "Val. How the fuck can you afford to buy a tablet for *four thousand fucking dollars?*"

"I can't." She gets a little aggressive with the mocha she's making, not that Jamie blames her. Four thousand dollars! What the hell. Sure, Val has a foot in the door doing what she wants. The theater loves her. And in reviews, Val's work always gets singled out for how superlative it is.

"So what are you going to do?"

"Rack up more credit card debt."

Like it's a joke, when it totally isn't. Jamie doesn't look at how much he's carrying anymore—he just pays off a set amount every month and doesn't think about it.

Val finishes the drink she's working on. "I'll start taking commissions. That person who always wants me to draw Ironman and Captain America banging DMed me last night and asked if I'm opening them up again."

"StonyColdCrazy?"

"I can't believe you remember that."

"Um, it's a pun on a Queen song, Val. Of course I remember." He fills two coffee cups with french roast. "Also, as I recall, they weren't just banging each other. Wasn't the request actually for Ironman to be a 'slutty bottom while Steve gives him the rawing of his life'?"

Val groans. "I should never have showed that to you."

"The most unforgivable part was that you showed me the request but I never got to see the finished product."

"And you're not going to."

"Was it hot?"

She ignores him for a second, then admits, "Yeah. It's a pretty fucking hot pic."

Jamie almost sloshes coffee over his hand as he laughs. "I hope all your porny art brings in enough for you to buy the drawing tablet of your dreams."

Just as he finishes the sentence, a customer comes in—so thank god they didn't hear him talking about smutty fanart of superheroes. It's one of the pickup orders, and the man is talking on the phone, Bluetooth earbuds stuck in both ears, so he doesn't acknowledge either of them as he grabs his drink and leaves. Val leans against the counter and arches her back in a stretch. "Too bad I'm not dating a doctor. I'd just ask if they could buy it for me."

"No you wouldn't," Jamie says.

"You're underestimating how much I want that tablet." She twists a braid around her finger. "Tall, Douchey, and Handsome isn't showering you with gifts?"

It's been a few days since the dinner party, but this is too close to Victor's insinuations for comfort. "No," Jamie snaps. "He's not my sugar daddy."

"With your thing for daddies? You sure?"

His face sours and he grabs a rag, heading to the farthest corner of the store to wipe tables. "Hey," Val says, following him. "I was joking. I know you have a whole self-sufficiency thing going on. Not relying on anyone else and everything. Which you might want to get therapy for, but what do I know?"

"Is this an apology or not?" Jamie asks through gritted teeth.

A beat of silence. "Yeah." She looks contrite. "Seriously. I'm sorry. I didn't mean anything by it."

Jamie huffs a sigh. "Fine. You're forgiven. And his name is Ben, by the way."

"Okay. Your *boyfriend's* name is *Ben.*"

"Yep."

"Your *lover's* name is Ben."

"Stop."

"Your beau's name—"

Jamie laughs. "We get it, okay?"

She straightens some chairs. "I can't believe you kept him a secret for two months. He came in here every day! I never would have guessed."

"Yeah." Jamie hopes he doesn't look shifty, because he feels shifty. "We wanted to keep it on the DL."

"It's almost like you weren't really dating," Val says.

Jamie freezes for a second too long.

"Ha!" Val crows. "I knew it!"

"Knew what?" Jamie asks. Shit shit shit shit.

She grins triumphantly. "You made the whole thing up. You're not dating him."

Shit shit shit shit.

Scoffing, Jamie says, "Why would I make up a fake relationship?"

"I don't know," she says. "I'm not the one who did it. You tell me."

"I can't, because I didn't." Jamie gives her a disdainful eye roll. At least the disdainful eye roll is his bread and butter, so he knows it's convincing. "Just because Ben and I kept things quiet until we were ready for everyone to know about us doesn't mean we aren't dating. We don't all have to post pictures on insta of our lease-signing three days after we meet."

He shoots, he scores. Val's nostrils flare and she folds her arms over her chest. "It was for a *rental car*, not an apartment, and I was young and stupid."

"It was two years ago," Jamie says. "You weren't that young."

She purses her lips. "You're purposefully changing the subject. Why are you pretending to date him?"

"I'm pretending to date him!" Jamie snaps. How dare she accuse him of that? Where does she get off? Obviously he *is* pretending to date Ben, but she doesn't know that, and he hasn't been obvious about it at all. Personally he thinks they seem very in love with each other, so why does she think it's not real?

Inspiration strikes. That's the way to get her to back off. "Are you suggesting there's something about my relationship that doesn't seem right? What are you accusing him of?"

"What?" Val looks alarmed. "I'm not accusing him of anything! Oh my god, why do you have to be so dramatic?"

"I just don't get why you think our relationship is a sham?" Jamie says, pitching his affront and hurt perfectly, if he says so himself. "I haven't been with a nice guy for like, years, and you're shitting on this one."

She looks intensely guilty. "I'm not implying anything about him."

"Good."

"As long as he's being nice to you."

"He is."

"And he makes you happy."

"He does." The lies come so easily that they don't feel like lies at all. Maybe they aren't? Ben is nice to him. Ben does make him happy. So really, he's not lying. It's just that both of those things are happening in the context of the relationship being fake, but minor detail.

"Does who make you happy, Jamie?"

Jamie practically jumps out of his skin, and Val starts too. They both turn toward the voice. Andy. Fuck. Exactly who Jamie didn't need to deal with today.

"Hey, Andy," Val says. Her eyes dart toward Jamie. Normally he considers her the Andy Whisperer, because she has an uncanny ability to divert the conversation away from what he's fishing for. But normally they aren't discussing Jamie's love life, because normally, he doesn't have one.

"You must be talking about your boo," Andy says. His walk is practically a slither as he crosses the coffee shop. Jamie prays for a customer.

"Er, yeah." Jamie tries to think of something that will end this conversation as quickly as possible.

Luckily, Val jumps in with, "I was just being protective."

"Ooooh, do you need protection?" Andy asks as he puts a scandalized hand on his chest. So that backfired. "You know I'm always just a text away, Jamie."

"She was being needlessly protective," Jamie says.

Andy puts his hand on Jamie's arm when choosing his shoulder would have done just as well. Once his hand is on Jamie's bicep, he squeezes. "Your boyfriend *is* treating you right, isn't he?"

How does he manage to make it sound so dirty?

"This doesn't even need to be a conversation," Jamie says. "Of course he is." Customer. *Please.* Customer. Someone, save him.

"But is he treating you right?" Andy asks. "If he's not—well, good thing you're both coming up to the house this weekend. You're still coming, right?"

Jamie makes a strangled sound that sort of passes for affirmation.

Andy's fingers squeeze Jamie's arm again, and this time, they don't loosen. "Maybe if you aren't getting the treatment you deserve, we could show him what you need."

The door opens before Jamie can jolt his frozen limbs into movement—movement away from Andy, who's just... ugh. He's so gross, but Jamie can't offend him, can't yank his arm away like he wants to, can't tell him where to shove his wildly inappropriate innuendo.

Val hustles to the counter. The customer doesn't pay any attention to the way Andy has Jamie backed into the corner.

"I can't wait for this weekend," Andy says, leaning too far into Jamie's space.

Jamie's skin crawls. Maybe he should call it off. He's got Marie's offer of help with Nina Noskova in his back pocket—but of course, he hasn't actually applied. He's opened up the application a few times this week, but when he starts to fill everything in, his heart pounds wildly and he has to walk away. When he convinces himself to come back to it, the sight of his information fills him with such overwhelming mortification and shame that he's closed the tab every time.

And he hasn't even made it to the work history section yet.

Is that why he hasn't told Ben about it? That feeling that crawls up his esophagus when he imagines trying to get something he wants, and failing?

Anyway, now that days have passed, Marie's kindness and encouragement seems like a fever dream. Plus, Ben and Jamie stormed out of her dinner party. That wasn't a great look. She probably doesn't even want to help him anymore. Andy's gross friends at his gross party are… well, gross, but they're also a surer bet. Andy will help, because he'll like the idea of Jamie owing him something.

The door opens again, and Jamie says, "I have to help Val."

Andy makes only a token effort to move out of the way, which leaves Jamie to brush against him to get past.

His eyes fall on the new customer. An involuntary smile dawns across his face.

"I know this isn't my normal time," Ben says wryly. The wryness is to mask something else, which Jamie can see so clearly now. It's to mask the fragile sincerity underneath, the sincere desire to see Jamie, and the fear blackening the edges of that desire that Jamie will… who knows? Scowl, or tell him to come back later, or maybe just look bored.

Jamie kisses him. Ben kisses back, a hand going up to cradle the back of Jamie's head.

A throat clears. Jamie grabs Ben's hand and turns to face Andy, who looks incensed. "No hanky-panky on the job," he says, sounding sulky, like he's five years old and Jamie just took away his favorite toy.

Ben squeezes Jamie's hand tighter. "You must be Andy."

Andy gives Ben a once-over, head to toe and back up again. "And you must be Jamie's boy toy." Andy offers Ben his hand, like he's expecting Ben to kiss it or something. Jamie fights not to roll his eyes. Ben looks a little alarmed, understandably confused about what the correct move is when a man offers you his hand like he's Henry VIII wanting you to kiss his rings. When Ben stays still, Andy withdraws his hand. "I don't think Jamie ever mentioned your name. That's funny."

"Ben. And yeah, that's on me. I'm a little weird about broadcasting my private life."

Andy's face brightens, which is never a good sign. "Oh, of course! Insecure about your sexuality? Worried your colleagues will see you differently? What do you do, by the way?"

Ben laughs. But it's so far from the laugh Jamie loves that it's like someone else is standing there producing the sound. It's this sharp-edged, dry, humorless sound. "Nope. Nothing like that. Just funny about random strangers knowing my private business." He glances toward

Jamie, and there's this half-second glimmer of mischief in his eyes, the tiniest upward tug to one side of his mouth. As he looks back to Andy, he says off-handedly, "I'm a surgeon."

"You're a surgeon," Andy repeats.

"Yeah. Need brain surgery?"

Finally, Andy laughs. It's the laugh Jamie doesn't like—the one that sounds like he's thinking of a way to screw you over. And probably screw you, too, because Andy's always thinking about screwing.

Jamie hates him.

"I'm taking my break now," Jamie announces. Everyone in the coffee shop looks at him because it's too loud. Whatever. He's going to own it. Looking directly at Andy, he adds, "You know how to make drinks, right?"

He doesn't bother to wait for an answer. He pulls Ben outside, their fingers threaded so tight that it's like they're trying to fuse into one person.

And that sounds like it could mean something else.

Jamie hasn't had sex with someone he's emotionally invested in for a long time. Not since his last boyfriend, David. The end of that relationship left a trail of wreckage all the way from here to Miami, where he ended up on an epic bender of tequila and Grindr notifications.

Tyler was the one who found him. Flew down to Miami to track him down, which he managed to do by following the clues Jamie left in his Instagram posts. When he wrung the liquor out of Jamie and got him on a plane home, Jamie knew he was going to get a call from Dad, that he was going to get scolded and told to come home. New York was too much for him, grad school was too much for him, he should come back to Hartford. Come work in the shop.

Dad never called. Which meant Tyler never told him. Which meant… something. Years later, Jamie still hasn't figured out what.

The point is, Jamie doesn't get Involved. He doesn't fuck people he likes. So the whole cheesy two-become-one thing he's thinking about with Ben—he's not going to do that. He likes Ben too much.

Ben's palm is warm; his fingers are strong. His shoulder knocks against Jamie's as they walk to the park down the block where they sat last week. It feels like forever ago. It feels like they really have been dating for two months. More than that. It feels like they've known each other for years.

He's falling in love with Ben.

Oh god oh fuck.

He's fallen in love with Ben.

They sit on a bench, and they keep holding hands, and it feels comfortable and right. And Ben looks at him and says, "If you want, I can help you fake a workplace injury to get some workman's comp out of him."

Jamie laughs and doesn't let go of Ben's hand, and he's definitely, absolutely, utterly, beyond a doubt in love.

Step one: remind yourself why being in love is a terrible idea. Step two: stop being in love. Step three: ??? Step four: be totally okay with everything once you're not in love anymore and don't feel brokenhearted every time Ben walks into the Daily Grind because you could have had something great and you stamped it out before anything could happen because you were too terrified of getting hurt, because you *always* get hurt, and why would this time be any different?

Shit.

# CHAPTER TWENTY

ON FRIDAY afternoon, Ben pulls up in front of Jamie's building. Jamie is outside, his JanSport backpack over one shoulder, one leg bouncing as he looks up and down the street. When Ben rolls down the window and says, "Hey, going my way?" Jamie's eyes light up.

Jamie puts his backpack in the back seat and gets in. "Unfortunately, yes." He looks mortified. "I mean. Unfortunately for you. And me. For both of us. Because of where we're going. It's good you're here and we're...."

By this time, Ben is grinning like a complete and utter idiot, his heart so full of light and happiness that he doesn't know how he's going to act like a normal person.

Acting like a normal person is part of his plan. Because he has one now—a plan to take this from fake dating to real dating. He's not going to muddy the waters by making a move before the natural end of their agreement.

As soon as he gets the promotion, and more importantly, as soon as Jamie gets a new job, he's going to make his move.

He can't stop thinking about Jamie. His wicked sense of humor. His smile, quicksilver bright. His blue eyes, mischievous and expressive and a window straight to his soul.

How could Ben have seen him every day and not tried for more?

He wants to bring Jamie flowers. He wants to take him to dinner. He wants to go dancing. He wants to say, *When I kiss you, it's real to me.*

"We're what?" Ben asks, because apparently he can't stick to his convictions for longer than five minutes.

"We're going to have to get each other through this weekend," Jamie says. He makes a face. "Just to warn you, you have to really think about the potential innuendo in anything you say to Andy. Like that? What I just said? Andy would turn that into *get each other off this weekend.*"

Now that image is in his head, not for the first time. Sitting behind the wheel of a car doesn't provide much opportunity for disguising where his blood is currently rushing to, so he forces himself to stop picturing how he might go about getting Jamie off. "Noted. I can see why you made up a fake boyfriend to get out of going to this guy's vacation house."

"One of his vacation houses," Jamie says. "Which he'll remind you of. Repeatedly. And expect you to make heart eyes at him for it."

Grimacing, Ben says, "My heart eyes are pretty rusty." Jamie smirks, and Ben changes the subject. "Hey, I got you something."

"Is it road-trip snacks?"

Ben chuckles. "I guess it can be? But I was kind of intending it for something else." He reaches into the back seat and grabs a plastic bag, then unveils the contents with a flourish.

Jamie's brow crinkles adorably. "Peanuts?"

"I thought you might want to make friends with the Poconos squirrels."

Wordlessly, Jamie takes the peanuts, and Ben's afraid he did something dumb. That he showed this part of himself that listens and watches and is breathlessly taken with softness. Maybe Jamie will think he's a dumbass for thinking about this at all.

Jamie puts the bag down on the cup holders between them, fists his fingers in Ben's T-shirt, and pulls him into a kiss. It's short, sweet like a burst of ripe fruit across his tongue, and over as quickly as it started.

There's a tiny heave to Jamie's shoulders as he rocks back. "We have to be used to doing things like that," Jamie says. "For. Um."

"Andy and his friends," Ben supplies.

"Yeah. Exactly."

"I think we should probably practice a few more times on the way."

A sly smile curls one corner of Jamie's mouth, and he's the one who leans forward again, his fingers sliding down the line of Ben's jaw in a way that doesn't feel fake, or for practice, and definitely not for show. It feels like it's just for them.

Abruptly, Jamie pulls away. Ben starts to wonder what he did wrong, but then he sees the way Jamie shifts and crosses one leg over the other, and—okay, it doesn't necessarily mean anything, because you know, biology and everything. But it still makes his heart pound against his sternum.

He pretends not to notice and starts the car. "Do you think we're primetime ready?" he asks.

"We weren't before? What were all the events with your coworkers? An off-Broadway production?"

Ben laughs and puts the car in drive, pulling into traffic. Jamie turns on the radio, and they flip through stations looking for the perfect song. Like all the time they spend together, the drive flies by, disappearing behind them just like miles under the tires.

The landscape gets wilder the farther they drive, signs of civilization dropping away. The road climbs into the hills, the deer crossing signs get more frequent, and the trees encroach on the road. It's pretty. It doesn't really remind Ben of where he's from, but it reminds him that he's not actually from New York. That there's something outside the city.

He's never told Jamie he's not from New York. It's not something he tells people. The Ben McNatt he wants to be is from New York. Definitely not from some podunk town in Ohio he couldn't wait to escape from. Definitely not the kind of place where you stayed in the closet, because if you didn't, you'd be lucky if the worst that happened was people calling you a faggot. He was from the kind of place where a rumor could go around once—once!—that maybe he was gay, and turn the boys' locker room excruciating for three weeks of tenth grade.

He never told Adriana. He's never told any of his coworkers.

"I grew up in a town that was out in the middle of nowhere like this," he says. Telling Jamie isn't as horrible as he always imagined it would be.

"Really? In Pennsylvania?"

"Ohio. About an hour from Cleveland."

"Let me guess, you didn't like it?"

With a snort, Ben asks, "What gave it away?"

"Stab in the dark. I mean, you bring it up so often."

The speed limit drops to thirty as they near a town. Ben slows as they approach a red light. It gives him a chance to look at Jamie. These days, looking at Jamie carries with it a pretty high probability of his breath being taken away. This is one of those times. Jamie's window is open, and the wind has made his hair a chaotic black tangle that Ben would give anything to smooth down, not because it looks anything less than beautiful, but because he just wants his hands in Jamie's hair.

"The light's green," Jamie drawls. There are blotches of red across his cheeks, so Ben's pretty sure he looked exactly as moony as he was feeling.

His face feels hot as he turns his attention back to the road. "Yeah, the town I'm from is just... the town I'm from. If I never see it again, I wouldn't be broken up."

"Oof," Jamie says. "That bad? At least I like Hartford, even if I don't want to live there."

"I don't know. It's just like... Ohio, you know? I was always going to leave. I always felt like I was born in the wrong place or something."

"I know the feeling," Jamie says. "Not fitting in. Like you were meant to be from somewhere else, or have some other life in a different place, and you just have to find it."

They're already out of the town. It was quaint and cute, exactly what you'd expect to find in the Poconos. "I think there might be something wrong with me, then," Ben says. "I figured New York was that life for me. Because New York is that for everyone, right? If you can't fit in in New York, you can't fit in anywhere. But I... don't."

There's a light touch on his leg. Jamie's fingers, brushing along the top of his thigh. "Maybe you just haven't found your New York yet," he says.

# CHAPTER TWENTY-ONE

THE LOW fuel light comes on, and they stop for gas in the next town. It's a whimsical, north-woodsy, log-cabin-y building with a sign in the shape of a bear, which reads, Black Bear Provisions and Diner. Four gas pumps and a small parking lot filled with cars, most with out-of-state plates. Ben pulls up to one of the pumps and shuts the car off. On impulse, Jamie gets out of the car after him.

"Want anything?" Jamie asks as he walks backward in the direction of the door. "Beef jerky? Maple syrup flavored water, or whatever they drink up here?"

Ben laughs. "I wouldn't say no to a cup of coffee."

"*Ben*," Jamie gasps. "You're going to cheat on the Daily Grind?"

"Does it count as cheating when you're still getting the coffee for me?" Ben asks, with this crooked little cant to his mouth that's way too sexy.

"I'll think about that," Jamie says, like it's a subject that requires deep deliberation.

Black Bear Provisions and Diner smells like grease, Fabuloso, stale cigarette smoke, and burnt coffee. The gas station convenience store takes up one side, with the diner on the other, a faded Please Seat Yourself sign and some worn carpet demarcating the border between the two.

Jamie wanders through the aisles, looking for an interesting snack and ending up disappointed. He grabs a Snickers and an Honest Tea.

On his way to the coffee urns at the front, an end cap catches his eye. It's filled with snow globes and little animal figurines emblazoned with POCONOS or LAKE GILES. There's a frog with a fishing pole, which doesn't make much sense, if you ask him. Do frogs eat fish? If frogs were meant to eat fish, surely nature would have given them the wherewithal to do so? Why isn't it a bear with a fishing pole, considering the name of this place, and also that bears *do* eat fish?

His eyes travel over the souvenirs until they land on a wood dowel displaying bracelets. They're made variously of leather, string, and hemp. Hemp, wow. Hi, 1998. They're actually not terrible, though. Definitely better than a frog with a fishing pole. Even the hemp ones.

One of them, braided and made of leather the color of walnut, has a single bead of sea glass on it. The color reminds him of Ben's eyes.

He unhooks it, gets Ben his coffee, pays for everything, and heads back outside. Moths, drawn to the light as the sun sets, flit in and out of view, their wings fluttering against the harsh glare of the fluorescent tubes overhead. As he hands Ben the coffee, he says, "I'm not sure you can ever come back to the Daily Grind after this."

Ben holds the Styrofoam cup up to his face and inhales with exaggerated pleasure. "Ah, the sweet smell of coffee, which will definitely be just as good as the overpriced stuff I buy in the city."

His smile makes Jamie want to kiss him. "How dare you," Jamie says, looking down his nose at Ben.

With a grin, Ben takes a sip of the coffee—and grimaces. "Yikes."

"All *our* coffee beans are sustainably sourced and roasted in copper-bottom pans in the traditional method," Jamie recites, which makes Ben laugh and choke on his bad coffee.

"I'll just go behind your back next time, baby," Ben says.

Which makes Jamie laugh. And also makes heat rush his bloodstream, like… well, insert sports metaphor here, probably. Jamie isn't the kind of guy who likes being called baby. Apparently, though, when Ben calls him baby, he is totally, 100 percent, the kind of guy who likes being called baby.

"Oh," Jamie says, trying to keep up with the joke and not give away that he's developing a semi, "lying *and* cheating, huh?" Ben gives him a goofy smile, and Jamie swallows hard. "I got you something," Jamie says. He holds out the leather bracelet. The glass bead catches the fluorescent light. His heart is beating way too fast considering it's a joke gift for his fake boyfriend.

Horrifically, Ben just stares. Shit. Abort, abort. "I guess I don't really know if you're a jewelry guy," Jamie says quickly. "But um, it's totally just something stupid. It reminded me of your eyes— You know what, I was totally kidding, I'll throw it away—"

"Don't!" Ben yelps. "Don't. Please. Sorry. I was just." His mouth hangs open soundlessly, and Jamie can see him cycling through different options to finish the sentence. Finally, he closes his mouth and smiles.

It's part wryness, part fragility. As though a man like Ben McNatt has anything to feel fragile about? He's wonderful. Amazing. Jamie would do anything to make sure he never felt like he wasn't good enough, or afraid he wasn't *enough*, just him, without the rest of the stuff he thinks makes him a success.

"You just surprised me," Ben says. He takes the bracelet, setting his coffee on the hood of the car so he can slip on the leather band. "I love it. Thank you."

Jamie hopes the gas station lights are doing their job and washing him out like they usually do, because he knows he's bright red. "I, um. Yeah. You're welcome."

They get back in the car, and Ben turns the key in the ignition. He reaches over and squeezes Jamie's hand. "Hey," he says. "If you need anything at this party—like, you need to leave the room or be alone or need me to make an excuse, or anything. Just hold my hand."

"Shouldn't we be holding hands anyway?"

"Oh." Happiness flashes over Ben's face. "Good point. How about hold the bead on the bracelet."

Jamie feels himself turning red, though he's not totally sure why. "You don't actually have to wear it," he says. "It was just something dumb."

"I want to wear it," Ben says, like it's the most obvious thing in the world.

Jamie squeezes Ben's hand back. "Well—okay. I'm glad you like it. And thanks."

Ben smiles, puts the car in gear, and gets back on the road.

# CHAPTER TWENTY-TWO

ANDY'S VACATION house looks exactly how Ben imagined. The light hasn't quite bled from the sky, but the house is lit up with floodlights. It's one of those sprawling places that aspires to Frank Lloyd Wright design. Or hell, maybe it *was* designed by Frank Lloyd Wright, who knows. Jamie once mentioned Andy was a trust-funder, so maybe his family hired Frank Lloyd Wright to design their vacation house.

"Vacation house" is obviously a misnomer. When Ben thinks "vacation house," what comes to mind is cabin-y, rough around the edges, with a gravel driveway and no garage, but definitely a boat. This place is bigger than the house Ben grew up in back in Ohio, and the shrubbery and garden beds that Ben can see in the twilight look impeccably maintained, a sure sign of a landscaping service. The driveway is paved, and there's a four-car garage at the head of it.

Parked in front of the garage are sports cars. Do they belong to Andy or Andy's friends? Why does Andy need a four-car garage for a vacation house?

The doors of Ben's Audi slam crisply in the gloaming. They get their bags from the back seat. Motion sensor lights click on, making Ben feel like he's in the middle of an operating theater. He meets Jamie's eyes over the top of the car, which has always felt swanky. Next to Lamborghinis, Maseratis, and Ferraris, it seems pedestrian.

The fear that's driven Ben for his entire life flares, a frigid flame of gut-churning terror. He won't fit in with these people. They'll see him for the fraud he is. He's not doing enough—not making enough money, not doing enough high-profile surgeries, not making enough of a name for himself. He's not enough.

"Fuck," Jamie says. "Look at this place."

Jamie doesn't look impressed. He doesn't look intimidated. He looks exasperated.

Shaking his head, Jamie adds, "It looks exactly the way I thought it would, though. How many Tom of Finlands do you think he has on the walls? Or maybe he just goes for straight-up porn...."

"Uh, isn't a lot of Tom of Finland's stuff straight-up porn?" Ben asks.

"Well, yeah. But it's artsy porn." He waves a hand. "Val did this whole project on him. She could tell you about it and be convincing. All I can tell you is that I was totally happy to let her rehearse her presentation for me, because she had a whole section on the Motorcycle Series and how it challenged... something. Or normalized. I don't know, honestly, I was just there for the pictures."

The fear curdling through Ben's stomach recedes in the face of Jamie being Jamie. "The Motorcycle Series?"

The floodlights are bright enough that he can see Jamie's face turn red. "Um, google it."

"I'm totally going to."

"No, good. You should."

"You're going to know I googled it when you least expect it."

"Ben," Jamie says mildly. "If you're even the slightest bit bi, I recommend you don't google it in front of other people."

Okay, now *Ben* is turning red. Did Jamie just—are they talking about Ben's dick? Technically they're talking about how Ben can avoid an inappropriate erection, but.... Jamie just—circuitously!—talked about Ben's penis. Is this mortifying or thrilling? Or a confusing mixture of both?

Figures pass in front of one of the picture windows, and Jamie's expression tightens. "I guess we should go in. Time for me to charm my way to a better job, right?"

Ben wants to grab his hand and run. Wait, that's stupid; they can get back in the car. The point is, he wants to get out of here. He doesn't want to go into this palatial vacation house full of creepy Andy's rich friends, who Jamie thinks he needs to impress. He knows with a certainty that sits deep in his marrow that no one here will be good for Jamie.

The roar of an engine makes both of them start. Headlights cut through the twilight as a car revs its way up the driveway. Yet another sports car squeals to a stop, blocking Ben in. Jamie's eyes are moving from the new arrival to Ben's car, so Ben doesn't have any choice but to do something about it. Anything to give Jamie one less thing to worry about.

A man swings out of the car. Tall, thin, hair that looks white in the floodlights but might be dyed silver or a pale purple. "Oh, *good*, I'm not the last to arrive!" he exclaims, though that's demonstrably not true.

"Do you mind moving your car so I'm not blocked in?" Ben asks.

The new arrival looks horrified. Good, they won't get into a yelling match. He apparently just didn't even realize he'd done it.

"Block you in? My dear fellow who I've never seen before, this is an Andrew Beaumont party. You'll have to be dragged away. Let's go, I'll introduce you."

"Yeah but, your car—"

"I know, it's a beauty, isn't it? Just drove it off the lot this morning!" He loops his arms through Ben's and Jamie's and tugs them up the path to the front door. "The color's called fuchsia sunset—I envisaged it! Fab, right? Porsche"—he pronounces it PORSH-uh—"*loves* me though. They're always *begging* for my help with their custom paint options for the new models. I always tell them, 'Well that *depends*, darlings, on whether or not I get first crack at *driving* the new models.'"

Ben glances at Jamie. Jamie looks like he's struggling to decide if he likes this person or not.

The man opens the door without ringing the doorbell, pulling Jamie and Ben through into a minimalist foyer. "Andrew!" he announces. "I'm here with—wait, what did you say your names were?"

Jamie speaks up first. "I'm Jamie. I work for Andy. And that's my boyfriend, Ben."

"Oh!" The man looks thrilled. "*You're* Jamie!" Raising his voice again, he singsongs, "I have Jamie and his *very real* boyfriend with me, Andrew! At last, we've arrived!"

Footsteps clack on the floor, which is probably solid wood—the most expensive solid wood money can buy—and Andy appears. A half-drunk cocktail sloshes in one hand. It's not his first, judging by the smell of bourbon wafting off him. He's wearing a button-up shirt that radiates dollar signs and is unbuttoned to his stomach. His skinny jeans look expensive.

"Jamie!" Andy enthuses, stepping forward to plant a sloppy kiss on Jamie's cheek. Jamie goes rigid, but he visibly forces the tension out of his body.

"Hi," Jamie says. "Andy, you remember Ben, right?"

Andy turns a smile on him, and his level of inebriation seems to drop precipitously. Giving Ben a chilly smile, he says, "How could I forget? The famous Ben, who managed to tempt our Jamie back into the dating pool!"

"Um, yeah." What the hell is he supposed to say? "Thanks for having us."

"I've been trying to get Jamie to spend some time outside work with me for years. It was like once I hired him, he didn't want to get together anymore!" Andy takes a swig of his drink while Ben shoots a questioning look at Jamie. *Anymore?* But that makes it sound like before Jamie worked at the Daily Grind, he socialized with Andy. And that can't be right.

"Well, let's go in!" says the man who escorted them to the door. "I'm Timothy, by the way, Andrew's beloved cousin."

The look that flickers across Andy's face doesn't say "beloved" so much as "pain in the ass," and that kind of endears Timothy to Ben.

Andy tells them to leave their bags at the door; someone will bring them to their room, which is at the end of the hall. A dull murmur of voices—all male—has been drifting through the house, punctuated now and then by a bray of laughter. "What do you want to drink?" Andy asks. "I'll have one of the boys make something."

"Just some club soda," Jamie says.

Making a face, Andy says, "*Jamie.* You *have* to have a drink!"

Jamie's eyebrows draw together in this kicked puppy look that looks, frankly, impossible to resist. "Maybe in a bit. I just get carsick, you know?" He laughs, a little titter that Ben hasn't ever heard before. "Gross. But I want to let my stomach settle."

With a heavy sigh, Andy says, "Oh, fine. But later. You have to have a drink later." Jamie makes a noncommittal noise that seems to satisfy Andy. "What do you want, Ben? Let me guess—Coors Light? Or are you more of a PBR man?"

Ben forces himself to smile. "I'll take a glass of red wine, if you're serving it."

Coors Light or PBR. Jesus. All the work he's put into not being a redneck from Ohio, and Andy still clocks his origins immediately. And like, yeah, sure, Ben shotgunned his fair share of PBRs in high school, but he doesn't touch the stuff now.

Timothy laughs. "Andrew, listen to yourself. Don't be such a bear." Poking Ben in the back with a finger, he adds, "We had a bet going that you weren't real. I said Jamie probably made you up to try to get out of coming. Andy didn't exactly disagree."

Ben feels his face getting hot. "That's—no. Jamie and I have been together for months."

Andy scowls but looks away so quickly that Ben isn't sure anyone but him saw it.

The house is more sprawling on the inside than it looks on the outside, and very mod. Or possibly seventies porno. The living room, or conversation pit, or whatever it is, is plushly carpeted with a recessed, stepped-down central seating area surrounded by square midcentury modern sofas. They're occupied by six men of varying ages, but they're all older than Jamie.

Andy waves to a table next to the door. "Party favors."

Ben turns. The table has a basket filled with condoms. Tiny bottles of lube are lined up next to it. Like. A lot of lube. Why is there so much lube?

With a gleeful cackle, Timothy scoops up a handful of condoms and drops them into Ben's hands, which he inexplicably holds out. He could have just let the condoms rattle to the floor. Now he's holding two handfuls of condoms. "Safer sex, boys!" Timothy says.

Ben is bright red. Jamie's face is set in a smile that looks like the effort to maintain it is burning more calories than a HIIT routine. "Andy, what kind of party is it, exactly, that you've invited my boyfriend and me to?"

Andy picks up a bottle of lube and a condom and stuffs them in Jamie's pocket. "I'm sex positive, Jamie. You know that."

"I'm in a committed relationship."

"Oh, did I make an assumption I shouldn't have? I figured you two were intimate."

"Oh my god." Jamie's face is getting splotchy with mortification. "Can we just—I'd really like to meet everyone. Introduce us to everyone."

"Since when are you such a prude?" Andy asks. "You weren't the last time we partied."

The smile is back on Jamie's face—the one it looks like he'd maintain even if explosions were going off behind him. "I guess I'm getting old. So, introductions?"

Timothy has been watching this exchange like he doesn't have a horse in the race—but he catches Ben's eye at one point and gives him a look that's impossible to read.

Andy's hand is still in Jamie's pocket, and Ben is frozen. Is he supposed to say something? What kind of boyfriend is he supposed to be? What kind of man does Jamie want to be with for real?

Before his brain can finish feeling out all the possibilities and pitfalls, words are coming out of his mouth. "Hey, Andy, I think Jamie would probably appreciate it if you'd take your hand out of his pocket. He just told you he's in a committed relationship."

The conversation from the porno pit has stopped. Oh god. Did it stop right at the moment Ben started talking? So all those men with pockets filled with condoms and lube, one of whom Jamie is depending on to offer him a job this weekend, just heard him call out the host of the party?

At least Andy takes his hand out of Jamie's pocket, looking the tiniest bit contrite.

"Oh, introduce them, Andrew. None of us are getting any younger," Timothy says.

With a smile that Ben wants to punch off his face, Andy leads them into the recessed seating area. All the men sitting there are white. The oldest is somewhere in his midsixties, and the youngest looks about Ben's age. They're all wearing designer clothing, and they all look like they probably stopped at a salon before coming here. Ben can't imagine his hair ever looking that impeccable. In fact, he can feel how ruffled it is right now, his bangs falling over his face, the cowlick sticking up in the back.

At least he trimmed his beard before they left Manhattan. He didn't think that hard about what he put on this morning, though. Something decent, because he wants to help Jamie impress these people. But the shirt is from—who the fuck knows. Banana Republic? It doesn't fit him the way these guys' shirts fit them, because he bought it off a rack.

A man with blond hair, probably close to fifty, with a pair of expensive-looking glasses perched on his nose, offers, "I'm Philip."

Pointing lazily at Philip, Andy says, "Philip Vitali." He rattles off introductions for everyone else: "Diederick Hamilton, Leslie Arana, Peter Lamasko, Luke Green, and Art Condon."

"Call me Derick," says the youngest man, the one that's close to Ben's age.

The man next to him leans back and puts an arm around him. "He hates being called Diederick. *Die*-derick, *Die*-derick!"

"Shut up, Art."

Art pinches his nipple. "Or?"

"*Or* you're not getting that sweet Hamilton bussy you've been waiting six months for."

"Derick!" one of the men gasps in mock-horror. Peter? Ben's pretty sure it's Peter, whose hair is auburn threaded with silver. He's devastatingly handsome. "Aren't you *seeing someone*?"

He sounds gleeful. Ben's discomfort with these people, with this party, crawls up his throat. This isn't his scene, and he doesn't know what he's supposed to do.

Shrugging, Derick says, "It's the Poconos. It doesn't count."

"It's Andy's place, so it doesn't count." That's Leslie. Next to him, Luke smirks. One of Luke's ankles is crossed over Leslie's. Are they a couple? Or are they just here to hook up because, apparently, it doesn't count if it's at Andy's place?

Somewhere in the house, glasses clink. A fit young man brings two glasses of red wine into the room and hands them to Jamie and Ben. At least, he holds it out to Ben. Ben stares at it for a beat too long. Over on the sofa, there's badly stifled laughter.

All these years later, and he's still the dumb, poor, closeted bi kid from Wakeman, Ohio. He can perform all the surgeries he wants, rise as high as possible in his field, make as much money as he can, but in the end, he's a joke to people like this. These men are supposed to be his community. They're queer, aren't they? But they're looking at him like they're wondering if he'll be doing an encore performance.

His hand shakes as he takes the wine from the young man. The server. He's a server. Andy has literally hired waiters to work this party. Wasn't there some salacious trial where the defendant was like, a Harvey Weinstein type who kidnapped young queer men and made them sex slaves? Is that what this is? Does he need to get a message to this kid? Like, blink twice if you need help?

"I like this crew better than the last one," Luke says. "Tighter asses."

Philip's lips thin and he exchanges a glance with Timothy, who also looks unamused. "You know they can hear you, right?"

Luke pouts. "Aw, did I push the trial lawyer button? Relax. It's not the first time that one's heard he has a tight ass."

Leslie pokes his tongue into the side of his mouth and wiggles it up and down before he says, "Think he'd be up for a threesome?"

With a tepid smack on Leslie's thigh, Luke says, "*Stop* it, Les, that's too naughty. But." He licks his lips. "Maybe."

Andy laughs, like this is hilarious and not creepy as hell. "I didn't pay for the full-service package, so you'll have to get his number if you want something more than alcohol and small plates."

"You must have skimped on the package you bought," Derick says, a sly smile on his face. "I can't even see most of the packages."

Art nods toward Ben and Jamie. "I think we're scaring the fresh meat."

"God, if you call them *fresh meat* again, can you blame them for getting scared off?" That's Philip. Ben isn't sure if he's actually the least terrible among these people, or if they're going to find out that he's all about #MeToo, but eats babies three nights a week.

Getting to his feet and stretching, Art says, "Sorry for our uncouth friends. They forget their house-training when you get a couple glasses of bubbly in them."

"Excuse *you*, I've had more than a *couple.*"

"Look at you!" Art says to Jamie. "You're just a little *baby*!"

"That's my skin routine," Jamie says. Everyone laughs. Ben feels like a cornered cat—he wants to make himself big and intimidating and scratch these people to keep them away from Jamie. But look at Jamie—he doesn't need Ben's help. Which is exactly what Ben has always known.

Instead, he wants the help of one of these men. Which is the one that has an open position? Which is the one that's definitely going to proposition Jamie at some point between five minutes and six months from now?

Ben looks at Jamie. Jamie meets his eyes with a focused gaze that says *trust me*.

So Ben takes another breath, anchors himself in Jamie's warmth at his side, and tries.

# CHAPTER TWENTY-THREE

ART SLIDES a hand over Jamie's hip. "So you're the famous Jamie. I can see why Andy likes you."

Jamie makes himself stay still instead of taking a gigantic step backward. "My reputation precedes me, I guess."

"He may have mentioned you once or twice," Art replies.

"Or a hundred times," Leslie adds, rolling his eyes.

"He's my best employee," Andy says, utterly unembarrassed. "And we get along really well. Don't we, Jamie?"

"Mm-hm, definitely." Jamie's super impressed with himself for not gagging on these words. They get along really well because Jamie wants a job. Now he isn't sure if Andy realizes that. Is it possible that Andy thinks Jamie genuinely likes him? Does he think Jamie genuinely might sleep with him? Does Andy think he's going to be using his party favors (god, ew) with Jamie? Tonight?

Well, in for a penny, right? That's the expression? Whatever. "Super well," he adds. "I mean, obviously!" He smiles brightly. "That's why we're here!" He loops his arm through Ben's. Poor Ben. "Right, baby?" Jamie asks.

"Right," Ben says, flashing the room a smile. Jamie squeezes his bicep in encouragement.

He leans in and brushes his lips over Ben's cheek, breathing, "Doing great."

"Awww, look at that," Art says. "Young love."

Peter cackles from the sectional. "I thought you and Derick were getting it on tonight?"

"Maybe Jamie and Ben want to join," Art says, batting his eyelashes.

Derick eyes both of them and says, "Mmm, I don't know. I don't put out for everybody."

"Jamie is Andy's favorite, darling!" Art's hand is now on Jamie's chest, and Jamie badly wants to remove it. "Anyone can make coffee, right? So you must be his favorite for some other"—a glance down—"reason."

There's energy thrumming off Ben that Jamie doesn't know what to do with. He's not going to throw a punch, is he?

To Jamie's surprise, Ben downs his entire glass of wine in one swallow, hands it off to a hovering server, and puts his arm around Jamie. "Sorry, guys, he's all mine. I do a really good jealous boyfriend. It's probably my best bit."

There's laughter and Jamie feels a tiny bit of tension seep out of his shoulders.

Luke and Leslie break apart on the sofa. Luke gestures expansively and says, "Ben, come here, I like you."

Ben doesn't let go of Jamie, which makes him realize Ben didn't put his arm around him in possessiveness or protectiveness. No, this is a grip of pure, unadulterated panic.

"Let's go sit down," Jamie murmurs, giving Ben a nudge with his hip.

And the night progresses. There's more wine, and then there's harder stuff—tequila, absinthe, liqueurs that are too sweet. The serving staff packs up and leaves. Derick and Art disappear to "get something from the kitchen," and look significantly mussed when they return. Ben keeps looking at Jamie, his expression edging toward panic each time. Every time, Jamie squeezes his hand and the panic recedes.

Eventually, Ben says, "Hey, can anyone direct me to the bathroom?"

"I'll show you," Leslie says. "I could use it too."

Ben squeezes Jamie's hand. Their gazes linger like Ben's going off to war or something.

Once Ben's gone, Jamie gets out his phone. There's a text from Val asking if he needs a rescue, because she can put a team together. He texts back that they're both still fine. No sex party yet.

She starts typing back, then stops, then starts again. There's a pause. Then: **I still can't believe you kept Ben a secret**

**You could have been sending me gross couples selfies**

**You must rly like this guy to not talk about it for 2 months cuz he didn't want you to**

Jamie responds by sending a selfie of Ben and him from their date day in Manhattan. It's one of the more adorable ones—they're kissing in Central Park, the sun bright behind them, shining through the leaves and dappling the light.

*Second date*, he types.

Andy plops down beside him and wraps an arm around Jamie's shoulders. "Having fun?" His breath is boozy enough to cause a contact high. "I hope you're having fun. I really, really want you to be having fun, Jamie. You're not having anything to drink! You should drink. Drinking makes things fun!"

His head drops to Jamie's shoulder, and he nuzzles his face into the crook of Jamie's neck. Jamie sucks in a breath and holds it. Shoving Andy off isn't the way to go.

He doesn't think he's going to get much help from this crowd. Derick is in Art's lap, and Jamie can't see all four of their hands. Luke is looking at something on his phone and snickering. Timothy cranes his neck to see what it is and shrugs. Philip is in the room's lone armchair, nursing a tequila. Peter is staring at him with naked longing. *Has* been staring at him with naked longing, actually, for a while. It's hard to tell if Philip is purposefully ignoring him or just in his own world.

Out of everyone, Philip seems the least horrible. Like, if Jamie walked out of here with a job offer from him, that would be okay. He's mostly been quiet, to the point that Jamie doesn't know why he's here, or if he's actually friends with Andy.

"I'm having fun," Jamie says, shifting away from Andy. He never wants Andy's mouth that close to his neck again.

Andy, shockingly, does not get the hint. He drapes both of his arms around Jamie and rubs his face on Jamie's shoulder, then shoves his face right into Jamie's neck again.

And ew ew *ew* god no fuck *Andy just kissed his neck* ahhhhhh NO he needs to have this skin removed from his body—what's that thing where all your cells are completely replaced every seven years? He can't take the chance that it's going to be *seven years* before he has new skin on his neck where Andy just put his lips.

"I always thought you'd smell like coffee, but you smell so much better," Andy says, his moist breath puffing against Jamie's skin.

"Andy," Jamie says, taking him firmly by the shoulders and straightening him up. Andy looks shocked to be righted. "I have a boyfriend."

"Maybe you should not have a boyfriend," Andy says, twirling a finger in Jamie's hair.

"But I do," Jamie says. "And I love him, and I'm really sorry, but no."

He makes sure Andy isn't going to grope him again, turns his head—

And meets Ben's eyes.

Ben, who is standing stock-still at the precipice of the living room, his eyes wide.

Jamie's first reaction is all adrenaline, all *oh god he saw another man crawling all over me and is going to think I wanted it*. His brain catches up to reality, but not before his stomach twists into sick, anxious knots and his heart starts cantering.

"Oh come on, I didn't mean anything. Nothing happened. Right, Jamie?" Andy nudges Jamie in the side and puts a hand on his leg, too high.

There's a set to Ben's shoulders. "Andy, Jamie mentioned that one of your guests was looking for someone smart and reliable to work for them. I'm sure they want to talk to Jamie, since you told them he's interested in a new position. Right?"

Andy looks flabbergasted. Jamie's torn between irritation that Ben stepped in and gratitude that he did. Because everyone's just getting drunker and no one's talking about a job.

"Oh," Andy says. "Yeah, I guess…."

Please say it's Philip.

"Peter, you're looking for someone, aren't you?"

Peter's eyes reluctantly leave Philip. "Hm? Oh yeah, Al's team has a consultant role open." His gaze grows more critical. "You're looking for a job?"

"Well—I—um." Jamie's neck gets hot, and suddenly his collar feels tight. "I—yes?"

What. The fuck. Is wrong with him.

"Any experience in finance?"

"Uh—"

Andy's head falls dramatically against the back of the sofa. "Come on, I'm telling you he's good."

"You didn't," Peter points out. Some of the criticalness fades out of his expression, though. "I can't talk shop after this many drinks. But yeah. Jamie, I'm looking for someone. If you're smart, it could work out. You wanna chat tomorrow?"

He *must* play this cool. He *cannot* look like an overeager, desperate loser, which of course is exactly what he is.

With an easy shrug, Jamie says, "Yeah, definitely. I'd love to chat tomorrow." He needs to make a joke about being smart, he has to acknowledge and confirm that he's intelligent, but he's also quick and clever. "I might be overqualified on the smart side, though. I mean, I was smart enough to wait for my boyfriend to leave the room before I let Andy get handsy, right?"

Peter laughs. Like. Peter laughs really hard. Derick turns around on Art's lap and lets out a surprised laugh too, and Art is snickering. Luke, who's just returning with another drink, asks, "What's funny? What did I miss?"

"Jamie dragging Andy," Philip says, glancing up from his phone. The expression on his face isn't quite readable. He looks amused, but also annoyed. Good thing he's not the one with the job opening.

"Noooo!" Luke cries.

Taking the shot at Andy doesn't feel as good as Jamie thought it would. He's been fantasizing about saying something like that for years, and now he finally did, and he just feels hollowed out. Peter, Art, and Derick are all still laughing, and once Luke and Leslie are filled in, they laugh too. What kind of friends laugh that hard at you? It's good for Jamie, because they're not insulted on his behalf, but like. Really? He totally just shit on their friend.

God. He feels bad. He feels bad for *Andy*.

Jamie clears his throat and stands up. "I think I'm going to go to the bathroom too."

"You up for a game of pool after?" Peter asks.

He's barely played pool since college. Tyler and his friends used to hang out at a tavern near home, and Jamie tagged along and got damn good at pool. For a while at NYU, he had a lucrative career hustling people. Then he actually made some friends and had things to do besides bilk tourists and drunks out of their money.

"Yeah," Jamie says. The old urge to play the ingenue surfaces. He bites his lip and furrows his brow. "I think I remember how to play? It's been a long time." He giggles. "I used to play sometimes in college."

Luke shoots him a wolfish grin. "Nothing to it. Like riding... a bike."

Everyone snickers. Jamie does too. He gets it. He's in on the innuendo.

Peter eyes Jamie appreciatively, but something makes him look to the side, and his expression falters. It's Philip, glaring over his phone at Peter like he wants to kick him in the junk.

Sooooo there's some history there, maybe? Is that something Jamie's going to have to care about when he's working for Peter?

Something defiant settles in the lines of Peter's mouth, and he looks back to Jamie. "If you can't remember how to play, I can help you.

Definitely don't want it to be Andy, right?" He cracks up at his own joke, and then everyone's laughing again. Well, except Andy. Philip doesn't look amused either.

Jamie takes a breath and smiles, then slips away to the bathroom. Once he's there, he spends a minute staring into the mirror. The image of that closed tab with its job application at Columbia swims through his head. The only reason he'd ever be up for that job in a million years is because he knows someone, just like the consultant job for Peter.

The consultant job is falling in his lap, though. If he hates it and he's bad at it, it's not like it's his dream. Who cares about rejection if it's something you don't care about, anyway?

# CHAPTER TWENTY-FOUR

PETER KEEPS trying to "teach Jamie how to stand," which mainly involves him pressing up against Jamie. He puts his hands on Jamie's hips a couple times. Each time it happens, Jamie meets Ben's gaze. He doesn't actually roll his eyes, but there's this thing he does, widening them just a little, his eyebrows twitching up, his stare going dead-eyed, like *kill me now; this is so obnoxious.*

While Jamie's looking at Ben, Peter keeps shooting glances at Philip. Every time he slips his arms around Jamie, there's a look toward him. Whatever's going on between those two, Philip's not biting.

When Jamie smokes Peter, sinking the eight-ball on some kind of trick shot that looks like it should be in the World Pool Championship (and probably is), the room erupts into laughter. Jamie chalks the end of his cue and blows the dust off like smoke from a six-shooter. "Thanks for teaching me the right stance," Jamie says, deadpan.

Peter looks sulky until Philip says, "I was rooting for you, Pete. I think Jamie just had beginner's luck."

"Definitely," Jamie agrees. "Anyone else want to play?"

There's some more laughter at Jamie's vamping, and then Leslie says, "I'll play. Maybe if you spent less time feeling up the competition, you actually would've had a shot, Peter?"

Andy laughs the loudest at that. It's amazing he's still upright. He's had more to drink than anyone, and none of these guys are going easy on the booze. Luke can't walk in a straight line, Art and Derick are doing more giggling than talking (and also more making out than breathing). Peter, Philip, and Timothy are the only ones who aren't sloshed, though Peter's well on his way.

Well, and Jamie and Ben. Since that first glass of wine, neither of them has had a drop.

Leslie and Jamie face off across the table. Leslie breaks and claims solids. Maybe Leslie's just a better player, or maybe it's because he's concentrating on the game instead of Jamie, but it's clearly more of a challenge. Watching Jamie play pool is an unexpected delight. He's good. The way he moves is hypnotic—his stalk around the table, sizing up the position of all the balls (a joke that has been made several times in the past hour), working out the angles in his head. The way he lines up his shot, careful and precise, and then snaps the cue out, it's oddly sexy.

Ben's face heats and he has to turn away.

Timothy is standing right behind him.

He makes Ben jump, but no one notices. They've all gravitated to the game, caught up in the drama.

"Your boyfriend's good," Timothy says.

"Oh—yeah. He is, isn't he?"

Timothy cocks his head and gives Ben a measuring look. From his back pocket, he pulls a pack of cigarettes, tapping the bottom on his palm. "I need one of these. Care to join me, my good man?"

"Er—" Ben looks at Jamie. Honestly? No. He doesn't smoke, and he wants to watch Jamie play. But he's conscious that he didn't make the best impression when they arrived. He embarrassed Andy for sure, and he probably didn't make Jamie's life any easier with that. Timothy is Andy's cousin, so… ugh, maybe he should step outside and be social. He doesn't want to be the reason Jamie doesn't get the job. Even though Ben really can't understand why Jamie would want to work with Peter.

"I guess I'll come out," Ben says.

"Huzzah," Timothy chirps, and Ben can't tell if he's being sincere or deeply ironic.

They step through the sliding door onto a wooden wraparound deck. There's no moon tonight, so the stars are bright even with the floodlights of the house. Insects, frogs, and toads sing in the still night air. The trees around the house stand like dark sentinels.

Timothy lights up and offers a cigarette to Ben. "I don't smoke," Ben demurs.

"Aw, come on. Bet you did once." Timothy rattles the pack. "Live a little. Peer pressure, baby! You gotta give in. All the cool kids are doing it. Don't be a square."

Something about Timothy makes it impossible to dislike him. He's ridiculous but seems like he's having fun with it.

"I don't think kids say 'square' anymore."

Timothy flips a limp wrist. "Oh, well, I never knew what the kids said, anyway. The point is, have a cigarette. One won't kill you."

With a wry smile, Ben takes one and accepts the light Timothy offers. The first drag makes him cough. Violently and mortifyingly. It's been a long time since he's smoked.

Timothy claps him on the back. "Breathe, kid."

"You're the one who peer pressured me into this," Ben says, getting his choking under control. "Jesus. I haven't had a cigarette since high school."

Timothy laughs before the two of them lapse into silence. The sharp, sweet smell of cigarette smoke cuts the earthiness of the mountain air. Ben leans against the railing, watching the pool game through the glass door. The long curve of Jamie's body as he leans over the table to line up his shot, the arc of his shoulder down to the bend of his waist, is the most graceful thing Ben has ever seen.

A long tail of smoke blows from Timothy's mouth. "So, you two are adorable."

Ben lifts the cigarette to his lips again, a flare of cherry red as he draws the smoke into his lungs. At least this time he doesn't cough. He exhales. "Thanks, I guess."

"Seems like the real deal. A perfect little gay fairy tale. I don't know which one of you is Prince Charming, though." Timothy thinks about that. "Is it you? The surgeon with the Manhattan apartment, swooping in and rescuing the down-and-out barista from his drab life of drudgery?"

"He works for your cousin," Ben points out. "And I'm bi."

"Darling, I use gay in the *loosest* possible sense, but for your inclusive sensibilities, I retract 'gay fairy tale' and replace it with 'queer fairy tale.'" The playful, ironic look on his face drops away. "I know he works for my cousin. I feel for him. I hope you rescue him from that."

Ben's glad for the cigarette because it gives him something to do while he processes that. "I don't think Jamie needs anyone to save him," he says. "I *know* he doesn't. He's really smart. He just...."

He needs to believe in himself. He needs to trust his own abilities. He needs to understand he's just as deserving of good things as anyone else.

"Once he realizes how amazing he is, he's going to be unstoppable," Ben says.

Timothy regards him, tapping ash from the end of his cigarette. "See? Totally adorable. You've got it bad, don't you?"

Inside, Jamie sinks a ball. He glances up, looks around the room, and catches Ben's eye through the glass. Ben waves, and Jamie gives him a little wave back. "I kinda do, yeah," Ben says, because Timothy is this odd, transient presence in his life, and it feels like he can say stuff like this to him.

Timothy takes another long drag. "You're not really dating, are you?"

The cigarette falls from Ben's fingers and lands on the deck. "Shit!" He stomps it out, grinding it under the toe of his shoe.

After that, he's not sure what he's supposed to do. He stares at his shoe, hoping Timothy will say it was a joke.

He doesn't. "Oh, I won't say anything. I just recognize the look on your face."

"You do?" Ben says weakly.

Smoke trickles from Timothy's nose as he laughs. "My dear, you look at Jamie the way Peter looks at Philip. You've never wanted something so badly in your entire life, and you have *no* idea how to get it."

"Uh." Okay, that's not going to do it. "I, uh. Yeah. I mean, no? I mean… it's a long story. But I guess, no. We're not exactly… official."

Timothy waves a hand. "Jamie didn't want to come here. Andy told him there was a job to tempt him. So Jamie got a convenient boyfriend. I'm not *surprised.* If I were him, I wouldn't want to be alone with Andy, either. Anyway, when you're a gay man of a certain age, you've seen a beard before." He frowns. "Not quite the same, is it?"

Ben watches Jamie. He's not going to fill in the blanks for Timothy and tell him the whole story. He doesn't want to talk about this at all, and how he's the idiot who real fell in love with his fake boyfriend. So he changes the subject. "What's the deal with Peter and Philip, anyway? Philip doesn't seem like he wants to be here."

"He doesn't," Timothy says cheerfully. "His family's firm has been representing our family for decades. Andy invites Philip because Philip hates it, but he knows he has to come or my family might no longer retain his family's services." Timothy blows smoke from his mouth again and goes on, "Peter and Philip have *history.* You would think it was just convenient sex, but no. Peter pines *beautifully,* doesn't he? Those soulful eyes, that jaw, those cheekbones. He's like a gay Rock Hudson."

"I thought Rock Hudson *was* gay."

"Oh, right. Well, you know what I mean."

Ben isn't sure he does. "Do any of you actually like each other?"

"Of course!" Timothy's cigarette has burned down, so he stubs it out on the railing and leaves it there. "But we all like each other a lot more once the G comes out. Shall we?"

"Um—" But Timothy loops his arm through Ben's and propels him inside.

As they walk through the door, Jamie takes his final shot. The cue ball makes one, two, three bounces off the sides of the table, hits the eight-ball with a clack—and the eight-ball spins into a pocket. Jamie smirks as Leslie throws up a hand in defeat.

"Remind me not to play pool with you," Ben says, crossing the room to Jamie. "I'd embarrass myself."

Jamie hooks an arm around Ben's waist and pulls him close. "Oh, I'd let you win," Jamie says, and kisses Ben lightly.

Ben can't do this much longer if it's not real. He can't keep holding Jamie, feeling Jamie's arms around him, kissing Jamie, if it's all an act to him. It means so much to Ben, and he can't bear it if Jamie's only playing a part.

He just wanted a job, not to fall in love. A job he's wanted for years, which he deserves, and which he's hardly thought about the last two weeks.

Ben clutches a fistful of Jamie's shirt in one hand, a wave of dizziness tilting his world on its axis. His job—nothing matters more than that.

When he gets the job, it'll be long days and long nights, and he'll have even less time for himself than he does now. Which is what he wants. Because his career is the most important thing. It's always been the important thing. Or is that the Ben-he-thought-he-needed-to-be talking? The Ben he now can't imagine re-inhabiting?

The person that he's been these last few weeks feels like an explosion of color against the tepid grayscale of the rest of his life. It's Dorothy's arrival in Oz, bright and technicolor. It's Mary Poppins, Burt, and the Banks children in the sidewalk chalk art.

How can he go back?

How can he *not* go back?

How can he let his dream go, even if from here it seems like less of a dream and more of a habit? Like he's on a game board and there's only one path. College, job, marriage, house, promotion, death.

"Are you okay?" Jamie asks quietly, so only Ben can hear.

He's clinging to Jamie like he's about to start sobbing. On impulse, Ben kisses his temple. "I'm fine," he says. This isn't the time for existential crises or epiphanies. They're still at this party, and Jamie still doesn't have a job offer, and didn't Timothy say something about drugs?

It's like the thought summoned him. Timothy reappears with a rose gold makeup bag. The fact that it says THIS BAG CONTAINS MY FACE in glittery letters becomes one of the weirder things about the night. "Come and get it, ladies!" Timothy crows, holding the bag high above his head.

"Finally," Luke says. He's the first to Timothy's side, accepting a little glass bottle.

"Share," Timothy says sternly. "Remember last time?"

"No," Luke laughs.

Andy comes up behind him and grabs a bottle for himself. As someone who's done his ED rotation, Ben can't help wincing. Andy's had too much to drink, and now he's going to take GHB on top of it. Great. Perfect. Is he obligated to do something? Is this covered under his Hippocratic Oath?

"*I* remember last time," Andy says sloppily, grabbing Luke's ass.

"We have it on video," Leslie says. "He doesn't remember, but he knows what happened."

When Timothy offers a bottle to them, Jamie shakes his head. "No thanks."

Ben asks, "Hey, you guys know that mixing alcohol and GHB is like, kind of dangerous, right?"

Everyone laughs. Art and Derick are already drinking from their bottles. Timothy pats Ben on the shoulder. "'You guys know mixing alcohol and G is dangerous,'" he says fondly, like Ben is a toddler who just said something adorable.

Things get more awkward from there.

Andy and Timothy dance, then Andy and Leslie dance. Then Andy tries to get Jamie to dance, swaying and grabbing at his arm and repeating, "But you're such a good *dancer*, Jamie, you're so *good* at it, I remember how good you are at it—"

Jamie snatches his hand back. Meanwhile, Peter and Philip are having a whispered conversation on one side of the room, which ends with Philip saying heatedly, "Then *get over it*," and storming off.

"PHILIP STORMED OFF! DRINK!" Derick yells.

After another few minutes, Derick and Art stumble off together, Art's shirt half undone already. Before long, Luke and Leslie are making out, and then Peter gets involved as Andy watches.

"Let's go to bed," Jamie says.

# CHAPTER TWENTY-FIVE

THEY FLEE to their bedroom. Jamie shuts the door and sags against it, letting his head thud back. "I need to bleach my brain."

Ben rubs his eyes. "Porn always makes threesomes look so hot. I feel lied to."

"Porn is fake, Ben! Aren't you old enough to know that? Also"—he arches an eyebrow—"tell me more about this porn you watch?"

Laughing, Ben says, "I don't. I mean, I've seen it, but it's not a habit."

"Who's your favorite on OnlyFans?"

"I'm not having this conversation!" But Ben's still laughing, and it makes Jamie light up inside.

The one bed looms. Jamie has no idea how to broach the subject of not sharing. Or maybe…?

Ben swings his bag onto the bed and unzips it. Jamie can't help peeking inside. It doesn't fit the theme of Ben's other possessions. It's old and well-used, brightly colored and two-tone. Pajamas are laid on top, then a couple pairs of boxer briefs. Shirts and jeans seem to have been placed side by side. Ben packs in reverse order of how he gets dressed. It's so him, and so cute.

Ben glares down at his suitcase, then looks at Jamie. "Do you want to take a walk?"

"Outside? In the dark?"

"Sure." Ben shrugs. "We have flashlights. Wait, are you tired? You can go to bed. I just… it would be nice to take a walk. Tonight was kind of a lot."

"I'm not tired," Jamie says. Watching Ben remove his button-down so he's just in a T-shirt and jeans makes him feel like he never needs to sleep again.

Ben seems oblivious to the way Jamie is staring. "Maybe by the time we get back," he says, folding his button-down and tossing it into his open duffel, "everyone will be asleep."

"Or deeply involved in an all-out orgy."

With a cringe, Ben groans, "You had to use the word 'deeply.'"

"I did, actually," Jamie says seriously. "I think they'll be *hammering* out the details."

"Oh my god, stop." Ben laughs, putting his hand over his eyes. "Are you coming or not?"

Arching an eyebrow, Jamie says, "Definitely a question being asked elsewhere in this house right now."

The laugh Ben lets out makes Jamie's stomach fizz. Yeah. He doesn't know how he's going to return to a place where he doesn't get to hear that every day.

Ben holds out a debonair hand, and Jamie takes it without hesitating.

They slip out of the house, tiptoeing like they're kids sneaking out. A floorboard creaks once, and they both freeze, waiting for—what? The SWAT team to descend? If it did, its members would all be wearing jock straps and bulldog harnesses. He'd say so out loud, but then Ben will make a joke about *members* and they'll both laugh and blow their cover.

Noises are coming from the part of the house they recently fled from—and Jamie is *not* going to think about what could be producing them, or who.

Once they're outside, Jamie lets Ben lead. They keep holding hands as they walk down a dark, quiet path. It leads into the woods, and when they round a bend, trees block out the light from the house.

The flashlight on Ben's phone blips on. "You were smoking with Timothy," Jamie says. "I didn't know you smoked. Or liked Timothy."

"I don't smoke. It just seemed like I should." He laughs, sounding embarrassed. "I guess I was thinking I didn't want to rock the boat any more than I already did. So you have the best chance of getting that job."

Something passes over Ben's face as he says that. "Do you want me to get it?" Jamie asks. He doesn't know why. It's not like Ben's opinion should matter. It's Jamie's job. It's Jamie's life.

"It doesn't matter what I want," Ben says. His tone says what his words don't. No, Ben doesn't want him to get the job. No, Ben doesn't want him to work for a creep who seems just as bad as Andy. No, Ben doesn't want him in the same situation he's in now, just more white-collar and on a higher floor.

"You think it's a bad idea, though," Jamie presses. Why? This is the whole point of the two of them carrying on this fake relationship. This was Jamie's price.

Because everything's different now, that's why.

The light on the path ahead jiggles as they walk. Ben doesn't say anything. They're headed downhill. The ground is uneven. There are low-hanging branches and an increasingly steep incline.

"I'm not going to tell you what to do."

"It's not telling me what to do if you say you think it's a bad idea."

Ben glances toward him again. "I just think you can do better than working for that guy. He seemed... like not the greatest."

With a snort, Jamie says, "Well, no. None of these people are the greatest."

What would Ben say if he knew Marie had offered to put in a good word for him with Nina Noskova? What would he do? Would he tell Jamie to quit stalling, quit chickening out, and apply for that damn job right now? Like *now* now, on his phone? It would infuriate Jamie. It would maybe give Jamie the kick in the ass he needs. It would fill Jamie with something he can't name, that someone might care about him enough to make him see something through, even if it's scary, even if there's rejection at the end of it.

That's probably why Jamie hasn't told Ben about the job with Nina Noskova.

They reach a set of stairs. They aren't as immaculate and well-kept as the house—they're like this path, uneven, roots growing under it and bowing the ground upward. The steps are cut into the dirt of the hillside and held into shape by beams of wood nailed into squares. The beams have seen better days. In the light of Ben's flashlight, it's clear how much they're rotting away. They must predate Andy's house.

As they descend, the air gets cooler and damper. It smells better. Fresher. Cleaner. Like there was a filthy film covering Jamie's skin in Andy's house, and the farther he gets from it, the more the dirt sloughs away.

The steps end and the path slopes downward a little more before leveling out. A few more yards and the forest opens to reveal the lake, placid and black in the still night. Small waves lap against the dock. Lights dot the lakeshore, winking through the dark, the other houses high on the hill just like Andy's.

Something in Jamie's chest evens out and settles. The still, starlight-mirrored surface of the lake makes Jamie's problems seem smaller.

Ben switches his flashlight off and puts his phone back in his pocket. "Sorry," he says. "It's none of my business."

"It's kind of your business, I guess." Jamie glances at him. "As my fake boyfriend."

A funny look crosses Ben's face. "Right, well. As your fake boyfriend, I think you have to make the decision that's best for you."

"Best for me." Jamie lets his gaze drift out over the lake, the way the dock sits ghostly pale on top of the water. He wants to say, *You know me now. Do you really think I have any idea of what's best for me?* He even opens his mouth—but the words don't want to come out. His gaze finds the dock again, and instead of saying anything useful or true or god forbid, honest, he asks, "Want to go out there?"

Ben watches him like he thinks Jamie has something more to say. Which is technically true, and maybe kind of scary that it's that obvious to Ben. His hand moves like he wants to take Jamie's, but then it stops midreach. A rueful smile quirks one corner of his mouth up. It's a very *What are we doing?* smile, but Jamie doesn't have an answer for that.

"Sure," Ben says.

The wooden slats creak and rattle as they walk to the end of the dock, where an aluminum ladder leads into the water. Jamie breathes deeply, holding the air in his lungs before letting it out.

Ben starts singing. "I'm sittin' on the dock of the bay, watchin' the tide roll away—"

"Ooooh," Jamie breaks in—pitchily—"I'm just sittin' on the dock of the bay, wastin' time." He grimaces. "Oof. I'm going to leave the singing to you."

"You have a nice voice!" Ben says. Jamie raises his eyebrows, but Ben doesn't flinch from the bald-faced lie. "Sing something else for me."

"No."

"C'mon!"

"No."

"We're alone," Ben wheedles. "And the acoustics are great with the water."

"That does not," Jamie says, "make me *want* to sing."

The grin on Ben's face is infectious. "Okay, the acoustics suck. Horrible acoustics. I probably won't even be able to hear you."

Jamie bumps Ben's shoulder with his. "You're kind of the worst."
"A little bit."

They both fall silent. Jamie looks over the lake before quietly singing a few lines from "Time After Time." Just singing about being lost and found, falling and being caught, as one does.

Mortification catches up with him and he squeaks on the last word. Heat rushes into his face, but at least the darkness hides that. He wants to question why he'd choose a love song to sing at Ben's request, but there's really not much to wonder about.

"You have a nice voice," Ben repeats, softer this time.

"Fake dating doesn't obligate you to compliment my singing," Jamie says. "I'm good enough for karaoke boxes. Barely."

"And picturesque lakes in the Poconos." There's a crooked smile on Ben's face. "Under the stars."

Why does Jamie feel like a teenager again? Why does this all feel so *new*? He's known he was gay since he was thirteen; he's been out since he was fourteen. The first time he kissed a boy was in eighth grade. He's had boyfriends. He's almost twenty-eight years old, and he's been around the block. This isn't new.

Except somehow, it is.

"Is it weird that I'm actually kind of glad we're here?" Jamie asks. "I mean, I know I totally ended up bringing you to a sex party, but some of it has been good." With physical effort, he musters every ounce of his courage. "Like. The parts that we've gotten to spend together. Those have been nice. This is nice."

The backs of their hands brush. "Yeah," Ben says. And then, "Yeah," again.

Warmth blooms in Jamie's stomach and chest. "Yeah?"

They sound like idiots. Like early man discovering the power of speech. What's next, multiple syllables?

The way Ben's eyes meet his makes Jamie's heart stutter. "Yeah. Though I guess if I'm being honest, I. Um. I'm kind of getting tired of us pretending we're dating."

The warmth flees. Totally, completely, and instantly. Ice fists in Jamie's intestines. How could he have—god, he's so stupid, so so stupid, he actually thought—

"Oh," he says. His voice seems to come from really far away. "Right. Obviously."

There's a pause as Ben's brow furrows, like he's picking back over what he said. Alarm flashes over his face. "Shit, that's not—oh my god. Jamie. It's just the act part. The pretending. Having to play a part. Not you. I'm not—I'm not tired of you. I couldn't be."

"Just tired of pretending to date me."

Ben rubs the back of his neck. "That came out wrong."

Jamie looks at him.

"Let me try again?"

Ben's body turns toward Jamie's, and with the way he's looking at him, Jamie can't say no. Even when he's contrite, Ben McNatt has this wry, crooked quirk to his lips, framed so neatly by his goatee, and Jamie's close enough that he can see the way lines are starting to fan around Ben's eyes, the way there's a furrow where his cheek dimples for his lopsided smile.

When Jamie nods, Ben says, "I'd rather spend my time being real with you than putting on a show for people who don't deserve our time."

"Better," Jamie says, and he shoots a smile at Ben to prove he's not upset. The smile he gets back creates an aching pressure in his chest.

There's a splash in the lake. It doesn't sound close; the noise just carries across the water. An owl calls and another answers. It reminds him of Hartford, and even though Jamie doesn't usually miss Hartford, it's nice. He feels calmer with the lake and the dark trees and the black dome of the star-spangled sky.

Ben kicks off his shoes and socks and lowers himself to sit on the edge of the dock. He rolls the bottoms of his jeans up and gingerly dips a toe into the water. Then, with a grin, he lets both feet dangle. "The water's really warm," he says, sounding like a little kid.

It's impossible to resist. When Jamie sits down, their thighs are pressed together.

His heart leaps and cracks itself back against his rib cage, and blood rushes to the surface of his skin. The heat of Ben's body through his pants soaks straight through to Jamie.

They sit there, legs pressed together, and it's perfect.

And then: "You want a really cursed image in your head?" Ben asks.

Jamie snorts. "No. But yes, obviously."

"Andy having a pool party."

Jamie laughs too loudly, and it echoes across the water. He claps a hand over his mouth, but Ben's grinning lopsidedly at him, cheek dimpling on one side, eyes twinkling, hair falling over his forehead. "I'm never forgiving you for that," Jamie says.

"Do they make sex furniture floats?" Ben muses.

"Dildo pool noodles."

Ben guffaws. "BDSM water wings."

Jamie lets his shoulder bump against Ben's. "It's cursed, but I think we might have something here."

"We could do a whole MLM thing," Ben says.

"Multilevel marketing targeted specifically to men who love men."

Ben kicks a foot and water splashes. When he shoots a wicked look at Jamie, Jamie says, "Don't you dare."

Laughing, Ben holds his hands up and says, "Okay, fine. I won't." His feet can't seem to stop moving now, though, and he leans over to dip a hand in the water. Jamie watches the way his fingers trail through it, leaving dark, soft ripples behind them. Then he straightens up and asks, "Want to go swimming?"

That's a joke. Right? Jamie laughs, but Ben doesn't. "Seriously?" Jamie asks.

"Sure. Water's warm. We have the lake to ourselves." Apparently that decides him, because he stands up and pulls his shirt over his head.

And Jamie is *not* ready for that. He's not ready for Ben's broad shoulders and muscled pecs. He's not ready for the darker blush of Ben's nipples or the hair across his chest. He's not ready for Ben's abs. He's definitely not ready for the line of hair leading under Ben's waistband from his belly button, or his V-cut.

Okay. Okay, this is fine. He can handle this. Just because Ben's stripping in front of him—and oh god his jeans are coming off now too— it doesn't mean Jamie has to react. He's in control of himself. He's not going to get a boner.

He sees the bulge of Ben's dick at the front of his boxer briefs, and his throat goes dry as he gets hard. Really hard. Too hard to pretend it's not happening.

He bolts to his feet and gets his shirt and jeans off at record speed so he can throw himself into the water.

Take that, inappropriate boner.

The water felt a lot warmer when it was just his feet in it. The shock of his body hitting the surface and sinking makes him yell underwater, bubbles streaming from his mouth. It's cathartic, actually. Maybe he should yell incoherently more often.

He surfaces and swipes his hair out of his eyes. Ben is still on the dock, looking very damp and very disgruntled. "I expected something more graceful from you than whatever that was," he says.

"It was a cannonball," Jamie replies, treading water.

"That wasn't a cannonball," Ben says.

A drop of water, glimmering in the light from the shore, slides along Ben's collarbone and down over one of those magnificent pecs. Jamie wants to lick it off.

Good thing his traitorous penis is below the water line.

Jamie smacks the water, sending a wave splashing over Ben's legs. "C'mon, this was your idea. Let's see your cannonball form."

"Prepare to be blown away," Ben says.

He takes his boxer briefs off.

Jamie flails, squeaks, and spins around, his eyes tightly shut even though he's facing the other direction.

There's a long silence before Ben says sheepishly, "Um, I meant my cannonball form, not... uh...."

"Please don't say 'package,'" Jamie says frantically, which— WHY? What the fuck possessed him? Now he wants to drown himself. Just swim a little farther into the lake and sink beneath the surface.

There's another pause. "No. I. Um. I wasn't going to say 'package.' Oh my god. Why did *you* say 'package?'"

Didn't your body get all bloated when you drowned? Or could they pull him out fast enough that he looked really pretty and tragic? He wanted to look pretty and tragic in death.

The aluminum ladder creaks, and once Jamie hears water gurgle, he turns. Ben's safely submerged up to his shoulders. His erection doesn't get the memo.

"I didn't realize we'd decided to go *skinny-dipping*," Jamie says.

"I didn't want to get my underwear wet!" Ben says defensively.

"Didn't you bring extra underwear?" Jamie asks, knowing full well he did, because he saw them folded neatly in his duffel bag.

"Yeah, but I didn't want to have to put my clothes on over wet underwear when we walk back up to the house."

"You could've gone commando," Jamie says, then sinks entirely below the water, dunking his head under. Seriously. What's wrong with him?

It turns out he can't hold his breath very long, so he pops back up. Ben is treading water, looking like he's still dealing with Jamie telling him to go commando. So obviously, Jamie says, "I guess I might have to go commando."

WHY.

"Bye," Jamie says. "When they dredge the lake and find my body, you can tell them it was self-defense. I couldn't stop talking about dicks, and you had to act. You did it mostly to save me from myself. No one would convict you."

Ben laughs so hard that he bobs underwater and comes back up choking. He's such a dork. The hard-on is still there, and still a problem, Jamie guesses, but there's something else sitting in his stomach too. It's a flippy, swirly feeling, a whirlwind of desire and happiness and... and love.

Ben does a few strong strokes, cutting through the water smoothly. Water shines on his biceps. He's still wearing the leather bracelet Jamie bought him earlier at Black Bear Provisions and Diner. It's the only thing he's wearing. He's a dork, but he's a cut, super hot dork, and he's naked except for something that Jamie bought him.

"You look good like this," Jamie says, which seemed like a good idea until the words leave his mouth. After they're out, he contemplates drowning himself again.

Ben stares at him, wide-eyed, and Jamie's about to turn it into a joke—somehow—when Ben says in a rush, "You look good too." He coughs like he swallowed lake water. "I mean, not like I just noticed. You're, um. You're really—like, I've totally noticed. Like, always? I noticed you the very first time I saw you in the Daily Grind."

"Well, yeah, you ordered from me. You kind of had to notice me," Jamie says, because he's the world's biggest idiot.

But Ben laughs. Ben laughs, bright and loud and beautiful.

That swirly, heady whirl of color and light in his stomach twists up through his chest and grabs him by the heart. He wants to shout, he wants to do something stupid and fun, he wants to seize this moment around its edges and make it last forever.

They're swimming, so *stupid and fun* presents itself immediately. He sucks in a giant breath and dives beneath the dark surface of the lake.

It's pitch-black underwater, but Jamie doesn't need to be able to see. All he needs to do is reach out and grab—

Even underwater, he can hear Ben's shriek. Such. A. Dork. Jamie loves him.

He breaks the surface, already laughing. His laughter turns to an outraged yell as Ben takes his revenge, launching toward him, grabbing him around the shoulders and pulling him underwater. They wrestle, submerged, for a few seconds. Jamie is in serious risk of drowning from laughing. He can't seem to stop.

They surface, still wrestling, and then there's tickling, and they're both laughing and yelling joyfully, and Jamie thinks, some people are with the person who makes them this happy forever.

Eventually, out of breath, they let go of each other and tread water. Ben's smile is blinding. He's looking at Jamie like Jamie makes him the happiest person alive.

Something lodges in Jamie's throat. Ben is so beautiful. Right now he's all starlight and shining water, hair plastered to his head, skin slick and glistening.

Jamie's chest tightens and swells, and his eyes track a droplet of water as it runs from Ben's hair, down the line of his jaw and throat to his shoulders, where it pools in the hollow of his collarbone. When he flicks his gaze back up, Ben's gaze is different. The happiness is still there, but there's something else now. Something hungry, something yearning.

Ben's throat bobs, and Jamie has never wanted to run his tongue along anyone's Adam's apple more. "Hey," Ben says, but stops and swipes a hand across his forehead. Water sluices off his bicep to his shoulder. And Jamie can't. Fucking. Breathe.

"Ben," Jamie says. A piece of Ben's hair is still stuck to his forehead. Jamie stretches a hand out, bringing them closer. His fingertips graze Ben's skin, wet and warm.

"Yes," Ben replies.

They move at the same time, a swirl of water and a desperate splash, and then they're kissing and kissing and kissing, and this is— it's like the kissing they've done before, but more. Hunger and heat and need, and Jamie's stomach drops out as Ben's arms go around him and Jamie pulls him close. Their legs tangle together. Ben's hands are in Jamie's hair and his beard scratches against Jamie's face, and Ben lets out a gasp, like the contact sent a physical shock through him.

Maybe it did, because every inch of Jamie's skin feels charged.

Jamie groans and sucks at Ben's bottom lip, runs his tongue over it, bites down, and Ben's mouth opens to his and it's just tongues and lips and the taste of Ben and oh god god god. They've kissed before. *They've kissed before.* So why is this so different? Why is this so much better?

Jamie's back hits the ladder, cold aluminum scoring his skin, and he squeals and bucks his hips into Ben's. Ben laughs into his mouth and slides his hands to Jamie's waist, where they rest at the waistband of Jamie's boxer briefs. Jamie's breath hitches and his hips push into Ben's again.

This time it's deliberate and slow, as he opens his mouth and glides his tongue against Ben's. Ben shifts, and Jamie shifts, and now—fuck.

Now, Jamie can feel how hard Ben is. Their dicks rub together.

Also: Ben is naked. Ben is incredibly naked and incredibly hard. Jamie's hands trail down his back, a long wet glide, starting above the water and ending below it as they settle at Ben's hips.

Ben nips at Jamie's lower lip. "Are you going to touch me or what?"

"Do you want me to?" Jamie asks, though he doesn't know what he'll do if the answer is *no.*

"Of course," Ben says. His hand cups the back of Jamie's neck. "So fucking much."

"Same," Jamie breathes as he slips his hands over Ben's ass and grabs two handfuls.

Then Ben's hands are on his ass, squeezing and stroking him through his underwear, and Jamie needs his clothes off, like, thirty seconds ago. He needs—he needs—Ben, and his back on the ground and Ben's weight on him, and maybe Ben's thinking the same thing, because suddenly they're both fumbling up the ladder, onto the dock, and then they're on each other and Jamie's gasping, "*Take them off, now, please,*" and there's the first scalding touch of naked cock on cock and Jamie's *gone.*

He could cry at the heat between them and how perfect Ben feels. Their bodies slide together, still slick and wet. Moaning, Ben breaks away from Jamie's mouth and licks down his throat to suck at his collarbone.

Breathing heavily, Ben moves down Jamie's body. He swirls his tongue around Jamie's nipple, which makes Jamie gasp. "I wanna know everything you like," Ben says.

"That," Jamie groans. "I like *that*."

Ben does *that*, and Jamie's hips arch off the dock. When Ben's teeth close around his tit and tug, Jamie cries out.

"God, I want you," Ben moans. His hand slips between them, but it hovers a finger twitch away from Jamie's cock.

Jamie spreads his legs and wraps them around Ben's back. Ben looks at him, and Jamie fists a hand in his hair. Their eyes stay locked on each other for a beat, then two, and Jamie is acutely aware of the beat of his heart, the hot blaze of his skin, the hard press of another body on top of his. The heaviness of his balls, the hard, aching length of his cock rubbing against Ben's.

"Then fuck me," Jamie says.

# CHAPTER TWENTY-SIX

BEN CAN'T go back.

He knows he should ask, *Are you sure?* But the way Jamie's legs are hooked around his back, the way Jamie's hand is in his hair, and the way—fuck—he just swiveled his hips to brush his cock against Ben's fingers, all of that seems like answer enough.

God, Jamie. His body is toned and lean and warm, hard in the right spots and soft in others. Ben wants to learn every dip of muscle and bone, but every time he tells himself to focus and memorize how Jamie feels, Jamie does something with his hands, his fingertips drawing sparks off Ben's skin.

"Yeah," Ben breathes. "Okay."

Like he hasn't spent every night thinking about this lately, about how he'll take his time, how they'll go so slow that Jamie will be begging for release, and Ben will be smooth and relentless, he'll keep Jamie on the brink, he'll keep himself in control.

Reality: Ben closes his hand around Jamie's cock, feels how it fills up his hand, and groans, "Oh fuck."

Jamie laughs and flails an arm, reaching for Ben's jeans. Ben doesn't know what he's doing until he pulls out the lube and condoms. "Thank god for Andy's creepy party favors."

Ben laughs helplessly. "Oh my god."

"I won't tell if you don't."

Ben kisses him, and Jamie's laughing underneath him. And then Jamie's hips roll, Ben tightens his grip, and Jamie lets out an uninhibited moan. Ben thinks he could maybe come just listening to Jamie's pleasure.

"Top or bottom?" Ben asks, playing with Jamie's foreskin.

"Bottom," Jamie grunts. His eyes slit open. "For now. If you're offering both."

Anything, actually. Everything. He's on fire. He feels drunk. He feels high.

"Yeah," Ben says. "I like both."

He sounds like an idiot. But something happens to Jamie's face. It softens, like he thinks Ben's endearing. "I want you inside me," Jamie says. "That's what I want. What I've wanted."

Electricity races up Ben's spine. "Wanted?"

Jamie groans and fucks Ben's hand. "God, Ben. Didn't you know I had a crush on you? All this time, and now we're *here* and—please just fuck me. *Please.*"

Ben has to bury his face in Jamie's neck, and Jamie's pulse is beating against his lips, hard and wild. He starts kissing, sucking, and god he wants to leave a mark.

Jamie's rocking against him, grinding, touching Ben everywhere. His fingers trail up and down Ben's back, along each knob of his spine. Hands squeeze his ass, and Jamie's exploring his cleft, from his tailbone down to his hole, to his taint and balls.

With a moan, Ben bites his shoulder, licks his collarbone, sucks one of Jamie's tits again before starting work on another hickey. Jamie makes this *noise* and Ben aches. This isn't gonna be the slow lovemaking Ben's been fantasizing about. Not with the way Jamie's squirming and pumping his hips underneath Ben. Not with the way Jamie grabs Ben's chin and pulls his face back up, the way he kisses Ben, all tongue, and bites his lips.

"Jamie," Ben whispers, and Jamie laughs. The sound pierces Ben's heart and this is perfect even if it's not perfect. It's them, it's Jamie and him, and Ben feels like he belongs.

He fumbles with the condom Jamie stuffs into his hand, then the lube. It's been a long time; does he remember how to do this?

Jamie rolls them over, flipping Ben onto his back. His hands run all over Ben, trailing through the hair on his chest, and Ben homes in on the way he's biting his bottom lip.

Jamie's hands make their way lower, touching Ben's stomach, then lower, lower, until he wraps his fingers around Ben's dick. His hips shift forward, and Ben can feel himself pressing against Jamie, hot and tight.

Jamie's eyes squeeze shut. Ben reaches up and runs his fingers over his face, and Jamie leans into him. He turns his head and kisses Ben's palm, and their eyes meet again. "You want this, right?" Jamie breathes.

"Yes," Ben whispers back, one hand sliding up Jamie's thigh until it settles on his hip, the other still on Jamie's face.

Hips shift again, Jamie opening and sinking down with a deep groan, Ben moving up to meet him. And then it's just—them. They're together, their bodies finding the right rhythm until they're moving in sync. Heat and the slickness of water and sweat and the lube still on Ben's hands. The slap of skin. Panting, moaning, gravel in his chest, all of this beyond words, beyond sound. Starlight silvering everything, Jamie's hair and his body, and the stars behind him that can't come close to capturing the feeling of infinity expanding in Ben right now.

It's never felt like this before, not with anyone.

He can't imagine wanting anyone else ever again, now that he's had this.

One of Jamie's hands finds one of Ben's. Their fingers thread together and hold on tight, hot and sweaty. Ben brings their clasped hands to his chest, right over his heart, and there are galaxies in Jamie's eyes as he looks down at Ben.

He looks like this is enough, just Ben inside him—but Ben's eyes dip to Jamie's cock, bobbing each time Jamie sinks down on him.

He wraps his hands around Jamie, and Jamie makes this *noise*. Jamie makes this noise that Ben hasn't even known to fantasize about, because he didn't know anyone could make a sound like that during sex. Jamie sounds wanton, and filthy, and—and—

And there's no way Ben can keep himself from careening into oblivion.

He comes so hard the stars overhead blur into one haze of white, and he's probably yelling. He's pumping hard into Jamie, uncontrolled and wild, one hand scrabbling for Jamie's hip to hold him in place and the other gripped around his cock and working it.

Jamie doesn't need to be held in place. He meets Ben stroke for stroke, teeth digging into his lip, panting, sweat and water dripping from his hair.

He lets out a choked, strangled gasp, and then pulls his cock, and Ben's hand, to his belly, holding it there. Ben feels the moment his cock twitches and pulses. He feels the moment Jamie comes, pouring himself onto his stomach and over his own hand and Ben's. He feels Jamie's labored breathing.

He feels the moment he can't ever go back. Not to before. Not to when he didn't have Jamie in his life. Not to when he didn't get to kiss Jamie. Not to when he didn't get to feel Jamie's body against his.

Jamie rolls off Ben, and his back thumps on the dock as he lies down. They don't move. They lie there, arms touching from shoulder to hand. The stars unstick themselves from each other and return to points of light in the sky. Water licks at the dock. Insects hum. It's quiet.

It's incredibly quiet. The two of them were not.

Ben chuckles to himself, then loud enough for Jamie to hear. "What?" Jamie asks. His voice sounds molten and lazy.

"Just thinking about who heard us."

"They probably heard us back at Black Bear Provisions and Diner."

There's a light touch at Ben's wrist. Jamie is running a finger along the leather braid of the bracelet he gave Ben earlier. His fingertip traces down, over the back of Ben's hand and his knuckles, then down his pinkie. It rests there, barely touching. A question.

Ben hooks his pinkie around Jamie's. It's the only place they're joined. It shouldn't send electricity thrumming through Ben's body, not after what they just did. But he feels every nerve lighting up from head to toe. Every inch of skin is hyperaware, and his pulse thunders in his ears.

"That was nice," Jamie says quietly. Seriously.

"Nice?" Ben asks, wondering if he should be insulted.

"Amazing." Tentatively, Jamie offers more of his hand. Ben takes it, interlacing their fingers.

"Yeah," Ben agrees. "It was amazing for me too."

Jamie laughs, bright and clear, and covers his face with a hand. Scrubbing it over his forehead, he says, "I can't believe I just told you that."

Something about Jamie's laugh, and the way his nose scrunches up, and the way he sounds so melodramatic but the furthest thing from upset, makes Ben grin. "What, that sex with me was amazing?"

Jamie laughs again and his grip on Ben's hand tightens. "Yes, okay? Yes, I can't believe I just blurted that out. That's so uncool. You never tell a guy the sex was incredible."

"Oh yeah? How come?"

"Because he'll assume you're emotional. And you'll want more than 'u up?' texts at two in the morning."

Ben props himself on an elbow. Jamie's hand is still resting on his forehead, but it's not covering his eyes anymore. There's a vulnerable look there, like even worse than saying the sex was incredible was saying why he shouldn't have said that.

He brushes his thumb over the back of Jamie's hand. "I don't send 'u up?' texts any later than ten."

Jamie snorts with laughter and surges upward. Their mouths meet in a kiss, which Ben expects to be hard and passionate.

It's not. It's soft, and Ben's mouth melts under Jamie's. This. This this this. He can't give this up.

When they break apart, Ben says, "I don't think emotional is a bad thing."

"No?" Jamie raises an eyebrow and looks like he wants to say something else. He doesn't. The expression smooths itself away.

All Ben can do is gaze at him, at the way his black hair is spread around his head in a halo, the way all his limbs seem liquid. And the way there's something in his eyes that now Ben knows isn't fake.

He runs his thumb gently across Jamie's cheekbone to follow the line of his jaw. He wants to tell Jamie the whole truth: that until this thing between them started, he did think emotional was a bad thing. Emotional people weren't successful. Emotional people didn't get to the top. Emotional people didn't become neurosurgeon-in-chief at thirty-seven.

The whole truth is that he loves Jamie.

Jamie takes his hand and kisses each one of his fingers lingeringly, then the center of his palm. "So, I should probably tell you that I have real feelings for you."

Ben can read him like an open book—the way the words terrify him, the casual way he says them to try to hide that fact, and to downplay it if Ben doesn't reciprocate. It makes his heart hurt that Jamie thinks he might not. It makes his heart hurt that Jamie thinks they could do what they just did, that it could feel the way it did, tender and perfect and full of love, even if neither of them said the word, and for it to not mean anything.

His breath catches, and he leans down to kiss Jamie gently. "Yeah," he murmurs against Jamie's lips. "I do too."

One kiss turns to two, then three. And then it's not separate kisses, but just one long continuous one. Ben runs his fingers through Jamie's hair, and Jamie's palms settle against Ben's hips. Jamie's knee nudges between Ben's legs, and their thighs fit against each other's. Everything is quiet. There's the lake, the lapping water, the whisper of the forest filling the night, and their hitched breaths.

Eventually, by unspoken agreement, they return to the house. They hold hands the entire way.

# CHAPTER TWENTY-SEVEN

WHEN JAMIE wakes up, he's afraid he dreamed the whole thing. But there's the warm, heavy weight of a body next to him in bed, an arm slung across his midsection. The room smells like lake water. Shouldn't it smell like sex?

Then again, the smell of lake water is pretty overpowering.

Jamie relaxes into Ben. He could stay right here forever.

A sharp rap on the door startles Jamie so violently that his heart leaps halfway up his throat, pounding hard as it settles back into the appropriate cavity in his chest. Behind him, Ben starts halfway upright.

"Good morning!" a voice trills outside. "Rise and shine, you sly little minxes!"

It's Timothy. How the hell does he sound so chipper after drinking as much as he did and taking G on top of it?

"We're up," Jamie replies, because he wouldn't put it past Timothy to waltz right through the door.

"Breakfast will be on the deck in half an hour!"

Footsteps trip away, and Jamie falls back into the mattress. And there's Ben, propped on an elbow and gazing down at him.

"Oh," Jamie breathes. "Hi."

"Hey." Ben smiles. It's the softest, warmest smile, and it turns Jamie's center into molten, gooey mush.

He didn't realize until now that his follow-up fear to "it wasn't real" was "Ben regrets it." One look at his face and Jamie knows that isn't true. Tentatively, Ben runs a finger along Jamie's collarbone, from his shoulder to the hollow at the bottom of Jamie's throat.

A smile blooms across Jamie's face. He buries his fingers in Ben's hair and pulls him into a kiss.

Kissing Ben would be a super easy way to spend the next half an hour. But Jamie still has to talk to Peter about the job, and ghosting on brunch probably isn't the best opening gambit.

Reluctantly, Jamie breaks the kiss. Or tries to. Ben doesn't let him. And Jamie doesn't fight all that hard to pull away. It feels too good when Ben nibbles on his lip like that.

When Jamie pulls away again, Ben groans in dismay, and Jamie laughs and puts his hands on Ben's face. His beard tickles Jamie's palms. The scratch of stubble is one of many reasons they have to stop now, before kissing Ben becomes a lot more. The way his stubble is rubbing coarsely against Jamie's face is doing things to him.

"Sorry," Jamie says. "If it's any consolation, I really wish we'd done this at your apartment so we could stay in bed all day."

Also he's pretty sure he has a splinter in his arm from the dock, but that's less romantic and/or sexy.

Worth it. He'd suffer a hundred splinters for the way Ben is looking at him.

Ben smooths hair back from Jamie's forehead—god, he doesn't even want to think about what it looks like right now—and tucks it behind Jamie's ear. "I thought I might've dreamed the whole thing," Ben says, wonder in his voice.

"I," Jamie says. And then, "No. Not a dream." He makes himself get up. "It wasn't a dream, but the way I smell is kind of a nightmare."

Ben laughs. "Eau d'lake water."

The sheet, which Jamie threw aside when he climbed out of bed, is draped over Ben in a way that looks artistic, but which covers absolutely nothing. Jamie loses higher cortical function.

Ben grins and stretches his arms over his head. Jamie's mouth goes dry. Muscles. Tendons. Body hair. V-cut. Dick, which is half-hard. Maybe a little more than half under Jamie's ravenous gaze.

"You were saying you wanted to shower?" Ben asks, his tone disgustingly nonchalant, like he isn't currently seducing Jamie.

"Mm. Um. Yeah. I… what?"

With another laugh, Ben climbs out of bed. The way the sheet falls away from him doesn't help Jamie's situation. Ben looks at it. "Maybe we can have a little making out in the shower," he says. "As a treat."

"Making out," Jamie repeats. His mouth has gone from dry to flooded with saliva. He's going to drool if he isn't careful. "Sure. We can call it making out if you want."

The bathroom is en suite. Yesterday, Jamie would have scoffed and rolled his eyes. This morning, he's thrilled they don't have to bother with clothes as they stumble into the bathroom, kissing and grabbing at each other.

They're only ten minutes late to brunch, which Jamie thinks is pretty impressive, considering.

It's a beautiful day. Bright, clear blue sky, crisp mountain air warmed just right by the sparkling morning sun, birdsong trilling through the forest. Granted, an unseasonable soup of sleet and freezing rain could blow in and Jamie would probably still sigh and think about how beautiful it was.

He and Ben are holding hands. Andy's eyes lock on their joined hands and he scowls, while Timothy asks, "Sleep well?" Pancakes and french toast are piled high on platters on the table.

"Yep," Jamie says.

No one else speaks. They all look rough. Luke is wearing sunglasses. Art is squinting, while Derick has a floppy sun hat pulled low over his eyes. Peter's eyes are bloodshot, and his hangover vibe is probably detectable within a three-mile radius.

Even Philip looks under-slept and over-drugged. There are puffy bags under his eyes, and the corners of his mouth are pulled down.

Timothy looks like he's fresh off the best night of sleep in his life. Jamie both admires and hates him.

"Are you cooking?" Ben asks, possibly because no one else seems compelled to fill the silence.

"Oh, *no*, of course not!" Timothy looks like this is the most ludicrous thing anyone has ever said to him, roughly on par with someone suggesting that Fort Lee, New Jersey, is a nice vacation spot. "Andrew hired the same company that took care of everything last night. Everything's already prepared, they're just heating it up. And I'm making myself *useful*, which makes a change from the rest of this crowd."

"Do you have to talk so loud?" Leslie asks hoarsely.

Timothy shakes his head despairingly and vanishes back into the house. Jamie and Ben take seats next to each other. Leslie winces at the sound of the legs scraping against the deck.

Once breakfast is served, Jamie disentangles his fingers from Ben's. Ben presses the side of his knee into Jamie's.

Timothy clinks the edge of his butter knife against his champagne flute, filled to the brim with mimosa. Art keeps looking at it like the fizzing is too loud. "To another fabulous Poconos weekend," Timothy says, to muted agreement. With a smirk, he adds, "And to aging, apparently. You're getting *old*, ladies. You never used to get hangovers."

"Maybe you're just inhuman or something," Derick grumbles, pulling the brim of his hat lower.

"Superhuman," Timothy corrects him.

Next to Jamie, Peter is cutting an omelet into pieces with the side of his fork. Is now a good time to bring up the job? Peter said they'd talk. Maybe he wasn't counting on being hungover? Or maybe he didn't really mean it. Maybe he just said it to get Jamie to shut up. What if he brings it up and Peter rebuffs him?

Jamie takes a slow, deep breath. What if he does? Jamie barely wants this job. He just wants to get away from Andy. The job he really wants is with Nina Noskova. Even though he knows what held him back from applying, suddenly it seems really stupid. Right now, with Ben's knee against his, he feels like he's brave enough to do anything, even apply for a job he already knows he isn't going to get.

His fork and knife ding as he rests them on the edges of his plate. "Hey, Peter, is now a good time to talk about the job?"

"Job?" Peter looks at him blankly. Realization flashes over his face. "Oh! The job! Right. Sorry. Look, can you use a computer?"

"Er, yeah?"

"Excel?"

"Of course." No, but how hard can it be?

"Great, job's yours." Peter takes a huge bite of omelet.

Seriously? Why is it so hard to get a job if those are the only qualifications?

"Oh—um, well, thanks!" Jamie's more bewildered than happy, but he makes himself not question it. If he says "Really?" then Peter might change his mind.

Jamie turns to Ben. "Did you hear that?"

"Yeah," Ben says, smiling.

He kisses Jamie. Right there at the table. "I'm proud of you, babe," Ben murmurs in Jamie's ear.

*Babe*. The pet name that wasn't supposed to mean anything. The pet name that makes Jamie's stomach flutter, and that, if Ben's still using it, means that it probably meant something this whole time.

If they both had real feelings from the start, and the pet names were what they would have used if they were dating for real, then… have they been dating for real?

Has Jamie been in a real relationship for the past two weeks without realizing it?

His stomach, intestines, heart, and several other internal organs spasm sickeningly. He doesn't do relationships anymore. This is like, a core part of who he is. *He doesn't do relationships anymore.* He can't. He can't get invested. He can't get his heart broken again.

If Ben leaves him—*when* Ben leaves him, that's it. Jamie has fake dated him for two weeks and no one could ever compare. If they try this and it falls apart, there's no hope. There's no *Well, maybe I could be happy with him….*

And the thing is.

He only wants to be happy with Ben.

He looks at his mimosa, bubbling cheerfully. Well. Shit.

While Jamie's having an existential crisis, Peter has secured a pen and is writing something on a napkin. "Here," he says, sliding it across the table to Jamie. "That's my number. When can you start?"

There's a temptation to say *immediately.* Andy's sitting at the other end of the table; Jamie could give notice right now and never go back to the Daily Grind. Something stops him. "A couple weeks," he says.

He makes himself not add, *If that's okay.* He's a catch, right? So they can wait a couple weeks for him. They're lucky it's not longer!

Right, sure.

Peter doesn't even blink. "End of June, then? Sure." He makes a note on his phone. "Text me when you have an exact date. I'll send you the office address. We'll get you set up with everything. We've been doing hybrid since the pandemic, so you'll have to come in a few times a week. Fosters culture, you know. You have dedicated office space at home, right?"

"Of course," Jamie says. He can dedicate his desk to being his office.

"Great." Peter winces, grabs his head, and scrunches his eyes shut. "*Fuck*, is that aspirin ever going to kick in?" He opens one eye, grabs his mimosa, and downs the entire thing in one gulp. Bracing his hands on the table, he says, "I need something stronger."

When he pushes away, Jamie carefully folds the napkin and pockets it. "I can't believe I actually did it," he says to Ben.

Ben takes his hand and squeezes it. "I can. You can do anything, Jamie. Anything you want. You're amazing."

Jamie's heart skips. "You think I'm amazing?"

"I—" Ben looks mortified before the embarrassment melts away. "I guess I can own it now, right?" he says, his voice softer. "I was always trying to stop myself from saying stuff like that."

"You've been thinking I'm amazing?" Jamie asks, sort of joking, but sort of not.

The way Ben's eyes catch his makes Jamie lean forward. "Duh," Ben says. The way Ben's mouth looks makes Jamie lean forward even more.

"Oh my *god*, can someone please stop those two from gazing adoringly into each other's eyes?" Art says from the other side of the table. "I feel sick enough."

"You're just bitter Derick doesn't gaze at you like that after you guys fuck," Luke says.

The moment is thoroughly stepped on, so Jamie and Ben draw back.

"Sorry for not gazing at you," Derick says to Art.

"Ew, no thank you."

In his pocket, Jamie's phone buzzes. It's too insistent for a text. "Shit," he curses when he sees Tyler's face and name on the screen.

"Everything okay?" Ben asks, instantly concerned.

"My brother's calling," Jamie says, pushing back from the table. "I better answer." Tyler doesn't call. Tyler only texts. Calling is bad. Calling means something is wrong.

Jamie's stomach twists. What if something happened to Dad? Their relationship isn't great, but he's still Dad, and Jamie's not ready for anything bad to happen to him.

"What's wrong?" Jamie asks in lieu of greeting.

"Jamie?" Tyler asks.

Jamie moves deeper into the house, not paying attention to where he's going. "Yes! Obviously! Who else would it be? What's *wrong*? Is Dad in the hospital?"

"Huh? Why would Dad be in the hospital?"

"Why are you calling, Tyler?" Jamie stops at an open door and goes inside. "Something bad happened, right? Just tell me."

"Nothing bad happened! Why do you think something bad happened?"

For god's sake. "Because you never call!"

"I just wanted to make sure I talked to you!" Tyler says, sounding exasperated. "I thought you might not see a text. Or you might not answer."

The last part is added in kind of an accusatory way, which… okay, fair. Sometimes Jamie doesn't answer texts from his family. But come on, who doesn't?

"I answered. What?"

"We're still coming down to the city today. Are you going to be around?"

Oops. Jamie hasn't exactly forgotten about the visit, but in the swirl of the last few days, it's gotten pushed to the back of his mind. And with last night… well, yeah. The last thing Jamie's been thinking about is his family.

"Are you still there?"

"Um, yeah. I'm at a thing today, remember? My boss invited me to his house in the Poconos, so… yeah, not sure when I'm getting home." He raises his eyes to the ceiling and pats himself on the back for his next words. "But I'm for sure still free tomorrow."

The other end of the line is silent until Tyler asks, "Your boss? Isn't he… I mean… haven't you said you don't really like being alone with him?"

Well, Tyler's going to meet Ben tomorrow anyway, right? Might as well break the news. "I'm not alone," he says, choosing not to touch the other part of that with a ten-foot pole while he's standing in Andy's house. "I brought my boyfriend."

"Your boyfriend? Since when are you dating again?"

"Since I met Ben." Wait, no. That doesn't jive with their story. "Since I started dating Ben. We've kind of known each other for a while. He's coming to dinner with us tomorrow, so you can grill him about it. That's okay, right? You and Dad don't mind if he comes with?"

Too bad if they do, because Jamie needs a buffer.

"Are you kidding? You're obligated to bring him. If you're actually dating a guy, that's like being married by normal person standards."

Normal person standards. That stings, even though he knows Tyler doesn't mean anything by it. "Yeah," he says, enough acid in his tone for Tyler to hear it loud and clear.

"Sorry. That came out wrong. I just mean he must be a really great guy, and you must really like him. You don't do casual."

"He is a great guy," Jamie snaps. He's legit annoyed, but maybe he needs to take it down a notch. Deep breath in, deep breath out. "He's a great guy," Jamie repeats, softer. "I think you'll like him. I mean, I hope you'll like him."

"If you like him, I'll like him."

"I'm way pickier than you," Jamie says, smirking even if Tyler can't see him.

"Ha, ha. So we're on for dinner tomorrow? Want me to pick a place?"

"Yeah, you and Dad choose the place. Text me the name and time. Ben and I will be there."

"See you tomorrow, Buttface."

"Drive safe, Farthead," Jamie shoots back.

Tyler laughs and hangs up. Jamie presses his phone against his sternum, feeling his heart beating against it. No turning back now. Ben's having dinner with his family, and it's not as a fake boyfriend, but as… a real one? They should probably talk about this.

"You rushed off," a voice says. It's not one Jamie wants to hear.

Jamie turns. Andy is in the doorway. For the first time, he glances around the room. A massive Mac sits on an equally massive desk. Bookshelves are hung at different levels on the walls. There are books on some of them, but they're mostly displaying what Jamie thinks of as "rich person stuff." There are small sculptures, a misshapen vase, some retro electronics that are the definition of form over function. There's a Tom of Finland print on the wall, because of course there is, and a leather loveseat.

This is Andy's office.

"My brother called," Jamie says.

"Everything all right?" Andy always does this thing with his voice where he sounds super sympathetic, but you know he isn't.

"Yeah, fine." Jamie keeps his phone out. How do you do the SOS thing again? "Him and my dad are coming down to New York today. He wanted to figure out details." Oh! This is perfect! "Actually, Ben and I should get going so we get back in time—"

"So Peter gave you the job?" Andy asks, cutting right over Jamie.

If he has to make his escape from the window, is he going to break a bone? Is it possibly still worth it? "Yeah," Jamie says, tilting his chin up. "He did."

Andy looks haggard. He's unshaven, his scruff growing in gray and uneven, and there are dark circles under his bloodshot eyes. Lines fan out from his frown.

Andy takes a step into the room. "I talked you up," he says.

Jamie holds his ground. "Thanks," he says, because it's the right thing to do. "You didn't have to. I appreciate it."

"You know, Peter's going to be a lot more demanding to work for. Not like me. He won't let you get away with stuff."

Jamie bristles. "What do you mean, *get away with stuff?* Are you saying I screw around at work?"

"I just mean Peter's not going to want to be your friend, like I am," Andy says, which is....

Which is, wow. Jamie barely stops himself from laughing. At the end of the day, Andy helped him get a new job, even if mentioning it was a transparent attempt to get Jamie here so they could fuck.

"I don't need a friend," Jamie says. "I just need a good manager."

"I'm a good manager," Andy says, sounding hurt. "You're my favorite! And I treat you like it!"

"You treat me like a toy," Jamie snaps before he can stop himself. "Do you think I like that? Do you think I'm into being groped at work by my boss? The guy who pays me? Who I have to be nice to so he doesn't *stop* paying me?"

Andy's mouth opens, but nothing comes out. Is it possible Andy doesn't realize how he comes across? Is it possible he never meant anything by it?

Did Jamie overreact? God, all this time, he's been telling himself he just has to take it, and the last couple weeks he's finally let himself see that he really does deserve better, that he doesn't have to put up with this shit at work. What if it's really him that just didn't get it?

"I thought you liked me," Andy says.

And Jamie realizes he's not overreacting.

"Not like that," Jamie says.

Andy comes closer. "We were great together. You have to admit that."

Jamie doesn't move. "We slept together *once*. It doesn't matter if I enjoyed it. It was *one time*, and I obviously wasn't interested in a repeat of the experience."

There's movement in the doorway. Jamie flicks his eyes over Andy's shoulder and sees—

Shit.

Ben is standing there. His gaze moves from Jamie to Andy, then back to Jamie again.

Everything inside Jamie wilts.

"I just wanted to see if you were okay." Ben's throat bobs.

The smile Jamie forces across his face must look ghoulish. Ben flinches, so—check. "I'm okay," Jamie says. "We should get ready to go. We have that thing with my family, remember?"

Without missing a beat, Ben says, "I figured you'd want to get on the road soon. I'll grab our bags."

This feels like a mockery of a normal conversation. A mockery of a relationship. The irony of it would be delicious if it were happening to anyone else: his fake relationship has never felt faker than this moment, when it should feel real.

Step one: extricate himself from this conversation. Step two: extricate himself from this house. Step three: extricate the awkwardness that's currently a thick, heavy curtain between Ben and him.

Step four: ???

"I'll be at work on Monday," Jamie says, maneuvering past Andy so he can leave the room.

# CHAPTER TWENTY-EIGHT

GETTING TIMOTHY to move his car is a chore Ben hopes he never has to do again. Not just because he hopes he never sees Timothy again, but because it takes twenty minutes too long.

First Timothy has to pack leftovers for them. And by "pack leftovers," it turns out he means "stand in the middle of the massive, chrome-plated applianced kitchen (seriously, there's more metal in this room than on the average car) and direct the catering staff what to pack for them." Then he has to exchange contact info with them, sending several photos of himself to "make sure he got their numbers right." Then he has to hug them and air-kiss their cheeks. *Then*, finally, he moves his car... only to rush out and hug them both again.

"Keep in touch!" he pleads.

When Ben spins the car around in the driveway, he glances in the rearview mirror. Everyone's already inside except Andy. He's standing forlornly, staring after their retreating tail lights.

Ever since Ben walked in on that conversation between Jamie and Andy, Jamie's been distant. Ben knows he has to say something, but— what? *Hey, it seems like you maybe thought that was a big deal, but it wasn't, so can we go back to the way we were when we woke up?* Every time he shoots a look at Jamie and Jamie refuses to meet his eyes, a blade scrapes against Ben's ribs.

What if Jamie doesn't want to talk about it? Ben doesn't want to make him. As far as Ben's concerned, there's nothing to talk about. Was he surprised to hear Jamie and Andy slept together? Sure, at first. But it's none of Ben's business.

They haven't hit the main highway yet when Jamie clears his throat. "So," he says. Ben waits. Jamie clears his throat again and picks at something invisible on his jeans. "So," he repeats.

"Please don't feel like you owe me an explanation," Ben says, unable to stop himself.

Jamie looks at him incredulously. "You just found out I slept with my boss."

"It's none of my business."

"He's a creep."

"Yeah, well, it's still none of my business." Something horrible occurs to Ben. "Wait, he didn't... I mean, was it... did you want...."

"It was consensual," Jamie says dryly.

Something untwists in Ben's chest. "Good."

There's a silence. The speed limit drops as they enter a town, passing Black Bear Provisions and Dining. The bracelet Jamie bought for him hasn't left his wrist since then, and he touches it now like it's a talisman.

Ben doesn't know what he's doing, but he knows he wants to try.

"It makes me realize there's a lot I don't know about you," Ben says. "But it doesn't change the way I see you. Why would it? It's not like I thought you were a virginal maiden or something."

"Yeah, but." Jamie pauses. "*Andy.* And you don't even know the worst part."

"You don't have to tell me. You don't owe me this information."

But Jamie keeps talking. It's like he wants to punish himself. Like he made this one decision however long ago he made it, and he's hated himself for doing it ever since.

"I slept with him so he'd give me a job." Jamie's voice is jagged. "I met him at a club, and I was kind of drunk. He was too. We were talking, and he kept saying how he owned all these different businesses, and like.... Ben, I needed a job. You have no idea how much I needed a job. I was about to graduate, and I just... I didn't know what I was going to do. I couldn't afford to keep going for a PhD. I have so much debt, it's— So I already knew I was done with grad school, and I'd been looking for jobs, but no one wanted me. So... I did that. I slept with him, and I gave him my number, and when he called me again I...."

There's such a long silence that Ben thinks Jamie is done. Finally, though, he finishes, "I said I'd love to see him again, but did he say something about a job? Maybe there'd be something for me?" Jamie folds at the waist, burying his face in his hands. "God, I've never said it out loud. It's awful. I'm awful. He's a creep, but I totally led him on. Why wouldn't he think he could be handsy after that?"

"Because no one has a right to your body or affection just because you said yes once," Ben says—feelingly, fiercely, needing Jamie to understand this. "Because you're allowed to do something and decide you don't want to do it again, and he shouldn't have expected it then, let alone all these years later."

He didn't mean to sound so fired up. But god, he wants Jamie to understand that even if he led Andy on, even if he used the implied promise of sex to get a job, Andy harassing him wasn't okay.

There's a tiny noise from the passenger seat that sounds like it might be a sob. And oh god. What does he do? Does he pull over? Does he keep driving and pretend that he didn't just hear Jamie probably crying? Is putting on the radio a bad choice? He could flip to the oldies station and they could both be appalled at how it's playing Foo Fighters these days?

"But I've had a crush on *you* for two years," Jamie says. The way his voice sounds makes it obvious he's trying valiantly not to cry. "And— that's a thing. We're... a thing. So maybe. I don't know. Maybe I led him on. Maybe it makes sense he didn't get the hint."

A blue sign flashes by on the right: SCENIC OVERLOOK.

Ben doesn't have to think. He knows the right thing to do.

He brakes hard and wrenches the wheel to the right. His Audi protests by flashing a dashboard's worth of warning lights at him, all of which he ignores. He stops, shuts the car off, and looks at Jamie.

Jamie's eyes are red and teary. His nose is red too, and leaking. He laughs in a weak, watery way. "So you're probably regretting what happened last night, huh."

"No," Ben said. He wants to make this better, but he doesn't know how. The only thing he can do is go with his gut. "Jamie, if you're saying us not making a move on each other for two years is some kind of weird justification for Andy not taking a hint, well, then... no. It's not."

Jamie scrubs a hand over his face. The tears seem like less of a threat now. Ben decides to take a chance. He reaches for Jamie's hand, letting his fingertips rest on Jamie's knuckles. When Jamie doesn't pull away, Ben lays his palm flat on the back of Jamie's hand. Jamie turns his hand over and interlaces his fingers with Ben's.

Ben's heart collapses and remakes itself into something new.

"Please don't feel shitty about this anymore."

"How do you know I've been feeling shitty about it?" Jamie asks.

"I just do," Ben says.

For a long, long moment, Jamie regards him. His throat bobs sharply. "I," Jamie begins. He swallows again. Ben waits. With a deep breath, Jamie says, "I really want to kiss you right now. But I don't know if that's something you're still, um, interested in. Since I just admitted to prostituting myself for a shit job. I should have just gone into actual sex work, the money's better, and I bet I could afford to be pretty choosy with my clients, right? Maybe I should've started an OnlyFans—"

"Jamie."

He stops talking and looks at Ben, his expression worried but trying to be stoic. "Yeah?"

"I really want you to kiss me," Ben says.

The trepidation falls from Jamie's face.

And he kisses Ben.

# CHAPTER TWENTY-NINE

THEY GO back to Ben's apartment. As Ben takes Jamie's backpack and disappears with it, Jamie drifts into the apartment, reconsidering—all of it. Nothing's changed since the last time he was here, but it all looks different. Before, it was Ben's apartment, Ben's furniture, Ben's space. Now, it's *Ben's* apartment. *Ben's* furniture. *Ben's* space. All of it has taken on a glow and a significance that objectively doesn't exist.

He rests a hand on the back of the leather couch. It's funny, because even though he's learned that Ben's so much more than the front he presents to the world, leather furniture still seems totally him.

Ben reappears, but he stops dead when his eyes fall on Jamie. Jamie turns to face him and asks, "What?"

Ben shakes his head. "Nothing."

"It's obviously not nothing."

A step forward. "It's just." The way Ben's Adam's apple bobs sharply makes a hard knot of desire form in Jamie's gut. "I thought about you being here. Not as like, part of a plan. But like…."

When Ben trails off, Jamie offers, "This?"

"Yeah. Like this." His chest rises and falls. "Do you want anything? Um, something to eat? Or a sparkling water or something?"

Jamie has a distinct sense of possibilities splitting, and how he's going to have to make a choice about what kind of person he's going to be. He knows what the smart move is. Shut this down. Remind Ben why they started this whole thing. Point out that Jamie got what he wanted—a new job—and now they should concentrate on getting Ben his promotion.

He doesn't do the smart thing.

He crosses the room to Ben. His breath catches and he can't fill his lungs, not with Ben so close. It's like stepping outside on one of those freezing Hartford winter days, when the snow's freshly fallen and the sun's shining, and everything is bright and glittering. When all the branches and windows are silvered with frost, argent and icy, and the world is still and quiet and perfect, and you don't want to breathe and break the spell.

Ben puts a hand to Jamie's face. His thumb traces a crescent across Jamie's cheek, and Jamie's heart jumps as he sinks into the feel of Ben's palm. Steady fingers trace his hairline before they burrow into his curls, and Jamie is—

Jamie is not *breathing*. He's staring into Ben's eyes and holding his breath. Ben's beautiful sea glass eyes, dark lashes framing them, fixed on Jamie. There's no chance. There's no choice. There's only this.

"I want you," Jamie says softly.

A small, helpless noise squeaks past Ben's lips. In his head, Jamie was sort of thinking he'd let Ben close the distance between them. Plausible deniability? It took the choice—the responsibility—from Jamie at the very last second, so later he could think to himself, *well, I might not have* actually *done it if he hadn't kissed me first.*

But that noise. That noise, and the way Ben's looking at him. The way his lips part and the feel of his palm on Jamie's face. His eyes and his body, warm and solid and inches away, and.

And Jamie slides his hands onto Ben's neck. Leans in.

Kisses him.

Ben lets out a moan when their lips touch and their mouths open to each other. Jamie is powerless against it. His defenses—still standing in name only—crumble to dust and swirl away. Bye, self-preservation. See you around, ironclad heart.

For a second, it feels like this might be like last night, frantic and needy, their bodies screaming and grasping for each other. When Ben touches him, though, Jamie knows it's not going to be like last night at all.

His touch is firm but slow. Purposeful. Ben starts at Jamie's hips, gripping, pulling Jamie into him. He slides his hands up Jamie's sides and around to his front. They rest flat on his chest, Jamie's heart thudding against his palms as Jamie lets out a gasp. His nipples have always been sensitive. The pressure of Ben's hands there suggests the pressure of his mouth, his teeth, tugging and biting like he did last night.

Carefully and deliberately, Ben inches his fingers around the top button of Jamie's shirt. He breaks the kiss bit by bit, allowing his lips to brush over parts of Jamie's, from the corners to the bow to the pout of his lower lip. The button stays closed, but his fingers also stay right where they are.

"Should we go to the bedroom?" Ben asks. Jamie hears every romance cliché in his voice all at the same time, and it makes him stumble even further into love. It's an open bottle of champagne waiting in an ice bucket. It's rose petals scattered across the bed. It's candles on every surface, lit and making the room glow.

"Yes," Jamie breathes.

Ben undoes the top button of Jamie's shirt and takes a step back toward the bedroom. Jamie can't do anything but follow.

There aren't rose petals or candles or champagne. There's an open closet and a bed, and then Jamie stops looking. Ben glances toward the light switch, but Jamie shakes his head. "Leave it on. I want to see you."

"Jesus Christ," Ben mumbles. It sounds rapturous.

Jamie laughs. "That's a good *Jesus Christ*, right?"

Ben's hands find their way to Jamie's buttons again. He doesn't hesitate this time as he works one through the buttonhole, then the next and the next. When Jamie's shirt gaps halfway open, Ben traces a single finger from the hollow of his throat, down his sternum to the bottom of his ribs. A shiver rips up Jamie's spine.

"By the way," Ben says with the kind of faux casualness that Jamie has come to find very, very sexy, "I'm totally intending to take my time."

Jamie holds his gaze, fingers slipping under the hem of Ben's T-shirt. When he brushes bare skin, Ben shudders. His eyelids lower to half-mast. Jamie hitches his shirt up with one hand, the other feeling along Ben's stomach. The perfect amount of hair makes a path from his pecs to his belly before it disappears under the waist of his jeans. "Please," Jamie says. "Take all the time in the world."

The next button falls open, and finally Jamie's shirt is all the way undone. Ben slips it off one shoulder and traces the curve with his fingers before lowering his mouth. Warm breath hits Jamie's skin a second before Ben's lips, and Jamie's fingers curl in Ben's chest hair.

Ben kisses so slowly, like he's mapping the topography of Jamie's skin with his lips, memorizing every tiny detail. Hot kisses move across the line of Jamie's collarbone. Teeth scrape, and the wet slide of tongue soothes the spot.

Before long, Ben's at his neck, kissing and sucking, and Jamie can't hold it together anymore. His head tips back and he moans, and Ben presses closer. He licks up Jamie's throat, over his chin, and flicks over his lips, and then they're kissing again, hotter and heavier than before.

Ben's shirt needs to come off *now*. When Jamie tugs it up, Ben doesn't resist, and then it's off, and—

"I know I'm not, well, thirty—" Ben begins.

Jamie kisses him to cut him off. "You're so fucking hot," he breathes into Ben's mouth.

Ben blooms with the praise. He lights up, and it makes Jamie want to tell him he's amazing in every possible way.

"Jamie," Ben groans, kissing him again. It's deeper this time, more desperate. Jamie presses his body against Ben's bare chest, excitement fluttering low and hot in his gut at the scratch of body hair, the heat of Ben's skin, the poke of his nipples. He knows he told Ben to take all the time in the world, but Jamie's need to be naked and tangled up together is burning.

With a helpless noise, Jamie kisses Ben hard, wrapping his arms tight around Ben's neck and rolling his hips. Ben makes a noise back and breaks the kiss long enough to ask breathlessly, "Can I take your pants off?"

"You haven't even taken my *shirt* off," Jamie replies. He's shooting for playfully aggrieved, but he's pretty sure he just comes off horny.

"So...."

"Yes, Ben. God, yes, take my fucking clothes off."

Ben laughs, and that's the thing about being with him, everything is fun. Sex has never been fun for Jamie. It's been hot, and it's felt good—like, obviously, because he kept having it—but he's never felt this joy. Is that what he's feeling? Is that what this ballooning, endless feeling in his chest is? He feels like he could illuminate a city block with the feeling. Maybe all of Nolita. Hell, maybe all of downtown Manhattan.

"Only if you take mine off too," Ben says, finally pushing Jamie's shirt off his shoulders. It flutters to the ground, landing in a pool of pale green around his feet.

With a growl, Jamie sucks at Ben's collarbone, then dips farther to lick one of his hard, pink nipples. Ben makes a noise of appreciation and pushes it into Jamie's face. Jamie grabs it in his teeth gently, applying more pressure when Ben digs his fingers into Jamie's back.

He puts some force into it, and Ben lets out a hoarse moan. His head falls forward and he moans again, mumbling into Jamie's hair, "That feels good, baby."

As Jamie switches his attention to the other tit, he works Ben's jeans loose. His fingers brush over the hard bulge straining against the fabric, and Ben gasps. The reaction makes Jamie smile so much that for a second, he loses his hold on Ben's nipple. "Do that again," Ben says.

"What?" Jamie asks, all feigned innocence. "This?" His entire palm rubs over Ben's cock.

Ben moans.

Before Jamie can get any further than unzipping Ben's jeans—the zipper's hot from pressing against his erection—Ben propels him toward the bed. Jamie doesn't resist.

They hit the mattress together. Jamie pulls Ben on top of him, and then they're kissing again, and Jamie's working off Ben's jeans and underwear, pushing them down his hips. Ben kicks them away, and they both laugh again. When Jamie reaches down and strokes Ben, the laughter turns to a completely different sound.

Jamie's pants come off, and they're naked together at last. Ben's hipbone digs into Jamie's leg, and Jamie smacks a hand down on his ass to pull him closer. Every inch of Jamie blazes with need and sensation. It's all the same passion and need as last night, but now they're taking their time, learning how each other feel, learning what the other likes. Jamie discovers that Ben squirms and pants if you trace featherlight circles on his inner thighs, and Ben seems thrilled to find that Jamie loves having his ribs stroked.

They're taking each other higher and higher without reaching a peak, but one of them has to get there first. As Ben slides Jamie's foreskin up and down, Jamie gasps and clutches at Ben's back and is pretty sure it's going to be him.

"Ben," he moans. "I need—"

Ben gives his cock a few quick jerks, which means all he can do is wait for the stars to clear from his vision and hope he returns to this plane of existence.

"What do you need, baby?" Ben asks, his voice all husky and pure sex.

"I need you." Jamie's hands are all over Ben's body, his leg is hooked over Ben's hip. He rolls over onto his stomach and grabs Ben's hand, guiding it to his ass. "I need you," he repeats.

Ben cups his ass and squeezes, and Jamie hisses between his teeth as Ben snakes one hand between his legs, pulling his dick so it's curved against his balls. All Jamie can do is bury his face in Ben's duvet, letting out a shameless moan. Ben keeps touching him, one hand stroking up and down Jamie's back while the other plays with his cock, his balls, his hole.

"I don't know if I have any lube," Ben says. With a groan, he adds, "We're not going to have to—"

Jamie snorts into the duvet. "Use Andy's party favor lube?" he supplies.

"Oh my god." Ben covers Jamie's body with his, burying his face in Jamie's hair. "Andy's fucking party favor lube."

Turning his head to kiss Ben—hard—Jamie says, "For what it's worth, it's good lube."

Their eyes meet, and for a second, they're suspended in this perfect, romantic, sexy moment, Ben's weight on him, his hair falling softly over his forehead, the light catching Ben's eyes and making them like glass, like light filtering through water.

Then Jamie snorts, and Ben does too, and they lose it. Jamie has a hand buried in Ben's hair and Ben's forehead bumps against his. The laughter slips into hard, messy kissing, all tongue and hot breath. They pull their bodies apart long enough for Ben to retrieve the lube from his bag and a condom from his nightstand. Ben tears the wrapper open with his teeth, and good fucking *god* if that isn't one of Jamie's turn-ons.

Ben spreads him and Jamie feels the hot pressure of him, right there, so close. His hips shift up—and Ben slides inside, the long, hot, beautiful burn of it making Jamie arch. Light shatters behind his eyelids, stars go supernova, and Ben thrusts in over and over, opening Jamie into his own expanding universe.

No one has ever, ever fucked him like this, with this care and passion. Jamie's had a lot of sex with a lot of guys. None of it has ever sent him whirling, gravity knocked out and all his senses going haywire. It's been forever since he handed another person any vulnerability and trusted them not to stomp on it.

With a moan, Ben presses his chest to Jamie's back, kissing his shoulders. His thrusts get slower, deeper, more deliberate. "Is this good?" he whispers.

He hits that sensitive spot deep within Jamie with these words, and Jamie gasps, pressing against Ben in return and wanting to mold their bodies so tight they're inseparable. He wants every barrier between them gone; he wants something deeper than skin to skin, than Ben inside him.

He doesn't know what that looks like, but he knows one thing that would get them closer. "I want to look at you," Jamie says.

"I do too," Ben replies, his voice cracking.

There's some maneuvering before Jamie's on his back and Ben's above him. Ben puts a hand on Jamie's face. As they lock gazes, Ben slides home again, buried deep. The look on his face is something like what Jamie wants so desperately.

As he arches up to meet Ben stroke for stroke, as they hold on to each other and climb closer and closer to their climaxes, Jamie realizes something: the look on Ben's face?

That's the look of forever.

# CHAPTER THIRTY

THE FIRST thing Ben thinks when the sun creeps across his eyelids, waking him the next morning, is: *I love him.*

The second thing he thinks is, *Fuck, I'm sore.*

The third thing he thinks is, I love him, and I have to tell him.

Jamie is warm and heavy in Ben's arms. Yesterday was… wow. Yesterday was *yesterday.* They eventually got out of bed about midafternoon for food and a shower. The shower was mostly touching each other and slippery, wet hand jobs. They made a halfhearted attempt to watch a movie, but before long, Jamie's hands were roaming, and then it just made more sense to go back to bed.

Jamie's face as he came is a beautiful cut gem of a moment that Ben has already tucked into his memory. The best thing was the way Jamie looked at him. Normally it scares Ben to tell someone he loves them. He's only done it once in his life, and does that even count, when it was all the way back in college? He wasn't even nineteen at the time, and love at nineteen is so different from love at thirty-seven.

He doesn't love easily. Falling in love has always seemed like a bridge he isn't able to cross. He can see it there, he can see what it would look like if he felt that way, but he doesn't.

Then Jamie came along, and Ben was so far across that bridge that he could barely see it behind him by the time he realized. Falling in love with Jamie has been the easiest thing in the world. It hasn't felt like falling—it's felt like slipping into honey, warm and sweet and syrupy.

It feels right. It's time to tell him. The fake relationship is over, and now they have… what? Something real, Ben hopes. It's the realest thing Ben's ever felt.

He breathes Jamie in and fantasizes about not getting out of this bed all day. Their legs are tangled together, the sole of one of Jamie's feet resting on top of Ben's. Being able to feel his calluses seems intimate and vulnerable.

It's crazy that this all started over a promotion.

Ben's joy stutters. The promotion. Work. His career. It seems obvious now that he allowed work to take over everything to fill the emptiness he'd cleared in himself, thinking a career was all there was.

Jamie helped him find those parts of himself he thought were gone.

Does he even want the promotion anymore?

Before he has time to consider the question—and somehow *question* doesn't seem like a big enough word for it—Jamie stirs.

Ben pulls Jamie closer, focusing on how Jamie's back feels pressed to his chest, how their hips fit together, how he can't tell whose leg is where or if he's smelling himself on Jamie or Jamie on him. "Morning," Jamie yawns.

Softly, Ben kisses the back of Jamie's head. Curls tickle his lips. "Morning, schmoopy," Ben replies.

There's a snort. Jamie wriggles against him, then rolls over with an *oof*. The backs of his knuckles graze down Ben's jaw, tickling against his beard. "Pookie," he says, arching an eyebrow.

"Honeybuns," Ben shoots back.

"Dreamboat."

"Aw, thanks."

Jamie smirks and kisses him. Ben's stomach drops out of his body and his head swirls. When Jamie pulls back, Ben wraps him up tighter and goes in for another kiss. Now's the time. They're warm and tangled together in bed, and the way Jamie's looking at him.... Ben's sure. He's not nervous. He's not scared. Yesterday, his head was telling him it was too soon. His heart, though—his heart knows this is right. Jamie's the one who helped him find his heart again. Jamie's the one who made him realize he had a heart to find and to fix.

"I love you," Ben says.

Jamie's eyes widen. The sunlight catches them, and the blue pierces Ben straight through his heart. "You... what?"

Ben holds his gaze. "I love you."

A slow, uncertain smile inches over Jamie's face. "Me. You love... *me*."

It makes Ben ache with competing happiness and sadness that he's so incredulous. Jamie deserves to be told how loved he is every second of every day. "Of course you," he says. He brushes his thumb over Jamie's cheekbone. "Of course."

Jamie's Adam's apple moves sharply. Something flickers in his eyes that Ben can't read, exactly, but can guess at.

"You don't have to say it back," Ben says. "I just wanted to tell you."

There's still a look in Jamie's eyes that Ben can't quite figure out. But he snuggles close and buries his face in Ben's neck, and he repeats against Ben's skin, "You *love* me," like it's still the most farfetched thing he can imagine.

Ben kisses his forehead and leaves his lips there, closing his eyes. He could stay in this moment forever—Jamie and him, the sun shining, and the truth finally out there. No more pretending.

Jamie's heartbeat echoes through Ben's body. His breathing is an adagio, and Ben feels like he's the cello it's being played on, resonant and deep, getting right into the marrow of your bones.

"What do you want to do today?" Ben finally asks.

"Stay right here," Jamie replies immediately.

"We can do that. At least until the thing with your family."

Jamie groans. "Maybe I'll tell them I'm sick."

With a chuckle, Ben says, "Don't. I want to meet them."

"Said no one, ever."

"I'm serious!" When Jamie snorts, Ben leans back so he can tip Jamie's chin up with a finger. "Don't get me wrong, it's pretty nerve-wracking, meeting your boyfriend's family."

"Is that who you are?" Jamie asks. There's a spark of mischief in his eyes. "My boyfriend?"

"If you want. Maybe you don't want that. Maybe—" Is he fucking this up already?

Jamie kisses him gently, and Ben's spiral halts. When Jamie breaks the kiss, he murmurs, "As far as my family is concerned, you're my boyfriend. As far as I'm concerned...." His fingers brush through Ben's hair. "I don't know what to call this."

"We don't have to call it anything until you want to," Ben says.

He hopes it's the right thing to say. Jamie doesn't give him any indication that it isn't, except that tiny shadow at the back of his eyes that won't fade, even with the sunlight gilding them.

"You're really, really lovely, do you know that?" Jamie asks.

No one's ever told Ben that before Jamie, so no, he doesn't. Of all the qualities he considers good about himself, being lovely has never ranked. Why be lovely when you could be successful?

The last two weeks with Jamie have made Ben want to be lovely. The way Jamie looks at him has made him realize a truth that he's been busy pushing down for decades: that sometimes the mark you make on the world is the people who love you for who you are.

He doesn't want the promotion.

It feels like something that needs time to sink in, but somehow it doesn't. Ben knows it fully and completely, like it's been engraved on him. He feels a little sick. His plan was to be the youngest neurosurgeon-in-chief at NewYork-Presbyterian. Ever. His plan was to have a plaque on the wall listing all his accomplishments.

And that's all he'd ever be. A plaque on the wall. A name in the hospital records. A dusty profile on LinkedIn. If he doesn't try for the promotion? He'd be Jamie's. He'd be the man Jamie Anderson loved. He'd be—a husband? A father, maybe? He'd have a brother-in-law and a father-in-law. They could get a dog. Or a cat. Or both!

Okay, he's totally getting ahead of himself here. The point is….

The point is, getting the promotion will bring him success. Creating something real with Jamie? That will bring him happiness.

His arms tighten around Jamie. He's about to say *I love you* again, but Jamie lifts his head and meets his eyes. They're nose to nose, and that shadow in Jamie's gaze is finally gone. "Ben," he says, "I—"

Ben's phone goes off. Both of them jump. It's the special ringtone he uses for emergencies, for when the hospital needs to get through to him. "Shit," he groans. "I have to get this. Don't move."

"I won't," Jamie says, smirking.

His phone is still screaming, so Ben rolls out of bed and answers. "Hey," he says as he walks out of the room, knowing it's the ED charge nurse on the line. He already knows what he's going to hear, too, because the charge nurse would only call for one reason: they're understaffed in the ED because the neurosurgeon called in sick; they have three critical cases from a crash on the Turnpike—airlifted to NewYork-Presbyterian. They have to go into surgery *now*, and there's no one in the building to do it.

"I'll be there as soon as I can," Ben says.

His brain kicks his body into gear and he's racing through the apartment on autopilot—sixty-second shower, pop a caffeine pill, throw on the first clean thing he can find. Jamie's standing in his bedroom when Ben strides out of the bathroom.

"I have to go to work," Ben says, his voice clipped.

"Oh," Jamie says.

He should eat something before he goes into surgery. He's still waiting for that caffeine pill to kick in, but when it does, he'll be jittery without food. There should be a few energy bars in the kitchen—he'll grab one on the way out.

"I don't know when I'll be back, but you're welcome to hang out if you want," Ben says, grabbing his shoes and jamming his feet into them. "I'll have to come back here and change before dinner. But if you have stuff to do, I can just meet you at the restaurant."

"Oh," Jamie repeats. And then, "Yeah, I'll… yeah. I have some stuff to do."

"Okay, just lock the door when you leave." He straightens up, crosses the room to Jamie, and gives him a quick kiss. His mind is whirring through what he's going to need to do to stabilize two of the three critical cases in the ED, because he can't operate on all three at once.

These are his patients now, and he does *not* lose patients.

"Dinner at eight? I'll see you there." And then he's gone, flying out the door, a couple energy bars jammed in his back pocket. It's not until he's prepping for surgery, changing into scrubs and shoving his clothes into his locker, that his fingers brush over the glass bead of the bracelet Jamie bought him, and his brain spins to a stop. Just for a second, he's the calm in the storm, the eye of the hurricane.

He remembers the expression on Jamie's face as he left.

He remembers that Jamie looked devastated.

# CHAPTER THIRTY-ONE

IT'S FUNNY how the most perfect, beautiful moment can turn dark with no warning. It doesn't take anything at all to douse even the most blazing happiness. One phone call. One reminder of what exactly all of this is. What it's always been. What it always, ultimately, will be.

Jamie doesn't want to look at the bed. He doesn't want to look at his clothes scattered on the floor. They got dressed to eat dinner last night, but Ben tore them off when they got bored with not being naked together. The memory of how hungrily Ben touched him, how hungrily Ben kissed him everywhere, is like a knife twisting in his gut. It's also arousing, and that makes him ashamed of himself, because look, here he is. Jamie the idiot, Jamie the sentimental dickhead who never ever learns.

Here he is, getting involved with a man against every single one of his better instincts. Here he is, convinced this man is The One, only for The One to blow him off for something more important.

And Jamie knows. He *knows*. Ben's a surgeon, and it was obviously an emergency, and when you're a surgeon, you don't get to say, *Oh sorry, I'm not feeling it—I can't come in and repair that person's severed spinal cord.* The fact that Ben left to do his job, his actually important job, doesn't mean what he said to Jamie isn't true. It doesn't mean he doesn't l— He was telling the truth when he said he's in lo—

Jamie takes a deep, centering breath, which doesn't do a fucking thing to center him. Oh god, is he supposed to hold the breath for five seconds? Eight seconds? He normally uses an app and he doesn't know how to breathe centeringly without it.

He squeezes his eyes shut and stands in Ben's bedroom. Last night, he was hyperaware of every part of his body, every inch of skin, every nerve. The same thing is happening now, only like, the worst timeline version of it. Now, he's hyperaware of every inch of his body, but all of it seems wrong and painful. His skin prickles like a dull razor is scraping over it. His head hurts, but like, along each seam of his skull? Is that possible? Can he feel the seams of his skull?

He can't breathe. There's something on his chest. He knows it's an anxiety attack, because he's had them ever since he was twelve, but it doesn't make it any easier to breathe.

Being here isn't helping. It smells like Ben; it smells like the two of them. It smells like sex. And this was stupid. They shouldn't have had sex. They shouldn't have admitted they had real feelings. Jamie knew better. He knew better and he went and fucking did it anyway, because of how Ben looks at him and smiles at him and laughs at his jokes, and just—

A sob grabs his throat, and he chokes it down ruthlessly, dashing the back of his hand across his eyes to take care of the tears that stupidly sprung up at the same time.

Getting dressed is torture, because he remembers the way Ben took off each and every article of clothing, right down to his socks. His cheeks are wet by the time he gets everything on.

Maybe he should have showered, but he can't stand the thought of smelling Ben's shampoo and soap. If he does, he'll lose it completely.

He takes the train home, his ratty JanSport backpack hugged to his chest. At least no one on the subway stares at you when you're obviously going through something. Everyone does the civilized thing, which is to ignore someone having Awkward Emotions.

He's never going to be good enough. He's not mad Ben had to go to work today. He *gets it*. Today it's legit life or death. That's just regular neurosurgeon stuff. But Ben's going to get that promotion, and once he does, will he have time for anything else?

Will he even want to have time for anything else? Because it was pretty clear, when they first started all of this, that the only thing Ben cared about was his job. This promotion. All of this—every photo, every date, every text, every conversation, every interaction—has been in service of Ben getting his promotion.

The last two weeks have been a great big fantasy. Real dating isn't like the last two weeks. Real dating ends with Jamie's boyfriend realizing he's not the kind of guy you want to stay with. Because he's wrong, somehow. Not good enough. Too boring, or too needy, or too anxious. Too in love, too ready to be all in.

And that was with exes who didn't have an amazing, important job. All his boyfriends leave him because they find something better. Jamie watches it happen every time. But Ben already has something better. The newness will wear off, and then Ben will be with a guy he never would have been with if not for their fake relationship.

Ben will realize he got caught up in a fantasy. He'll leave, because that's what everyone always does. Jamie isn't good enough to make them stick around.

It's the most agonizing feeling, because he won't, he can't, he refuses to be anyone but himself. But that means living with the fact that who he is just isn't that great.

He gets home. Showers. Thinks about getting dressed and doesn't. Instead, he crawls into bed and pulls his comforter over his head.

Ben didn't even seem sad about not spending the day together. Doesn't that just prove that every single one of Jamie's worst fears is true? Ben's important. His job is important. He saves lives. He doesn't have time to waste his breath with apologies or *I really wish I didn't have to go in but I have to operate on all the most adorable children in the orphanage. I'll make it up to you. What kind of flowers do you like?*

Would Ben have gotten him flowers? Maybe he would have bought more peanuts so they could feed squirrels together.

In the stuffy darkness under his duvet, Jamie laughs. And then he sobs. And then he shoves the duvet into his face, because he's not going to sob, he's not going to fucking sob. He won't. So what if the peanuts Ben gave him when they left for Andy's the other day are still in Jamie's backpack? So what if he was looking forward to sharing that with Ben? It's dumb and silly, but no one's ever humored him about it before, and Ben did.

Ben did *now*. But it wouldn't take long for it to go from endearing to irritating and stupid, an idiotic, childish thing that someone with nothing important to offer society does.

That's the other thing it comes down to, isn't it? Ben is important. Maybe Jamie's going to be working in finance in a few weeks, doing whatever he'll be doing for Peter, but it's not neurosurgery. Jamie suspected at the very beginning of all this that Ben thought he was better than him because of his job and his money. Then he thought he misjudged Ben, and a lot of what came off as arrogance and snobbery was just Ben being awkward.

What if he was right? What if Ben always thought he was better? What if he saw himself as Jamie's savior?

Jamie's phone buzzes. He ignores it. He doesn't want to talk to anyone. He doesn't want to see anyone. He might never come out of this room.

His stomach turns over. Dinner. He's supposed to have dinner with Dad and Tyler and Ben.

The thought makes his chest screw so tight that for a minute he really, honestly thinks he's suffocating. He throws the duvet off and sucks in shallow breaths through his mouth. The air feels fifty degrees cooler without the duvet covering him, which would be great, except he can't breathe. His lungs won't fill; it's like they're half-full of sand or sludge and the air only penetrates part of the way.

If just the thought of dinner is giving him this bad of an anxiety attack, what's the actual dinner going to be like? How the fuck is he going to get ready, get there, face Ben and his family and pretend like nothing's wrong?

He's been pulling off this fake relationship like he's an award-winning actor playing the role of a lifetime. But pulling off a real relationship when he can feel the whole thing falling apart barely twenty-four hours after it started? That's beyond him. He can't fix this. There's no point in trying.

He pulls the duvet up to his chin and closes his eyes. His phone buzzes again.

Jamie turns it to Do Not Disturb.

# Chapter Thirty-Two

It's after six when Ben leaves the hospital. He's exhausted and he feels shitty about the way he left Jamie. What must Jamie have thought, the way Ben rushed out of there? He's just so used to being on his own and going into doctor mode when he has to. Habits are hard to break.

He picks up a sad bouquet of yellow and orange roses in the hospital gift shop on his way out, and thank god he notices the little Get Well Soon card stuck in them before he gets home. Not that he thinks Jamie will still be there. But he still kind of hopes.

Jamie's not there. Ben tempers the disappointment by texting him: *At home getting changed now. I'll definitely be on time!*

He stands in the living room waiting for Jamie to respond. Jamie doesn't. Why should he? Is Ben envisioning him staring at his phone, waiting for a text?

But he didn't have a single text from Jamie when he got out of surgery. He was hoping maybe…. Okay, but no, that's stupid. Jamie said he had things to do; he was probably just busy.

Except Jamie always found time to text him over the past few weeks, even when he was at work.

Ben rakes a hand through his hair, puts his phone on the wireless charger, and strips his clothes off to shower. He tidies up his beard and puts on some cologne, and there's no text from Jamie when he's done.

By the time he leaves, there's still no text, but Ben's determined to stop thinking about it. Maybe Jamie just went to hang out with his dad and brother early and he's not checking his phone. Being present, or whatever.

He arrives at the restaurant twenty minutes early, popping inside to look for Jamie. Still no text. But it's okay. He's early.

At five to eight, two men go inside. Ben eyes them, thinking maybe the old one has Jamie's eyes? Maybe the young one has the same jaw? But Jamie isn't with them, and Ben's pretty well talked himself into believing that the only reason Jamie hasn't texted back is because he's with his family, so he dismisses the idea that this could be the family.

Then the young man who maybe has Jamie's jaw comes back out, looks up and down the sidewalk, and finally focuses on Ben. "Hi, sorry, this is weird, but I think you're my brother's boyfriend?"

"Are you Tyler?"

"Yeah. Um, Jamie never actually told me your name."

Ben offers a handshake and introduces himself, adding, "I figured Jamie was with you."

Tyler's forehead crinkles. He looks a lot like Jamie when he does it. "Dad and I haven't heard from him since yesterday."

Unease creeps through Ben's stomach. "Really?"

"Yeah." Tyler shrugs. "But that's pretty normal for Jamie. He's bad at texting back."

Ben checks his phone again, just in case he missed the buzz of an incoming text. Nope. Still nothing.

"Well." Ben eyes the time. It's eight, and this is a popular restaurant, and they're not going to hold the table forever. Even though it's not going to make Jamie text, he still opens his messages and looks. Nothing. Not even three dots to show Jamie's typing. His most recent message is unread.

The unease in the pit of his stomach grows.

"They'll seat us now," Tyler says. "Dad's probably already at the table. He's sick of being on his feet."

"Yeah, uh—" Ben checks up and down the sidewalk for Jamie again. Nothing. "Yeah, let's go in. We can at least get a drink or something."

They're brought to the table, where the older man who maybe has Jamie's eyes is sitting. He eyes Ben sharply. Jamie hasn't said much about his family, but it's pretty obvious the relationship between his dad and him is complicated. The only thing he's ever said about his mom is "she left" in the kind of tone that Ben's socially adept enough to know means *back off this conversation.*

"Hello, sir," Ben says. "I'm Ben McNatt."

Jamie's dad gets to his feet. His hair is mostly white, though here and there are streaks of black—the same black as Jamie's hair. Under the wrinkles and lines in his face, Ben can see the same sharp nose and cheekbones that give Jamie his angles and character.

"Gary Anderson." His handshake is firm. "Tyler tells me you and Jamie are seeing each other."

"Yeah," Ben says. "Yeah, it's been…." Is he really going to lie to these people? What choice does he have? He can't tell the truth and then let Jamie get blindsided by them knowing when he gets here. "It's been a few months."

"Hm." Gary regards him, sizing him up. Ben feels deeply inadequate, which man, would have pissed him off a few weeks ago, because how dare someone make him feel inadequate? He's a damn neurosurgeon; no one should be able to make him feel inadequate.

That version of himself seems far away now. Now he's wondering if he can measure up to what Gary Anderson wants for his son.

Their waiter arrives at the table and Tyler says, "Dad, you can grill Ben once we have something to drink."

Gary lets out a snort of laughter, and that's pure Jamie too. Maybe that's the problem with their relationship—they're too much alike.

They all order drinks—wine for Ben, beer for Tyler and Gary. And still no Jamie. Ben checks his phone. It's starting to feel like a nervous tic. His last text is still unread, and Jamie still hasn't sent anything. He hasn't tried to call, either. Should Ben try to call him?

"So, Ben," Gary says. "What do you do for a living?"

"I'm a surgeon at NewYork-Presbyterian." Ben has to pause as their waiter brings the bottle of wine and waits for him to taste it.

Once he's given his approval and they all have their drinks, Tyler says, "That's cool. Surgery! So you're like *Grey's Anatomy*?"

"Not as dramatic," Ben says, sipping his wine.

"Do you do open-heart surgery?" Tyler asks.

Ben always got the impression that Tyler really took after their dad, but he doesn't actually look or sound much like him. Tyler's hair is a light brown instead of black, and there's less sharpness in his face.

"Neurosurgery."

Gary looks surprised and pleased. "How in the world did you meet Jamie?"

Tyler looks at him and makes a face. "You know there are more ways to meet people than at school or work, Dad. Come on."

Waving a hand, Gary says, "I'm just asking. It's a normal question. Isn't it, Ben?"

"Yeah, no, it's normal," Ben says, though the way Gary asked was definitely on the catty side. "We met at Jamie's coffee shop, actually."

"You mean the coffee shop Jamie works at," Gary says with the air of someone correcting a particularly idiotic spelling mistake. Ben has no idea what Jamie's dad does for a living, but he hopes it's not teaching elementary school kids.

"Right, the Daily Grind," Ben says, figuring he's not selling Jamie out if he's noncommittal in his agreement. "I go there every day, and… well, yeah, one day I was ordering my regular drink and I finally asked him out."

Tyler cocks his head. "Jamie said you asked each other to dinner at the same time after you walked him to the train station."

"So you do talk to your brother," Gary says, sounding mildly affronted.

"Yeah, but you know how he is, it's like pulling teeth to get him to tell you anything." Looking back to Ben, he adds, "It stuck out that he told me that. It's sweet. Jamie deserves that."

"He does," Ben agrees.

"But you just said you asked him out when you were ordering coffee."

"Uh, I asked if I could walk him to his train," Ben says, thinking fast. "I guess in my head I think of that like our first date." Shit. Jamie wouldn't have fucked up their story. Where *is* he?

Tyler's checking his phone too, looking uncertain for the first time. Ben would love to say, *Hey this is weird, right? Jamie usually doesn't do stuff like this?* But the truth is, he doesn't really know if this is weird. Maybe Jamie is habitually late, and he was on good behavior for Ben.

There's an awkward silence. Feeling like he needs to fill it, Ben says, "So, what do both of you do for a living?"

Looking unsurprised, Tyler says, "Jamie's never mentioned it?"

"Uh…."

"I own one of the oldest operating repair shops in Hartford," Gary says.

Can Ben get away with pretending he just forgot? "Oh, right," he says. "I can't remember if you specialize in European cars or not."

Tyler snorts into his beer, which is Ben's first clue he just stepped in it. Gary looks tired. "It's a vacuum repair shop."

Ben surreptitiously checks out the space beneath neighboring tables to see if he can crawl underneath any of them.

"Jamie's always been embarrassed by it," Gary says. "He didn't want anything to do with the business."

"He's not embarrassed," Tyler says. "He just…."

"He's embarrassed, Tyler. He hasn't even told his boyfriend what we do."

Tyler leans across the table. "He just felt trapped, Dad. C'mon. He wanted bigger things."

After a gulp of beer, Gary says, "Something better than anything I could offer him. Just like your mother."

Looking pained, Tyler says, "Let's talk about something else." He shoots an apologetic smile at Ben, who couldn't agree more. Jamie can get here any time now.

He doesn't. Fifteen minutes pass, then thirty, then forty-five.

It is, without a doubt, the most awkward forty-five minutes of Ben's entire life. He can't decide whether he should be worried about Jamie or mad at him, and neither Gary nor Tyler are giving him many clues. They both seem to think that if something bad happened to Jamie, Ben would know about it—but Ben doesn't know about it, because he's never even been inside Jamie's house, because they've only been pretending to date until the last forty-eight hours, and something's wrong. Something has to be wrong, because Ben sees the way Jamie looks at him and it's real, and it means something.

But it doesn't change that Jamie isn't here, and their waiter is getting less subtle with his hints that he wants them to leave if they're not going to order any food.

After a particularly brutal four minute and twenty-seven second stretch of silence, Ben says, "Um, Jamie should be here by now."

"Jamie should have been here an hour ago," Gary says brusquely.

Yeah, that doesn't solve anything or help the situation in the slightest.

"I'm calling him," Tyler says decisively. Which helps a little more. It also leaves Ben and Gary alone while Tyler gets up to make the call.

A minute passes. Ben's given this dinner up for a lost cause, and he's trying to catch the waiter's eye to pay for their drinks.

"I don't mean to be hard on him," Gary says. Ben glances over, wondering if he's talking to someone else. Nope. No one else within earshot. "He was the sweetest little boy. Looked at me like I was his hero." Gary takes another swallow of beer. "I don't know what happened. He got older, and we didn't understand each other anymore. Maybe I didn't handle the gay thing right. It didn't matter to me. He's my kid. But I didn't know how to talk to him about it."

Ben just sits. Gary doesn't expect him to respond, does he? Gary coughs. "You get along with your parents?"

"My parents passed away when I was thirty," Ben says. "I guess we got along. We weren't close."

"Yeah." Gary shakes his head. "Fathers and sons. It's hard. I didn't get along with mine."

The conversation sputters out, and Ben cranes his head to look for Tyler. His hope that Jamie's going to show has died, and he's pretty much resigned himself to sitting here stewing until Tyler comes back.

"Do you love Jamie?"

Gary's voice startles Ben. The question startles him even more. "Yeah," Ben says. "Yeah, I do."

Gary nods and gruffly replies, "Good."

The waiter swings by again, not bothering to smile. "Are you ready to order yet?" he asks flatly.

Before Ben can say no, and can they please get the check, Tyler reappears. "He answered his phone."

Ben's on his feet, though he doesn't remember standing. "Is he okay? Where is he?"

The look on Tyler's face is exasperated and sad at the same time. "He's… I'm not supposed to say where he is."

Fear clenches tight in Ben's chest. "*Is he okay?*"

Tyler hesitates, looking like he's choosing his words carefully. "He's not in any kind of trouble."

The world telescopes in this weird, sickening way, and Ben hears himself say, "He's at home, isn't he?" Tyler doesn't answer, and that's the answer. Ben drops two hundred dollars on the table, says, "It was nice meeting you," and then he's gone.


THE DOOR of Jamie's building is propped open, music spilling out onto the street. Bass thumps from an apartment and people throng the hall, which is hazy with pot and cigarette smoke. Ben gets halfway down the hall, saying, "Excuse me," on a robotic loop, before he realizes he doesn't know which apartment Jamie lives in. He doesn't even know what floor. But he gets lucky, and the third person he asks is one of Jamie's roommates.

The door to the apartment isn't locked. Ben shuts it behind him and stands in the living room, his head and heart pounding in time with the music he can hear through the walls.

"Jamie?" he calls.

There's no answer, but a shadow moves across the light showing under one of the closed bedroom doors. Ben slowly walks toward it. "Jamie," he tries again. "Are you okay?"

"I'm fine. You should go."

Ben's heart leaps at the words. Well, at the fact Jamie's talking to him. "Can I come in?"

"No."

"Please, Jamie."

Silence. He can't be fine. Something obviously happened. He should have brought the flowers in, but they're still sitting in the passenger seat of his car.

"You don't seem okay," Ben says, leaning his forehead against the door. "You wouldn't have ghosted your family and me if you were okay."

The door swings open. Jamie's face looks puffy; his eyes are red. "You think so?" he demands, a strangled note in his voice. "You really think so, Ben? How do you know?"

Ben doesn't retreat. "Because I know you."

"You don't. You think you know me. Guess what?" Jamie looks a little wild. "This is it! This is the real me! I flake on plans. I turn off my phone. I'm not a perfect little fantasy boyfriend!"

The first spark of irritation flares in Ben's chest. "What are you saying? You didn't show up because you were trying to prove something?"

Jamie clenches his fists and looks away. Ben waits. And waits.

And then he realizes.

Nothing's wrong. Nothing happened. Jamie didn't show up because he didn't feel like it.

And that. That fucking hurts.

His voice souring, Ben begins, "We agreed I was going to help you with your brother and dad—"

"Well, aren't you just my *hero*," Jamie spits.

The venom in his voice takes Ben aback. His mouth snaps shut. But then his own defensiveness rears its head. After everything, how can Jamie act like the last two days never happened?

"I was never trying to be your hero," Ben says.

Jamie laughs, a hard, bitter sound. "Oh, well, you could've fooled me. You sweep in and ask me if I want to be a glorified escort, like you're a fucking white knight, because obviously I need help, with my stupid shitty coffee shop job—"

"Are you serious right now?" Something is bubbling up in Ben's chest, and he can't tell if it's frantic, insane laughter at the way everything is falling apart so spectacularly—or tears. "That was never—I didn't—"

"You've always thought you were better than me!" Jamie's voice is a crack straight through the foundations of Ben's heart. "And that I need your help because you're a doctor and you've got your shit together, and you could just stroll in and solve all my problems, and you think—you think—"

Ben wants to fight back, to defend himself, to be cold, precise, unflappable Doctor Ben McNatt. But that's not who he is anymore—and it's because of Jamie. He's just Ben, the guy who wears a roller skate tie, who dances like a fool at a gay club, who does silly dinosaur imitations. Just Ben, who found the heart he tried so hard to bury and fell in love with a man who made him feel like himself for the first time in his whole life.

Now that man is shoving him away. Pushing him into freeway traffic. Onto the third rail. Off a bridge.

Jamie's shoulders heave. Anything Ben might have said is knocked away by his accusations. Maybe Jamie's right. Maybe deep down, Ben did think those things.

"I think what?" Ben asks, wanting his voice to come out strong and hard, like he has a handle on himself. Like he's not crumbling into a million pieces.

He fails. He sounds small and sad, and exactly like he's crumbling into a million pieces.

Jamie looks wound tight enough to crack. Something blazes in his eyes, something that looks a lot like fury. Or maybe misery. Or loathing. Or all three mixed together in a toxic slurry.

"You think I'm a loser who needs you. But I don't," Jamie snarls. "I don't need you, Ben. So just—leave. Leave me alone. Get out."

Ben does.

He turns around. He walks out of the apartment, through the crowded, hazy hallway, out the front door, and down the sidewalk to his car. He gets inside, and he starts it up. The flowers on the passenger seat look sad and wilted and pathetic. He pulls away from the curb.

He makes it across the Macombs Dam Bridge before he has to pull over, because he's crying too hard to see.

# CHAPTER THIRTY-THREE

THE ONLY good thing about the next morning is that Jamie and Val are on the schedule together. Knowing he gets to spend the day with his BFF is a lifeline for Jamie's emotions. Even if he wanted to talk about what happened, he can't, because Val thinks Ben and him were together for months, and he's not planning on coming clean with her.

Jamie gets there earlier than normal because he can't sleep, so he's done with the opening stuff before Val arrives. "Don't say I never did anything for you," he jokes when she comes in.

She takes a look around the coffee shop, grunts, and walks into the back.

It's not like her. Maybe she's tired.

She's like that all day, though. When Jamie tries to make conversation, her answers are monosyllabic. When she looks at him, which isn't often, she's glaring. By lunchtime, Jamie's stomach is churning, because something's obviously up with her, and he's positive it has to do with him. But he doesn't know what he did wrong.

The fact that he feels the shittiest he's ever felt in his entire life and she's making him feel even worse makes him mad, which he knows is unreasonable. His heart is too wrung out to be reasonable, though. His stomach feels like anxiety has gnawed a hole through it. He needs a friend. He expected a friend.

The minute Jamie locks the door at close, he rounds on her. "Okay, what did I do?"

She stops mopping. "Are you serious?"

"Yeah, I'm pretty fucking serious!" His voice catches and goddammit, he's not going to cry, no matter how much he wants to. "You know, I'm feeling really shitty right now, so if you have a problem with me, why don't you just fucking say it?"

She shoves the mop in the bucket so hard that water sloshes over the sides. "Okay, Jamie, I'll *fucking say it*. Why did you lie about you and Ben?"

Hearing Ben's name is like a punch to the gut. "What?"

"You. Lied. About. Ben." Her glare makes every ounce of his irritation with her disappear. "I straight-up guessed you two weren't really dating, and you insisted you were. But you weren't. I was right. You lied to me. So yeah, I'm pissed at you!"

His first instinct is to deny the whole thing was fake. It's over now, so what does it matter if it was fake for 90 percent of the time and real the last 10 percent, until Jamie fucked it up? "I didn't lie—"

"Oh my god." She drops the mop handle. The entire bucket tips over, spilling soapy beige water. It pools around her ankle boots and creeps across the floor. "That picture you sent me the other day? Of you two on your 'second date?'"

Jamie's all in now, so he has to commit to the lie. "Yeah? What about it? We went to Central Park—"

"I was with you when you bought that shirt, asshole," Val interrupts. "It was three weeks ago."

His stomach shrivels. She's right.

He opens his mouth, but he doesn't know what to say. Val's face goes from angry to hurt to frigid. "Yeah," she says. "Exactly."

"Okay, I'm sorry I lied about it," Jamie says quickly. "It was a whole thing, it was this whole…. It doesn't matter, but I really needed Andy to not find out I didn't have a real boyfriend, because he invited me to that party and I said I had one, and one of his friends was going to offer me a job, so I couldn't piss him off—" He's not explaining this well at all, and Val's expression is getting more and more incredulous with each word his mouth vomits out. "I had to get out of this hellhole, you don't get it—"

"Because this is all I'm good for?" Val snaps. "Because I don't have a college education too? Because I'm not completely overqualified for this place? I actually have another job, in case you forgot, Jamie!"

"No, that's not… I didn't mean that." This conversation was never on the rails, but it's currently careening into the East River. "I just didn't want you to let anything slip to Andy, because then he'd be pissed off at me—"

Val rips her apron over her head and flings it on the ground. It lands in the water. "I get it. You think I can't keep a secret, even when it's important to you. You didn't trust me not to blab to Andy."

"I trusted you, it's just that sometimes you tell people stuff and it gets back to the person who isn't supposed to know—"

"Oh my god, fuck you!" She laughs, hard and unamused. "Fuck you so much, Jamie. Have fun with your fake boyfriend and your new job with Andy's friend."

With that, she throws open the door to the back. Jamie can hear her gathering her stuff, and he's trying to figure out what to say to her when she comes back out. But she doesn't.

The door to the alley slams, and Jamie is left alone in the Daily Grind, water creeping around his Chucks—just one more mess to clean up.

It takes him an extra twenty minutes to mop up the water and close everything by himself. When he's done, he takes his apron off and hangs it up. For a minute, he stares at it.

Is he really going to come back here for the next two weeks before starting his new job with Peter's company? For what? The opportunity to get groped by Andy a few more times? Strained shifts with Val, assuming she doesn't get her schedule changed to avoid him? Watching the clock tick down to six fifteen, dreading and hoping he'll see Ben walk through the doors, just like always?

Jamie gathers his things, sets the security alarm, and locks the coffee shop. Before he walks away, he opens a text to Andy.

*Hey it's Jamie from work. Today was my last day*

He blocks Andy's number, then opens another text.

*If I take the train up to Hartford tomorrow, can you pick me up at the station?*

The reply comes back immediately. **Are you srsly asking me to pick you up after yesterday**

*Yeah isn't that what big brothers are for?*

This time there's a pause. Then: **I'll be there**

*Thanks Tyler. Love you*

**Love you too, buttface**

A smile doesn't quite manage to crack his face, but his misery feels slightly less miserable.

The urge to look back at the Daily Grind prickles at the back of his neck. Jamie forces himself to keep his eyes on what's in front of him.

The solution to his problems was never going to fall in his lap. Ben coming along with the perfect fix for everything was always too easy. A nice fantasy, but it was never going to be real. No one's going to fix anything for Jamie except Jamie.

Everything he's let go wrong sinks through him and hits iron at his core. Maybe he can't fix everything, but he can try to fix some of it. He has a tab in his browser history that seems like the right place to start.

# CHAPTER THIRTY-FOUR

NOT MAKING the six fifteen trip to the Daily Grind feels wrong.

On Monday, Ben drives out to Montauk and watches breakers roll in. He reschedules surgeries on Tuesday so they'll take place during that time. Walking over there to ~~see Jamie~~ get his evening coffee goes beyond habit. It's so ingrained that on Wednesday, when he doesn't fill the time with something else, he gets outside the hospital before he realizes he can't go to the Daily Grind ever again.

Okay, that's dramatic. He can't go to the Daily Grind until Jamie moves on to his new job. Except why would he want to go to the Daily Grind once Jamie moves on to his new job? The coffee isn't that great. It was always the staff. It was always Jamie.

Ben remembers what he thought the first time he walked in. It wasn't on his way to anything—not home, not work. He was just taking a walk through the neighborhood, and he's always up for trying a coffee place that isn't Starbucks.

He pushed open the door and saw this gorgeous man behind the counter, tall and lean and laughing at something his coworker was saying. And he thought, *It would be an amazing feeling to make that man laugh.*

As he stands on the sidewalk in front of the hospital, Manhattan heaves around him. Ben forces himself to let the city flow past. He forces himself to stand there. To feel it. To feel what it is to stand still while everything else moves, while the whole wide world throws itself into life. Into heartbreaks and failures. Into missed opportunities and roads not taken. Into long shots and not-part-of-the-plans. Into living life for *life*, living it for yourself, and not for what someone else expects you to be—even if that someone else is yourself and your misplaced ideas of what it means to be a success.

This is who he's been. He's been standing still while life moves around him. He thought he had it all figured out, but he never did. Not until Jamie reminded him that there was another Ben McNatt, the long-buried Ben McNatt willing to take a chance. The Ben McNatt who isn't terrified to be who he is, because who he is is *enough*.

He touches his wrist. Leather meets his fingertips, and smooth glass warmed by his skin. Being a person who made Jamie Anderson laugh, who Jamie Anderson wanted to be with, even if it was only for a few weeks, made him happier than all the awards, all the accolades, all the money ever did.

Even if Jamie doesn't want to be with him, no one can ever take that away. He'll carry it forever, a warm, untouchable glow to light his way when he feels like he's not right, or not enough, or that he'll never belong.

He touches the bracelet again.

*Even if it was only for a few weeks.* Who is he kidding? A few weeks wasn't enough. What Ben feels for Jamie, that's once in a lifetime stuff. Love of your life stuff. Ben knows he can't just let Jamie go, but—

But he also knows there are things about him that need to change. Not for Jamie. For Ben, because now he knows what makes him happy, and he knows what's incompatible with that happiness. He knows he can't just do the right thing, call Jamie up, and say, *Guess what? I have my priorities straight now. Can we pick up where we left off?*

That's not how it works. Who knows if Jamie wants him? Who knows if Ben wants Jamie, after that fight?

That's stupid. Of course Ben wants Jamie. He'll want Jamie until every last synapse in his brain fades to black, until every electrical pulse in every neuron and soma and axon sends its last signal.

He checks his watch. He knows what he has to do. He's known what he had to do, he thinks, for days.

So he turns around to go and do it.


"I'D LIKE to withdraw my name from consideration for neurosurgeon-in-chief."

Marie Kidjo looks at him like he's pranking her, and she doesn't want to look stupid for falling for it. "You do," she says, not a question at all, just a flat statement, like, ha-ha, I know you're pulling my leg, good one.

"Yes," Ben says.

Marie's smile fades. "I don't understand. This position has been in your sights for years. You've made it clear it's what you want."

He rubs the back of his neck. "Yeah. Yeah, I did."

"Because you know, we're very close to making a decision."

A twist of longing screws into his sternum, but—no. It's not longing. It's an echo of longing. The habit of it. She's right. This is what he's been gunning for. Now he's walking away. His amygdala hasn't caught up. Hell, he's probably got his desire for this job imprinted in his neural network.

"I assumed you were," Ben says. "That's why I wanted to let you know as soon as possible."

Marie's expression has gone from confused to full-on flabbergasted. "Ben, this is… shocking. I'm not exaggerating when I say this is the last thing I expected."

Does she think he's under duress? Like he's being put up to this? Is she afraid he has a bomb wired to his chest?

"I know it's coming out of the blue." Ben runs the pad of his thumb along the bracelet. "It is for me too, kind of. But the right move for me is staying where I am." The glass bead on the bracelet winks as it catches the light. He remembers that student approaching him in the locker room, thanking Ben for inspiring him to become a surgeon. Once, a long, long time ago, Ben was driven by the desire to help people too. Maybe it's not too late to get back to that.

"What if I told you you're the search committee's top choice?"

If he said he wasn't tempted, he'd be lying. His stomach lurches with victory, and the old surge of I'm-the-best adrenaline tears through him.

The temptation burns itself out. Ben keeps his fingers on the bracelet. "I'd say I'm honored by your regard for me, but it doesn't change anything. I no longer want to be considered for the position."

There's nothing more to say, so he stands. Marie still looks shell-shocked. "Another opportunity like this may not come along at New York-Presbyterian for decades," she says.

"I know," he says. He checks his watch. It's six forty-five. If he hurries, he can probably get to the West Village before seven. "I guess I'll just have to play things by ear."

A smile cracks her face. "Ben McNatt, something's come over you."

"Yeah," he agrees. "Tell me about it."

Six forty-six. Fourteen minutes until the Daily Grind closes.

Ben doesn't know if Jamie wants to see him, but he's not going to give up on them.

# CHAPTER THIRTY-FIVE

THE LAST few days have been a whirlwind, and now Jamie is sitting through an hour and a half of experimental theater. Without falling asleep. Without even yawning! Val isn't answering his texts, so he's making sure he talks to her by seeing her current production. He fucked up, he hurt someone he loves, and he's going to fix it.

When the show's over, Val clomps across the tiny stage in her ankle boots and thumps down in the seat next to him. "What are you doing here?"

He kind of deserves to be hated for the way he's treated people lately, so he's glad she's giving him a chance.

He leans forward, his elbows propped on his knees, and looks up at her. Her spine is ramrod straight and her lips are pursed, and she doesn't look like she wants to forgive him. He's going for it anyway. "This happens to be a stop on this month's Jamie Apology Tour."

"You have a monthly one, huh?"

"Yeah, well." He shrugs. "We used to do them biweekly, but maturity and self-reflection started cutting into the profit margins and we couldn't fill the seats."

She snorts and looks away.

Jamie sits up straighter. "Val, I'm really sorry. Lying was a dick move, and it was an even dickier move to do it because I didn't trust you. I do trust you. I panicked, but I was wrong."

There's a long silence. There's a low murmur of voices in the building. Finally, Val looks at him. "Why does everything have to be about dicks with you?"

Jamie tries not to grin. "I mean. I do have a thing for dicks."

She rolls her eyes, but a smile flashes over her face. "Ugh, you're impossible to be mad at when you do that kicked puppy look."

"Excuse me? I was *not* doing a kicked puppy look! I'm genuinely very sorry!"

"You're doing it now."

Jamie arranges his face into an angry grimace, but Val shakes her head. "I don't think you're capable of looking scary and angry for real."

He laughs, but he thinks about how he must have looked when he went off on Ben. And he's pretty sure she's wrong.

He's such an idiot. The worst part is not knowing if he did the right thing or not. On Sunday, he thought so. On Monday, when he went up to Hartford for the day to apologize to Dad and Tyler, he was less sure. Yesterday, when he went for the interview with Nina Noskova, all he wanted to do was call Ben to tell him.

Today, he's trying to sit with it. He made the choice to blow it up. If he wants to fix it, that's on him too—like he fixed things with Tyler and Dad. Like he's fixing things with Val. Like he's trying to fix the things in his own life he has control over.

And like—*fixing*. Fixing sounds so final. Like there's a set end point: you're here, and when it's fixed, you'll be *here*, and you won't have to work on it anymore.

That's not true. Sure, his relationship with Dad is strained. Jamie never bothered trying to make it better, because he didn't think it could be fixed. He couldn't envision a point where everything was better. He's never understood that it's okay to be fixing something forever. It's a work in progress.

Val elbows him. "Hey. Are you okay?"

This time when he smiles, it's sadder. "Oh, you know."

"Not really," she points out. "You've been lying to me for weeks."

"Okay, I deserved that."

"Yeah you did."

The voices from backstage get louder, and four people appear. They're Black, and they're also the kind of theater people that Jamie's always found intimidatingly cool.

"Hey Val, you coming or what?" one of them asks.

Getting to his feet, Jamie says, "Sorry, I should let you go out with your friends—"

Val stands and grabs his hand. "You're my friend too, idiot. And we're going to REBAR, so you pretty much have to come."

Hanging out with Val and her cool theater friends at REBAR sounds amazing. He turns to them. "Do any of you mind?"

A man with a shaved head, glittery eyeshadow, and wearing a dress with a *V* slit all the way to his belly button gives Jamie a once-over. "You're V's white friend with no friends, right?"

He shoots her a dirty look.

She grimaces. "Thanks a lot, Khalid. I had him feeling real bad for fucking up."

Khalid shrugs, a smile cutting across his face. "I'm down," he says. His eyes linger on Jamie. If it was a month ago, he would've been all over that. Especially after what happened with Ben. Jamie's definitely tried to cure heartbreak with hookups, but now....

He returns Khalid's smile but tries to imbue it with Thanks, you're hot and I appreciate the interest, but not tonight.

The person who asked if Val was ready hops down from the stage. They push their hair, curly and natural, out of their face. "Yeah, come along. I'm Joss."

"Joss the boss," the two women rounding out the group chorus.

Joss groans. "Y'all *need* to stop with that."

Khalid snickers. "That ain't happening."

Squeezing Jamie's hand, Val says, "Joss is our stage manager. Khalid's costumes. Ororo"—the woman with her hair in a ponytail waves—"does lighting, and June's our intern."

The other woman, the youngest out of everyone, says, "*Unpaid* intern, so y'all are buying tonight."

Val turns to Jamie. "Come out with us. It'll be fun. Also, I'm never gonna forgive you for lying about the fake boyfriend if you don't, so."

"The *what?*" Khalid asks, sounding delighted. "Okay, he's sitting by me in the Uber."

Joss yanks their phone out of their pocket. "Shit! The Uber. He's here. We gotta go before he leaves without us!"

As the six of them pile into the Uber, Jamie finds himself smiling for a longer stretch of time than he's smiled in days.

WEDNESDAY NIGHTS are quiet at REBAR. The dance floor is crowded but not packed, and you can usually find a space at the bar. Tables aren't impossible to find.

The six of them do shots before heading out to the floor to dance. Jamie dances with Val, with Joss, with Khalid, and finally, on his own, just like Robyn said.

Sweaty and tired, Jamie finds their table and flops into a chair. Val joins him, and the two of them sit in companionable silence, listening to the Hayley Kiyoko remix playing. Eventually, Val says, "So are you going to tell me why you're so sad?"

"Am I sad?"

She stares pointedly.

Slouching in the chair and rubbing his hands over his face, Jamie says, "Ugh."

"Good start, keep going."

"My fake boyfriend wasn't fake at the end."

When he risks a look at her, her eyes are wide. "Shit," she finally says.

"Yeah."

"You said *wasn't*."

"Yeah, I…." God, it sounds so stupid. "I broke up with him? I guess?"

"You caught real feelings for your fake boyfriend."

"Right."

"And then you broke up with him."

"Yeah."

To her credit, she's trying not to be mean. "Guess you decided really fast he wasn't boyfriend material?"

No, he decided really fast that *he* wasn't boyfriend material. He always knew he wasn't, but he let himself get swept away by his feelings for Ben.

"I guess," he says, because there's not much else to say.

Val drums her fingers on her leg. "Must have been a pretty good reason, considering he came by the coffee shop tonight looking for you."

An ache knifes through Jamie's chest. LO fucking L. It sure felt like a good reason when Ben showed up, finally privy to the one-step-above-squalor Jamie lives in. The hot, creeping shame that crawled over him in that moment makes him feel ashamed now. On top of everything else, Ben seeing Jamie isn't just broke in a funny ha-ha millennial way, but poor, was just… too much.

His IKEA mattress that should have been replaced years ago, the scuffed, beat-up desk he spotted outside another building and dragged five blocks because it was an actual *desk* someone threw out. It's the nicest piece of furniture he owns.

It got mixed up in his head. There was the knowledge that the Ben he was in love with wouldn't care, running headlong into his own self-doubt, wondering if maybe what attracted him to Ben was his money, after all.

He's mad at himself for thinking Ben might care and mad at Ben for not caring. He's mad at Ben for defying his expectations. He's mad at Ben because if he's not mad at Ben, he has to admit he was wrong, and he'll have to turn all that anger on himself.

He might not be doing as good of a job sitting with it as he thought.

Why would Ben come looking for him? He hasn't texted or called, and he could have, because even though Jamie thought about blocking his number, he couldn't bring himself to go through with it. Maybe Ben assumes he did.

"Did he seem pissed?" Jamie finally asks.

With a shrug, Val says, "He seemed sad."

Well.

Fuck.

"But I said you quit, and he seemed happy about that," she adds.

Fuck.

Crystal clarity hits Jamie, filtered through pounding bass and the barest alcohol haze. He's been hellbent on doing things his way his whole life. He'd move to New York, he'd get through college and grad school, he'd hack it here no matter what, and he didn't need any help from anyone. He didn't want Ben to save him, but he stuck Ben in the position of saving him anyway. He asked for help, and he got it. And then he punished Ben for it.

And Ben never wanted to save him, did he? Sure, Jamie accused him of it, but did Ben ever try? Did Ben ever do anything but make Jamie feel like he could do whatever he wanted all on his own? All Ben ever offered was his support, and Jamie—

Jamie got scared.

Who knows why Ben went to the Daily Grind tonight. Maybe he wanted to chew Jamie out. Maybe he wanted Jamie to do a work thing with him. Jamie kind of fucked that up for Ben.

There's a tiny, remote possibility that Ben came by because he doesn't hate Jamie. That's the one Jamie latches on to. What if everything isn't ruined forever? What if it's possible to repair the damage he did?

"Weird question," Jamie says. Val cocks an eyebrow. "Was Ben wearing a bracelet?"

She thinks. "Actually, yeah, he was."

"Leather?"

"Maybe? Why?"

The last few weeks have been the happiest of Jamie's entire life. He's laughed more, had more fun, felt more seen and listened to than he ever has. No boyfriend has ever made him feel like this. It's terrifying, but also? He'd be crazy to walk away from that.

The DJ interrupts the music to remind everyone about REBAR's Pride dance party on Friday night. Val lets out a whoop, but all Jamie can feel is something hollow rattling around his rib cage. He wanted to bring Ben to Pride.

Maybe he still can? If Ben's wearing the bracelet... if Ben came to the Daily Grind because he wanted to see Jamie, because he misses Jamie the same way Jamie misses him....

It's the tiniest, remotest possibility. Nevertheless, Jamie says, "Val—I think I know what the next stop on the Jamie Apology Tour is."

Step one: admit you fucked up. Step two: own up to your mistakes. Step three: face the possibility of rejection.

Step four: reach for happiness anyway.

# CHAPTER THIRTY-SIX

MANHATTAN IS a colorful, joyful shitshow during Pride. Jamie wouldn't trade it for anything, but holy hell is it impossible to get anywhere. It's not like you can be mad, not when everyone is so ebullient. Jamie loves Pride in New York. He'll never forget the visceral connection between everyone the first time he attended. These were his people, and he found them, and they were all in this together.

That's the feeling he wants Ben to have, even if Jamie ruined what was between them. The sadness in Ben's eyes when he said he didn't go to Pride anymore because he felt like he didn't belong? No one should ever feel that way. Especially not at Pride.

But also, if Ben doesn't feel it, that's okay too.

It'll also have to be okay if Ben doesn't want anything to do with him. It's *not* okay, but Jamie won't keep himself from living because he's too afraid of being hurt. If he can't open himself to the possibility of heartbreak, then how can he be open to its opposite?

Jamie clutches his sweaty hand tight. Cellophane crinkles and cuts into his palm. It was easy to be all inspirational and mature in the days leading up to this moment, but now that he's standing in front of Ben's door, this seems like maybe the worst idea he's ever had.

Maybe he and Ben will have a big dramatic moment where Ben chucks the flowers in Jamie's face, which totally feels like it should be from some classic romcom, but Jamie's wracking his brain and he can't come up with one. Maybe it's a TikTok.

Maybe he should stop thinking about this and knock on Ben's door, because he's never going to know how it all works out if he doesn't at least try.

He raps his knuckles on Ben's door. Footsteps thump inside and the door swings open.

Jamie's heart, his stomach, and at least half of the rest of his internal organs drop out of his body as he meets Ben's eyes. It's only been a week, but seeing Ben slots something into alignment within him that's been off-kilter since that night.

For the longest moment in the history of the planet, all they do is stare at each other. Ben's hair looks ruffled. There's stubble growing in around his beard. He's wearing a Jimmy Eat World T-shirt that's seen better days and joggers sitting low on his hips.

The bracelet Jamie bought him is cinched around his wrist.

He looks good. The unkempt, it's-Saturday-morning-and-I-have-nowhere-to-be look suits him. In another universe, Jamie would be inside the apartment with him, and maybe they wouldn't have gotten out of bed yet.

"Hi," Jamie says, because he has to say something. Ben looks like he doesn't know how to handle that, so Jamie thrusts the bouquet at him. It's a spray of blooms and color, dyed rainbow-hued for Pride, baby's breath dipped in glitter and a unicorn that would make Lisa Frank proud stuck right in the middle.

They weren't the *most* extra flowers, but they're pretty close.

Ben doesn't take them, but he also doesn't slam the door in Jamie's face. Jamie sucks in a breath. "I know you don't have any reason to talk to me like, ever again. I suck, and I don't blame you. I was a total asshole, and it wasn't you. It was never you, and it was always me and my shit, and I…." He prays Ben will take the flowers. "Will you come to Pride with me? Even if it's just as friends?"

Ben still looks like he doesn't know what to say. When he speaks, it's not what Jamie expects. "It was kind of me, though. Wasn't it?"

Jamie's arm is getting stiff, and the flowers are seeming like a worse idea the longer they stay in the space between them. "It wasn't. I just—" It's hard to say this out loud. But if Jamie can say the bad things, the horrible stuff that's the worst of him, then he should be able to say the good stuff too. The things that are the best of him.

Deep breath in. Deep breath out. "I got scared," he says. "I always go all in, and then I get hurt. The guys I've been with… they always left me, and it had to've been me, right? Like, something about me not being good enough. Maybe I wasn't worthy of love. So I got into the habit of pushing them away, and then when they left, it was like they were proving me right. I wasn't enough for them to stick around for."

There's this look in Ben's eyes that makes Jamie feel brave. "And with you… I thought, if I'm not enough for you, if you leave like everyone else always does, then I'"—something that feels like a sob crawls up his throat—"I couldn't stand it. I couldn't stand having you and losing you, so I thought it was better to just never have you. And just, why would I be enough for you, when you have your job, and… I guess what I'm saying is I have my shit. And I need to work on it. I *am* working on it. Fixing things. It's a work in progress. But I…."

He swallows. The longer Ben doesn't take the flowers, the more Jamie's heart falls. "But I was so wrong. The things I said to you. I'm so sorry. I don't want to be scared. Or at least, I don't want to let being scared stop us from trying this."

"I turned down the job," Ben says.

His words ring in the space between them. Jamie wonders if he misheard. "You… *what?*"

Ben rakes a hand through his hair. "I mean, I didn't actually get the job. I withdrew myself from consideration."

"I don't…." Jamie can't wrap his head around this. "You wanted that promotion."

There's a wry quirk at one corner of Ben's mouth, like, *yeah, no shit*. "I had kind of an epiphany about my priorities. And the things that make me happy."

"The things that make you happy?" Jamie asks, hope flaring in his chest.

Finally, Ben reaches for the flowers. His fingers brush over Jamie's, and the warmth of them goes straight to Jamie's core. "The people," Ben says. "One person."

Instead of taking the bouquet, Ben puts his hand on top of Jamie's. Jamie feels his pulse pounding in his fingers—or maybe it's Ben's. Jamie's voice catches in his throat as he says, "I'm a mess. You know that, right?"

"I kind of am too." Ben swallows. That crooked smile makes a reappearance. "This guy I know said something really smart about how that stuff is a work in progress."

"That was like, a minute ago," Jamie says, unable to stop smiling.

"Yeah, well. It was a good line."

Jamie's rib cage feels open. His heart is exposed. "I wanted to make you hate me all at once instead of despising me slowly," he says. "And it was wrong. Can you forgive me for the way I treated you?"

"Jamie." Ben's grip tightens. "I forgave you the minute I walked away. I went by the Daily Grind to talk to you, but Val said you quit. I've been trying to work up the nerve to call you, but I figured you blocked my number."

The hope in Jamie's chest grows warmer. "I didn't," he says. "I didn't block your number. I couldn't, because... Ben. I don't want you to leave me alone. I never want you to leave me alone."

A stupid, goofy smile spreads across Jamie's face. It doesn't matter how idiotic he looks, because an answering smile is on Ben's, bright sunshine and the brilliance of a rainbow after a storm. "Can I kiss you?" Ben asks.

Jamie sucks in a deep breath. "That," he says, "is a stupid question."

The next thing he knows, the flowers are crushed between them, and Ben's hands are on his face. Jamie's fingers thread through his hair, and—they're kissing. They're kissing and kissing and kissing, and Ben's lips are so soft and warm, and the two of them fit together so perfectly, and Jamie's never going to walk away from this again.

It could have been a desperate kiss, because that's how Jamie's been feeling. But it's not. It's slow and soft and intimate. It's their breath mingling, their hearts beating in time, their hands clasped. A thumb across a cheekbone, the rasp of stubble, fingers tracing along a jaw. It's their mouths open and the taste of coffee on Ben's lips, on his tongue, and Jamie's never liked coffee—not until now. Now, it's the sweetest thing he's ever tasted.

The kiss is a promise, not a plea, and it's a promise Jamie wants to keep making forever.

Kissing forever also seems like a really excellent plan, but Jamie shifts closer and the movement makes the flowers fall to the floor. They both reach for them at the same time. Jamie gets there first and presses them against Ben's chest. He's already covered in glitter, so what's a little more?

Jamie puts his hands on Ben's face and drinks in the beautiful blueness of Ben's eyes. "I love you," he says. "I should have said it back. I love you."

A blinding smile flashes across Ben's face before he leans in and kisses Jamie. "Come in," he whispers against Jamie's lips.

"You never said if you'll come to Pride with me," Jamie whispers back.

"I'll go anywhere with you," Ben breathes, before they kiss again.

When they come up for air, they've managed to get into the apartment. Jamie swings the door shut and brushes Ben's hair off his forehead. Outside, it's a sunny day, and the streets are painted in rainbows. Here, Jamie is all light, all glitter. He'll go anywhere with Ben too. He'll do everything he can to make Ben feel like he's enough, just the way he is. Because he is. He makes Jamie want the world. He makes Jamie want to be better.

It's a work in progress.

Jamie's twenty-seven years old, and he's fixing things.

And it's fine.

# Chapter Thirty-Seven

*Six months later*

BEN SURVEYS the kitchen. The vegetarian coq au vin is simmering, the salad is made, the bread is baking, and the wine is chilling. The table is already set, flowers in a vase in the center and a couple candle tapers ready to be lit. He has time for a shower before Jamie gets home from Columbia. From work—from his first day as an adjunct lecturer of Russian history, a position he was elevated to after five months of working for Nina Noskova.

Pride and love crowd Ben's chest. He knew Jamie could do it. He knew Jamie was unstoppable. He knew his talented, determined, brilliant boyfriend could do anything he set his mind to.

Jamie thinks Ben's in surgery right now and that they're going to go out for a celebratory dinner, but Ben rescheduled the surgery weeks ago so he could be here when Jamie got home. He's been getting his priorities straight—shorter hours at work, more time for hobbies. He discovered he loves cooking, and he's wanted to make something special for Jamie for months.

Having a life outside of work and an identity outside his career is a revelation. They took a vacation to Vermont in the fall to look at leaves and learned they both love hiking. Now they find parks to visit. Ben reads for pleasure. They go to shows—Val's theater has one running right now—and see bands. They've done the Museum of Natural History for real. He finally let Jamie read some of his professional writing, and Jamie was the perfect, supportive boyfriend, really giving it his all, until Ben said, "I know it's boring. You really don't have to read it."

Jamie looked at him, that little wrinkle between his eyebrows that makes Ben's heart skip, and said, "It's not boring. I just don't understand any of it!"

So Ben taught him about neurosurgery, and it was the final push to reawaken his love for his profession. Last week in the ED, he operated on a man who had fallen from a ladder and broken his spine. When Ben came out of surgery to tell the wife her husband would make a full recovery, she hugged him—and he hugged her back.

It turns out he likes who he is when he's more than the sum of his awards and accolades. He likes who he is now that he's unlocked his heart.

The timer for the bread goes off as Ben is buttoning his shirt. He grabs his outfit's finishing touch and goes to retrieve the bread. It's cooling on a rack, and Ben is checking his appearance one more time in his reflection from the microwave, when Jamie arrives.

"Ben? I thought you had a surgery this afternoon?" Jamie pokes his head into the kitchen, and his smile makes Ben's insides squirm and flutter. His hair is tied back in a bun and he's wearing a blazer with elbow patches. The first time Ben saw him wearing it, he pushed him against a wall and took it off, and they missed their time slot for the Halloween thing at Van Cortlandt Manor.

"Congratulations on your first day," Ben says, his heart a blob of mush.

Jamie's flabbergasted expression is too much for Ben. He puts his arms around Jamie's neck and kisses him. "I'm so proud of you, babe."

Jamie's arms wrap Ben up and hold on tight, fingers digging into Ben's back as he deepens the kiss. "It was just syllabus stuff today," he murmurs.

Ben nips his lower lip and Jamie makes a muffled noise that's half protestation and half groan. "Stop. You're amazing. You're teaching a class. You're a hot professor now."

Jamie arches an eyebrow. "*Oh.* This is new. You have professor fantasies?"

With a lopsided grin, Ben says, "Maybe. I could be the struggling student who comes to your office hours, willing to do anything for a better grade."

This wasn't a fantasy Ben was aware he had, but now he's into it. Judging by the hint of red in Jamie's cheeks, he is too. Sex is obviously part of tonight's activities, but dinner first. Ben kisses Jamie quickly. "Sit down. Dinner's just about ready."

"Let me help!"

Ben gives him a little push. "Sit down, Professor."

"Bossy." Jamie smirks. "Maybe you'll order me to strip later?"

The way Ben's eyes drop to Jamie's mouth, then his crotch, is involuntary. "We'll see," he says, in the most totally unconvincing way imaginable. Uh, yeah, he'll tell Jamie to strip. The blazer with the elbow patches really does it for him. So does the hair bun.

The direction of his gaze definitely doesn't go unnoticed. Jamie shoots him a smile that promises very good things.

The recipe is new, so Ben's nervous about how it turned out. It's perfect. After the first few bites, Ben holds up his glass of wine, looks Jamie in the eyes, and says, "To my brilliant, amazing, and very real boyfriend." Jamie laughs, and Ben's expression softens. "Watching you pursue your dreams has been incredible. Getting to be by your side while you do it? That's been a huge honor."

Jamie's face is red with pleasure, and he's battling an irrepressible smile. "You're making a bigger deal about this than it is," he says, but it's obvious how much it means to him that Ben's making a big deal.

And Ben means it. He's so, so proud of Jamie. He's proud of him every time Jamie takes a risk that scares the hell out of him. He's proud of him when Jamie meets rejection head on, gives it the middle finger, and tries again.

"This isn't making a big deal," Ben says. "I was thinking about renting out one of those wedding palaces in Jersey and really turning this into a thing."

With a laugh, Jamie says, "That would've been a lot of coq au vin."

Ben clinks his glass against Jamie's. They drink, and then Jamie reaches across the table to hold Ben's hand while they eat. Their fingers interlace; their palms fit together perfectly.

"I got some good news today," Jamie says, in that casual way that means he's actually been dying to tell Ben about it. Ben squeezes his hand. "My paper got accepted for publication in *Kritika*."

"Jamie!" Ben goes around the table to pull Jamie into a tight hug. Jamie laughs and hugs him back, burying his face in the side of Ben's head. "That's fantastic," Ben says. "Congratulations."

Lips graze Ben's ear. "It's kinda your success too," Jamie says. "You had to proofread it like, a million times before I started submitting it to journals."

"I mean, thanks, but no. This was all you." Ben pulls back just far enough so he can tilt Jamie's face toward his. Jamie beats him to it, pulling him into a deep kiss. Ben lets out a groan. He can't help it, not when Jamie kisses him like this, when their tongues slide together and Jamie's breath hitches.

Fingers walk across Ben's chest, and he feels Jamie pull his pocket square loose. They break their kiss, and the first thing Ben sees when he opens his eyes is Jamie's bright smile, his eyes sparkling as he says, "Don't think I didn't see this."

"I was wondering when you'd say something." Ben tucks a piece of Jamie's hair that's come loose from his bun behind his ear.

"Roller skates," Jamie says fondly, slipping the pocket square back into Ben's jacket. "I love you."

"For my fashion sense?" Ben asks.

Leaning his forehead against Ben's, Jamie says, "For everything."

Ben wants to kiss him again. Ben wants to take him to bed. He wants, like he does every day, to make Jamie feel like the most loved person on the planet. "I love you too," he says, and kisses Jamie deliberately.

The kiss gets heated, then urgent, and soon Ben's getting his wish to take Jamie's blazer off—along with everything else. They're naked and tangled together in bed before long, Ben tracing paths with his tongue along Jamie's body that he memorized months ago while Jamie writhes and moans under him. When they fuck, Ben holds Jamie's wrists over his head, drinking in the taut definition of his biceps, the graceful line of him every time he arches in pleasure.

He feels so good. Every time they make love, it gets better. Ben didn't know that was possible. Then again, with Jamie, everything seems possible. And yeah, that's cheesy as hell. But it's true.

"Ben," Jamie moans, his fingers scrabbling for something to fist. "Please...."

"Please what?" Ben asks breathlessly, dropping his head to kiss and suck Jamie's neck, to bite his collarbone.

As he draws out and buries himself again, Jamie's mouth drops open and his eyes squeeze shut. "Harder," he manages, his hips rocking up to meet Ben's thrusts.

"How about slower?" Ben makes good on that, rolling his hips slow and deep.

Jamie lets out a strangled sound, half laugh, half moan. "Asshole."

There's a joke there, probably, but Ben can't think—he can only move, feeling Jamie under him, slick and panting and clenched around him.

Jamie makes a noise that sets Ben on fire. "Feels so good. Fuck, Ben. *Fuck*—mmph god come here—"

He's panting when Ben leans down to kiss him, and he knows by the way Jamie's moving how close he is. His hard, hot cock digs into Ben's abs, smearing precum between them. "That's it, baby," he breathes into the kiss. "Come all over me."

Those words push Jamie over the edge. He cries into Ben's mouth, desperate and incandescent. The hot, wet mess of him spilling over his own belly and slicking across Ben is too much to handle. There's no amount of control that can stand up to that feeling, to Jamie shuddering and moaning underneath him, to the tight clench of him around Ben's dick.

He comes, and he's annihilated. He's a supernova collapsing in on himself, scattering his atoms to the stars. But Jamie's there to pull him back together. And Ben's there for him, kissing him slowly, drawing him back to himself. When Ben releases his wrists, Jamie's arms go around him, a hand in his hair. His mouth is soft and open and pliant against Ben's.

Their kissing tapers off until their lips are just resting against each other's. Jamie's nose pokes into Ben's cheek and their breath mingles. Moments like this were what Ben thought wouldn't make him happy. He was such an idiot. Now that he's here, sharing this with Jamie, he knows he never even knew what happiness was.

"I think we should move in together," Jamie says, his voice lazy and satisfied.

Ben props himself on an elbow and plays with Jamie's hair, twirling it around a finger. "Yeah?"

"Yeah." A mischievous smile flickers over Jamie's face. "I mean, I'm going to marry you, so it just makes sense."

Ben lets out a startled, happy laugh. "You're going to marry me, huh?"

"Mm-hm."

"Is this you proposing?"

"Don't be stupid," Jamie says loftily. "I don't even have the rings yet. You'll *know* when I'm proposing to you."

God, he looks gorgeous, lazy and sprawled on the bed, hair loose and a mess of frizzy curls, his smile lopsided and the sexiest bedroom eyes. One of his legs is hooked over Ben's, and his arm is around Ben's back, fingers trailing from shoulder blades to ass.

"You sure? I can be pretty clueless."

"Trust me." Jamie stretches, his lean body arching, and Ben slides his palm from Jamie's pecs to the dark hair in his crotch, where his dick is nestled, limp and spent. "It'll be a whole thing. I have Khalid lined up to do my makeup. Joss has a flash mob staged. Val's making the rings. And Adriana's going to get you to the Hudson Yards observation deck so you can see the Empire State Building just at the right time, which will say"—Jamie pauses for effect—"Will you real marry me, Ben McNatt?"

What in the world is he supposed to do except laugh? Which he does, before leaning down and kissing along Jamie's jaw. "You have it all planned out."

"Yep." Cupping his hand over Ben's face, Jamie tilts his head so they can look each other in the eyes. "Would you say yes?"

"Can we negotiate on the flash mob?"

Jamie shakes his head. "The flash mob's non-negotiable. I'm really going for those 2009 vibes."

Ben's heart is too full to do anything except laugh again. He buries his face in the crook of Jamie's neck and breathes in his scent. "Okay. Fine. You can keep the flash mob."

Jamie kisses Ben's forehead. "So?" he asks, his voice quiet.

Like it's even a question. Like Ben would have to think about it. "When you real ask me to real marry you, I'll real say yes."

There's nothing in the universe as bright as Jamie's smile when he's happy. Ben wants to lift his face to that sunshine and let it warm him forever. And he will. He will, if Jamie wants him.

Wait—he never actually addressed Jamie's first suggestion, did he? "And you're right. We should definitely move in together."

Jamie pulls him into another kiss.

Ben is right where he belongs.

# ACKNOWLEDGMENTS

To my favorite English teachers: thank you for fostering my love of writing and for your encouragement to stick with it. Special shoutout to Mrs. Brzezinski for letting me write during the unit on grammar in eighth grade.

My parents always encouraged my love of reading. There was never a book that I wasn't allowed to read, and in this era of book bans, I'm more grateful for that than I can say. My sister read most of my early writing. Thanks, Frannie, and also, I probably owe you an apology for subjecting you to some of that.

Thank you to Anke Schönle for beta reading, as well as those I sent snippets of this manuscript to while I was writing it. The team at Dreamspinner Press has been wonderful to work with. Thank you so much for answering all my new-to-publishing questions and for making The Boyfriend Fix the best that it can be!

If you've ever left me a comment on AO3, please know that you gave me the confidence to write original fiction. Your support means a great deal to me.

And finally, thank you to my wife, Laura. Meeting you was the best thing that ever happened to me. Your unwavering love and support is romance novel levels of swoony.

Keep reading for an exclusive excerpt from
*Strangers to Husbands*
by Lee Pini!

# CHAPTER ONE

LEWIS IS drunk off his ass when he decides riding the mechanical bull is an awesome idea. After finding his pockets disappointingly empty of cash, he gets Stacy—also super fucking drunk—to spot him ten bucks.

When he gets back, some guy is handing over a ten to the operator. Lewis leans his elbows on the railing to wait his turn, and the guy looks over and meets his eyes.

Lewis's stomach swoops, and it's not just the six shots of tequila he chased the pitcher of beer with. The guy has this beautiful head of auburn hair, curly and thick, gorgeous cheekbones, longish, pointy nose, a sharp chin, and an even sharper smile. He's T-A-L-L, taller than Lewis, all legs in tight black skinny jeans. Jesus fuck it should be illegal for someone to walk around with a bulge like that.

The guy smiles slowly and says something to the operator, who shrugs and nods. "Wanna join me, cowboy?" Tall, Dark, and Gorgeous drawls to Lewis.

"Um," Lewis says. The guy unsteadily crosses the crash pad to the bull and puts one foot in the stirrup. Lewis's eyes go straight to his ass.

Damn. He is tooootally not a one-night stand kind of guy because he believes in LOVE, that's L-O-V-E Love. Or wait, no? He doesn't, not anymore. Love is dead! Love is dead, so he should blow this guy in the bathroom.

Hot Mystery Man's shimmery black tank pulls taut across his chest. Muscles in his forearm pop as he holds the pommel on the bull's saddle. The divots of his collarbone look like the perfect place for Lewis to put his tongue.

Does he want to join? Um, *yeah* he wants to join. He wants to join so bad he trips over his feet as he stumbles across the crash pad.

"How's that going to work, though?" Like he cares about anything except getting closer to this man.

The guy's gaze travels from Lewis's head to his feet and back up, lingering at his hips, his chest, his shoulders, and his mouth. Heat floods Lewis. His jeans tighten as his cock stirs.

"You'll know what to do once we start." The guy swings into the saddle and pats what little space is left beside him.

Yeah! He will, totally. He will, and—oh shit. Lewis knows he shouldn't ogle but he gets an eyeful of what's between the guy's legs, and. Nnnng. That is. He is. Okay they're in a western bar so the joke is *right there* but—

Okay. Fine. Yeah. The guy is well-hung. And Lewis's mouth is literally watering.

If he was sober, he'd wait his turn. But he's not sober. He is not at allll sober. So he climbs on and finds himself basically in his new friend's lap, Lewis facing forward and the man facing backward. The heat of his legs pressing into Lewis's brings the stomach swooping back.

"Shouldn't we face the same way?" Lewis asks.

Up close, he can see Mystery Man's blue eyes and a thick scatter of freckles that start on his cheekbones and spill down his neck. How far down do they go?

The guy's smile gets wicked, and he leans forward. His lips brush Lewis's ear. And then it's all hot breath and gravel as the guy says in a low, dirty voice, "I like to look at men when they're giving me a good, hard ride."

"Fuck," Lewis breathes.

The guy draws back, looking ridiculously pleased with himself. And ridiculously drunk.

Lewis puts his hands on the guy's knees, and at his nod, slides his palms up his thighs to his waist. The man arches into his touch, and his body is warm and firm and Jesus—will Stacy be cool if he bails on the bachelorette party to take this gorgeous man back to his hotel room?

The mechanical bull starts rocking slowly, swinging in a gentle circle, and Lewis absolutely cannot tear his eyes away from the way the man moves. His hips roll, all fluid sex on legs, and one of his arms loops around Lewis's back as he shifts closer. He slides into Lewis's lap, and they're moving against each other, grinding their hips, and Lewis is so hard it hurts.

There's a rope overhead, and the guy pulls himself up with it. Lewis gets a view of his abs and treasure trail, and he wants to put his mouth there and lick and suck his way down, down, down—

His mouth waters. The guy's legs hook around his back, and he rubs his hard cock against Lewis's stomach.

Lewis can't breathe.

There's a shrill whistle and a couple catcalls. Without looking, Lewis knows it's the bachelorette party. A small, slightly more sober part of his mind informs him he's never going to hear the end of this—he's basically fornicating on a mechanical bull in the middle of a honky-tonk during his best friend's bachelorette party.

But as Lewis pushes the guy down to the bull's neck and ghosts his lips over the man's jaw with its prickle of stubble, it's pretty hard to care.

He smells like gin and rose; spice and wood; *sweat*, and Lewis has never wanted to take someone to bed so bad in his entire life.

The bull slows and stops. Lewis is still on top of the man. Their faces are inches apart. The man's freckles are like stars. Lewis's pulse pounds in his fingertips and in his crotch. His skin is on fire.

"Lew!" Stacy yells. "Who's your friend?"

The guy grins, and where before he was all sultry and sexy, now he looks a little shy, a little giddy, like maybe he can't believe he just did that. It's adorable.

Lewis grins back. "I think I should probably ask your name?"

"Tad," the man says, biting his lip and watching Lewis's mouth.

Lewis shifts off him as Stacy's friends keep whooping. "I'm Lewis. And I would really, *really* love to buy you a drink, Tad."

"I would really, really love if you bought me a drink," Tad replies. He slides to the ground and helps Lewis down, and the two of them stumble into each other's arms, crash pad undulating beneath their feet.

Lewis laughs and leans into him, Tad's arm goes around his waist, and before Lewis knows it, they're jammed together at the bar, doing shots. "Aren't you here with someone?" Lewis asks.

"My brother and his friends." Tad flaps a hand. "They're not *here*. I left them at some casino."

"You left them to come ride a mechanical bull?"

"I left them because they're boring."

"What about me? Am I boring?"

Tad's hair falls in curly wisps over his forehead. He has the clearest, prettiest blue eyes Lewis has ever seen. "I don't think you're boring. You're like, the least boring person I've ever met."

Leaning into him, Lewis says in his ear, "I don't think you're boring, either." He trails a finger along the line of freckles on Tad's neck, down to where they disappear under the neckline of his tank. "I like these," he adds, because it seems really important for Tad to know.

"Really?" Tad sounds awed.

"Mm hm." Lewis leans in. It's easy to dip his head to Tad's neck, because Tad is taller than him. He kisses the spot where the freckles spill onto Tad's collarbone and disappear under his clothes.

It's happening, isn't it? Finally. Love at first sight *is* real. Take that, Jonah! And Diego, and Liam, and Jayden, and every other ex-boyfriend who ground him down and made him doubt true love was out there waiting for him. The rom-coms and Disney movies he loves are right, after all! Because his stomach's fluttering and his heart's pounding and every inch of his skin has this buzz pulling him toward Tad.

Sure, Lewis is drunk right now—really, really drunk—but Tad is definitely a person Lewis falls in love-at-first-sight with.

Tequila seems like it will make him fall even more in love with Tad, so he gets another one of those. And so does Tad, and the night turns to a hazy blur of dancing and singing along to Garth Brooks and Dolly Parton and Carrie Underwood. Tad yells to Stacy at one point, "I'm sorry I didn't get you a gift!"

Stacy yells back, "I'm just really happy you're here, Chad!"

"It's Tad!"

Slinging an arm around Lewis's neck, Stacy pulls him in for a sloppy kiss on the cheek and shouts over the music, "Lewis looooooves you, I can tell! Maybe someday you guys will get married! Lewis, I really want us both to be married."

Goddddd Lewis wants to get married so bad. Ahhhh it would be *amazing*. Stace is getting married, which he is like, *so* happy about! They can both be married to the loves of their lives, which Lewis is now like 99 percent sure Tad is. Stacy will marry Alang, and Lewis will marry Tad, and everyone will live happily ever after.

Tad presses into his side. He laughs and nuzzles his face into Lewis's. "We'll have a long engagement."

Which is like the funniest thing Lewis has ever heard, and now he knows he's in love-at-first-sight with Tad.

They leave the bar, and—stuff happens? Stuff must happen, because Lewis is having a blast, he's having so much fun; his hand is in Tad's, he's kissing Tad, and there's champagne. It's the best night Lewis can remember having in forever, even if he already can't remember most of it.

DESERT SUN on his eyelids wakes Lewis. His mouth is gummy, his stomach is sour, and his eyes are sandy. Something is twisted around his legs. Hotel sheets? Hotel sheets. The air conditioner is blowing on him, which is when Lewis realizes he's super naked.

He rolls over, groaning—and discovers he's also super not alone.

But hey, if you're going to wake up in bed with a man you've only known for twelve hours, it might as well be the most beautiful man you've ever seen.

The most beautiful man Lewis has ever seen opens his eyes groggily. His hair is in curly snarls on the pillow. A flash of hot memory scorches through Lewis's body—his fingers twisted in that hair, a warm, wet mouth on his cock.

Mr. Beautiful, He-Of-The-Best-BJ-Lewis-Is-Pretty-Sure-He's-Ever-Had, stretches, and Lewis's eyes track down and back up his body. He's lean and gorgeous, rangy strength, legs for days, *very* nice cock currently providing a nice display of morning wood. The freckles are all over his body. Lewis vaguely remembers trying to kiss all of them before getting distracted by the aforementioned very nice cock.

Lewis hopes his breath isn't toxic. "Hey."

Looking sated and wrecked, Mr. Beautiful says, "Hi."

What are you supposed to say in the morning to the gorgeous guy you drunkenly hooked up with?

"It's Tad, right?"

Which isn't his best effort, but he's rewarded with a bright, beautiful smile. "Yeah. Lewis?"

Well, Lewis doesn't remember a whole lot else about last night, but at least they remember each other's names.

He extends a hand for a handshake. "Lewis Mancini-Sommer."

Tad's smile gets a little crooked and a lot mischievous, and Lewis's heart swoops. "You don't do this very often, do you, Lewis Mancini-Sommer?"

"Dry hump a stranger on a mechanical bull and then hook up with him? Not really."

Tad laughs. It's hoarse, but—it's such a nice laugh. Sounds out of practice. His hand slides into Lewis's and they shake, which is when Lewis realizes there's definitely cum caked in the creases of his palms. Like. Kind of a lot.

"I don't," Lewis says. "I mean, obviously not the mechanical bull stuff. But… yeah, the like, drunk hooking up."

There's a sad little twist to Tad's mouth for a second and he pulls the sheet up to his waist. Maybe Lewis is still drunk, but the sight of Tad being unhappy makes him want to fix it. "Hey, um. Is there, like. Anything you want to… do? Like breakfast? Or, I don't know, coffee?"

Or sex? Because Lewis is leaving Vegas today and obviously never going to see Tad again. So… sex?

Tad's eyes flick to Lewis's. "Can we do each other?" He bites his lip. "Sorry! God. I'm actually usually not like this, like, at all. Slutting it up isn't really my thing. I mean, it's fine if it *is* your thing, like, no slut-shaming! I'm just, like, not that way. Usually. I was last night I guess? Sorry, I just—I was here with my brother and his friends, and they make me feel invisible, and—wow, did I really just ask if you want to fuck and talk about my brother in the same breath…?"

That's a lot of words that Lewis's brain can't really process, not after the ones at the very beginning. "I think we should do each other." He slides a hand over Tad's stomach and up to his chest. His stomach is just defined enough, but still soft. His pecs, on the other hand, are hard and warm, and Lewis has a faint memory of sucking Tad's nipples and him really, *really* liking that.

So he brushes a thumb over one. Tad's eyes close and he breathes in hard, and Lewis rolls on top of him. Tad grabs his hand and brings it to his mouth, then stops. His eyes widen.

"You're married?" he demands.

"What?" Lewis laughs. "Um, no."

Tad jabs a finger at one of Lewis's. "You're wearing a wedding ring. Why would you be wearing a wedding ring if you weren't married?"

"I'm not—" But Lewis's eyes flick to his own hand, and—

He is. He *is* wearing a wedding ring. He's wearing a rose gold band (gay, wow) with a viney, scrolling pattern.

"What the fuck?" Lewis asks, looking at Tad, even though Tad's made it pretty clear the existence of the wedding ring was unknown to him until this moment.

"I don't sleep with married men," Tad says in the same tone you might say *I don't sleep with serial killers.*

"I'm not married!" Lewis repeats. Tad rakes a hand through his hair and starts to get out of bed, but Lewis grabs his wrist. "Um, hey, excuse me, Mr. I-Don't-Sleep-With-Married-Men? What's that on your hand?"

"What's *what* on my—" Tad looks at his left hand. There's a ring there. Tad stares. "What the hell?"

"Fuck if I know," Lewis says. "I don't know where mine came from, either."

Their eyes meet. Lewis's mouth goes dry, and Tad scooches back into bed with him, holding out his hand until it bumps against Lewis's.

Tad's is also rose gold, with the same pattern of vines and flowers.

The rings match.

The rings. Fucking. *Match.*

"Do you remember what we did last night?" Tad asks slowly.

"Well." Lewis looks at him meaningfully. "I remember doing a lot of things."

Tad's face colors. "Before that."

"Um." Lewis is saved from answering by his phone buzzing. He dives for it and opens the text from Stacy.

"Oh," he says. "Fuck."

*I found this in my purse???* Stacy's text says. Beneath it is a photo of a marriage certificate. Lewis can only see four pertinent words on it: Lewis Mancini-Sommer... and Thaddeus Pierce.

# Scan the QR Code
# Below to Order!

LEE PINI is a queer author who has been writing since they could pick up a pencil. They have lived in England, Northern Ireland, and Florida, and currently live in their home state of Minnesota with their wife and cat. Lee studied archaeology at the graduate level but currently uses their degree primarily to chuckle knowingly at classics memes. When they aren't at their day job or writing, they're reading vociferously, listening to music, enjoying nature, or nerding out. Their dream is for someone to one day write fanfiction about their characters.

# When We Finally Kiss Good Night

# LEE PINI

Jake lost his Christmas spirit when his husband left him on December 26. This year, when a friend offers him her reservation at a resort in Florida, he jumps at the chance to get away. No snow, no Christmas trees, no problems.

Except the resort does a Christmas Golf Cart parade every year, and Alex, the man in the neighboring cabin, wants Jake's help with his.

Jake just wants to be left alone… until he spies Alex's design. Maybe working together won't be so bad. Can an unexpected friendship reawaken more than Jake's holiday spirit?

## SCAN THE QR CODE
## BELOW TO ORDER!

In a last-ditch effort to finish a manuscript, Thomas Kovacs packs up his teenage daughter, Alexis, and relocates to a small town in northern England. Things have been strained between them for months, but the closer Thomas gets to the end of his book, the more distant Alexis becomes.

Krishna Singh came to Corbridge to open a bookstore and start a family. After two years, his business is thriving. His family? Well, he hasn't gotten around to that yet. Actually, he hasn't even dated. The closest he gets is bonding over books and music with an American teenager who comes into his shop.

When it turns out the teenager's dad is none other than Krishna's favorite author, he wastes no time in getting to know Thomas. But attempts at something more go about as well as Thomas's writing, or his relationship with Alexis. Can Krishna convince Thomas that they all deserve a happy-ever-after?

## SCAN THE QR CODE
## BELOW TO ORDER!